"If you would love to lose yourself completely in a book, this is the book."
—*News Virginian*

"One of William Hoffman's best tales."
—*Winston-Salem Journal-Sentinel*

"Here is one book that can be summed up in one word: Superb!"
—*Springfield (IL) State Journal-Register*

"A bitter, moving, funny chronicle of a time none of us wants to endure again."
—*Wichita Eagle*

"Hoffman skillfully blends shock and sensitivity. He writes with tremendous perception and brilliance."
—*Newport News Daily Press*

"The life of enlisted men in camp and on leave and the politics of the officer caste are reported in detail, with hilarity at times, as well as with sympathy. . . . A vigorous war novel with convincing characterization, ranging from the serfdom of barracks life to the terror of battle action."
—*Library Journal*

VOICES OF THE SOUTH

WILLIAM HOFFMAN

YANCEY'S WAR

Louisiana State University Press
Baton Rouge

Copyright © 1966 by William Hoffman
Originally published by Doubleday and Company, Inc.
LSU Press edition published 2005 by arrangement with the author
All rights reserved
Manufactured in the United States of America

14 13 12 11 10 09 08 07 06 05
5 4 3 2 1

Library of Congress Cataloging-in-Publication Data

Hoffman, William, 1925–
    Yancey's war / William Hoffman. — LSU Press ed.
        p. cm.
    ISBN: 0-8071-3069-9 (pbk. : alk. paper)
    1. World War, 1939–1945—Fiction. I. Title.
    PS3558.O34638Y36 2005
    813'.54—dc22

                                                    2004022765

The paper in this book meets the guidelines for permanence and durability of the Committee on Production Guidelines for Book Longevity of the Council on Library Resources. ∞

For
Ruthie and George

YANCEY'S WAR

1

Unlike the rest of us, Marvin Yancey was not young. His skin had a reddish tinge, and he bulged with fat. He couldn't have been more than an inch or two over five feet tall. His short legs were thick at the thighs, and his dark, thinning hair grew out of a pale, flaking scalp. Most of us were draftees. We were standing at ungraceful attention under a blazing Virginia sun after coming west from Richmond by train the evening before to a raw, new induction center set among pines. Chiggers buried in us, and ticks sucked our blood. Shouting, exasperated noncoms herded us like dumb cattle through the battery of processing—the inoculations, the aptitude tests, and the VD movie.

We had just been issued uniforms. They were creased from being folded on shelves in the unpainted supply shed. The new khaki, which shone and was stiff, chafed our skins and caused us to sweat. We put our civilian clothes into cardboard boxes provided by the Army. The boxes were to be mailed home postage free.

Yancey, in the first squad of the platoon, was oozing sweat. His khaki shirt had turned dark under his armpits and down his back. Compared to him the rest of us appeared lean and tough, though not nearly so lean and tough as the waves of men who had come to fight in the first years of the war. At twenty-five I was near the average age. A few were in their early and middle thirties. Yancey, however, was well into his forties.

He sagged in the yellow-hot sun like a stick of butter set on end. The soft blubber of his rolypoly body hung over his shirt collar and drooped about his belt. The web belt itself seemed to be keeping his belly from popping out his shirt and spilling to the ground. As he stood at attention, he made me think of a slapstick comedian who at any instant would go into an act ridiculing the Army.

That he was a volunteer and hadn't been drafted—a fact we learned from his serial number—made him even more of a curiosity. Noncoms and officers at various stages of processing called out his name, glanced in his direction, and were startled. They believed he was some sort of mistake—a short circuit in the machinery of preparing men for war.

We were assembled on bare ground outside the supply shed. After inoculations the scorching heat was making us sick. Men sucked their dry tongues. A noncom ordered us to carry our new equipment to the barracks and to go to the mess hall for lunch.

Nobody was hungry. When we finished pushing our food around on tin trays and again reached the hot, resinous barracks, we sank to our bunks in the hope of resting a little before the next frantic shrilling of whistles. I felt a tick crawling up my leg. I flung him from me, groaned, and closed my eyes.

Yancey's bunk was next to mine. I heard him bustling around and humming. I peeped at him. He winked as if the two of us were conspirators. Behind the lenses of rimless glasses his light brown eyes were large and watery. Winking was a habit with him. He did it to everybody.

"Processing takes about three days," he explained as if I'd asked him. "The job is important and I don't begrudge the inconvenience or the time. They have real problems putting the right man in the right slot. The Army may be slow, but it usually knows what the score is."

I turned my head slightly on the rough blanket covering my pillow to stare at him. His voice was high-pitched and strident. Its timbre rasped the nerves. He talked like a high-pressure salesman attempting to move the goods. As he sat on his bunk, he removed his glasses to clean them. Without glasses his face looked exposed. He patted his stomach, which thumped like a ripe melon, and belched.

"Of course I can save them a lot of trouble," he went on. "I knew exactly what I wanted before I came into this man's Army, and I can tell them where I'll do the most good. I already told them when I put my John Henry on the dotted line."

Unlike most of us who spoke in the soft, slow manner of Southerners, Yancey's speech shot out fast and explosively. Each time his oversized lips moved, fine saliva sprayed across a shaft of sunlight. His words carried the length of the barracks, and other men lying on bunks were listening. Like mine, their faces were bewildered and disbelieving.

Yancey turned away. He pointed at a young draftee who was trying on a new pair of leggings.

"You're doing that wrong," Yancey told him. "You have to change the hooks from the inside of your calves. They could cause you to get hung up and trip. Put the hooks on the outside and you'll be okay. This might be a modern war, but the Army's been using the same leggings ever since the AEF went after Kaiser Bill."

He shifted back to me. I saw beads of sweat on his white scalp. He ran pudgy fingers over his thin hair.

"Yes, sir," he continued, reaching into his duffle bag for a can of polish to shine newly issued shoes. "I know what I want and what I'm going to get. It's the old blue-cord infantry for me. Forty men, eight mules, and Mademoiselle from Armentières. I want to be up front where they have all the fun."

Somebody on a bunk farther along the line snickered. Had we not been hot, tired, and sick, we might have been convulsed with laughter because if ever a man had obviously not been cut out for combat it was Yancey. With his shortness, his sausagelike body, and his watery eyes, he was a parody of the warrior. He belonged in a soft spot—perhaps a cook, a baker, or a ward boy in a base hospital. He was definitely not meant to hurl his doughy flesh against enemy guns.

Yet apparently he was serious. He went on talking as if it were a foregone conclusion that infantry was where he would end up. He kept winking as if he had the lowdown and everything had been arranged.

"How about you?" he asked while buffing his shoes. "What branch you want?"

"I'm mulling it over," I answered as if the Army had given me a choice. I closed my eyes and wished he would leave me alone.

"Well, just remember when everything's said and done infantry are the boys who win wars. You can take all the glamour pants in the Air Corps or Navy and they look pretty in parades, but the old dogfaces are the people who get the job done. Me, I want to be where the men are."

The words contradicted so forcibly his ridiculous appearance that snorts and whistles sounded up and down the line of bunks.

"Of course it's tough," Yancey said, nodding seriously and ignoring both the reaction he was causing and my attempt to rest. "I know it's tough. But like anything else it has to be tough to be worth the effort. You can't name anything good that doesn't have to be worked for. Besides a man has to live with himself. How can he do that if he's in the Medics or Quartermaster?"

I'd had enough. I stood and walked to the latrine. I didn't want him to get the idea he and I had anything in common. Furthermore I hoped to make it plain to the others I knew him no better than they did.

Just as I lighted a cigarette, whistles blew. The barracks emptied. We milled in the street as we tried to form a company. A sergeant ordered us to change from khakis into fatigues. He started on the whistle again before we finished dressing. We stumbled out pulling on pants and jackets. Yancey was hopping as if in a potato race.

In the wilting heat we marched to a dusty field and went through calisthenics. The exercises were supposed to prevent our arms from becoming stiff. As we jumped in vague cadence to the sergeant's commands, our civilian bodies ached and grunted. Given a ten-minute break, we sought the shade of loblolly pines where we lay as if in shock.

"They're doing the right thing," Yancey informed us, himself gasping for air. "Calisthenics are the best medicine in the world to keep muscles from contracting after inoculations. You have to remember all this has been thought out."

"By an idiot," a surly, blowing draftee said.

"Well, to some of you boys who aren't familiar with the Army it might seem that way," Yancey answered, smiling and winking. "You have to remember the Army has everything down in the book."

He stopped talking a moment to suck for breath. Men glared at him in outrage. The sergeant, who stood apart as if he might become contaminated by close association with us, watched.

"Yes, sir, the old Army has it all down on paper," Yancey continued. "They tell you how to brush your choppers, when to change your shorts, and the best way to dry between your pinkies. In that book it says after inoculations calisthenics are good to prevent stiffness. So don't think the Army's stupid, though it might look that way. There's always a reason for doing things, and usually it's sensible."

4

We were disgusted. He was obviously playing it up for the sergeant.

"If you have any questions, I don't mind answering them," Yancey said. "I want to be all the help I can to you fellows."

2

Yancey chose me to attach himself to. Each day when released from formation he hurried to my side. The fact I walked off in mid-sentence or turned my back didn't stop him. He refused to be snubbed.

I couldn't escape him. He followed me into latrines and squeezed beside me at the mess hall. In ranks he maneuvered to stand next to me. He pretended not to see my annoyance. Wherever I looked, I met his watery, winking eyes.

"You may wonder why I've been trailing you," he said to me on the evening of the fourth day as we were returning to the barracks after chow. His fat legs pumped to keep up with me. "I don't mind telling you. I saw right away that you and I are a lot alike."

I clenched my fists and didn't answer.

"What I mean is I could see you were somebody before you came to the Army," Yancey said, half-running now. "The rest of the fellows are fine—don't misunderstand me, they're the salt of the earth. For the most part, though, they don't amount to much. They worked in gas stations or drove delivery trucks. They're young, but most of them won't go much further. You and I don't really belong with them. I happen to know you're a college graduate like me. I also know you worked in a trust department of a good bank."

He had undoubtedly peeked at my records as we stood in line during classification. I quickened my step and clamped my teeth.

"I'll lay you odds it wasn't a lackey's job either," Yancey continued, and I was certain if I glanced at him one of his great brown eyes would wink at me. "I bet whatever your position it involved responsibility. Me, I'm in the construction business, and in the construction business you have to learn quickly to size a man up. I sized you up as being somebody."

We had reached the barracks. I walked first to my bunk and then to the dayroom to lose him. He followed.

"I was in a position of great responsibility myself," he said. "In fact I still am. My company has government contracts. I won't tell you how much we're grossing because it's a trade secret and a lot of people in the industry would like to have that figure. I'll just say it's plenty."

In desperation to be rid of him, I gathered my towel and soap for a shower. The steam drove him back, and the roar of water muffled his voice. He appeared with his own towel. He took a shower next to me and went on talking. He borrowed my soap.

For me his voice began to dominate the induction center. It was the first thing I heard each morning and the last thing at night. As soon as I opened my eyes, the mouth would be there, spewing forth words. The voice weaved around me until my head ached from it. I heard it in my sleep.

Moreover Yancey was constantly giving advice. He whispered as if sharing a secret, and his eyes darted about.

"Don't use so much polish on your shoes. Too much and you don't get a good shine. Don't use dubbing either. Overseas use it, but as long as you have to stand inspections dubbing prevents your shoes from taking on a high gloss. It's better to have wet feet than gigs for wearing shoes that won't shine."

He advised me to carry all my uniforms to a tailor and to have them altered to fit snugly as he had done with his own.

"It doesn't cost much and you'll look sharper," he said. "You should always try to look sharp. You want to show the noncoms and brass you care. They're watching. I'm telling you a fact."

About the only peace I had from him were the times he was on the telephone. He claimed to be making long-distance calls to his construction company. I didn't believe he owned a construction company, and I was suspicious the calls were staged for the benefit of me and the other men. Yancey would leave the door of the booth open and talk loudly about "subs, I beams, and headers." There was a good possibility he wasn't speaking to anybody at all but into a dead telephone.

As I did not believe what he said about his business, I also doubted his loudly professed wish for the infantry. That, I thought, was just another facet of the blowhard. He knew he would never have to go to the infantry and he was safe in making his brag.

I was standing behind him the second afternoon we filed through the classification center. We waited in line for our turns to sit at desks where clerks worked over our records. Collected information was to be assessed by personnel officers. They were to make recommendations about what would happen to each of us.

A thin, studious-looking corporal motioned Yancey forward. Yancey sat down in front of the desk and winked.

"I can save you a lot of trouble," he told the corporal. "Just put me down for infantry."

"That's not up to me," the harried young corporal answered. "Can you ride a motorcycle?"

"I want to speak to the officer in charge," Yancey said.

The corporal raised his eyes slowly. Yancey smiled at him in a friendly manner. Behind me the long line of men had heard. The line bent around a little to watch.

"Look, soldier, I have to ask you these questions and you have to answer them," the corporal said, his face stern. "Now just tell me whether or not you can ride a motorcycle."

"I'm not telling you anything until I speak to the officer in charge."

Men behind me drew in their breaths. The corporal put down his pencil. He frowned at Yancey in an attempt to intimidate him. Yancey crossed his fat legs and continued to smile pleasantly.

"You don't want an officer," the corporal said. "You better believe me."

"You might as well get him," Yancey insisted. "Otherwise I'm not going to co-operate."

The corporal was the one intimidated. He'd pulled his rank and failed. He was unsure what to do next. Angrily he rose from his chair and strode to the back of the shed where a group of officers were gathered. He talked and pointed. A lieutenant stepped away from the group. The corporal followed the lieutenant to the table.

"What's the beef?" the lieutenant asked, scowling at Yancey.

If anything the lieutenant was younger than the corporal. He wore a shiny new gold bar on his khaki shirt collar. Just out of OCS, he was attempting to appear ferocious, but Yancey—old enough to be his father—was not cowed. He stood at attention and saluted.

"I always believe in going to the top man," Yancey said. "It saves time and confusion. Now I enlisted in this Army for the infantry. That's where I want to be because that's where I can do the most good. So why bother with a lot of red tape when you can just mark me down for a dogface and save everybody trouble? You fellows won't have to waste time worrying about me, and I'll be happy."

7

"What you thought you were enlisting for doesn't bind us here," the lieutenant answered, his voice threatening. He picked up Yancey's records and inspected them. He was aware of the line of men watching. "You'll be evaluated according to established procedures. Now get the lead out."

The expression sounded false coming from him. He was still too virginal for tough Army talk. Believing, however, he had solved the problem, he dropped Yancey's records onto the desk and walked off. Yancey, remaining at attention, called to him.

"Lieutenant, I don't think you understand," he said. "One way or another I'm going to the infantry."

The tone Yancey used wasn't that of a man making a request. He was defying the lieutenant, and the lieutenant realized it. He turned, his face red. He felt his authority as an officer was being challenged. He came back to the desk and leaned across it toward Yancey.

"Mister, you'll go where your weighed score dictates you be sent. That's the long and short of it. Now sit down there and answer the corporal's questions or you're in big trouble."

"I suppose I have to go wherever you send me," Yancey admitted, his expression crafty—like that of a horse trader about to sell a spavined, wind-broke nag. "That doesn't mean I'll stay. I'm just trying to save the Army a lot of trouble. What good's it going to do to make trouble? That won't help win the war, will it? All you have to do is make certain marks on my records and everybody'll be happy."

Not only men in the line, but also the clerks were watching. The whole classification process had stopped. As Yancey talked, he was moving around the desk toward the lieutenant. The lieutenant believed he was facing a mutiny.

"Get back around that desk!" he shouted, his voice cracking. "I'm ordering you back around that desk and to answer the corporal's questions. If you don't answer the questions I'll personally place you under arrest for insubordination and have you taken to the stockade."

"Yes, sir, but you ought to think it over," Yancey answered, retreating only a step. "Putting me in the stockade won't help this country win the war. I'm not asking anything disgraceful or unpatriotic. I want to be where I can fight for the U.S.A. Millions of guys don't like infantry and you can trade me for one of them."

"Not another goddamn word!" the lieutenant ordered, his voice trembling. His hands were up as if to ward off Yancey. The lieutenant was breathing hard.

"Sure, sir," Yancey said.

"Sit in the chair and answer the questions."

"I believe you at least ought to consider my side of the argument."

"In the goddamn chair!"

"Yes, sir," Yancey said, lowering himself to the chair.

"And everybody get to work around here!" the lieutenant hollered. His face was flaming, and his fists were up. He cast one final, ominous look at Yancey before returning to the group of officers who'd been watching. Clerks raised their pencils, and the classification process again commenced. Men in the line were whispering. Yancey winked at the corporal.

"A ninety-day wonder," Yancey said. "He's young and uncertain of himself. That's why he's so excited. When he thinks over what I told him, he'll understand I'm right."

"Can you drive a motorcycle?" the corporal asked warily.

"You bet I can but that doesn't mean I'm going to."

"You don't have to convince me. I just work here. Previous military experience?"

"I was infantry during World War I. In France."

The information traveled back along the line. Though Yancey acted as if he owned the Army, he'd never told us he'd been a part of it. He wasn't lying because he'd know his service records were on file in Washington and would eventually catch up with him. He spieled off his old serial number as well as the name of a famous division.

"I'm no rookie," he said. "I've seen a hell of a lot more than that lieutenant. I'll tell you something else. Wars might change but armies don't. The infantry wasn't much different in the time of Caesar."

Yancey talked so much the corporal had difficulty getting in questions. Those of us in line were confused. Yancey would have been more in character avoiding combat altogether than pursuing it.

"You can give the lieutenant a message for me," Yancey instructed the corporal. "Tell him I'll go AWOL from any outfit except infantry. Tell him he might as well use me to win the war."

Yancey stood. The corporal looked distraught.

"He'll see it my way when he thinks it over," Yancey said. He put on his overseas cap and winked.

9

3

I watched him leave the shed. Even in tailored khakis his buttocks stuck out obesely, and his walk was something between a strut and a waddle. He was whistling happily. I lost sight of him. The corporal motioned me to take the chair Yancey had just vacated.

"Can you ride a motorcycle?" the corporal asked.

The questions were on a mimeographed sheet before him. Unlike Yancey I answered them gladly. The infantry was a part of the service I definitely did not want. If I could help it, I wasn't about to get myself shot at. Because of my college degree and experience at the bank, I hoped I would be assigned to some administrative branch of the Army. And, of course, I was counting on OCS.

The corporal went into detail about my work at the bank. That fact reassured me the Army really was trying to use me properly. I described my duties in the trust department. The corporal's pencil flew across his answer sheets.

When he finished, I left the shed. Yancey was waiting outside, leaning against the shady side of the building. He quickly fell in step with me.

"Surprised you, didn't I?" he asked. "I mean about being in the Army before."

"You surprised me," I answered and hurried on. If I couldn't get away from him, I'd make it as uncomfortable as possible for him to keep up with me.

"You didn't think I knew what I was talking about. I could see you didn't. Well, I fool a lot of people. Not that I'm worried about that lieutenant. Once I'm shipped out I'll never see him again, and he can't hurt me. I'm not kidding myself either. The infantry's going to be a bitch. I'll have to sweat off a lot of fat. I'm not going to worry about it though. That's what cadre gets paid for."

At the barracks I lay on my bunk. Yancey sat on the edge of his and kept talking. Covering my eyes with an arm, I let his words wash over me. He was again on the construction business. He acted as if he were a major contractor.

"We do a lot of business at Fort Myer," he said. "They needed a new administration building. I figured I didn't have a chance on it and bid blind. That means on the high side. The job dropped right into my lap. I don't know where I'll get the labor to finish it. A man can't help making money with a war on."

Whistles shrilled. We ran outside to form for drill. With the exception of Yancey, we were awkward and unco-ordinated. He, however, was able to execute close-order commands with oily smoothness. He was so good the sergeant called him from ranks and made him a temporary instructor. Yancey behaved like a general, and his petulant voice nagged us.

"Hup, hup. Watch your distance! Don't you know your left from your right? Close it up!"

He was a lot tougher than the sergeants, and by the time we were dismissed late in the afternoon some of the men who had formerly been amused at Yancey now actively disliked him. They grumbled and shot him resentful looks.

He ignored them. He was happy at being in command. He sought me out and followed me to the mess hall. I hardly spoke to him, but he carried on both sides of the conversation. I finished my meal quickly, stood, and hurried from the building. He called my name. I didn't look back. I ran to the barracks for a box of stationery and went to the dayroom where I began writing my mother.

Yancey found me in less than ten minutes. When he appeared in the doorway, I pretended not to see him in the vain hope he wouldn't bother me. He came straight to me and pulled up a chair. He peered at my letter, obviously trying to make out the words.

"Who you writing to?" he asked.

"My mother," I answered, my voice cold.

"Say, that's nice. I ought to write my wife. I have a knockout of a wife. Can I borrow some paper and an envelope?"

"They sell stationery at the PX."

"Oh sure. I have stationery. I brought a whole bunch of it from home. I just don't want to have to go back to the barracks."

Without waiting for me to offer him my box, he reached in and helped himself. He did have a pen. Instead of moving to another table, however, he used the end of mine and jostled my arm. His pen scratched, making it difficult for me to think. He covered one sheet of paper and took a second from my box.

"I'll pay you back," he told me. "I always return anything I borrow. I expect people to do the same to me. Now a couple of sheets of paper and an envelope aren't worth much. They're not worth more than a few cents. Still I always believe in paying and getting paid no matter what the amount. I've found that's the best basis for friend-

11

ship. If you don't owe anybody and they don't owe you, then there's nothing to get sore about."

I closed the box, sealed my letter, and rose to leave.

"Wait a minute, Charley," he said, hastily trying to finish his own letter.

I hated for anyone to call me Charley. My first name was Charles, and I hadn't given him permission to use even that. I didn't wait. I reached the steps leading from the dayroom to the street. Yancey's chair scraped, and he was right behind me.

"Slow down a little, will you?" he asked. He was licking his—or my—envelope.

I walked toward the mailbox nailed to the outside of headquarters building. The evening was humid and still. Against a dark sky pines were motionless.

"Let me tell you something about this man's Army," Yancey babbled on. "You got to think ahead. You have to ask yourself where you're going to be the day after tomorrow. Will you slow down?"

I didn't slow. I dropped my letter into the mailbox and headed for the barracks. Yancey came after me, caught my arm, and stopped me. Using my first name was bad enough, but even worse was his thinking he could put his soft, white hands on me. I jerked my arm from his grasp.

"Calm down, will you?" he said. "What you so touchy about? Let's have a beer."

"No," I answered, starting away from him. He ran around in front of me.

"Come on now. It's not going to hurt you to drink a beer with me. They have the genuine article at the PX."

I didn't want to drink beer or anything else with him, but it occurred to me that by doing so I might have a better chance of freeing myself. I would have one beer and leave. He would probably stay on. I changed directions in order to walk to the PX.

"Now you're talking," Yancey said.

Beer was sold in the basement of the PX. Outsized foaming mugs were only a nickel each. The room had a low ceiling and sawdust on the floor. There was a battered counter and a large table at which noncoms were allowed to sit. Draftees stood around drinking, conscious of the newness of their uniforms. Steel guitars twanged and wailed in a multicolored jukebox.

"I'll flip you for the beer," Yancey said.

I didn't want to flip. He had already borrowed my stationery, and he had invited me for the beer. I might not have let him pay for it, but he should at least have offered. He both tossed the coin and called it. He then informed me I had lost. When the colored bartender brought the beer, I reluctantly put my money on the counter. Yancey was chuckling. He had gold inlays in his teeth. He smacked his lips.

"The old Army ain't so bad when you can get beer like this for a nickel," he said.

"It cost me a dime," I reminded him.

"It sure did." He laughed loudly. He wiped his lips with the back of his hand. "Listen, how about calling me Marvin. That's my first name and what my friends use. I have friends all over the country. Marvin. Okay?"

I pretended to be very busy with my beer.

"And let me tell you something, Charley, it's good to have friends. Especially in the Army it's good. Without a buddy the Army can be hell."

He drank from his mug. Foam stuck to the skin above his lips and to his nose. He licked at it.

"You're not married, are you?" he asked.

Again he was pumping me. I didn't want to answer him, but he was staring at me with his moist brown eyes. I shook my head impatiently.

"I didn't think you were," Yancey said. "You have a restlessness about you a married man doesn't. It's my belief a fellow will never really amount to anything until he's hitched. If it wasn't for my wife, I'd probably be a bum. I don't mind telling you I've made a little money in my time, and I owe most of it to her. She's a real dish."

I could imagine the type of woman who would marry Yancey. She would be no dish.

"Of course she didn't want me to come into the Army. I didn't have to come either. I could have stayed home and concentrated on socking money in the bank. I felt it was my duty to join up. Remember what old Robert E. Lee said. 'Duty is the sublimest word in the English language.' He knew what he was talking about."

"'Most sublime,'" I said, thinking of the contrast between this noisy, brash clown and the quiet dignity of General Robert E. Lee.

"Huh?" Yancey asked.

"Robert E. Lee said 'most sublime.'"

"Well, it means the same thing. Why split hairs? To tell you the truth English is my weak subject. But you can't fool me on figures. I have an instinct for figures."

"I'm going to have another beer," I told him, not because I wanted it, which I didn't, but curious to see whether he would offer to pay for the second round.

"Not me," he said, stepping back from the counter. "I never drink but one beer. The stuff will bloat you. Besides it's bad for your wind. To get through infantry basic you're going to have to be in condition."

"I have hopes of not going to the infantry," I answered, annoyed at him for dodging the beer.

"Well, any basic is tough. Of course I think you're making a big mistake about infantry. What you going to tell your children?"

"I'll try to think of something."

"Don't be sarcastic. Sarcasm gets you nowhere. Besides you'll really want your children to be proud of you." He looked at an expensive gold watch on his wrist. "Lordy, it's almost eight-thirty. I have to make some calls. See you in the morning."

He hoisted his pants over his sagging belly, walked off, and came back. As he leaned toward me, he lowered his voice.

"I wouldn't drink too much if I were you. They're putting us on KP tomorrow, and it's tough."

"Thanks for the advice."

"Don't mention it."

"And for everything else," I said, holding up the mug of beer.

"Oh sure," he answered, smiling and not getting the point.

I watched him go. He hadn't thanked me for the writing paper, the envelope, or the beer. Furthermore at the steps he winked a last time, and before I could stop I found myself winking back.

4

Yancey was right about KP being tough. At four in the morning noncoms ran through our barracks blowing whistles and stripping off covers. We stumbled from bed in astonished disorder.

Only Yancey was cheerful. He walked through the room to the latrine calling "Rise and shine." As he shaved, he sang in a trembling off-key voice. He slapped men on the back. Growls followed him.

"KP, KP, KP," he said. "This old Army hasn't changed much. They

14

used to treat us this way back in the First War. You fellows better get used to it because we'll be working the mess hall from now till we're shipped out. Go at it slow and steady. Spoon out your energy."

In a whisper he advised me to hurry. He wished to reach the kitchen early because of his belief that the first men received the easiest jobs. I didn't want him to wait for me, but he did. Purposely I dawdled. He fretted until I left the barracks.

We walked through the cool morning darkness to the huge central mess hall. Coal smoke rising from chimneys turned the air acrid. Inside, a porcine sergeant sat at a table drinking coffee. His assistant, a first cook who held a duty roster, assigned Yancey and me to filling sugar bowls.

"What'd I tell you?" Yancey asked. "We got the soft stuff. Think of those poor fish on pots and pans."

The doors opened at seven. Soldiers crowded into the room we had made immaculate for them. I ran back and forth between the kitchen and serving line carrying tubs of food. Men were yelling "Hot stuff!" The kitchen was an inferno of boiling kettles and swirling steam. KP pushers shouted orders.

When the doors closed, the mess hall was in shambles. Yancey was put to washing tables, and I scrubbed floors. I used brown soap, a bucket of water, and a stiff brush. I had to get down on my knees. My new fatigues were soaked from ankle to thigh.

After the floor was clean, a KP pusher sent me with others to the refrigeration chambers where we carried out bloody carcasses of pork and beef. Grease coated our fatigues. We chipped ice from tubing as smelly water from the ceiling dropped on us.

The porcine mess sergeant was a lordly figure. He never spoke directly to any of the KPs. He was followed wherever he went by the first cook who gave the orders and did the chewing out. The mess sergeant acted pained by what he saw around him. He resembled a man enduring long suffering.

At noon we had to be ready for another horde sweeping in from the doorways. A different shift of cooks came on, but the KPs were not allowed even a ten-minute break. Pots and pans were stacked chin-high around the draftees assigned to scouring them. The eyes in their blackened faces rolled without hope.

Again I hustled tubs of food from the stoves to the serving tables. A KP stumbled and spilled an urn of boiling, bubbling coffee. The black coffee swirled across the floor. Men did a crazy, high-stepping dance to escape the heat under their shoes. Nobody was hurt, but

15

the KP who spilled the coffee was officially chewed out by the first cook and sent to clean grease traps.

After lunch the mess sergeant found a new job for a dozen of us. The building had rafters thirty feet above a cement floor. He decided the rafters were collecting dust and ought to be washed.

Doing so was a difficult, frightening task. Holding buckets of soapy water, we climbed swaying ladders. The height caused me to feel giddy. My back ached, and my eyes burned from dust. The rungs of the ladder became slick with soap. One man's feet slipped, and for a moment he dangled over space. His bucket crashed to the floor. By the time he was down safely, he was unnerved and shaking. The first cook exiled him to pots and pans for dropping the bucket.

My shoes were wet from soapy water slopping into them. My arches hurt, and my legs were tired from climbing the ladder. All the while KP pushers moved below us to see we weren't loafing. They were arrogant, pimply-faced men of no rank who were drunk on delegated power.

I hadn't seen Yancey for several hours. I didn't realize he was operating until I went to the kitchen for more water and heard his voice. He was outside on a steel ramp where trucks were unloaded. He sat among cooks and KP pushers. Like them he was drinking coffee.

"A lot of ignorant people don't realize how important cooks are," he was saying. "Cooks don't get much glory, but I'd like to know where this Army would be if it wasn't for the men at the stoves. Cooks and mess sergeants are unsung heroes. If I had anything to do with it, I'd see there was a medal especially for them. They deserve recognition."

"You ain't birding," a big-assed KP pusher said and spat.

"After all an army travels on its belly," Yancey continued. "You guys might not be in the front line, but if it weren't for you nobody would."

It was the most blatant and obvious kind of sucking up, yet the cooks and KP pushers were loving it. Yancey's voice had captured them. They sat nodding in agreement while he told them how great they were. I listened until a KP pusher came up behind me and shouted at me to get back to work. I hurried to my ladder.

I had to spend the rest of the afternoon among the rafters. I was filthy, my eyes were inflamed, and my neck had a crick in it. From my position up there, I could see Yancey boring in constantly among the cooks. They had an apron on him and were allowing him to cut meat. The apron gave him authority. He was ordering other KPs around.

When those of us in the rafters finished cleaning them, the first cook sent us to the loading ramp to wrestle garbage cans onto the trash truck. Yancey was trailing the first cook.

"Cheer up, fellows," Yancey said as he passed. "Remember it'll be worse tomorrow."

"Why don't you ram it?" a KP, outraged at Yancey's getting out of work, asked in a hissing whisper.

"Now, now," Yancey answered, smiling and winking. "There's no use being sore at anybody. Being sore only makes it worse. The thing to do is stay cheerful. That's my advice. Look on the bright side and stay cheerful."

He waved and hurried after the first cook. The two of them went into the mess sergeant's office. Later Yancey ate at the mess sergeant's table where he shared steak, cold milk, and fried eggs. The rest of us got stewed chicken on stale toast.

We weren't let off until nine-thirty that night. We had been on KP for over seventeen hours. During the last of those hours exhaustion stunned us. We shuffled about dazed, our eyes dull. At times we heard Yancey's merry laugh. The cooks were having a card game in the mess sergeant's office, and Yancey was playing.

Leaving the mess hall, we were bent, slack-jawed, and stiff with grease. We staggered through the night to the barracks. We almost went to sleep standing in the showers. Nobody talked. Each man fell on his bunk and groaned. On my bunk were two sheets of stationery and an envelope. Under the paper clip holding them together a note was fastened: "*Marvin Yancey always pays his debts.*" I crumpled the stationery, envelope, and note, and threw them against the wall.

At four the next morning we were again assaulted by whistles and sent to the kitchen. Yancey had to go too, but he lived a different life. He ate with the cooks and spent a leisurely day following the mess sergeant or sitting in the office. He had steak sandwiches whenever he wished. At night he got off earlier than the rest of us and was snoring by the time we reached the barracks.

We believed he had at last revealed himself. He wanted no infantry. Rather he figured the best way not to get a thing in the Army was to desire it. What he was really after was a cushy job in the mess hall. When we shipped out, we'd leave him behind.

We were beat down. Strong brown soap shriveled our skins. Grease became so enmeshed in our clothes that no amount of washing

17

would remove it entirely. We had dark pouches under our bleary eyes. Like coal miners early in the century, it was dark going to the job and dark returning. We reeled into the barracks too weak to complain. As we passed the PX on some of those nights we heard Yancey's laughter. He sat drinking beer with the noncoms at their table. He was buying.

On Sunday our shift was given the day off. That morning nobody moved in his bed, not even the country boys who were accustomed to rising with the chickens. We lay like corpses. I intended to sleep the entire day. A hand shook my shoulder. I opened my eyes. Yancey was bending over my bunk.

"You awake?" he whispered.

"Of course I'm awake," I said angrily.

"I been waiting for you. Want to go to church?"

"I want to sleep."

"They have a nice little church right here on the post. We could attend services and go into town for a chicken dinner."

"Get the mess sergeant and first cook to go with you."

Yancey was blinking down at me through his thick glasses. His large brown eyes were never still.

"You're sore," he said. "You're sore because you have to work harder on KP than I do. Admit it."

"It's your business if you want to brown the cooks. Just leave me alone when I'm sleeping."

"Now, Charley, brown's a pretty strong word."

"It's the word everybody's using. You've been buying the cooks beer."

"I've bought a few beers and I admit it, but you have to understand conditions are only temporary. I mean we're not going to be here long and frankly it's kind of a waste of talent to make people like us scrub floors or wash pots. If a person can get out of the dog work, I think he's entitled to do it."

I was glaring at him. I longed to return to the velvet depths of my sleep. He waved his pudgy hands over me.

"Don't get sore," he said. "When the time comes I'll do my part. Old Marvin'll be right in there with the rest and best of them."

"Will you let me sleep?"

"Well okay," he answered, adjusting his tie. "I just thought you might like to go to church. Now that we're friends and all I was afraid you might get sore if I went and didn't ask you. In this man's Army, good buddies should stick together."

I pulled the blanket over my face.

18

5

On Monday everybody except Yancey was again assigned to KP. He didn't have to get up in the wet darkness but slept on in his cozy nest. Later in the morning he came to the mess hall and ate breakfast with the mess sergeant. The induction center was supposed to ship a man out as soon as his processing was finished, but by the tenth day most of us who'd been on the train from Richmond were still in the kitchen. We yearned to leave. Anything would be better than the exhausting inhumanity of the labor we were doing.

Each afternoon we were allowed a few minutes off to listen to a master sergeant call out the names of people who would be moving the next day. It was an exciting time. The sergeant stood on headquarters steps and milked the suspense by reading his list slowly. When a person heard his name, he straightened and sometimes clicked his tongue or snapped his fingers. I wanted badly to hear my own.

"They're saving us for infantry," Yancey said while I worked at the serving tables in the chow line. We had just come from the latest session with the master sergeant. Our names had not been called. "I knew they would."

"Look, you don't have any more information than I do," I told him, irritated with myself for talking to him at all but feeling I couldn't let his knowingness go unchallenged.

"Maybe yes and maybe no. I happen to have a source of information. He's a certain sergeant who works in Classification is all."

I didn't believe him. There was no doubt he'd been snooping around, yet the unit to which a man shipped was purposely kept secret. By so doing, the Army avoided both protests and AWOLs.

Nor was I greatly worried about being sent to the infantry. I didn't think the Army would waste me in that way. Better use of my background and experience could be made in almost any other branch of the service. To my mind the infantry was the lowest of the low, and only men with whom Classification could do nothing else were sent there.

The master sergeant called my name on a Friday. I was jubilant. Others on KP were hearing theirs too. We smiled at each other. As I moved back toward the mess hall, however, I heard Yancey's name

19

and felt cheated. I would not be leaving him behind. He swaggered into the mess hall and acted as if he'd been aware all along he would be on the list.

"I knew it would be today," he boasted. "I just happened to see the roster on a certain sergeant's desk. Of course it's going to be tough down there. One thing we can say for sure is that it's not going to be any picnic. I'm out of shape, and I know it. It'll be a pleasure to feel these old muscles harden up again."

"Down where?" we asked, curious in spite of our determination not to speak to him—fish rising to the bait.

"Well, I can't say exactly. My source couldn't give me that info. That's up to the transportation officer. He keeps travel orders locked up in a safe. Odds are, however, it's the Deep South. Most infantry basics are down there because they have plenty of room to maneuver."

"You're wrong," I told him. I considered Yancey himself the best argument against our going to infantry. They wouldn't be sending anyone as unwarlike as him into combat training.

"Friend, I have the word," he answered.

"I'm not infantry material. Neither are you."

"Dogfaces we're going to be," he maintained stubbornly.

"Not a chance," I said, feeling my temper rise at his smugness.

"Bet you ten dollars."

"Done," I told him.

"Actually you'll like infantry," he said, heading for the icebox to get himself a waxed carton of cold milk—a privilege forbidden the rest of us KPs. "There's the pride of being in a tough outfit."

Except for Yancey, we didn't get off KP early the night before we left. We worked until ten and went wearily to the barracks to pack. Yancey had finished. He attempted to help us. We were suspicious and wouldn't let him touch our equipment.

In the morning he was the first up. He hurried to the latrine in order to be certain of having hot water for his shave. Later he bustled around the barracks giving advice. He looked rested and clean.

"Put all your breakables in the middle of your duffel," he directed. "Wrap your towels and blankets around them. And keep a towel, soap, and shaving gear at the top so you can get at them easily. You might have to live out of those bags a while."

We had twenty minutes for breakfast. That seemed a long time after the way we had been treated on KP. The men being left and still working looked at us enviously.

"You ought to give up coffin nails," Yancey told me as I lighted a cigarette to smoke with my coffee. "They cut your wind."

"Where I'm going I won't need wind."

"Money in my pocket," he answered.

"We're going to chemical warfare," a man who in civilian life had been a shoe salesman said. "I heard it from one of the cooks."

"Not a chance," Yancey countered, smiling superiorly.

"Field artillery," a young draftee put in. "That's what's needed most. I read it in the newspaper."

"Talk, talk," Yancey said, his attitude of omniscience infuriating. "All talk, talk. We'll be in infantry three days from now."

Whistles began to blow. We ran to the barracks and fell out with our duffel bags. As noncoms read our names, we answered by calling our serial numbers.

Buses were waiting. For lack of seats some of us had to stand. Not Yancey. He elbowed his way in.

The buses drove into town. At the rail depot we were lined up for another roll call.

"We'll go right down the coast," Yancey said. He wasn't speaking to me as much as to men around him. "It's the most direct route."

He kept talking. We tried to ignore him by looking up the tracks for the train. When it did come, nobody was happy. Coaches were old and grimy. Floors had not been swept since the last soldiers in transit. Seats were covered with a rough green material. The antique light fixtures had apparently been converted from gas to electricity.

As soon as I had a seat, Yancey pushed in beside me. He rolled his duffel bag onto the rack.

"We're really on the way now," he said, rubbing his hands.

I wanted to move. I'd have done so had not all other seats on the coach been taken. I sat lost and glum, staring through the dirty window at the sooty depot. Yancey prattled on.

The train didn't pull out for two hours, and its progress was maddeningly slow. After chugging a few miles up the track, it stopped for thirty minutes. Next it backed as if the engineer couldn't make up his mind where he was going. Naturally the coaches were not air conditioned, and we had to raise the windows. Men whistled at girls along the street, but the girls acted as if they were used to troop trains and rarely turned their heads.

I found myself attempting to analyze types. I felt if I got some sort of composite impression, I'd have a pretty good chance of determining what kind of basic we were going to. I walked from coach to coach searching faces of soldiers and classifying them into intelligent or dull categories. Since the infantry received the dregs, the two categories seemed all that were necessary.

I counted. Our shipment contained over five hundred men. There were some poor specimens, but we didn't resemble castoffs by any means. I returned to my seat feeling my ten dollars was safer than ever.

"Where you been?" Yancey asked as if he had a right to know. He was in my place by the window.

"You're in my seat," I answered, waiting for him to move.

"I'm watching scenery. You don't mind if I watch scenery, do you?"

"I mind if you're doing it from my seat."

"Okay," he said, sliding across to his own. "Okay, okay."

Yancey was right about our going down the coast. That fact didn't mean anything yet, but he continued to act smug. He had a road map he was marking with a pencil. At every station he'd lean across me to peer at the name of the city or town. Each confirmed his belief in our destination. He kept winking. I turned my head from him.

In spite of open windows, the train was hot. Within just a few miles I felt unclean. Coal smoke twisted along the sides of the coaches, and grains of soot fell into our laps. I went to the latrine to wash. There was no hot water. Even with soap it only reluctantly removed dirt.

For lunch we ate K rations. The wax boxes cluttered the floor of the coach. As soon as we finished, we attempted to catch up on our sleep, an act Yancey made difficult. He announced the name of each station loudly. He walked up and down the aisles. Unlike the rest of us he was not worn out from KP.

"What's the matter with everybody?" he wanted to know. "Is this a funeral we're going to?"

No one answered him. Already we had learned to put on a certain mask whenever he came around. The mask was forged of distaste and forbearance.

"You ought to be happy," Yancey was saying. "You ought to be living it up. This is a big day."

Our eyes remained closed. He walked to the front of the coach and banged the flat of his hand against the metal wall. Eyes opened. Yancey was smiling.

"Come on, fellows, get with it. Let's do some singing to pass the time. That's the way the British operate. That's how they keep their upper lip stiff. You all know 'The Caissons Go Rolling Along.'"

He waved his arms as if he were a conductor and started singing. Nobody joined him. For a moment his own unmusical tenor trembled above and below the melodic line. His voice petered to a stop. "Can't you fellows sing? Or do you think you're too good? You're no better than the British and remember how they saved the bacon for us. Now come on, let's go. On three. One, two—"

"Can it!" somebody in the back of the coach yelled.

"Ha, ha, ha," Yancey said. "I'll ignore the remark. Let's see how much noise this outfit can make."

Again his voice wobbled up. It wavered halfway through the first verse before stopping. Yancey looked hurt that no one had joined him. His slick, rubbery face worked into an expression of annoyance.

"I'm only trying to help. I don't think you fellows have the right spirit. If you want the truth, they ought to put the whole bunch of you in the quartermaster instead of the infantry."

"Blow it out!" somebody else shouted.

Yancey's face reddened, and he returned to his seat beside me. For maybe five minutes he was quiet. Yet he couldn't keep silent long. He squirmed and fooled with his map. He went to the front for a drink of water. On the way back he tried to talk men out of their magazines and newspapers.

He was an odd combination of brass and subservience. He would approach anybody and start conversing in a loud, arrogant voice. At the same time he seemed to be figuratively holding his hat in his hand as if wishing to be humble and liked. All the while his eyes were at work. They could have belonged to an Arab trader in the bazaar.

He found a crap game in the vestibule between coaches and crowded into it without being asked. When he came back, he had wads of dollar bills stuffed in his pockets and clutched between his fingers. Sitting by me, he smoothed the bills out on his fat thighs. He laughed to himself.

"Nobody beats me playing craps," he said. "I know the percentages. I have a mathematical mind and can figure them in a second. I never lost a dollar gambling in my life."

He filled his wallet. It held not only money won at craps, but also tens and twenties. He flashed the wallet. He was trying to impress me, but he didn't. I believed he was carrying all the money he owned.

23

Though I faced the window and away from him, he wouldn't stop talking. He began telling me about his house in Virginia. He said he lived in a mansion two hundred years old located in the hunt country. He bragged about the horses in his stables. He described the bloodlines of his bird dogs and a Hereford bull which had won prizes all over the state.

Everybody in the coach heard him. There were exhalations of disbelief and disgust. We knew he was lying. He continued to pile the lies up. He claimed his civilian clothes were tailored. His shoes were hand tooled by a New York firm. He had shotguns made in England. On his farm was a stallion he'd paid eleven thousand dollars for. The lies were so farfetched we couldn't even laugh.

A thunderstorm beat against the train, and we had to close the windows. Immediately the air became stale. My eyes burned. Yancey, however, never ceased talking. My head ached from his voice.

For supper we filed into a baggage car. Field ranges had been set up in boxes of sand. We ate out of our shiny, new mess kits. The food was lukewarm and tasteless. I dumped most of mine into a GI can and walked back to my seat. Night was falling. I tried to sleep.

Yancey's voice roused me. He was arguing with men at the front of the car.

"You don't know any more than the rest of us."

"I'm taking bets," Yancey said. "I'm making book. I'm warning you not to bet against me. I'm lucky."

Other men—dirty, cramped, provoked—were getting into it.

"Infantry's the first thing they fill up," one of them said. "They've already done that. Now they're putting together the service units to back them."

"How much would you like, friend?" Yancey asked, pulling out a small notebook and a pencil. "I can handle your money."

By late that night he had bets throughout the train that we were going to the infantry. He didn't reveal how much money was involved, but it must have been a considerable sum. As I tried to sleep, he gloated over his figures and made mysterious marks with his pencil.

"Like taking candy from babies," he said. "Oh yes, like candy from babies."

I was not able to sleep. The seat wasn't large enough for me to get comfortable in. The rough green nap rubbed my skin raw. My neck and back ached. I worked my tongue against the roof of my mouth in an attempt to dislodge the film there. My eyes, like those of the men around me, were sunken and stark.

Breakfast was as bad as supper had been. Again we filed into the baggage car. The cooks were disorganized from working in such narrow quarters. A second time I threw away most of my food. I was living on candy bars I'd had foresight enough to buy at the PX before leaving. Yancey, however, had a big appetite. He ate the pale, watery eggs with gusto. I couldn't bear to look at him as he hunched over the mess kit spread across his knees.

"Nothing wrong with Army food," he said loudly. "It's scientifically prepared to give a soldier the vitamins and minerals he needs. Eat up, fellows. Your old uncle is thinking of you."

After twenty-four hours on the train our seats had become instruments of torture. No matter how a person writhed he could not find relief. Men moaned and ran their hands over their faces.

Cinders and soot flying in the windows were turning our skins dark. We had given up trying to keep ourselves clean. Even going to the latrine had become an act of courage. The commode was clogged and stank foully. My own sweat had become sour. I reeled up and down the aisle as if drugged.

Yancey managed to get some sleep. He spread newspapers on the floor and wiggled under the seat. He was short enough to make it. Occasionally one of his arms would stick out and touch me. I moved my legs away quickly. His snores mocked us.

By the second night men were so desperate for rest they stretched out in the aisles. They no longer cared about their new uniforms. At first some of the transportation officers tried to stop them, but the officers were also tired and after a while gave up. To move through the coach, one had to step carefully over bodies.

In the vestibule a continuous crap game went on. The players were red-eyed and absolutely quiet as they rolled dice in what seemed slow motion.

"We were supposed to have sleepers," a draftee whined as if he might cry. "I read in a magazine the Army's supposed to provide sleepers for troops moving by train."

"Cheer up, fellow," Yancey called, looking refreshed after a nap and on his way to the crap game. "It'll be worse tomorrow."

"How does your buddy do it?" a soldier across the aisle asked me.

"He's no buddy of mine."

What I'd been afraid of was happening—people were beginning to associate him with me. I decided to become ruder than ever to

25

make him understand I didn't want him sticking to me. When he returned from the crap game with more money, I refused to answer his direct questions. He didn't notice. He was whistling and counting his loot.

By the morning of the third day we resembled damned souls escaped from Hell. Our eyes were unseeing, and our mouths agape. We had lost the power to propel ourselves. We sat rocking listlessly to the motion of the train.

Even Yancey was somewhat subdued, though he was still maintaining our position on his map. He continued to call out the names of towns we passed. He was particularly vocal at state lines. He was constantly consulting his notebook and giggling to himself.

In the afternoon the heat boiled us, and we were shuttled to a siding in the middle of a palmetto field. Brackish water stood in dark pools beside the track. The coaches became ovens. We sat in hot cinders on the shady side of the train. We panted like dogs.

Yancey spied colored children peeping through the palmettos. He shouted hello, but they were scared of him and ran. He went after them, following them to a ramshackle cabin under a dusty cedar tree. He went inside the cabin. A few minutes later he came back pushing a rusty wheelbarrow.

In the wheelbarrow were cold watermelons. Yancey set up shop right there beside the train. He cut the fat melons with a pocketknife and handed out dripping slices. Men, officers included, shoved and snarled at each other to get to him. Yancey sent the colored children with the wheelbarrow to bring in more melons.

"No charge, boys," Yancey kept announcing. "This is my treat. I got tired seeing you all look so sad."

The red, cold meat tasted sugary to our dry throats. We gorged ourselves and returned for more. We threw rinds along the track. Flies buzzed around them. Our chins and shirts were wet from juice.

Yancey talked the ragged, barefoot children into playing a harmonica and dancing. They clapped and kicked among cinders.

"Oh damn," Yancey said happily, still slicing melons. "Have plenty here for everybody and no cover for the floor show. Step right up and get yours."

By the time the engine whistle blew for us to climb aboard, we were stuffed to the point of stupefaction. Men found themselves thanking Yancey, though the rocking coaches caused some of them to become sick. They stuck their heads from windows and spewed out red streamers.

That evening about five we reached a section of eastern Mississippi. Our train squeaked and rattled to a stop at a small town where moss hung from trees. Officers roused us. We stumbled from the coaches carrying duffel bags onto a sandy field which had been bulldozed clean of Spanish bayonets.

Trucks were driving around the field and stirring up dust. Noncoms in fresh, stiff khakis walked along the sides of the train shouting and attempting to get us into formation. After a roll call we climbed on the trucks.

There weren't enough of them. Seats were quickly filled, and many of us had to stand. We fell against or stepped on the feet of the sitters. They cursed us with weary profanity. I went limp and allowed myself to be pushed in the direction of lease resistance. Yancey had maneuvered himself into a place near the tailgate. He was leaning out to see where we were going.

Some twenty minutes later the trucks slowed. Yancey almost toppled from his perch. He whooped and waved an arm. He had been able to see a sign which arched over the road leading into camp. On the sign were crossed muskets.

"We're dogfaces!" Yancey yelled. "It's an infantry training center. Get out your money. This is old Marvin's payday!"

6

We were given no time to be disappointed. As soon as we jumped down from the trucks, noncoms marched us into an area of huts painted gray. The training center had been knocked together hurriedly, and the huts were little more than cardboard. They shook whenever a person crossed the floor. I could have punched a fist through their flimsy sides. Wasps which had been nesting on the ceiling buzzed angrily around our heads.

Before we could move in, we had to scrub floors and wash windows. While we worked, Yancey crawled around collecting bets. He had his little notebook he slipped from his shirt pocket when no noncoms were looking. He got my ten dollars. For those who couldn't pay him immediately he extracted promises of money at the first of the month. Men stared at him in hate.

He was literally bulging with money from crap games and bets. He could hardly bend over for the lumpy wads of bills in his pockets. He smiled happily.

We were ordered from the huts. As I stood in the dusty company street, I could see across a hot, treeless plain. The view was desolation. Mosquitoes had discovered us, and we slapped at them. A draftee hollered in fear. He had stepped on a snake crawling from under a hut.

Our platoon sergeant, a hulking Slav named Bulgan, was already harassing us in the best tradition of basic. He never spoke when he could yell. He formed us into a platoon. Like other sergeants up and down the line, he made a little speech he had undoubtedly memorized and used on each new shipment of trainees.

"We don't baby you here," he said hoarsely. He was wearing immaculate khakis, and his web belting and leggings had been bleached. "In case you don't know, the purpose of the infantryman is to kill the enemy. I'll see you learn your trade. You ain't going to like me, and I'll cry myself to sleep every night worrying about it. You think you can whip my ass, I'll meet you behind the barracks any evening of the week and all day Sunday."

Next he called our names. When we answered, he glared as if sizing each of us up. Sight of Yancey made him pause. Bulgan approached for a closer look.

"I'll take some of the lard off you, fat man," Bulgan said.

"I'm in your hands, Sergeant."

"What's that?" Bulgan asked, unsure.

"I want you to take the fat off me. I know I'm not in condition, and I realize how important it is for an infantryman to be trim. I'd also like to say I thought your opening remarks to the platoon were very well put."

Bulgan wasn't actually dumb. He merely possessed the ungainliness of a large man. For a moment, however, he appeared dumb.

"Are you trying to brown me?" he asked.

"Not me, Sergeant. I thought your speech hit just the right note. A lot of these men don't understand how lucky they are to be in infantry training."

"Goddammit, you are browning me!"

"You're mistaken, Sergeant. I've just always made it a practice to tell a man when he does a good job. I believe in giving the Devil his due. Of course I don't mean you're the Devil."

"Close your yap!" Bulgan shouted. Yancey was quiet. Bulgan scowled at him. "What's your name again?"

"Yancey. Y-a-n-c-e-y. A lot of people call me Marvin."

"Well, I don't call you Marvin. I call you a stupid, fat yardbird.

You better learn one thing right now. You don't talk back to me in formation unless I ask you a direct question. Nobody talks back to me unless I ask them a direct question. Got that?"

"Sure, Sergeant. I've been in the Army before."

"Then you ought to know enough to keep your mouth shut."

"I do know it. This being our first day, however, I thought some latitude might be permissible."

"Will you shut up? I don't want to hear one more goddamn word from you."

Yancey was silent. Bulgan, an inch or so from his face, was glowering. He whirled, walked quickly to the front of the formation, and ordered us to double time it to supply to draw our bedding. As we stood in line a freckled country boy named Honeycutt snickered.

"What's so funny?" Yancey wanted to know.

"He's got you figured," Honeycutt answered. "You better watch out."

"Figured how?"

"You got caught with brown on your face. You ain't going to get out of duty in this hole."

"Now look here," Yancey sputtered, but before he could continue he reached the counter where the supply sergeant stood eying him.

I was hoping for quarters different from Yancey's, but Bulgan assigned us to the same hut. Yancey immediately set up his bed next to mine.

Bulgan showed us how to make the beds. It was strange watching the massive, ungraceful man doing a housewife's duty. He demanded our blankets be stretched so tight that a fifty-cent piece would bounce from them.

To his surprise and confusion the first man to get his bed right was Yancey. Bulgan reluctantly allowed him to go to the showers. The rest of us had more trouble. Bulgan came into huts like an angry bull, bellowing and turning over beds which didn't suit him. He threw our blankets into the air. We were exhausted from the trip, and I had the sensation I was condemned to an eternity of bedmaking. Men looked on passively as Bulgan kicked over their cots.

"Garbage!" he shouted, throwing a mattress across the room.

I had to do my own bed four times before Bulgan judged it right and motioned me to the showers. A simple pleasure long denied can seem a paradise. That's what the shower was. I lifted my grimy face into the streams of water and sighed. Just as I soaped myself, however, the hot began to give out. Those men who were last to finish their beds had to wash under water so cold that their teeth chattered. Yancey, of course, had used plenty of the hot for himself.

When I reached the hut, he was sitting on his cot studying his notebook. All his clothes had been hung in accordance with mimeographed instructions nailed to the back of the door. His wooden footlocker was ready for inspection. His pack and helmet liner were strapped to the foot of his bed. His shoes were shined and in a neat row.

"Make sure the laces are tied," he advised us. "When you hang up your shirts, button the pockets. Roll your socks and put them in the footlocker with the smooth side facing out. You want the inspector to see the best of everything."

He really wasn't giving us information we couldn't have learned for ourselves. All the rules were contained on the mimeographed sheet. He'd had more time to read it than the rest of us and was now posing as an expert.

Bulgan whistled us out for chow. Compared to what we'd been served on the train, the food was good. After eating, we returned to our huts and collapsed on our beds—all, that is, except Yancey. He roamed the company streets trying to find men who hadn't paid him. He didn't come in until we were asleep. He woke us by turning on the lights. Hatfield, a lean, dark coal miner from West Virginia, rose from his bed. He switched off the lights.

"Say now," Yancey protested.

"Leave them off," Hatfield told him in a soft but deadly voice.

Yancey left them off. We heard him bump around in the dark and finally lay on his bed. Before most of us could get back to sleep, he filled the hut with his snoring. We yelled at him. Honeycutt tossed a shoe. Yancey rolled over and smacked his lips.

At reveille Bulgan stormed among huts. He blew a whistle and pounded on the flimsy walls with a wooden billy. We ran into the street for roll call, and he told us that after breakfast we would police our areas for inspection.

The inspector was our platoon officer, a young second lieutenant about half the size of Bulgan. Bulgan followed him around with the protective loyalty of a faithful dog. The lieutenant was out to humble us by finding mistakes. He reprimanded us for such slight faults as having our shaving brushes improperly placed or arranging our handkerchiefs so that they faced in the wrong direction. Only Yancey got by without a gig. His area was perfect.

As soon as inspection was over, we were marched out for close-order drill. Yancey again shone. Whereas the rest of us tripped over our feet and bumped into one another, he executed Bulgan's orders without effort. He moved in the easy, gliding manner of fat men. Bulgan was puzzled but impressed.

Yancey had other advantages over the rest of us. The first days of basic were largely a matter of learning the small tricks of soldiering. He already knew them. Each night before going to bed he laid out his clothes on his footlocker in order to be able to dress quickly and reach the latrine first for a hot-water shave. He had a special way of getting a high gloss on shoes by heating the polish and letting it soak into the leather. He shined his brass with a Blitz cloth and painted clear fingernail polish on it to keep it gleaming.

When we were issued rifles, he was familiar with his. He blind-folded himself and practiced field stripping it until he could do it in a matter of seconds. His chubby fingers raced over the parts. He ran a patch cut from his Blitz cloth through the barrel so that it looked as if it were made of silver.

He also got the jump on us in classes. Most of the men didn't take seriously the instruction manuals passed out by Bulgan. Yancey, however, studied his. He used what he learned to brown unmercifully on the three afternoons a week we sat in the hot classrooms which smelled of new-cut lumber and tarpaper.

Either the officers didn't realize he was browning or else they liked it. They treated him as their star pupil. When they asked a question, they automatically glanced at Yancey. He, smiling and alert, was quick to stand with the answers.

"All right now," our second lieutenant asked. "Why is the muzzle velocity of an 03 higher than an M-1?"

He nodded to Yancey, and Yancey came to rigid attention.

"Because the M-1 uses some of the released gases to cock the piece and thus dissipates a portion of the explosive force. Such dissipation reduces the thrust of the projectile."

"That's correct," the lieutenant said, frowning at the rest of us. "Don't you others ever study?"

Yancey pretended not to hear our whispers or see our angry looks. He strutted about the hut giving us advice in the strident, high-pitched voice which rubbed our nerves.

"You ought to pay more attention to lectures," he told us. "I know it's hot in there and you get sleepy, but one of these days you might hear something that'll save your life."

Or, "Don't pull out your blankets when you get in bed, and at reveille you can slide over the head, smooth the blanket a little, and your bed's already made. That'll keep you from wasting a lot of minutes in the course of a year."

Or, "You should always wear two pair of socks so you won't have blisters. And if you strap your packs high, they won't feel as heavy on your shoulders."

Yancey's mistake was becoming overconfident and cocky. He was not only certain he knew more than the rest of us, but also at least as much as the cadre. One hot afternoon he misunderstood Bulgan's commands and did a right flank instead of an oblique. His error caused collisions and milling about. Bulgan started shouting.

If Yancey had just kept his mouth shut and let Bulgan yell, nothing would have happened. Yancey, however, apparently believed he was incapable of fault.

"I don't think I'm entirely to blame," he told Bulgan, and Bulgan's eyes popped.

"Well, just who in hell do you think is to blame for God's sake? You trying to pass the buck?"

"I'm merely trying to explain what happened. I couldn't hear the command clearly. Flank and oblique sound something alike. They have to be enunciated distinctly."

"You telling me I don't enunciate?" Bulgan shouted. "I'm a sergeant and you're a buck-ass private and you're telling me I don't know how to call close-order drill?"

"I didn't mean to reflect on you, Sergeant. You're a superior noncom and good at your job. What I'm attempting to explain is that I also know a little about close-order drill, and it's highly unlikely I'd execute such a fundamental command incorrectly if I could hear it. Usually your commands come in well, but perhaps the angle of march deflected it from my ears. I'm certainly not intimating you're at fault. I think our platoon's lucky to have such a noncom."

"You're browning me again."

"No, Sergeant."

"And you're talking too goddamn much. It's like Niagara Falls coming out of your mouth. Now shut it up and double-time around the drill field. I mean now."

The drill field's perimeter was easily half a mile, and it was dusty from battalion close order. Yancey carried his rifle at port arms. He began to jog. Bulgan ordered him to go faster. Yancey's pale fat bounced. The rest of us were marched into the shade and allowed to smoke.

On reaching the platoon again, Yancey was in bad shape. He was covered with sweat and breathing hard. His clothes were disheveled. His face was very red, and he kept opening and closing his mouth like a fish. At the hut, for once he had nothing to say. He lay blowing on his back with his arm over his eyes.

That was just the beginning. His double-timing it around the drill field had shown just how bad off Yancey was physically. Although Bulgan never again caught him in a mistake at close-order, we had already started taking marches once a week. On the marches we wore full-field packs and helmets as well as carried ammunition and rifles.

When the marches grew longer, they became a special hell for Yancey. He was at the rear of his squad because of his size, and a column has a tendency to act something like an accordion. One moment it's bunched up and the next strung out. That meant Yancey was either taking dainty steps or running to catch his squad. Those of us farther forward in the platoon could hear him scurrying behind us.

He was determined. He gave the hikes everything he had. The trouble was that physically he didn't have a lot to give. After the first few miles he began to slump. All the while the sun burned down and dust rolled from under our feet. His clothes became soggy with sweat. He would get the fish look on his face and wheeze. Bulgan yelled at him constantly.

"All right, Yancey, close it up goddammit!"

Yancey managed to flap along at our rear until we had a five-miler. That march caused his breath to rattle. He was covered with a gray film of dust which stuck to his sweat. His eyes became blank, and he reeled. He acted as if he weren't sure where the road was. Finally we heard a crash. He'd fallen into a drainage ditch and was lying on his back, his stomach humped up because of his equipment. No amount of yelling from Bulgan could raise him.

We in the platoon smiled at each other. We figured it was retribution for the way Yancey had acted on KP at the induction center and for the money he'd taken from us on the train. Of course he had provided the watermelon, but that didn't make up for his browning.

He had to ride back in an ambulance. On marches meat wagons followed each company. One carried Yancey to the door of our hut. He entered with his head lowered. His helmet had slipped over his eyes so that he looked something like a hermit crab. He fell onto his bunk and lay staring with watery, unblinking eyes toward the ceiling. When he gathered strength enough to heave himself up for a shower, he got the cold water.

It became the same every week for Yancey. Somewhere in the first five miles he always ended up in a ditch. His example helped the rest of us because falling out of ranks would have joined us shamefully with him. None of us wanted that. Thanks to him our platoon had the best record in battalion for finishing hikes intact.

Feeling sorry for Yancey did not pay. The hikes were hard on him, but he had the ability to recuperate fast. Within twenty-four hours he was almost as cocky as ever. He would be out looking for crap games or at the service club on the telephone. He had no genuine humility in him, and he explained away his failures as if they were slight.

"Breathing's the important thing," he announced as if somebody in the hut had asked him. "I have to learn how to breathe again. You may think it's a natural function and when you're young it is. As you grow older your lungs become lazy. They're out of shape and can't carry enough oxygen. That's why I'm working on my breathing. Soon as it's right, you fellows better watch out. I'll be walking right over you."

He would then go through his exercises. He stood in the center of the floor with his palms pressed flat against his body. As he lifted his arms slowly, he gulped in air until he was puffed up like a toad. He held the air as long as he could. His cheeks swelled, and his face became scarlet. Lastly he dropped his arms with a slap against his thighs and exhaled explosively.

Each evening he did the exercises twenty minutes while the rest of us were trying to write letters or catch a little sleep. We turned our backs on him and put our hands over our ears to shut out the sound of his puffing and blowing. We all wished him dead.

7

In addition to weekly marches, the obstacle course turned out to be another serious difficulty for Yancey—not all of the course, but only the wall. The wall was approximately ten feet high and made of reinforced oak planks. Trainees were supposed to run at it, grab the top, and pull themselves over. Yancey, being short and fat, could not jump high enough.

"Do it again," Bulgan ordered.

Yancey tried. He ran at the wall as if pursued by a tiger, his thick, meaty legs pumping furiously. He sprang, and his chubby fingers clawed at the top. They missed by only fractions of inches. His soft body thumped against the boards, and he crumpled to the ground.

"Again!" Bulgan shouted.

Yancey picked himself up, went back to the starting point, and flung himself at the wall a second time. He hit it with such force that his helmet bounced from his head, and he was dazed from the impact.

"Again goddammit!" Bulgan yelled.

Though Bulgan didn't particularly like Yancey, the noncom was not being any tougher on him than he would have been on any of the rest of us. Bulgan was simply concerned with finishing the training schedule which stated that each man should complete the obstacle course. He had never previously been confronted by a person who could not climb the wall. Bulgan felt it was his duty to make Yancey go over.

"You're stupid," he shouted. "You have to reach the top before you can pull yourself up. Now jump!"

Yancey jumped, but his fingers would not reach. He lay in the dust of his collision.

Bulgan kept him at it until Yancey was battered as a fighter. By then the rest of us would have already finished the course. We were allowed to sit around smoking. We were delighted with Yancey's misfortune.

Once or twice Yancey's fingers did manage to hook over the top of the wall. He couldn't, however, pull the rest of his flabby body over. He struggled, kicked, and twisted, but his foot would not make it. He hung for a moment before letting go. Bulgan screamed at him so loudly that Yancey hunched his shoulders as if against a storm.

Naturally he attempted to talk his way out of it. He apparently believed he could get out of anything by talking.

"It's only a simulated wall," he said to Bulgan. "It's highly improbable that one would meet with such a situation in actual combat. The purpose of the wall is physical training."

"Huh?" Bulgan asked.

"I said the purpose of the wall is merely for training. Chances are a million to one that anything like this would be encountered under combat conditions."

"Listen, fat man, the training schedule says you got to complete the entire obstacle course. Now get your whale tail over that wall."

Yancey was taking a terrible beating from the wall. The sound of his soft body hitting the boards was like that of an overly ripe melon. Bulgan would keep him at it until the platoon had to move on to another phase of the day's training. Yancey limped after us looking as if he'd been run over by a truck.

Bulgan refused to accept the fact Yancy would never get over the wall. After chow each evening he took Yancey to the obstacle course so that he could practice. The rest of us were allowed to go to service clubs or post movies, but if we stood at the edge of the company area we could hear Yancey's body thumping against the wall with regularity. Bulgan held a flashlight in order that Yancey might see in the dark. Later, just before taps, Yancey staggered in bruised black and blue, splinters in his fingers, his knees bloody. He fell on his bed like a dying man.

"The whole secret is breathing," Roberts said unmercifully. "If you breathe deep and get enough air in your lungs, you'll be light enough to float over the wall."

Yancey, his jaw slack, didn't open his eyes.

"That's right," Bailey added. "Or you could tie coil springs on your shoes and bounce over."

"He ought to try farting," Honeycutt, the country boy, said. "I always let me a big fart just as I reach the wall. Shoves me right over."

For once in his life Yancey didn't have answers. He was too weary. He went to sleep without undressing and lay snoring. By his snoring he was still able to inflict punishment on us because he sounded like a boar hog rutting. In the morning there was always a pile of shoes around his bed.

We wondered how much longer he could last. The strain of both the marches and the wall was wearing him away. Not only was he marked with lumps and bruises, but he was also losing weight. His uniforms began to look baggy on him, and his shoulders sagged. He was too exhausted to spring up quickly in classes with answers for the officers.

To make matters worse he had trouble on the infiltration course. The course had been created in order to reproduce as faithfully as possible simulated battle conditions. Machine guns shooting live ammunition traversed the area. Explosive charges were buried in the dirt to give the effect of artillery or mines. They were detonated from a control shack at the end of the course. Sounds of rifles, mortars, grenades, howitzers, and naval guns roared from metal loudspeakers set on tripods.

By platoons we were sent to a trench at the beginning of the course. We squatted and listened to bullets zinging. At a command from the loudspeakers, Bulgan started us over a parapet two at a time.

I was near Yancey. He was nervous. For once it was a cool day, but he was sweating. He licked his lips and clutched at his rifle. When he noticed me watching him, he winked.

"Nothing to it," he said. "A man couldn't get hurt if he wanted to." He didn't look convinced.

Bulgan tapped Yancey and me on our helmets, the signal to start. I wiggled over the parapet and crawled along the ground, my rifle folded in my arms, my head low. An explosive charge went off to my right. Bullets were hissing overhead. Yancey was behind me, his nose almost touching the ground.

I reached the barbed wire. Our instructions were to roll on our backs and squirm under as we held up the bottom strand. I had no trouble. Dirt rained around me from an explosive charge.

As I continued, I heard whimpering. When I was a boy my father had bought me an Angora rabbit. A bird dog had caught the rabbit, and its soft cries of terror were very much like the sounds I was hearing now. I looked behind me.

Yancey was caught in the wire. His belly, ballooned by his pack, had pushed right into the barbs. Panicked, he was making rabbit noises. I was afraid he might try to raise up and be punctured by bullets.

"Back up and start through again," I called to him.

"I'm stuck."

"If you back up, you'll pull free."

"Honest to God I can't budge. Help me, Charley!"

I had no choice. I changed directions and crawled to him. Another explosive charge went off. My head ached from the concussion. I reached the wire. Yancey was trembling so badly his equipment rattled. His eyes were shut. I attempted to unhook barbs caught in his fatigues.

"Get hold of yourself," I told him roughly.

"I can't move."

37

"You can move. Open your eyes."

He opened his eyes slightly. They shifted about. He would have appeared comical had it not been for the bullets.

"All right, now back up a little," I ordered him. "As soon as you get your weight off the wire, I can finish unhooking you."

I shoved on him. He moved maybe an inch. I twisted the barbs from his fatigues. He was still shaking. There was another explosion close by. He pressed to the ground. I grabbed his collar and pulled. As I held the wire up, he came under.

Once through, he sped along the ground. He was shaking and held his head low, but he kept up with me. Powder charges were going off. Each caused Yancey to flinch. We both looked as if we'd been digging ditches.

When we reached an area no longer under the traverse of machine guns or mined with explosives, Yancey quickly became more confident. He crawled ahead of me toward the end of the course and dropped into the trench. I followed him. As I straightened, I pushed back my helmet and eyed him. He was bloodless and dirt stuck to his sweat. He gasped for air. Bulgan was shouting.

"What the hell was going on out there?" he demanded of Yancey and me.

I turned to Yancey. So did Bulgan. Yancey licked his lips and tried to smile.

"Nothing unusual, Sergeant. I just got hooked on the wire. You all string wire differently than we did in the Great War. In the Great War we put less tension on the bottom strand."

"The hell with the Great War. You're supposed to come across the infiltration course unassisted. Now go back and do it again."

"Sergeant, I feel it's necessary to tell you I've been in combat, and sending me through a second time is a waste of my energy and yours."

"Don't give me no backtalk."

"You're hazing me."

To use a word like "hazing" was typical of Yancey—as if all this were some sort of blithe college affair instead of preparation for war. Bulgan was completely taken aback.

"What'd you say?"

"I believe in being a good sport," Yancey answered. "Frankly, however, I think you carry things too far."

The whole platoon was watching and listening. Bulgan sputtered. His tongue actually seemed to flap.

"Good sport? Why you fat garbage, you go back and come through that course again or I'll see you're court-martialed for disobeying a direct order."

"I'll go, but I got to say I'm greatly disappointed in you. You have all the qualities of being a first-class noncom and now you're compromising them by abusing your authority. You shouldn't try to humiliate a volunteer and a veteran."

With that, Yancey walked away. For once Bulgan was incapable of speaking. His mouth worked, but no words came forth. His hands opened and closed convulsively. He howled and ran to the control shack.

A few moments later Yancey came over the parapet. Immediately explosions erupted around him. Bulgan himself was working the detonators in the control shack. Like a mad scientist, he was pushing in plungers. As Yancey crawled slowly toward us he was bounced off the ground. Streams of fire from three machine guns slashed the air above him. The metal loudspeakers quivered with a paroxysm of sounds.

We wondered whether Yancey could survive. Bulgan seemed trying to destroy him. At times Yancey was completely hidden by dirt and debris thrown around him by explosions. He was a chip on a raging sea.

Soldiers from other companies were watching. Officers stood near the control shack and looked through binoculars. Somehow Yancey kept coming. I was sure he was terrified and his eyes would be shut. Perhaps he was making the rabbit sounds. Geysers of earth shot up practically underneath him. One blast turned him over and rolled him along the ground.

He reached the barbed wire, wiggled through without catching his fatigues, and dropped out of sight into a crater. He came up again and inched forward like some sort of brown, pulpy worm frantically trying to escape extinction.

When it was certain he was going to make it, we might have cheered had it been anybody except Yancey. Those of us watching were tormented by mixed feelings. We didn't want him to succeed because of the things he had done, yet we hoped he would because he was also one of us.

He finally reached the safe area and tumbled into the trench. He was the color of dirt, shaking, and panting for air. His watery eyes had streaked his face, and his glasses had been knocked awry. I believed he was going to fall, but he leaned against the trench. He

39

pulled at his throat as if choking, and I saw the mushroom paleness of his skin.

"Now you can claim you been through the infiltration course," Bulgan said, coming from the control shack.

"You're an irresponsible noncom," Yancey answered in a quivering voice.

We couldn't really believe we'd heard him correctly. Yancey was a bootlicker. Bucking authority didn't fit him. Bulgan was completely confused. He looked around at the rest of us as if he wanted us to confirm Yancey's words.

Up to that point I don't believe there was anything personal in the way Bulgan had treated Yancey. Bulgan was merely a cadreman doing his job in the blustering tradition of infantry basic. From that moment on, however, he saw Yancey as the enemy.

Bulgan swelled with anger. It was as if he grew before our eyes. To get at Yancey, he double-timed the platoon back to the company area. Yancey was not only out of shape but twice as tired as the rest of us. When we reached the huts, he reeled in ranks like a tree about to fall. We had to guide him through the doorway.

Bulgan never let up on him. The giant of a man would start at reveille and keep after Yancey until taps. For the slightest misstep Yancey was ordered to run around the drill field or given extra details of policing the grounds. Bulgan talked to the cooks so that on KP Yancey automatically was assigned to pots and pans.

Bulgan would call the company to attention and walk up behind Yancey. He would breathe on the skin of Yancey's neck. If Yancey so much as shivered, Bulgan punished him by making him march at attention with rifle and full-field pack along the company street.

Yancey had appeared pitiful before, but now he was ghastly. He looked like a person caught in a disaster he couldn't understand. His pale flesh sagged, and the circles under his eyes became deep pouches. He trudged through the area with an unseeing, vacant expression, his rifle at a crazy angle and his shoulder humped up. After dark as we lay in our beds, we could hear the listless shuffling of his aching feet.

He was always tired, and as soon as he sat down he went to sleep. Even in the classrooms he could not remain awake. Once the officers' favorite, he quickly became the butt of their displeasure. They first threatened, then gigged him, which caused more company punishment. No matter how hard Yancey tried to sit straight, his chin inevitably dropped to his chest and he would snore.

The extra punishment piled up. On Saturday afternoons or Sundays—times the rest of us were able to store a little energy for the next week's assault against us—he walked penalty tours or cleaned the grease trap at the mess hall. We saw him black and stinking with grease, his head bowed, his body bent like a hunchback's.

Bulgan was so relentless and Yancey so miserable some of us began to feel sorry for him. We found ourselves helping him. When he stumbled into the hut at night too exhausted to undress, we unbuttoned his clothes and removed his shoes. We unrolled his pack, cleaned his rifle, scrubbed his area, and arranged his footlocker for inspection.

"I think Bulgan's going too far," Carter said. Carter was a young man of eighteen from South Carolina who was imbued with a sense of Civil War glory. He descended from cavalry generals. Other than Yancey, he was the only volunteer in the company, and he also was proud of being infantry. The kindest among us, he had an old-fashioned sense of fair play.

"You're damn right he is," Jennings agreed. Jennings was a fertilizer salesman from Norfolk. A budding guardhouse lawyer, he talked aggressively about what the Army could or could not do to him. "We might as well be living in Germany. It's like having the Gestapo snapping at your ass."

Carter, being shot through with honor, let Bulgan see how he felt. Bulgan was double-timing Yancey around the drill field. Yancey tripped over his own feet and fell. Without asking permission, Carter left ranks to help him up. That evening and for the rest of the week he joined Yancey on penalty tours.

"We could go to the first sergeant," Carter argued at the end of the week when his tours were completed. He considered himself a good soldier and believed he had been punished unjustly. "He ought to know what's going on in this platoon. It's our duty to tell him."

Nobody answered that. Though we didn't like what was happening to Yancey, in our limited world the first sergeant was a distant and majestic figure. He appeared only at inspections. The sleeve of his blouse was stiff with service stripes. His lair was the orderly room —a mysterious place none of us had ever entered and from which issued the orders and directives that controlled our lives.

Carter convinced himself his mission was righteous. He started talking it up. He came after me, but I evaded him. Feeling sympathy for Yancey was one thing. Sticking my neck out in a way which

41

might jeopardize my chances for OCS was another. The Army had a long memory.

Carter believed we should go as a platoon. He walked from hut to hut in an effort to persuade men. He converted Timberlake, the other college graduate besides Yancey and me—if Yancey was at all which I doubted. I had already sized Timberlake up as competition for OCS. He was a tall, towheaded law student who habitually frowned.

With Timberlake on his side Carter's cause kindled fire. I was the last holdout. Everybody in the platoon stared at me as if I smelled bad. Reluctantly I agreed to join them.

We made our march on a Thursday evening after chow. Yancey was on KP, toiling among the filthy pots and pans. Each of us had on clean khakis. Carter led the way. I stayed in the rear, hoping I would not be noticed.

At the screen door of the orderly room Carter acted resolute, but his knock sounded timid. I wondered whether I could slip around the corner of the supply shed. The trouble was men from other platoons were gathering to watch. I was unable to escape without their seeing me.

The company clerk, a small man with a mustache, came to the screen door and looked out at us with no change of expression.

"We'd like to talk to the first sergeant," Carter told him.

The company clerk's eyes swept over us. I was sure he was taking names and tried to appear as inconspicuous as possible.

"He ain't here," the company clerk said.

"We'd like to make an appointment," Carter insisted.

"You think this is a dentist's office. We don't make appointments."

"We have a right to see the first sergeant," Carter, the idealist, maintained.

"You got a right to wait," the company clerk answered, turning from the door.

We stood outside in the street for over forty minutes. At first we didn't realize the first sergeant was in the orderly room all the time. Only when he passed the screen door without even glancing at us did we understand. He was with Bulgan, and they were laughing together. I wanted to leave. It was obvious the first sergeant wasn't going to have anything to do with us.

"Maybe we ought to come back tomorrow," Jennings, the guardhouse lawyer, said. He had lost his nerve and was sweating.

"It might not be a bad idea," I agreed, knowing that I wasn't coming back tomorrow or any other time.

"We can't leave now," Carter protested. "That's what they want us to do."

"Carter's right," Timberlake said. "We have to stick it out."

"Not me," Jennings told them. "I'd like to stay, but I got fish to fry."

I was glad he left. His doing so allowed me to get away without catching great blame for it. I slipped off and walked up the street past men from other platoons who were whispering and watching. I didn't wish to be the first one to reach the hut. To keep from it, I circled the area before going in. When I entered, others were there. We avoided eyes.

Carter, his stubborn southern blood up, stuck it out for two hours. In the end the only men who remained with him were Timberlake and Hatfield, the coal miner from West Virginia. We'd been shocked to discover Hatfield was being treated twice a week at the infirmary for syphilis. He had no love for Yancey, but he did have a sort of dumb friendship toward Carter. Besides, Hatfield would never back out on anything.

Though they stayed in front of the orderly room until lights out, they never did get to talk to the first sergeant. He left by another door. Carter, Timberlake, and Hatfield came to the hut.

"You're brave men," Timberlake accused us. "You're a real bunch of lions."

The next day Carter tried to talk us into returning to the orderly room. The attempt was half-hearted because he'd been whipped and realized it. As he spoke, men were busy shining shoes or studying. In the end Carter too was silent.

Yancey was obviously finished. He was so beat down he was going to goof badly and end either in the stockade or the post hospital. Most probably he would eventually be discharged under a convenience of the government regulation. The quicker he left, the better it would be for us. Once Yancey was gone, Bulgan would ease up on the platoon.

On Sunday we had a dress parade for a visiting general from Washington. At the sounds of whistles we all hurried from our huts buttoning our blouses and adjusting our caps. Bulgan was shouting. When we were in formation he automatically looked down toward the end of the second squad where Yancey was. Bulgan stared and

43

then squinted. He looked angry. With fists balled, he strode to Yancey and stood before him.

"What the hell's that on your blouse?" Bulgan demanded.

"My ribbons," Yancey answered, his voice broken and weak. "I'm entitled to wear them."

"Who entitled you?"

"I won them in the last war. It's on my service record. You can look on my record and you'll see."

By then everybody else in ranks had turned his head in an attempt to see. Bulgan was blinking. When he spoke, he sounded uncertain and a little afraid.

"What are they for?" he asked.

"One's the Victory Medal," Yancey said. "Everybody got that. The second's the Purple Heart. The last is the Distinguished Service Cross for gallantry in action in France."

8

Yancey a hero! The idea was so fantastic our minds could not work with it. I who'd seen his terror on the infiltration course thought the ribbons must be a desperate move on his part to save himself. If that were true, he was in real trouble.

As soon as the dress parade was over and the formation dismissed, Bulgan rushed to the orderly room to check on what Yancey had told him. He found he could not. Yancey's old service record had not yet arrived from Washington. In the meantime Yancey continued to wear the ribbons on his blouse, and Bulgan felt powerless to act.

Yancey gained immediate relief. While the officers and noncoms waited for the service record, he was no longer put on extra duty or company punishment. Bulgan stopped double-timing him around the drill field. At the obstacle course Bulgan glanced the other way when Yancey reached the wall, and Yancey ran around it. Instead of getting pots and pans on KP, the cooks put him to work sweeping floors or helping with rations.

With the pressure off, Yancey was able to recuperate. He caught up on his sleep, and his shoulders firmed. The black pouches faded under his eyes. His voice grew stronger, and inside a week he was nearly his old self.

"Most of you guys eat too many potatoes," he said. "Now potatoes are all right in cold weather where you're burning off energy, but you ought to go light down here in Mississippi. Too many potatoes clog up your pores with starch. Then you don't sweat, and a man should sweat. It's healthy to sweat."

All of us, enlisted men, noncoms, and officers, watched him in awe. We could not accept the fact he really deserved medals, but on the other hand we didn't believe he would be foolish enough to lie. Until we knew for sure, we kept silent. Yancey enjoyed our bewilderment. His expression became sly.

Although an urgent request was put in for Yancey's old service record, ten days passed before it arrived by registered mail. The company officers and cadre gathered to read it. The record verified that each of Yancey's ribbons had been duly entered. Thus Yancey officially became a celebrity. Men who had previously regarded him with contempt now watched him in envy.

To our surprise Yancey displayed a degree of modesty. He removed the ribbons from his blouse. Of course he didn't need to wear them any longer. Everybody knew he had them, and that was just as good as putting them on. Still it would have been more like him to flaunt the medals than to spare our feelings.

Because of the medals, Bulgan in particular became a subdued and disturbed man. He respected the infantry. Moreover he himself had never been in combat, and he now felt inferior to Yancey, who had. Bulgan would hardly look at Yancey for fear he might be accused of picking on him. In his confusion Bulgan stopped shouting altogether. His commands sounded meek.

Yancey began to lead a charmed life in the company where only a few weeks before he had been the object of persecution. No directive had to be issued that he be given special privileges. Men in authority instinctively softened his life.

For example if long marches were scheduled, he would either be assigned as a battalion runner or put on fire guard. During field exercises he was chosen for latrine or hot-water duty. When we came stumbling back weary and covered with dust, Yancey would be stretched out on his bunk clean and full of life.

"What a sad bunch of warriors," he taunted us as we struggled with our heavy equipment. "If the enemy could see you guys now, he'd consider the war won."

Once somebody like Hatfield would have told him to shut his fat mouth, but now nobody dared talk back to him. We'd lost the right to. Yancey had moved from the province of ordinary trainee into more worldly realms. He seemed closer to the cadre than to us. He could bang our ears with advice, and we had to suffer silently.

"You fellows ought to buy arch supports," he told us after we returned from a particularly cruel forced march he'd missed. "A dogface is no better than his feet. If they ache, he's whipped before he gets into battle. I'm telling you what's a fact."

Each day he became surer of his own self-importance. He'd gained back most of his weight and strutted as if he personally were directing the company. The noncoms not only allowed him to get away with it, but even treated him with deference. He now had access to the orderly room where he was permitted to sit around and chat with officers. He was seen paying for the first sergeant's beer at the PX. The two of them were drinking and laughing together like old cronies.

I'd hardly spoken to Yancey since he got into trouble with Bulgan, but on Sunday he called to me as I was walking to the service club. I was still trying to fit his behavior on the infiltration course to the medals he'd won. I'd come to the conclusion the difference was a matter of age. He would have been only eighteen or so during the First War. Over the years he could have lost his nerve.

"I want to thank you, Charley," he said when he caught up with me. We went on toward the service club.

"Thank me for what?" I asked.

"I know you're one of those who went to the first sergeant about me. I really appreciate it."

I looked at him closely, thinking he might be speaking sarcastically, but he wasn't. He actually seemed to believe I'd exposed myself for his sake when I'd done everything I could to get out of it. I didn't tell him the truth now. He was becoming a power in the company, and I was aware he could be an asset to me.

"Well, that's what buddies are for," I answered, not sure I could get away with it. Certainly I'd never considered myself his buddy. He, however, didn't mock my words.

"You're right," he told me seriously. "I want you to know I'll never forget it either."

From that afternoon on, we were together daily. I didn't like it because I realized I was browning him. I should have been ashamed, but I'd learned about browning people long ago at the bank. My belief was that everybody did it some time or other. Office boys browned tellers, tellers cashiers, cashiers vice-presidents, vice-presidents the president, the president the chairman of the board, and the chairman of the board the big stockholders and industrial accounts. If I had to be nice to Yancey, I could do it.

I soon saw his power working for me. During inspections Bulgan hardly glanced at my footlocker or bed. On KP I got the easy jobs. When I passed noncoms on the company street, they nodded or smiled at me. Because of Yancey, they had talked me over.

Undoubtedly the fact I had seen Yancey's cowardice on the infiltration course bothered Yancey as much as it did me. Naturally I never mentioned it. He made reference to it one afternoon on the rifle range. He was observing while I shot.

"Don't listen to everything they tell you out here," he said in a low voice. "When you get in combat, shoot with both eyes open. That's how all the old-timers do it. Here you just play the game."

He looked over his shoulder as if to be sure nobody was listening.

"None of this is real," he continued. "No matter how hard they try they can't create combat conditions. To know combat you have to be in it. That's why my nerves acted up a little the other day. I remembered the way it was in France. To tell you the truth, I'm glad it happened. I got all that mess out of my system. I'm clean of it."

His excuse sounded half logical, but I had reservations. There was an unreal quality about Yancey, a cunning. He was a man who figured percentages and angles. I wondered whether instead of my using him he was using me.

There was a definite change in our relationship. He no longer followed me around—I followed him. I trailed him to the service club, the PX, and the barber shop. I waited while he made his telephone calls. I played Ping-pong with him in the dayroom.

He was too good at the game for me and most others. He had a fast, clever serve which utilized lots of spin. He feinted constantly and waddled in with a smashing forehand. Each time he made a point he laughed, and I decided laughter was part of his game. It irritated his opponents into making errors. They became red-faced and flailed at the ball.

That he wasn't liked worried him. He talked about it a good deal. "I'm not popular," he said. "A lot of the fellows don't like me. Well they don't know everything. I sent the money I won from them on the train to the Red Cross. I didn't need the dough. I give a hell of a lot to charity."

He was probably lying, though perhaps he had felt an impulse toward generosity and was puzzled by it.

47

Yancey was the one who mentioned OCS. We were returning from the service club and could see the cluster of yellow buildings set apart from the rest of the camp. As we walked he said he believed qualified men ought to be allowed to enter officer training without having to go through basic. He told me he would be glad when eight weeks were up so he could apply.

"Apply?" I asked. I intended to make my own application, but I never thought about Yancey's doing it.

"Sure," he answered and winked. "I've already talked with the CO. In my case getting in is just a formality."

I didn't answer. If there was one thing Yancey was not, it was officer material. He was a horse trader, but no leader of men.

"I feel it's an obligation," he said. "I can put my experience to the best use. I'll be able to teach rookies a lot. War hasn't changed. The essentials are the same. In the end it's always experience that counts."

"Did you know I'm thinking of OCS myself?" I asked carefully.

"Sure I know. I picked you out immediately. You and I belong. Most of the other guys are peasants. The two of us'll make the best line officers in the infantry."

9

Yancey, who continued to live his privileged life within the company, scared me about OCS.

"Getting in might be a little tougher than I'd thought," he told me on a Monday evening when he returned from the orderly room where he had been talking with the noncoms. "It looks as if the competition's going to be rough."

"How rough?" I asked, immediately uneasy.

"Well, it's more complicated than it used to be. The Army now has a pool of officers. You might say many are called but few are chosen. Still we ought to be able to make sure you get in."

I'd never before seriously considered the possibility that I might not make OCS. As my mother would have said, "Our men have always been officers." I found myself worrying about Timberlake, the law student. He had been made a temporary squad leader, and I had not. That meant the noncoms thought more of him than they did of me.

Yancey claimed he was working for me. He was definitely friendly with the first lieutenant who was our company commander. The lieutenant had also been in the construction business, and he allowed Yancey to use the orderly room telephone for his calls to Virginia. Yancey said that whenever he could, he slipped in a good word about me.

I was leery of his help. There was always the danger that a man like Yancey might overdo it. If he stumbled in his intricate manipulations, the bad feeling would be held against me as well.

On the other hand it seemed to me I had to use him. At the moment anyway he did have the inside track with both noncoms and officers. I, as a result, found myself being especially nice to him. When we drank a beer at the PX, more often than not I paid for it. I listened to his talking and braggadocio without complaint. I could no longer afford to be rude.

He knew he had a hold on me. Whenever he spoke of OCS, his expression became crafty and he dug at me.

"Maybe you don't think I'm such a bad guy after all," he said, holding a bottle of beer I'd bought him and smiling.

"I never thought you were a bad guy," I answered, the lie tasting bitter in my mouth. "Where'd you get that idea?"

"I could tell what you thought. I don't mind because I don't believe in holding grudges. Maybe you learned a lesson. It shows you how wrong first impressions can be."

We both had the basic requirements for OCS, which were few and simple. We must pass a physical and have IQ's of at least 110. Yancey claimed, however, that because of the glut of officers all company commanders had been instructed to cut down on nominees, restricting their lists to men who were truly exceptional. Those men in turn would have to appear before a regimental board of examining officers.

"It looks as if only eight of us from battalion will be allowed to appear before the board," Yancey reported after further talks with the lieutenant. "That's the official figure. Qualifications don't count so much any longer. Everything works on quotas."

"Eight isn't very many," I answered, knowing that in the four companies a lot more men would want to go.

"It's enough. Just stick with me."

"I hope you're right."

"I'm right," Yancey assured me. "I've been banging the lieutenant's ears about what a great guy you are. I can tell you you're definitely being watched."

The idea I was being watched put more pressure on me than ever. I had naturally been doing my best, but now I was constantly afraid of making a mistake which might influence somebody's judgment of me. The compulsion to be perfect made me tense with anxiety. Yancey on the other hand was fat and relaxed.

Just as he had predicted, a notice was tacked to the bulletin board of the orderly room four weeks before the end of basic. The notice stated that any men qualified for OCS could submit application by reporting to the company commander at seven o'clock Thursday evening. I shined my shoes and polished my brass. Others in the hut glanced at me as if I were betraying them for wanting to be an officer.

The initial step was easier than I'd expected. At the orderly room the first sergeant sent us one at a time into the company commander's office. We saluted and gave our names. The lieutenant, a burly, heavyset man, wrote down our names and told us our records would be assessed by the company officers and noncoms. He seemed somewhat bored by the whole business.

There were six applicants from the company—a number which was unnerving in light of what Yancey had said about only eight being allowed to go before the regimental review board from the entire battalion. The company commanders would have to purge their lists mercilessly. Walking back to the huts from the orderly room, our eyes shifted about as we tried to size each other up. Only Yancey was unconcerned.

The officers and noncoms met Friday evening to cull the list. Lights stayed on late in the orderly room. When they went off, Yancey hurried out of the hut into the dark. He returned at midnight and whispered that the company was sending up three men—himself, Timberlake, and me.

A notice posted the next morning made it official. Those who had been butchered from the list glared at those of us who had not. They could do nothing. There was no right of appeal.

Naturally Yancey had already found out details about the review board at regimental headquarters. The board was composed of a full colonel, two lieutenant colonels, and four majors. They were not bound to find anyone who appeared before them officer material.

Timberlake, Yancey, and I went up to regiment on Monday morning. As we walked along the edge of the road, we attempted to keep dust off our shined shoes. Headquarters building was a sprawling frame structure which had been freshly painted. Candidates from other companies and battalions were gathering in front. There were at least forty men.

Each group stuck together protectively. Yancey, however, moved about the yard as if the whole affair were a social. He talked about the great responsibility of being an officer and said a person should feel a deep sense of certainty before becoming one. He made everybody nervous.

"It's tough too," he told them, obviously enjoying the discomfort he was causing. "It makes basic seem like a Girl Scout picnic. I hear they scratch half the class."

I wished Yancey would shut up. He kept winking. I was eying the others and trying to calculate my chances.

"Breathe easy," Yancey whispered. "Look as if you're certain of yourself."

A sergeant came out of regimental headquarters. He held a roster and called the name of a man from 1st Battalion. That man remained inside approximately fifteen minutes and reappeared looking ashen. As he walked off, he would say nothing even to the group from his own company.

Every fifteen minutes or so another name was called. At noon neither Yancey, Timberlake, nor I had gotten in. We stood in the sun, afraid to sit for fear of messing our uniforms. The review board adjourned for lunch. By that time I was so tense I couldn't swallow food.

After lunch Yancey, Timberlake, and I returned to regimental headquarters. Our collars, like the dry, crackling grass we stood on, wilted in the heat. At a few minutes after three, Yancey's name was called. Winking, he swaggered into the door.

Timberlake and I did not speak. He had little regard for me because I hadn't stuck it out with him, Carter, and Hatfield when the platoon went to the orderly room on behalf of Yancey. I didn't care in the least what he thought of me.

While Yancey was inside, I believed I heard his laughter, but I decided it was my imagination. I considered it impossible that anybody could laugh under such conditions.

I waited for him to come out. I'd examined the faces of all men leaving, in the hope of learning something useful. Each had been silent and wan. They would answer no questions. Answers might give somebody who had not been inside an advantage before the review board.

When Yancey opened the screen door, however, he walked to me and led me away from Timberlake. Timberlake scowled at us.

"They'll ask you why you want to become an officer," Yancey whispered. "Shoot them a little bull. Tell them you want to serve your country and think you can do it best as an officer. They'll also make you give a speech. They asked me to talk about red foxes."

"Red foxes? I don't know anything about red foxes."

"Neither does anyone else. The important thing is not what you say but how you say it. Just be sure you keep going. They'll be looking at you to see how you react under pressure."

He slapped me on the back and told me he'd wait for me at the company. He walked away whistling and snapping his fingers. His quivering buttocks were wider than his shoulders.

"He tell you anything?" Timberlake asked, edging toward me and smiling ingratiatingly.

"Nothing," I answered, and Timberlake's eyes narrowed with hate.

When the sergeant called my name, I straightened my blouse and entered the building. I followed him down a corridor along which clerks worked at desks. They glanced at me with the same expression of betrayal I had seen in the company. At the end of the corridor was a double door.

"Walk in, salute, and state your name," the sergeant instructed me. He went to his desk.

Squaring my shoulders and holding my hands along the seams of my trousers, I stepped forward. I entered a large room at the end of which was a long table where the review board sat. Each member had a pencil, pad, and folder before him. The full colonel sat at the very center, and the other officers were evenly divided on either side of him. I approached the colonel, stopped three feet in front of the table, and saluted. The colonel returned my salute.

"Private Charles Talliferro Elgar reporting to the review board as directed, sir," I said, standing at rigid attention.

None of the officers answered. Their eyes moved over me as if I were a piece of meat. They made me stand that way a full minute before any of them spoke. I found it difficult to breathe quietly.

"Questions!" the full colonel snapped, causing me to flinch.

"Private Elgar, why do you believe you should be an officer?" a lieutenant colonel asked.

"Sir, I've considered that question, and it's my belief a man should

52

strive to utilize himself fully," I answered, not looking at the lieutenant colonel but straight ahead at a smudge on the brown wall. I was trying to throw the bull as Yancey had indicated. "I think I can best serve my country as an officer."

Of course it sounded completely false. Somebody should have laughed. Lateral vision showed me a cynical smile on the face of a major.

"So you want to serve your country?" the major asked.

"Yes, sir, I do."

"You think perhaps you're doing your country a favor?"

"No, sir."

"You think maybe you'd better yourself and get on to a good thing?" another major said. "You think officers have it soft?"

"Definitely not, sir."

"You like the infantry, do you?" the second lieutenant colonel asked.

"I consider it a privilege to serve in the infantry, sir," I lied.

"You're a college graduate," a major said, leafing through a folder. "Were you pretty good in college?"

"I had a B average, sir."

"That's not so hot. Did you hold a class office?"

"No, sir."

"Play football?"

"I played tennis, sir."

"I didn't ask whether you played tennis. I asked you about football."

"I didn't play football, sir."

"What makes you think you're capable of leading men into combat?" the full colonel asked.

"Well, sir, I'm not without experience in leadership. Where I worked in a bank I had employees under my supervision. Intra-office relationships were excellent."

"You think running a platoon of infantrymen is like working in a bank?" a major asked.

"No, sir. I did, however, have to exercise responsibility and command."

The major grunted. A lieutenant colonel tapped his pencil on the table.

"Tell us about red foxes, Elgar. Being a Virginian, you must know something about the red fox."

"Well, sir, the fox, red or otherwise, has a reputation for being a very sly animal. I'm sure you've heard for example about the fox who couldn't get the grapes. The grapes were ripe and delicious, but they were too high for him to reach. After he tried to get them and failed, he made the comment the grapes were probably sour anyway."

"How do you know that wasn't a gray fox?" one of the majors interrupted.

"Sir, I must admit it might have been either a gray or red fox. I don't remember the author's being very definite on that point. Naturally the gray and red foxes are brothers under the skin. I assume they both like grapes. Also, in the French book I studied in prep school, there was a picture of a fox rearing for the grapes and in that picture he was red. Of course the painter could have been ignorant of the true facts in the case. It's entirely possible he had never seen a fox in his life either red or gray and was going entirely on hearsay."

I paused for breath, hoping they would allow me to stop, but they were watching sternly. They looked as if they had bitten down on something bitter. I hurried on.

"The red fox is generally larger than the gray and has been known to steal chickens," I said, desperately searching my memory. "He also kills many partridges and ruffed grouse. He has been observed leading a pack of hounds across a railroad track in front of an approaching train in an attempt to kill them. People who hunt foxes on horses have a different attitude toward them than farmers. The horseman considers the fox a good citizen and resents any effort to stamp him out. The farmer on the other hand thinks the fox is a predator. As you can see, the matter depends on what angle you look at it from."

I again allowed myself the slightest pause. There was no spit in my mouth, and my voice was shaky.

"In some sections of Virginia they trap the fox," I said, remembering an article I had glanced through in a dentist's office. "They boil the traps to remove the man scent and use a powerful fragrance to attract the fox. If I'm not mistaken, the male fox has a difficult time resisting the smell of the vixen's urine. Even when he's suspicious of a trap, he can rarely pass that up."

"Vixen urine?" the full colonel asked, blinking and looking interested.

"That's the way I understand it, sir."

"Where do they get it?"

"I don't know, sir."

"Certainly a female fox doesn't report to the infirmary and piss in a specimen bottle."

"I wouldn't think so, sir."

"Still it's an interesting fact. If it's true. It better be true. I intend to do some checking."

"Yes, sir."

"Proceed."

"Well, sir, a great many people use fox tails to tie to the antennas of their automobiles," I said, frantic now because I had nearly run out of things about foxes. "Some people also buy fox coats. It might be claimed a fox is known as much for his coat as his craft."

"Squirrels' tails are what people tie to their antennas," a major corrected me. "There wouldn't be enough fox tails to go around."

"I believe you're right, sir. Of course there is some similarity between a fox and squirrel tail."

"I take exception to that," the major said. "Proceed."

"Yes, sir. I'm certain all of us here are familiar with the fox in the Brer Rabbit stories. It's an interesting reversal that the rabbit is made more intelligent than the fox. Naturally in real life a fox is a lot smarter than a rabbit which is not smart at all."

"Bedtime stories," the major said. "You're telling us bedtime stories."

"Sir, I thought it might be worthwhile to trace the development of the rabbit and fox in our folklore."

"We want to know something profound about a fox," a lieutenant colonel put in. "Can you come up with something profound?"

"Well, sir," I said, feeling sweat run down from under my arms, "I've heard that if a hunter is on a deer stand and a fox comes by the hunter shouldn't shoot because often an old buck will be following the fox. Evidently the deer believes the fox will lead him to safety. I consider that pretty profound."

"I would consider that makes the deer profound, not the fox," the other lieutenant colonel said. "Moreover, I don't believe it."

"Sir, although I can't vouch for it personally, I've heard hunters swear it's a fact."

"I think it's an old wives' tale," the lieutenant colonel said. "You're spinning stories here."

"You also took part in a demonstration against authority," the full colonel said.

"Demonstration, sir?"

"We have a report here which alleges you and a group of trainees marched on your company orderly room."

So they knew about that too. The Army and its long memory. I cleared my throat.

"Sir, I'd like this board to understand I didn't want to go. I was forced into it by others in my platoon. I'm sorry about it, and I'd never again do such a thing."

"Allowing yourself to be forced into a situation isn't a sign of leadership ability, is it?" the major asked.

"It isn't, sir, but I can assure you I've learned my lesson."

I humbled myself. I didn't want them to have any doubts that I was really sorry. At the same time I wondered what Yancey would have thought had he heard me disowning him.

"Period up," a major at the left end of the table said. He held a watch.

"More questions?" the full colonel asked. The other officers sat at attention. The colonel blew his nose and spoke to me. "You may leave. A list announcing this committee's findings will be posted on your company bulletin board."

"Sir, I'd like to remind everybody he didn't tell us anything profound about a fox," the major said.

"Furthermore I intend to do some checking into that vixen urine tale," the full colonel added.

"Yes, sir," I told him, backing toward the door and repeatedly saluting. I was like the lowly born leaving the presence of an Oriental potentate. Still saluting, I reached the corridor where the clerks were. They stared at me contemptuously.

I hurried from the building. Other men were waiting in the yard. They looked hot and unhappy. Timberlake watched me hopefully, but I went past him without speaking. I was sweaty and trembling. I found Yancey in the hut lying on his bed. The rest of the company was out drilling. He waved a hand.

"How'd you do?" he asked.

"Miserable. Really miserable."

"What makes you think so?"

I told him everything that'd happened except the part about being sorry for going to the orderly room. I said I had failed to come up with anything profound about a fox.

"Don't worry about it," he assured me. "The important thing was to keep talking and use good English. You did that, and you'll come through."

I wasn't so sure. Timberlake was just as capable of talking and using good English as I was. In spite of Yancey, I couldn't lay my fears. I felt my future was on the line.

From that day on I couldn't pass the bulletin board without the sensation that it was taunting me. Each morning I rose wondering whether at some moment while I was sleeping the company clerk had tacked up the announcement. I tried not to let others see my anxiety, but as soon as I was free I'd rush to look. I got to know every dog-eared order and directive on the board. Once in the middle of the night I became so apprehensive I crept out of the hut and read by flashlight.

As if waiting weren't bad enough, the last weeks of basic were hellish. The cadre realized they would have only a few more cracks at us and seemed determined to make us as wretched as possible. We went on a forced march which carried us twenty-five miles into the swamps. We bivouacked at the edge of dark, fennish water and were bitten by mosquitoes until we whimpered. We killed rattlesnakes as thick as our arms. During the blazing heat of the day we maneuvered on our bellies among Spanish bayonets and sand spurs which stabbed and rubbed us raw.

Yancey escaped the worst of it. He was made company runner and spent his time either in the shade of headquarters' tent or with the cooks drinking iced tea. On a night when it rained and streams of water washed through our pup tents, he slept dry in an ambulance.

"You want to look good," he kept telling me confidentially. "People are still observing you."

"Are they observing you too?" I asked. Like everybody else I was half dead and limped on blistered feet.

"Sure they are," he said and winked. "I volunteered to be company runner. They love volunteers."

That afternoon we dug foxholes and squatted in them while tanks rattled and roared over our heads. The iron treads threw down clods of dirt, and the engines filled our holes with oily blue exhaust fumes. As a tank thundered over me, I heard laughter from inside.

During the night I was on guard with Timberlake. He was as nervous about OCS as I was. We avoided each other as we patrolled the area. He hated me and I him for the reciprocal threats we posed.

Going back to camp the company was put through another forced march—this one the most brutal of all. We spent more time running than walking. The sun burned down from a perfectly clear sky, and thick dust coiled around us. Stragglers littered the side of the road like battle casualties. Ambulances were so packed they could pick up no more men. Even the cadres' faces were drawn and pained. My feet bled into my shoes. I kept going only because of what Yancey had said about my being observed.

We reached camp late Saturday night and stumbled down the street to our huts. Thirty-seven men out of an entire company had made it. Timberlake was one of them. I'd hoped he would drop out and help my chances. In the hut I had to peel my socks from my blood-encrusted feet.

The moon over camp gave it a ghostly appearance. As soon as I'd showered, I hurried to the bulletin board where I struck a match. No announcement about OCS had been posted. On returning to the hut, I saw Timberlake sneaking through the dark to look.

I flopped on my bed. Yancey had not yet come in. I closed my eyes and was immediately asleep.

When I woke, it was daylight and somebody was shaking my shoulder. Yancey was bent over me.

"You got it," he whispered. "I've seen the order."

"You sure?" I asked, coming instantly awake.

"I'm sure. I was in the orderly room while the lieutenant was going over the stuff that'd come down from regiment. Me and you. Timberlake was scratched."

As much as I wanted to, I couldn't believe it. I had to see the official announcement. I made a dozen trips to the bulletin board. The neatly typed list wasn't posted until late afternoon. I stood staring at it. Yancey's and my names were there. Timberlake joined me. He read and closed his eyes.

"Tough luck," I told him, able to feel sorry for him now.

"Oh sure," he answered and walked away with his hands in his pockets.

I telegraphed my mother the good news, and after supper Yancey and I went to the PX for a celebration. I didn't mind buying the beer. Sitting on a wooden crate across the yard was Timberlake. His shoulders were hunched, and his head was bowed. He got so plastered he fell off the crate.

The next week Yancey in talking with the company commander was able to learn that the board had had a difficult time deciding between Timberlake and me. Apparently I owed my selection to what I'd said about fox trapping. The full colonel had checked my facts and found them correct. He was now passing the information around the officers' club as if he'd made the discovery himself.

"It's great," Yancey told me, laughing and slapping my shoulder. "You're bound to be the only guy in the history of warfare who owes his commission to the male fox's irresistible urge for the pee of a vixen."

10

The Army had already taught me a lot about what generally are called breaks—the soldier's term for luck. When the breaks were with you, good fortune came in streams like sausages tied together. When the breaks were bad, however, a man could win at nothing and might grow lean in the belief that his destiny would never again be propitious.

The breaks for Yancey and me during the last days of basic were golden. Not only were we accepted as candidates to OCS, but we also found we were to receive a furlough. We had expected to finish basic and go directly into officer training on the other side of camp. As it happened, officer school was slightly out of phase with regiment. Thus though other men in the company were given nothing, Yancey and I had seven whole days.

I sent another telegram to my mother telling her I was coming. Yancey quickly solved the problem of the long train trip and the time we would lose traveling. He had the company commander obtain priorities for us from regimental headquarters. With the priorities we had no trouble getting reservations on the airlines. The two civilians who were bumped to make room for us were important-looking men with brief cases. They were angry.

All the way to Richmond Yancey insisted I come to his town in northern Virginia to visit him.

"You got to," he told me. "I realize you have family commitments, but we'll go bird hunting. I own the best dogs in the state."

I didn't believe he really wanted me to come. He had done too much lying about his house, horses, and dogs. Undoubtedly he felt safe inviting me, knowing I was unlikely to accept his invitation. He could afford to keep his lies intact.

Although he was going on to Washington, at Richmond he left the plane with me and walked toward the terminal.

"Now you promise me, Charley," he said. "You can spend at least one night with us."

He made a good show of it, pushing the invitation right up to the edge. As he talked, I saw my mother on the terminal steps. She was wearing a dark coat and a hat with a veil. She held her umbrella as if it were a weapon. She appeared genteelly out of style, yet she had dignity too. If she'd needed help, colored redcaps would have abandoned big tippers and scurried for her.

I put my arms around her. Under her clothes she was thin and hard. I smelled the familiar odor of soap and cologne. Her clear blue eyes picked at me, searching for change.

"You've lost weight," she said.

Her eyes turned from me to Yancey who was standing close and watching. She regarded him. He held out his hand.

"I'm Marvin," he said. "I only have a minute, but I want to put it on record you have a fine son here, Mrs. Elgar. I know I'm not telling you anything you're not aware of, but you can be proud of your boy. He was a ball of fire during basic."

He'd caught my mother's hand and was shaking it vigorously. She was startled. She disengaged her hand and looked disapproving.

"What did you say your name is?" she asked, leaning toward him as if deaf. Her eyes examined him closely.

"Marvin Yancey, mam. I met your son at the induction center and we've been soldiering together ever since. We're just doggies, but we like it that way."

"Doggies?" my mother said, glancing distastefully at me.

"Infantry term," Yancey explained. "Just an old name for the foot soldier. Charley and I been looking out for each other."

My mother flinched at his use of the name Charley. I'm sure she'd never heard anyone call me that before. Yancey didn't notice. He went on talking loudly about basic, probably believing my mother was hard of hearing. People passing by turned to look at us.

"Well I have to be going," Yancey said when loudspeakers announced his plane was loading. "In another thirty minutes I'll be home. My man'll meet me at the airport. Normally that would be unpatriotic with gas rationing, but I guess the government can spare a few gallons for a soldier boy. Your son's coming to visit me, Mrs. Elgar. We're going to shoot quail."

He held out his hand to my mother a second time. Gingerly she shook it, releasing her fingers as quickly as she could. Marvin, fat and middle-aged, hurried down the steps toward his plane. He ran stiff-legged. He wanted to be certain nobody got his seat by a window. On the ramp he turned and waved.

"Where did you pick him up?" my mother asked, her voice critical.

"I'll tell you about him later," I answered, lifting my bag. I offered her my arm. We walked through the terminal toward the taxi stand.

"He's common," she said. "I hope he's not one of your friends."

"Well he's an Army friend. That puts him in a special category."

"I don't approve."

"I don't either, but he has helped me."

"I find that difficult to believe."

"He's been in the service before and knows the ropes. In fact he's an authentic hero with medals to prove it."

She looked at me questioningly. We had reached the other side of the terminal building. The single taxi was already partly loaded. The driver was waiting to fill it up. My mother sat in the rear and I in front. She held her hands on top her umbrella and seemed so queenly that the other people talked in whispers.

Richmond was bright with autumn. Trees were at the height of color, and the cool air was perfectly clean. We passed statues of Confederate generals. The cab stopped several times to let people out. She and I were the last ones. I got in back with her.

"Does he really have a man?" she asked, still assessing Yancey.

"It's doubtful. He exaggerates."

"You mean he's a liar."

"I guess I do."

"Well, he seems an extremely odd person for you to have taken up with. You're not really going to visit him, are you?"

"No."

We were almost home. I watched the street along which I had walked so many times. The yards and boxwoods in the fashionable section were well kept. The driver pulled up before our house—a two-story brick with columns and a circular drive. Sam, our colored man, was raking leaves. I shook hands with him.

Inside, Lucy, our maid, was waiting. I also shook her hand. My mother removed her veil and hat. She stood in front of the hall mirror and patted her gray hair which she wore in the old-fashioned manner of parting it precisely in the middle of her scalp and gathering it in a bun at the back.

Lucy carried my bag to my room while I accompanied my mother into the immaculate parlor furnished with the heavy Victorian

61

pieces my father had loved so. There were gilt mirrors, curlicued table legs, and lamps with stained-glass shades.

My father's picture was over the fireplace—a portrait of him in his judicial robes painted just before he died. In the painting he looked severe, which he could be on the bench, but he had not been that way at home, though he'd believed in absolute correctness and had given me a lecture once for playing craps with the cook's two sons. He hadn't minded the gambling as much as the fact I might lead the cook's sons into believing a familiar relationship existed between us when it could not.

I sat on a blue velvet sofa and refrained from lighting the cigarette I wanted, knowing how my mother worried that I might drop ashes on her bright Persian carpets.

"I'm pleased you're going to OCS," she said.

We talked of the Army. She had no real conception of what it was. Her ideas had been formed in another day, and her head held a vision of the polo-playing British who drank tonic on the verandas of white, pagoda-like hotels.

"Of course you must go by the bank," she said. "Mr. Edwards will want to see you. You'll also have to visit your cousins. They constantly ask about you."

We ate dinner in the large, formal dining room, the walls of which were decorated with flowered paper. Lucy had cooked an enormous roast beef that I sliced as thin as possible, using a bone-handled knife which had been in the family for years. We drank red wine, and my mother toasted my homecoming. She reached across once to put her finely veined hand on mine.

"I don't like your associating with him," she said, suddenly switching back to Yancey.

In her way of viewing life, people belonged in carefully separated pigeonholes. I was incapable of convincing her that the Army had a habit of scrambling the normal gradations of the civilian until they became meaningless. I could imagine her horror had I told her about Hatfield's being treated twice a week for syphilis. She would protest to the Secretary of War.

"I more or less have to associate with him," I answered her. "He's also going to OCS."

She lowered her fork.

"I thought the standards were high."

"Well, he does have the medals. They can't very easily ignore a hero."

She questioned me, drawing out just about everything I knew of Yancey.

"There's something wrong," she said when I finished. "Not only the lies. None of the pieces fit into place."

After dinner we drank coffee and talked until it was late. I was tired. I found my head nodding. She realized I was about to doze off. She came to me, raised me from the sofa, and kissed my cheek. "You're worn out, and I'm prattling on like a fool. It's good to have you home, Charles."

I slept soundly until six in the morning—the hour reveille would normally have wakened me at camp. I tossed, unable to go back to sleep. Finally I got up to shave, dress, and fix my breakfast. Lucy brought me coffee in the garden. Already I had the feeling of time pressing in.

My mother came down later in the morning. I was reading the newspaper. She looked me over critically.

"You simply can't be distinguished in an enlisted man's uniform," she said. "I suppose the Army wants it that way. At any rate you'll make a handsome officer, and people will take notice. Don't be afraid. You have nothing to be afraid of."

"I'm not."

"Just remember your blood is better than theirs."

In the early afternoon I walked down to the bank. I faced the Roman façade with its huge Corinthian columns flanking a doorway. Over the sidewalk hung a large American flag. Brass had recently been shined. I pushed inside.

The first thing I saw was a wooden plaque listing employees who had gone into the service. I picked out my own name. I continued on into the marble room where golden light fell from a line of crystal chandeliers. The sounds of adding machines and money changing hands were muffled. I passed bronze tellers' cages. Men who had gone to war had been replaced by young women who appeared both businesslike and efficient. The guard, an old man, gazed at me with no sign of recognition.

At the rear of the bank one of the assistant cashiers saw me and stood to say hello. Others came to speak to me. They asked perfunctory questions about the Army and congratulated me on my going to OCS. Mr. Edwards was in conference but would talk with me when he was through. I told his pretty secretary I'd be in the trust department.

I went up to look at my old desk. It was just the same, except my replacement was using it. He was an older man named Buster Berry who had been deferred from the draft because of asthma. As I stood quietly in the doorway watching him go over a list of securities, I had the impulse to kick him the hell out of my office. Actually there was no reason for me to be upset. Mr. Edwards had promised my job would be waiting after the war.

Buster, realizing he was being observed, spun around and smiled.

"Well, Charles," he said, standing and holding out his hand. The hand was soft, reminding me of Yancey's. "How does the old salt mine look to a soldier boy?"

"It doesn't resemble a salt mine. After basic, it's a featherbed."

"We haven't had it altogether soft. A lot of work's piled up. We've been shorthanded."

I went down the corridor among the secretaries to see Old Pope, who was senior trust officer. His white hair was neatly brushed. He was sitting at his desk watching pigeons strut on a ledge. He began to talk pompously.

"We've made strides here," he said. "We're getting an increasing percentage of the trust business. This department hasn't lost its zip because of a little thing like a war."

Old Pope's telephone rang. Mr. Edwards was waiting for me. I told Old Pope and Buster good-by. They wished me luck. I went downstairs to Mr. Edwards' office. The pretty secretary held his door open.

"Charles, you look just fine," Mr. Edwards said from his desk. He was a graying, distinguished-looking man with a narrow face. He shook my hand. "We heard about you going to OCS. The Army must think highly of you. I knew once you got them organized we'd start winning the war."

He was a busy man, but he never allowed anybody to be hurried in his presence. For many years he had been a friend of my father's, which was the main reason I was able to get the job with the bank, though I did have the proper qualifications. He indicated I was to sit, leaned back in his leather chair, and folded his hands over his stomach.

"I was in the infantry during the last one," he told me. "I can remember being envious of my seemingly more fortunate friends in the field artillery or air corps. Now I don't regret it. Between you and me, infantry's for the real men. Of course I never got across the water."

"Yes, sir," I answered, thinking he was talking a little like Yancey.

64

"We're doing well enough here at the bank. In fact we're doing shamefully so. I wouldn't want my board to hear me say that. The truth is war is good for business. We do have some employment problems. Many of our new people we wouldn't have considered once. Frankly the quality of the work is terrible. Secretaries spend vast amounts of time in the ladies room. They know we can't fire them."

We had a pleasant visit. He was always cordial, and he reminded me a second time that my job was waiting. He walked me to the door with his arm about my shoulder.

"We're proud of you here," he said. "Confidentially I wish I could be with you. When you get across the water, give them Old Nick for me."

11

I was quickly bored by my furlough. I couldn't escape a sense of the clock's ticking. I felt I should be doing something exciting every moment, yet there was little I could do.

I, of course, went to see my female aunts and cousins—most of them kind old ladies who served me tea and asked my opinion of the war. Though they were nice and I loved them, visiting them was not the relief from the Army I needed.

I had a few dates with girls I'd squired before being drafted. For the most part they belonged to the Junior League and various organizations like the Red Cross and canteen clubs. They were atune to war. We danced at the country club or drank beer at road-houses.

The trouble was I had grown up with them all. They were friendly and concerned about me, but there was no chance of anything more than a little impersonal necking in the car. Most of them were pining for their warriors away in the service.

I did some work around the house. I helped Sam rake leaves and burn them. I cut a large limb from a red oak which had been struck by lightning. I covered the wound with black pitch, painting it on with a brush. I then sawed the limb into precise fireplace lengths and stored the wood in the garage.

On the fifth night as I sat with my mother in the parlor and tried to keep from yawning, the telephone rang. I answered it. The voice was Yancey's. He was enthusiastic.

"Freedom it's wonderful," he said. "You having fun?"

"Oh sure," I told him.

"You don't sound as if you mean it. What you need is me to cheer you. Come on up."

"You really want me?" I asked, still not believing he did and that he would squirm at the actual threat of my doing so.

"Of course I want you. You think I'd be wasting money on a call if I didn't?"

I found myself hoping he was sincere because I saw visiting him as an opportunity of escaping ennui.

"Wait a minute," I said and went to the parlor. I explained to my mother who it was and what I wished to do. She didn't object nearly so much as I'd expected her to.

"I don't like him, and I don't like your associating with him," she said to me. "On the other hand this hasn't been much of a leave for you. You deserve more pleasure. I won't stand in your way."

I returned to the telephone and told Yancey I was coming.

"Now you're talking," he said. "Give me a ring when you hit town. I'm in the phone book."

I rode the bus—there was no train—the next morning. It was crowded with soldiers, and the air was foul. A drunk puked.

As we drew closer to the small town in northern Virginia where Yancey lived, I thought about him. I was still sure the stories he had told in basic were untrue. I assumed he meant simply to brass his lies out. Certainly any house he owned would be small. As to bird dogs, even a poor man could afford to keep a few of those. There would be no blooded horses. The beautiful wife he talked about would more than likely chew bubble gum and use toothpicks.

The town itself had a population of less than five thousand. It was basically a farm community, but it was rapidly becoming a sub-urb of Washington as the city spread west along the Potomac. The section was one where planters had established great estates in colonial times and many men had died during the Civil War. The split-rail fences looked as if they had been put up to accommodate fox hunters rather than to enclose land. It was not the kind of coun-try a person associated with Yancey.

The bus station was located next to a fertilizer store. From a pay telephone I called Yancey's number. A woman's voice, low and impersonal, answered. She said Yancey wasn't in and suggested I

66

try his office. She gave me the number. I dialed, and another woman answered. When I asked for Yancey, she wanted my name. The telephone clicked.

"You're here are you, buddy?" Yancey said. "I'll be right down."

I had the impulse to tell him just to send his man for me, but I did not. Since I was visiting him, I intended to be as pleasant as possible no matter how badly he had lied. All I wanted from him was that he take my mind off myself.

I stood in front of the bus station. The town was an odd mixture of farmers and chic wives of men who worked in Washington. A hound dog lay sleeping alongside a store which sold expensive clothes. The fire department had a steeple on it.

A gray Cadillac drew up and stopped. For an instant I didn't recognize Yancey. He honked at me. He was so short he could barely see over the wheel. The car was in a no-parking zone. He opened the door and hurried to me. Instead of a uniform, he had on a pair of tan slacks and a sports shirt. He shook my hand with both of his.

"Come on now, tell me you missed me," he said.

I felt better just seeing him. Rolypoly and ridiculous in the yellow shirt, he seemed more comical than ever. He was talking fast.

"You don't have to tell me you missed me. I know it. Admit you've become used to the old man. After all who's been making your decisions for you?"

He put my bag in the rear of the car and held a front door open for me. A policeman was watching because the car was parked illegally, but Yancey merely waved. The policeman touched his cap.

The Cadillac was big as a hearse. It was undoubtedly meant to be driven by a chauffeur. The fact Yancey owned it did not impress me. Like poor whites everywhere, he probably blew most of his money on automobiles. Without a chauffeur, the car was a joke.

He pulled away from the curb, driving in a jerky, aggressive manner. He acted as if other automobiles were out to smash him. He glared like a person surrounded by peril.

"You have to watch these country jakes," he said. "They think they own the road."

At that moment a muddy pickup truck swung out from a feed store. Yancey stomped the brake. The big car bucked. I threw out my hands to keep from hitting the windshield. Yancey stuck his head from his window and yelled at the other driver—a dignified old farmer who looked surprised and unknowing about the entire incident.

"They ought to take your license," Yancey shouted. "You ever hear of checking the road behind you before you pull out?"

Leaving the farmer open-mouthed, Yancey drove on. He scowled and talked to himself. He said he should have got the man's number to report it to the police. He was still grumbling as we reached the end of the street. He turned right. On a rise of ground was a neat brick building.

Pounded into grass was a large sign with the legends YANCEY CONSTRUCTION CO., YANCEY PLUMBING CO., and YANCEY ENTERPRISES. I glanced at him, astonished to realize that at least part of the bragging he had done must be true. He parked on gravel behind the building. In a field were rows of yellow construction and earth-moving equipment.

Yancey led me into the building by the back steps. We entered a long room lighted by fluorescent tubing. Men were working at drafting tables. Yancey held a door for me. We crossed a reception room furnished with carpets and leather chairs. A lovely young secretary smiled professionally from her desk. Yancey and I walked into his office which was pine paneled and had photographs of construction jobs hung on the walls.

"What you think?" he asked me proudly as he pushed the button on an intercom box. "Send Blackburn in here."

"I think I might owe you an apology," I answered.

"I knew it. I could tell all along you didn't believe me. Remember I didn't have to go into the Army either. I could have lain around here and let fruit drop into my mouth. I volunteered."

I was impressed. He was obviously the center of a going concern, and those telephone calls he had made from basic must have been real. The Cadillac no longer seemed absurd.

There was a tap at the door, and a burly man in soiled khakis entered carrying a roll of blueprints. He and Yancey unrolled them on the big desk.

"They promised the steel," Yancey said. "I've got it in a letter." He pressed the button on the intercom. "Bring me the file on the Grierson job," he ordered.

The lovely secretary came in holding a manila folder. Yancey leafed through it impatiently until he found what he wanted.

"Get me Cleveland," he said to the secretary.

She went out. He returned to the blueprints. The intercom buzzed. Yancey snatched up his telephone.

"Grant, you promised me the stuff last week," he said, frowning.

For a moment he listened. I heard indistinct words coming from the other end of the line. Yancey tapped a pencil against an ashtray. "I don't see it that way," he said, interrupting. "I got men on the job and a completion date. Without the stuff I lose money. Some of you fellows better realize the war's going to be over one of these days and Yancey Construction's going to need a lot of steel. Yancey is definitely going to remember its friends."

It was a side of him I'd never seen before. He was a person very much in control. He no longer appeared comical or a blowhard. Even if the performance was partly for my benefit—which I suspected—it was a good one.

"The steel men think they run the world these days," he said, putting down the telephone. "Everybody licks their boots." Then to Blackburn who stood in front of the desk: "Look, Mike, take some metal off the Myer job. We can make a switch when this comes in."

"You going to clear me with the inspector?"

"I'll take care of it this afternoon."

My impression was that Yancey had decided something not quite ethical. Blackburn rolled up the blueprints but hung back at the door.

"What about Taylor?" he asked.

"I'm sending him a check," Yancey answered. "A thousand dollars. That ought to ease his pain."

Blackburn went on out. Yancey turned to me and smiled.

"Taylor's a foreman who got hurt. He was painting his house and slipped off his ladder. Broke his neck. He won't be coming back here. I don't have to send him anything. I paid him good. I just feel sorry for the guy."

Yancey the humanitarian. I remembered what he'd told me about sending his bet winnings to the Red Cross. Perhaps after all under the blubber and bluster there lay a streak of goodness.

"The trouble with owning a business is you have to make all the decisions," he said. "No one wants to accept authority. Now you understand why I had to keep in touch from camp. When I get up in the morning all I see is a mountain of decisions facing me."

We left his office. He told his secretary she could reach him at home. We went down to the Cadillac and drove out the gravel road. I again read the sign with the three companies listed on it.

"A matter of taxes," Yancey explained, answering a question I hadn't asked. "Everything a businessman does these days is a matter of taxes."

He told me he had one more stop before we went to his house. By route markers I could see we were headed toward Washington. On the Virginia side of the Potomac we came to an Army installation surrounded by a high wire fence. Yancey showed a pass to an MP at the gate.

We drove between rows of barracks to the skeleton of a large building. Men were mixing concrete and carrying it in wheelbarrows up a wooden ramp. Yancey left me in the car while he went to talk. I guessed he was taking care of the inspector as Blackburn had requested.

"That's that," Yancey told me when he returned to the car. "Actually we're ahead of schedule here. We got no real worries unless the weather caves in on us."

We left the Army installation, drove back through town, and out into the country. The land on either side of the twisting road became rolling. I could see mountains. Farms along the way appeared prosperous. Doves swooped into harvested fields. Because of a chill in the air, Yancey put on the heater.

Naturally I was now curious about his home. After seeing his office, I was ready to believe anything possible. Well, almost anything. I was certain his place would be expensive. I was also convinced it would be garish and in bad taste. There would probably be tassels on the sofa pillows and potted palms in the hallway.

As we rounded a slight curve, he slowed the big car. Enclosing a field to my right was a freshly painted white plank fence. Land undulated back from the road to the base of a wooded mountain. On lush pastures sleek cattle and horses grazed. Cedar trees grew along the fence.

We turned in at a fieldstone gate which had electric lanterns on it. A drive wound among alternating magnolia and dogwood trees. I could look out across a meadow and see a large new barn with a green roof. A pond glistened.

The drive straightened, and we faced the house. It was a very old Georgian colonial which appeared perfectly restored. Ivy grew up outsized brick to a slate roof. The headers were glazed, and at each end of the house were two chimneys. Along the walk in front were English boxwoods as large as I'd ever seen. Shaded by giant tulip poplars, the whole setting gave the impression of quiet grandeur and was enough to make me catch my breath. It was a place I'd have sold my soul to own. I was too shocked to speak.

Yancey drove to the rear of the house where a garage had been converted from what once had been either slave quarters or a kitchen. Two silky English setters came running toward us. A Negro walked from the garage. He was wearing rubber boots and holding a chamois. He had been washing a red convertible and was obviously the man Yancey had bragged about. I felt humbled.

"This is all yours?" I asked as I looked at the house and the magnificent sweep of the land.

"Hell yes it's mine. You think I borrowed it just for your visit."

"I think you're a very lucky person."

"You don't have to tell me. I've always been lucky."

He left the Cadillac in the drive. The colored man touched his cap to me and got my bag. Yancey patted his English setters. We went to a back porch and up steps. A pretty, light-skinned Negress in a white uniform opened the door for us. Yancey introduced her as Bessie.

I was all eyes for the inside of the house. At least here, I believed, some of Yancey's gaucheness was bound to show. I was wrong. As he led me from room to room, I saw that each article of furniture was a genuine period piece. Tables, washstands, and cupboards of walnut or cherry glowed with the rich sheen of age. On a sideboard was old silver, and daylight distilled through panes of Williamsburg glass created a golden softness.

We went into the hallway where a staircase curved to the second floor. I could imagine the days when ladies glided down in stiff, rustling dresses. Gentlemen in knee breeches and powdered wigs would have snapped their snuff boxes shut and bowed gracefully.

The only flaw I could find in the house was that everything was a little too perfect. There was no warmth. The rooms felt cold and unused. They gave no sensation of living or wear.

Yancey delighted in showing me around. He was enjoying my reactions. He pointed out his finest pieces to me as if afraid I might not understand their value. He stopped me before a walnut secretary with hammered brass fittings. Lord Cornwallis himself was supposed to have used the secretary in writing dispatches to the king.

"It's lovely," I said, touching the wood gently and with reverence.

"It is now," he answered. "It wasn't when I first got hold of it. Neither was the house. The first floor looked as if the owners had used it for chickens. There were holes in the ceiling. Termites had eaten part of the foundation. In some places you could jump through the floor. I had men on my payroll I could send out here to work when they had nothing else to do, but this house cost me a for-

tune to restore. If I told you how much, you wouldn't believe me."
I thought he was going to tell me. Instead he took my arm and showed me upstairs to my room. It was on the back of the house, and the windows looked to the mountains. The room was furnished with two small tester beds, each covered by a silk comforter. The wallpaper was patterned with golden fleur-de-lis. A low doorway led to a completely modern bathroom. The night table had the latest magazines on it. In front of a fireplace fitted with brass andirons was a wing-back chair. My clothes had already been put away.

"Clean up a little, but don't be all afternoon," Yancey said. "You got to see the rest of the place."

He left me. Repeatedly shaking my head in wonder, I showered quickly, changed shirts, and went to look for him. Moving along the carpeted hallway, I passed a closed room from which I caught just the faintest scent of perfume. I was definitely interested in seeing Yancey's wife, but I was no longer sure she would chew bubble gum and use toothpicks. I was afraid to guess about anything now.

Downstairs I found Yancey in the den. Other than the kitchen, it was the one modern room on the lower floor—pine paneled, a bar, overstuffed furniture. Shelves held modern novels. On the walls were framed pictures of dogs. Over the fireplace was a pretentious painting of Yancey himself.

He'd already changed his clothes and fixed drinks. He wore brown riding pants, boots, and a tweed jacket. His fat buttocks made him a travesty of the country squire. He put on a hat which had a grouse feather in the band.

We carried our drinks outside. As I wondered when I'd meet his wife, he showed me the rest of the farm. We went first to the stables. The floor was paved with concrete, and each stall had its own water fountain. All the horses were hunters—highly bred, tense, wild of eye. Their names were painted on wooden plaques above the stalls. While Yancey patted their necks, the horses' nostrils flared and they tossed their heads.

"Martha loves to ride," he said, mentioning his wife for the first time since I arrived. "She's the equestrian. It's all I can do to keep up with the field. I didn't have much opportunity to fox-hunt when I was a boy."

I hoped he would say more about himself, but he didn't. He showed me his tack room. Fine bridles and English saddles hung from nails. Each bit and stirrup had recently been polished.

We left the stable. Using a pickup truck, he drove me across a pasture to the new barn I'd seen earlier. He showed me his prize bull. It was a huge, sullen animal. He locked its head in a special steel cage so that we could get close. The bull's eyes rolled balefully. Yancey stroked him proudly.

"Got the highest rating in the state," Yancey said. "A dairy interest from Ohio offered me twenty thousand dollars for him. Wouldn't take twice that. Wait till you see his daughters."

The daughters were penned up individually and had heavy, bulging udders. Yancey talked about butterfat and production records, none of which I could follow. I merely tried to look knowledgeable.

He showed me a special piece of equipment which resembled an instrument of Inquisitional torture. The thing was a rack to support the bull when he mounted cows. Without it his great weight on the cows' backs might smash their spines.

Yancey next took me to his milking barn with its automatic equipment. Electric fans turned, and loudspeakers piped in soothing music. Colored men moved among stalls throwing down hay and adjusting machines. The barn floor had been freshly hosed.

"I make money on the dairy," Yancey said. "It's the only place. The rest of the farm costs me even with the tax angles. Of course I'm constantly improving the property."

We drove through gates and across fields to the foot of the mountain. The leaves were a blaze of pinks, reds, and burgundies. We were high enough so that we could look down on the house in the distance. The sun was lowering, and the tulip poplars were casting long shadows. I realized I was envious of Yancey—a condition I wouldn't have been able to conceive of only hours ago. He no longer appeared the same to me. A man can't patronize what he envies.

"We'll shoot birds tomorrow," Yancey said. "That means getting up early. You can handle a shotgun, can't you?"

"I know what end to hold to my shoulder."

"Well, that's a good start. I'll coach you. We'll slay them."

We returned to the stable in the pickup truck and walked from there to the house. I had become cold. In the den Yancey lighted a fire of red oak logs. He made fresh drinks. I noticed that in spite of the war and rationing he had plenty of good liquor under the bar.

"I bought a couple of cases of everything I could get my hands on the day after the fight started," he explained. "Of course I could get it anyhow. I have connections in Washington."

Yancey and I put our feet up on a rough-hewn coffee table and drank. He was lapping me on the whisky. I was still wondering when his wife would come down and listening for her. Yancey, however, was the first to hear her footsteps. He stood quickly. I followed him into the hall.

I didn't think I could be surprised again, but I was. The woman walking down the stairs was in her middle thirties. She was small and dark. She wore a simple black dress and a string of pearls. Her ankles were so delicate they seemed fragile. She looked completely self-possessed and untouchable.

She moved slowly, carefully, sensuously. Her hair was pulled back in the old-fashioned manner one sees in paintings of Civil War belles. Her neck was long and aristocratic.

Reaching the first floor, she smiled slightly and held out her hand to me. I expected her skin to be cold. It was not.

"It's good to have you with us, Mr. Elgar," she said in a voice which was almost a whisper. "Forgive me for not coming down sooner. I had a headache."

Even in high heels she hardly reached my chin and had to tilt her head to see into my face. Her eyes were a dark brown, almost black. She had on just a trace of lipstick. She folded her hands at her waist.

"You can't call him Mr. Elgar," Yancey told her. "Try Charley."

"I'll compromise," she said and smiled a second time. Again I had the impression of coldness. The smile had come automatically, meaninglessly. "I'll call him Charles. I've never liked Charley."

Those were my own feelings exactly. I was more than ever convinced she was a lady.

"There's nothing wrong with Charley," Yancey said. "It's a good, solid American name." He beamed on her with the same pride of possession he had displayed showing me his prize livestock and blooded horses. "Ain't she something?" he asked.

She shot him a glance. Done with a creasing of her forehead and a thinning of her lips, it was definitely a reprimand and a warning. The effect on Yancey was startling. For an instant he lost his composure. He even stuttered.

"I just meant you're beautiful, honey," he said, and I had the sensation he was about to break into a sweat.

She turned from him to me. The slight, controlled smile came back. She was again the gracious lady of the manor. I was thinking it was her taste which had furnished the house, not Yancey's.

"I hope your room's comfortable," she said.

"It couldn't be more so."

"Let me fix you a drink," Yancey offered, eager to make amends.

"I don't mind," she answered.

We went into the den where she sat on the sofa in front of the fire, crossing her legs and pulling her dress over her knees. Yancey was at the bar making drinks. She reached to the coffee table for a cigarette. Her nails were long and painted a deep red. I lighted the cigarette for her. Her dark eyes shone in the match flame. It seemed impossible she could belong to Yancey.

"She doesn't like me to say she's pretty," Yancey told me as he came with the drinks. "I can't help it. Everybody can see it anyway. You can't hide beauty under a bushel basket. She's got family too. They settled in this part of the country two hundred years ago. She can't walk up and down the street without bumping into cousins."

As he talked, she sat quietly, but there was a tenseness in her small body like a person steeling himself. It was as if under her skin a drawing up of muscle and nerve were taking place. It was as if she were expecting a blow.

"I wanted to marry her the first time I saw her," Yancey explained, drinking freely. The liquor made him more reckless. He sat beside her on the sofa and didn't notice the looks she was giving him.

"Believe it or not she was in the choir of the Presbyterian Church when I first saw her. She was an angel up there in white robes. I can tell you just seeing her made a Christian out of me. I started going to church every Sunday, and I sat in the front row. Of course she wouldn't look at me. I used to try to will her to do it."

Yancey finished his drink and rose to make another. I'd never seen him tight before. His skin was ruddy, and his eyes blinked constantly behind his glasses.

"She wouldn't have anything to do with me," he said from the bar. "If I called her on the telephone, she'd hang up. I couldn't blame her. I didn't have the best reputation in town. She couldn't get away from me though. She was working as a receptionist for a doctor, and I always made a point of being around when she went out for lunch. Didn't I, honey?"

"Yes," she answered, her whispered voice absolutely toneless. It was as if the word had come up through ice. Yancey should have been warned off, but he was running with the bit in his teeth.

"I used to watch her walk down the street," he continued. "Whenever she passed my window, I'd hurry to give her the eye. She had the prettiest, most dainty, ladylike walk in town. She took little steps and held her head up high. I'd follow her into the drugstore and always try to sit on the stool beside her. She didn't like that. She even got up and moved. It didn't do her any good because I did the same thing myself. The way she looked right through me made my heart stop, but I couldn't give her up either."

Martha sat rigid. She stared into the crackling fire. The fingers around her glass were clutched so tightly that the blood was squeezed from them.

"Let's all have another quickie before dinner," Yancey said. He stood and took my glass. He reached for Martha's. She hadn't moved. He saw she hadn't drunk her drink.

"What's the matter, honey?" he asked. "I make it too strong?"

"I'm not thirsty," she answered, her mouth severe.

"Well, you ought to join the celebration," Yancey told her, refusing to see her expression. He went to the bar. "Old Charley and I don't have the privilege of drinking good whisky together very often. I can tell you what we been through down in Mississippi was rough. It was pure hell and makes a man thirsty."

Martha kept staring at the fire. Bessie, the good-looking colored maid, came to the doorway to announce dinner was ready. Yancey insisted we all carry our drinks with us. Martha walked out straight-backed and angry. Yancey and I followed, he with his arm around my shoulder.

On the dining-room table, candles burned in a silver candelabrum. Yancey held Martha's chair for her, sat heavily, and said the blessing. Without pausing for breath, he began to explain that the walnut table had come from an old plantation in the Tidewater. He lifted the linen tablecloth to show me how pegs had been used instead of nails.

All the time he talked I was glancing at Martha. Her eyes were lowered. She merely pushed at the food Bessie brought in for us to eat. Yancey switched from the table to the china we were using. He said it had been in Martha's family for years. He next pointed out the silver candelabrum at the center of the table.

"Look at the metal work," he said to me. "That's real fancy stuff. You can't find craftsmen to work like that these days. Also belonged in her family. Her mother kept it in a trunk. Martha's great-grandfather was a general in the Civil War. He once hung a Yankee sergeant from a maple tree just down the road. He caught the sergeant stealing chickens. I can tell you that everything in this house is authentic. Of course I had to buy most of it."

He was very tight, and he was drinking as he ate. His eyes were glassy. He wobbled in his chair and was having trouble getting food onto his fork. Her face had become a mask. Only the muscles of her throat revealed her resentment. She gave the impression of being a woman who had suffered often and long.

"I've never liked cheap stuff," Yancey said. "Get the best I've always believed. It lasts longer and pays off over the years. It also looks better as it grows older. That's a fact nouveaus don't understand. If I told you how much money I have the stuff in this house insured for, you'd think I was lying."

He pushed back his chair, stood, and went to the sideboard where he picked up a silver bowl. He brought it to me. The metal had been hammered out until it was as thin as a wafer.

"Look at this now," Yancey instructed me. "Is it or is it not a beauty? Worth a thousand dollars if it's worth a penny. I had it appraised by experts in Richmond. Tell him what it was used for, honey."

"Walnuts," Martha answered, not raising her face. Her voice sounded dead and as if she were reciting by rote.

"That's right," Yancey said. "Walnuts. Belonged to one of her aunts. The old lady didn't know or care about silver. The bowl hadn't even been shined. It was black."

As he talked on, Martha lifted her eyes a moment. They seemed to apologize to me for Yancey and to be full of pain. She again looked toward her plate.

"You ever hear of such a thing?" Yancey asked. "Walnuts, by God. I bought it from the aunt for twenty-five dollars, and she thought she was gypping me. Of course I sent her more money later. I'd seen a picture of a bowl like it in an antique book."

Martha was sitting so quietly she could have stopped breathing. He didn't notice. He talked with food in his mouth and drank whisky.

When he finished eating, we carried coffee into the den. Outside, a wind had risen, and panes of glass were steamed. Yancey threw another log on the fire. Martha sat in a chair to herself. She dutifully answered Yancey's questions in monosyllables, but she made no attempt to carry the conversation.

Yancey was showing his shotguns. He had unlocked the glass door of the gun cabinet to bring them out. They were finely and expensively made. His personal double had been tailored for him in London. He pulled it to his shoulder and shot an imaginary quail. He spoke knowledgeably about patterns, loads, and bores. Martha stood. Her face was strained.

77

"Good night," she said softly, moving toward the door.

"It's early yet, honey," Yancey told her. He was sweating and weaving before the crackling fire.

"I have a headache," she answered, not turning to us. She walked quickly from the room, her back very straight. As she climbed the steps, sound of her faded.

"Ain't she something?" Yancey asked proudly. "Tell me the truth now, you didn't think I had me a wife like that, did you?"

"No, I didn't."

"You don't have to tell me. I knew you didn't. Boy, I'd like all those peasants down in basic to see her. I'd like to have her get really dolled up and parade down the company street. Would their eyes pop out or not? You notice how she's dressed? I encourage her to buy good clothes. All the Washington stores have her measurements. They send stuff down for her to try. I like to see her licked and slicked up fit to kill."

He spoke of her not as a person he loved and shared his life with, but as if she were a device to make other men envious. He hauled out more guns and continued to talk. She was very neat, he said. She never raised her voice. She sat a horse as if she had been carved upon it. She could play Mozart on the piano.

"There's nothing like marriage," Yancey said, going for brandy and glasses. "Marriage anchors a man. I used to be nervous as hell. Don't laugh. You think I'm nervous now, but it's nothing to what I was. I couldn't sleep more than a couple of hours each night. I lived on milk and toast my stomach was so jumpy."

He put the guns back, wiping his fingerprints from each with a flannel cloth. As he concentrated, his sweaty face was serious. The comical had dropped away from him like a clown who had removed his make-up.

"I wish I had some children," he said. "Not having any is one of the great disappointments of my life. Somehow it just never happened to Martha and me. Well, there's always hope. I could do a lot for a son. I'm making plenty of money, and I'm going to make more. I'd like to have a son see me in uniform."

In spite of his grossness and vulgarity, at that moment I liked him for the first time—I mean really liked him for himself and not for what he could do to help me. His wish for a son was obviously sincere. It left him human and, in contrast to the way he had been acting all evening, pathetically deflated. For a few seconds his face was hurt and sad. To my surprise I felt sorry for him.

"I'm talking too much," he told me, shaking his head as if to fling off the effects of the liquor. He set down his brandy glass. "We ought to get some sleep. We have to be up early. I'll wake you."

We switched out lights and went up the stairs together. He walked with me to my room, patted my shoulder, and moved off unsteadily down the hall.

After I undressed, I opened my window a crack. Cold air off the mountains washed into the room. I slipped in between sheets.

I intended to sort out my thoughts about Yancey, but I went right to sleep. Light woke me. I thought I'd forgotten to turn off the lamp. I brought my wrist watch close to my eyes. I'd been in bed less than an hour. I smelled cigarette smoke and reached to the ashtray. I jerked back my hand as if I'd been burned.

Martha Yancey, in a white silk housecoat, was sitting on the other tester bed. Her black hair had been let out, and on her small feet were white fur slippers. Her legs were crossed. As she jiggled a foot, she watched me. The window had been shut. Like a maiden, I pulled the covers to my chin.

"You don't sleep with your mouth open," she said matter-of-factly. "Marvin does. The pillow's always damp with his spit in the morning."

"Where is he?" I asked.

"Snoring." Lazily she inhaled smoke from her cigarette. "He always sleeps like a baby. Are you frightened?"

"I'm definitely frightened," I answered, glancing toward the door and remembering all those guns in the den.

She was amused. She continued to jiggle her foot. One of my shoulders pressed against the wall.

"There's nothing to be afraid of," she told me, her voice completely calm. She could have been discussing a flower arrangement. "We share separate rooms, and he won't come looking for me. He's drunk."

She leaned to the night table to use the ashtray. At the same moment she smiled—a smile no longer thin and cold. Rather it was lascivious. On her proper, ladylike face it was shocking.

With a slow, deliberate movement, she crushed out the cigarette, stood, and crossed to my bed. Her housecoat rustled. I smelled her perfume. She sat beside me, and the bed sank under her weight.

"It's chilly out here," she said, hugging herself. "Why don't you let me in there with you?"

"What about Marvin?" I asked, the words sounding ridiculous to me as I spoke them. I wasn't really thinking about Yancey. More than anything I was scared of being caught in a situation I couldn't handle. I simply wasn't prepared for this and was scared of seeming a fool.

She sighed and rose. She was still smiling a little, but now it was the patient expression a woman would use on a backward child. Without another glance at me, she walked from the room in her fur slippers and closed the door behind her. For a long time after she was gone, I lay clutching the covers and gazing at the door. Her perfume lingered. She didn't come back.

12

After I turned out the lamp, I slept only fitfully. I thought she might return and listened for her.

At daylight Yancey shook me. I needed a moment to remember what really had happened. For an instant I thought her visit might have been part of a dream. Then, while Yancey stood beside me, I saw her cigarette in the ashtray, lipstick on the tip. I pushed out of bed and across the room to draw Yancey's attention away from the night table.

"The morning's just right," he was saying. "We want to get moving before the birds do."

He was wearing mustard-colored hunting pants and a chamois shirt. I maneuvered him to the door, promising him I'd be down as soon as I dressed. When he was out of the room, I grabbed the ashtray and flushed its contents down the commode. Yancey came back. This time he had on a red cap and was rubbing his hands. He sat on the bed where Martha had been last night.

"Don't shave," he instructed me. "You can do that later. We ought to have our limit by ten o'clock."

Instead of hunting clothes, I put on an old pair of corduroys and high-top shoes. I'd used them working around my mother's house before going into the Army. Yancey was hurrying me. As we went down the hall, I pulled a sweater over my OD shirt. I was very much conscious of passing Martha's closed door. I thought of her sleeping in there. I looked at Yancey and remembered her saying they shared separate rooms.

Yancey cooked breakfast, but I could hardly eat. He piled my plate high with pancakes, sausage, and biscuits. He had already put guns by the door. He explained he had chosen an automatic for me. His jaws bulged with the great amounts of food he was swallowing. As I forced down drafts of hot coffee, my head throbbed from the liquor we'd drunk. He began dumping shells into the pockets of his hunting jacket and talked enthusiastically about the hunt. I wondered whether Martha slept with all house guests or had merely been driven to me by the way he had acted last night.

The sun was bright, yet the air was cold. On the grass at the back of the house a frost crunched under our feet. The two English setters saw us coming and jumped against the wire of their pen. Their breaths, like Yancey's and mine, steamed. While I smoked, Yancey went for the pickup truck. He put the dogs in the rear. As we drove away from the house, I looked at it and again thought of Martha lying warm in her bed.

"The thing to do is pick out only one bird and shoot at it," Yancey was lecturing me. "The covey rise will scare you but don't fire blindly. Actually you have plenty of time."

Not really listening, I let him talk on. I was still under the spell of Martha's presence. He drove down a dirt road to his hay fields. Fringes of lespedeza had been left uncut to support birds. Yancey was so happy I decided he couldn't possibly suspect anything about his wife. He stopped the truck and let out the dogs.

The English setters were lean, sinewy animals who sped across the field as swiftly as greyhounds. He immediately started yelling at them. They paid no attention but romped through a covey of birds. He was furious. He had been bragging about his dogs, and they were shaming him. He had a silver whistle attached by a chain to the shoulder strap of his hunting coat. He blew the whistle until he became red in the face. The dogs didn't even look around. They were having a marvelous time busting up birds.

"Wait till I see the trainer," Yancey threatened. "He told me they were right. I paid five hundred dollars for the pair and sixty a month to have them conditioned. They might as well be rat terriers."

As the sun rose higher, the land warmed. I began sweating a little under the heavy clothes. Yancey continued to shout at the dogs. We went from field to field but had no shots at birds. By ten o'clock Yancey was so angry he cussed furiously.

Then, unexpectedly, a setter went on point along a fence row. The second dog circled and backed. Both stretched out stylishly. Yancey became happily excited. He hurried me toward the dogs.

"Now we'll move right in behind them," he said. "Don't take off your safety yet. Wait for the birds to get up. Delaying the safety helps keep you from shooting too quickly. Remember what I told you about picking just one bird. And don't look for them on the ground. That'll just confuse you."

He was a lot more nervous than I was. Part of it was that I'd never believed in hunting. I had always considered killing animals a bogus manly ritual. Moreover I was haunted by a lascivious smile. I walked calmly to the dogs. I really didn't care whether birds rose or not. The setters' eyes bugged, and their bodies trembled.

The bobwhites hurled out on the other side of the fence. I was not especially unnerved by the sound. Following Yancey's advice, I picked out a bird, sighted along the barrel, and pulled the trigger. Nothing happened. I had forgotten to take off the safety. I could hear him banging away.

All the birds should have been gone, but a last straggler came up, his wings thrashing against a tangle of honeysuckle. He flew to my left. The safety was already off, and when I shot, the bird dropped as if clubbed. The setters found and retrieved it. I heard Yancey cursing.

"You killed a bird on your first shot?" he asked, his face red again.

"Luck," I told him, taking the bird from the setter's mouth. The quail was warm, moist, and quivering.

"Luck is right. I shot under mine. The birds didn't move in the direction I expected. You had a gimmie."

He was resentful of it. I suppose that was understandable. He had been instructing me, and I was one up on him. He marched toward the woods where the singles flew. I wasn't interested and wanted to return to the house. Yancey, however, wore a grim, purposeful look.

At the edge of the trees the dogs pointed a single. When the bird came up, Yancey missed it with two shots. He sucked in his bottom lip. A few feet farther on, another bird rose. He wasn't loaded. I really didn't aim. I just pulled the gun clumsily to my shoulder and jerked the trigger three times. On the third shot, the bird sailed down.

The dogs retrieved it. Yancey was glaring at me accusingly. He thought I had been holding out on him when I told him I'd never hunted before. Another single exploded up right under his feet. He missed it. He called in the dogs who were innocent of fault and beat them. He was acting like a child. I felt the liking I'd had for him last night washing out. What's more I was beginning to wish I had slept with his wife.

"You been kidding me," he said, scowling. "You dropped that bird like a pro."

"Why don't we just go on back to the house?"

"I'm not going back as long as you have more birds than I do. I'm the one who should have the birds."

"You can take these," I said, offering mine to him.

"That's not the way it's done."

"Nobody'll ever know. I want you to have them."

"Listen, you don't have to kill birds for me. I'm an excellent shot."

At that instant he kicked up a single which flew straight away from him. He missed it clean.

We hunted on. The dogs had settled down and to my inexperienced eyes were working well. They stood a covey in a field. I purposely shot my gun high to prevent even the possibility of hitting anything. Yancey got a bird with his second barrel. When he saw I'd missed, he looked fleetingly victorious.

He wouldn't quit until he'd beat me, and though I fired my shotgun at the open sky, it was noon before he could do that. I was hot, and my nose was running because of stubble we had stirred up walking through fields. With more birds than I had, he again became the good fellow—friendly, laughing, generous. Watching his change of moods was disgusting. At one moment he was practically snarling, at the next amiable and joking. On the way to the pickup truck he put an arm around my shoulder.

"What can beat this life?" he asked happily. "Are we living or not?"

By now, of course, I was convinced Yancey knew very little about bird hunting. He had read or heard it was a sport gentlemen engaged in and had taken it up as part of his country squire routine. Moreover I was certain he had done so only recently.

As we drew closer to the house, I stopped thinking of him altogether and again considered Martha. I wondered how I was supposed to greet her. What did the etiquette books say about a guest thanking his hostess for coming into his room during the night and offering herself?

At the kitchen porch, Yancey and I removed our boots and shoes. He left the birds on the sink for Bessie to clean and brought two bottles of iced beer from the refrigerator. He poured the beer into frosted glasses. Carrying them, we walked to the den.

Martha wasn't there, but I could feel her in the house. Yancey called up the stairs. She answered from the parlor. Sitting in a window seat and holding a fashion magazine in her lap, she was wearing a tweed skirt and a cashmere sweater. Her black hair was parted in the middle. Again she appeared completely cold and untouchable. She smiled at me as if it had been the most natural thing in the world for her to come to my room last night.

"Any luck?" she asked, her voice low. She was looking directly at me. I felt heat in my face.

"Not much," Yancey answered. "Birds weren't feeding as early as I thought. We're going to have to watch this boy though. He could be a great shot. I had to work like hell to show him who's top gun around here. The dogs were lousy. I'm not going to pay the trainer. He can take me to court."

As she turned her dark eyes from me to him Martha's expression changed. It was as if a hardness settled over her features. Her red mouth became smaller.

"I'd better pack," I said. "I have to be on the afternoon bus."

"Not leaving us so soon?" she asked, and I heard mockery in her voice.

"I promised my mother. She's expecting me."

"Bessie will pack for you."

"Thanks but I can do it."

"I'll see about lunch," she said.

She stood from the window seat and smoothed down the front of her tweed skirt. It was a simple, feminine gesture I had seen many times, yet I found it suggestive and meant for me. It was as if she had traced with her hands the shape of the belly I had not uncovered. As she passed close in front of me, I smelled the perfume she had worn last night.

I went to my room, showered, shaved, and put on my uniform. I packed my bag and carried it downstairs. The table in the dining room had been set. While we ate, Yancey tried to talk me out of leaving.

"Stay one more night," he said. "We'll snooze a little and go hunting this afternoon. We'll have our limit by four o'clock."

"We'd be delighted to have you," Martha told me.

I stared at her. I thought staying another night might mean I would again see her in my room. I felt as if she were teasing me for fleeing her. Or was she? Even as she smiled, I couldn't be certain.

Yancey was still upset about his dogs. He kept apologizing for them. I believed that by blaming them he was trying to shift some of the responsibility for his poor shooting. He went to a desk in the den and came back with papers to show me their bloodlines. Though I hardly heard what he was saying, I pretended to be interested. I kept glancing at Martha. She had withdrawn into herself and acted as if she had forgotten either of us was at the table.

When it was almost time for my bus, Yancey picked up my bag to put it in the Cadillac. Martha came to the door. I went through the business of thanking her for her hospitality. For me it was an awkward moment. She arched an eyebrow and held out her small hand. I didn't know whether its warm pressure meant anything or not.

"You must come again soon," she said, smiling.

"He will," Yancey broke in. "I'll make him promise."

"Yes, do that. Make him promise."

Yancey and I got into the car. As we drove off, Martha was still standing on the rear steps, her feet held together, her hands clasped behind her back. She waved once. The corner of the house cut her off, and the Cadillac moved under the trees.

On the way to town Yancey talked about his dogs and the perfidy of their trainer. I was thinking he must have plenty of gasoline to drive the Cadillac in spite of the C sticker on his windshield. I was also remembering Martha on the steps. We arrived at the station just as the bus was about to pull out.

"You had a good time didn't you?" Yancey asked.

"Of course."

"Well, it was fine having you. I could tell you really made a big hit with Martha."

I looked at him, wondering whether there was possibly any hidden meaning in his remark. Apparently he was sincere. His face was suffused with candor and good will.

"This lousy war," he said. "After we win it, you can spend a month here and we'll really kill some birds. We'll try a fox hunt too."

I could imagine his fox-hunting fat as he was—bouncing along with determination and hogging the gates. Still he obviously meant it about having me. The bad manners he'd used about the birds that morning actually weren't important. For the second time in as many days I found myself liking him. Of course the feeling was now complicated by Martha.

I got onto the bus. It drove off just as I found a seat by a sleeping sailor. Yancey waved. Settling back, I closed my eyes, but I couldn't stop seeing Martha. I still wasn't sure how I should have acted. To her I undoubtedly resembled a schoolboy. On the other hand she

was Yancey's wife, and I was glad I hadn't touched her. I told myself
I was.

In Richmond I rode the streetcar rather than waste money on a
taxi. I found my mother sunning herself in the solarium.

"Was it worth doing?" she asked, raising up from a chaise.

"I'll tell you about it," I answered and sat beside her. Of course I
didn't tell her everything—just the fact Yancey hadn't been lying
when he spoke of his money, house, and wife. My mother listened
carefully, tapping her finger on the arm of the chaise.

"He sounds utterly parvenu," she said.

"He is utterly parvenu."

"I don't know what's happening in this world. All the wrong people have the money. There's no longer any order."

That same night after dinner I wrote Martha a thank-you note. It
was conventionally impersonal. I could imagine her reading it and
smiling mockingly.

13

During the last day of my furlough I worked around the house. I
washed the car and mulched boxwoods against the winter. I hoped
to hide my desire to return to Mississippi. I had no love for the
Army, but I was anxious to get on to OCS and my part in the war.

"Will you have a leave after graduation?" my mother asked me.

"There's a good chance of it."

"You must have your picture taken in your officer's uniform."

"Suppose I bust out?" I really didn't believe I would, but I had
at least considered the possibility.

"Don't be ridiculous," she answered me.

The morning I was to leave, my mother and I rode to the airport.
She held her umbrella.

"Keep your eyes open," she instructed me. "As long as you're in the
Army, make use of it. It can be an educational experience."

"I'll try."

"Watch your associates closely. Of course the quality should improve in OCS. You ought to be particularly careful of this Yancey
person."

"Maybe he's not so bad."

"I think you're mistaken. You'll do well avoiding him. Certainly never put yourself in a position where he can hurt you. Remember a war record can be a real asset to your career. Now kiss me before I weep."

When the plane came in from Washington, we saw Yancey. He hurried to us and shook my mother's hand. Her face was set. She didn't like him, and hiding her feelings was difficult.

"I'm glad you're not late," Yancey told me. "We don't want to get into any trouble reporting in. The thing to do is start right. Don't give them a chance to find flies on us."

I'd checked my equipment and had my ticket stamped. We stood at the wire gate. Because of minor trouble with the hydraulic system, our plane was twenty minutes late in leaving. During that time Yancey fidgeted and assaulted my mother's ears with complaints about the undependability of the airlines. She was reprieved by loud-speakers announcing the plane was loading. I kissed her good-by a second time. Small and lonely looking, she waited at the fence until we took off.

"I bagged fourteen birds yesterday," Yancey bragged, unfastening his safety belt before the sign told us to do so. "Used twenty shells. Best shooting I've done in years."

I didn't believe him. He couldn't shoot that well ever. Nor had he been hunting for years. He was attempting to whitewash the miserable performance he'd shown me. Still I didn't challenge him. I wanted no squabbles. Furthermore I was wondering about Martha.

"Incidentally, you were nice to write the wife," he said as if he had plucked the thought from my mind. "I explained to her you always have proper manners. She wanted me to be sure and ask you to come back."

Again I stared at him, searching for some hidden meaning to his words. His face was as uncomplicated as a child's.

"How long have you all been married?" I questioned him, hoping I sounded casual.

"Fourteen years come December. We got hitched just before a Christmas, and she's always accused me of doing that to gyp her out of a present. That's a joke because I'd give her anything I own. She knows it too."

Abruptly he stopped talking. He turned his head from me and looked out the window. The clown's make-up came off, and for an instant worry creased his face. I wondered whether he was thinking about her or some complication in his business. I didn't question him closely for fear he'd grow suspicious.

87

The plane lost fifteen minutes between Richmond and Charlotte and another ten minutes in reaching Memphis. Yancey was concerned about it. He kept checking his watch. Our orders required us to report to OCS by five o'clock. The delay was cutting our schedule pretty close. He complained to a harried stewardess.

We, of course, had a little information about OCS. Yancey had begun investigating as soon as he was sure we were going. We knew the cadre made life as rough as possible for candidates in the hope they would quit. There was a quota of men allowed through, and it was ruthlessly enforced.

"The thing we have to do is prepare ourselves mentally," Yancey said. "We ought to tell ourselves it's going to be hell but that a lot of men no better than we are have gotten through. We can stand it if they did."

He was worried. Though he had finished basic, he had been allowed the soft duty ever since he put on his medals. He was, as a result, not in the hard physical condition the rest of us were. His belt cut into the fat of his belly. He was undoubtedly thinking there would be more Bulgans at OCS.

By the time we took off from Memphis the plane was an hour and eight minutes late. Yancey decided to take action. He caught the pilot as he was entering the plane from the terminal. The man had gray hair.

"We have to be there by five," Yancey said. "It's very important."

"I'll do my best, soldier. We're bucking a headwind."

"Here," Yancey told him, reaching for his wallet. He removed a twenty-dollar bill. "It's yours if you make it."

The pilot didn't even glance at the bill. He was angry.

"Keep your money. I'm no bellboy."

He walked on to the pilot's compartment. Yancey winked at me.

"I knew he'd turn it down. He thinks he's above being tipped, but watch him goose this plane."

Yancey was right. The pilot did make up some of the time, for when we landed in Mississippi we were less than fifty minutes behind the airline's schedule.

Yancey and I still had to move fast. The taxi driver at the airport wanted to wait for a full load. Yancey waved a ten-dollar bill in front of him, and we sped off. At the post gate, however, we had to start walking because taxis weren't allowed inside the military reservation. We hurried along the road and passed our old company area. It looked deserted. In the hope of finding a ride, we stopped by the orderly room. The clock read five minutes after four.

"A ride?" the company clerk asked. "You must be kidding. I couldn't get a ride myself around this hole."

We walked on. With the exception of rifles, which we'd turned into supply before leaving basic, we were carrying all our equipment—duffel bags, gas masks, helmets. We kept looking for a post bus. None came into sight.

Instead of sticking to the paved road, we crossed a sandy drill field. We had been careful to stay clean on the plane, but under the hot sun our uniforms were becoming wilted and sweaty. Yancey was puffing.

We jogged across the field, bent over under the weight of our equipment. Yancey had difficulty keeping his balance. Our feet kicked up dust. We could see the group of isolated yellow buildings a long time before we reached them. They appeared mysterious and sinister.

When we did arrive at the area, we hoped to save a few minutes by walking among the complex of buildings rather than going around by the street. A window banged open.

"Get the hell off the grass," a voice shouted at us. It belonged to a young second lieutenant who glared at us from an office.

"Yes, sir," we both answered, lowering our equipment in order to salute.

"And succor those blades of grass as you back up."

"Succor, sir?" Yancey asked.

"Goddammit, soldier, can't you understand English? Succor them!"

The lieutenant slammed the window and disappeared. Yancey and I glanced at each other and at the grass.

"How does one go about succoring a blade of grass?" I whispered. We were both still at attention.

"I'm not sure. Let's stand here a little longer and see what happens."

We waited, thinking perhaps the lieutenant would reappear to explain. Yancey looked at his watch. We had less than fifteen minutes to report in.

"Let's slip away quietly," Yancey suggested.

"We could go in and find out," I said.

"I'm against that. He might not want to be disturbed, and there's no telling what we'd run into. We might foul up worse."

Silently we shouldered our duffel bags, retreated from among the buildings, and hurried to the street out front. We ran along a board-walk. Several hundred yards ahead we saw the sign marking headquarters building. We could make it all right. Then a second window opened, and another lieutenant appeared.

"You didn't salute me," he yelled at us. "You'd have gone right on by without saluting."

"We're sorry, sir," Yancey answered as we dropped our equipment to salute. "We didn't know you were there."

"I was standing in plain sight by this window. You're supposed to see things. How do you expect to be officers if you're not observant? Suppose I had been a machine-gun emplacement? You and your men would be dead."

"Yes, sir," we agreed.

"When you report in, notify the sergeant I've given you five gigs each. From this point onward salute everything you pass that's over twelve inches tall. Got me?"

"Yes, sir."

As he closed the window, we saluted him. We also saluted the building and for good measure all the windows too. Hoisting our equipment to our left shoulders and feeling entirely foolish, we saluted telephone poles, barracks, GI cans, and mailboxes. Our hands flew continually up and down. Our arms ached. We were uncertain about a small sign warning us to keep off the grass. It didn't look quite twelve inches high, but just to be on the safe side we saluted it. No sooner had we done so than a third lieutenant opened a window and shouted at us.

"You don't have to salute that sign. Not high enough. That's five gigs. Tell them when you report in."

We had little time left to do that. We began to run along the boardwalk and salute at the same time. A window banged up. Another lieutenant told us that it was against regulations to salute from a running position and added five more gigs.

When we reached headquarters, we saluted the sign, the building, and the door. We left our equipment on the stoop. Just as we entered, we saw the second hand on a large electric clock swinging toward the number five. Also watching the clock was a master sergeant who sat at a desk. In the room behind him were two pfc's.

"Here come the horses' asses," the sergeant said to the pfc's. "You are the horses' asses, aren't you?"

"Yes, sir," we answered, standing at rigid attention.

"You're dumb too. You don't have to say 'sir' to a sergeant. If you're so dumb, what makes you think you're officer material?"

"We believe you can teach us," Yancey said, trying a little soft soap.

"If I could teach you, I'd be an officer myself. It's a silly answer. Give me a better one."

"We think we can best serve our country as officers," Yancey told him, pulling out that old chestnut.

"Bullshit. Your answer makes me sick to my stomach. Pass the puking bowl."

The pfc's snickered.

"Frankly I'm not impressed with the two of you," the sergeant continued. "You look like hell. You're sloppy. Your sloppiness is going to cost you five gigs. Now hand me your orders."

Yancey gave him the orders, which were sealed in a brown envelope. The sergeant tore open the envelope. The two pfc's were smoking and watching. The sergeant checked our names against a mimeographed sheet which lay on his desk. He stood and indicated we were to follow.

We crossed the hall to another room. The room was bare except for blackboards which covered three walls. On the blackboards were horizontal lines and men's names in chalk. The sergeant printed our names at the bottom of one of the boards.

"This is where we keep score," he explained without turning his head. His chalk scratched. "This is where you measure up or go back to being peons like the rest of us."

"How many does it take?" Yancey asked.

"Shut up," the sergeant said. "You got a big mouth and I should gig you for it. You don't talk around here unless you're spoken to."

He wrote 5 after each of our names, the number representing the gigs he'd given us for sloppiness. I'd already observed that every name on the board had gigs. That fact made me feel somewhat better, though we still hadn't told the sergeant about the fifteen we'd received coming down the company street.

"All right," the sergeant said. "A hundred gigs and you're out. Each day you go without a gig reduces your total by one. You don't have to worry about keeping count because we'll do that for you at no charge. You're now cluttering up my office. Get out of here and report to supply for your bedding and rifles."

Yancey moved, but not me. I frowned. We couldn't just leave without mentioning the gigs we'd received from the lieutenants. I

91

wondered whether Yancey had forgotten or was deliberately attempting to get away with something. I spoke up.

"We have fifteen more gigs to report, Sergeant."

"That doesn't surprise me," the sergeant said. "If I ever saw two screwups, it's you guys."

He changed the totals after our names to twenty. I still wasn't greatly disturbed. Twenty was about the average score on the board.

"Now get out of my sight," the sergeant told us. "You stink to me."

"We don't know where supply is," Yancey said as we backed from the room.

"How do you expect to be officers if you can't even find supply?"

"I guess we can find it, but we thought you might advise us."

"Just get the hell out of here is what I advise you. And if you want my frank opinion you'll both be doing yourselves a favor by quitting and saving misery. You'll never make the grade in this place."

We were still backing out. We got through the door and stood on the stoop.

"Sergeant," Yancey called through the door.

"You guys still here?" the sergeant asked. "You're going to be late for inspection."

"You didn't tell us which barracks."

"Do I have to tell you two screwups everything?" He consulted a list. "See what you can find in 820."

We picked up our equipment, left the stoop, and hurried along the boardwalk saluting.

"You shouldn't have told him about the gigs," Yancey whispered. "Those lieutenants wouldn't remember us."

"They might make a point of remembering around here. I don't want to take any chances." I was disappointed and annoyed at him for even trying such a trick.

"In this life you have to take chances," he snapped at me.

We searched along the street for a sign which would show us where supply was. The door opened in the headquarters building we had just left, and the sergeant yelled to us.

"You forgot to salute the stuff in the office," he said.

We had to return to the office and salute wastebaskets, water cooler, and filing cabinets.

"That doesn't get you out of the penalty," the sergeant told us, picking up his piece of chalk. "Five more gigs. Now beat it."

Again we left. We bent under our duffel bags. I was worrying about the inspection the sergeant had mentioned. Our arms moved like semaphores as we looked for the supply room.

Behind us was more shouting. When we turned, we could see the sergeant and an officer running toward us. I recognized the lieutenant who had been first to open a window and who had chewed us out for being on the grass. We lowered our equipment and saluted.

"There they are," the lieutenant accused, pointing at Yancey and me. "They failed to succor the grass."

"I knew they were screwups the minute I set eyes on them," the sergeant said.

"I gave them a direct order to succor." He scowled at us. "Do you deny it?"

"No, sir," we answered.

We were braced at attention. In spite of the fact I was aware this was all a part of the game, I was alarmed. We had the inspection coming up and hadn't even found the barracks. We were bound to get more gigs from the lieutenant. He peered at us distastefully. His lip curled as if we were trash.

"These men are sloppy," he said.

"I already gigged them for it," the sergeant told him.

"They look as if they've been rooting with the hogs. I've never previously had men fail to succor the grass on a direct order."

"Begging your pardon, sir, but we just didn't know what succoring the grass meant," Yancey said.

"You have a mouth, don't you? Obviously it's functioning. A universally accepted practice is to ask questions when you need answers."

"We thought we might disturb you, sir."

I wanted Yancey to shut up. He should have realized talking wasn't going to change anything. If he had let me go in to ask the lieutenant as I'd wished, we wouldn't be in trouble now.

"Mouth," the lieutenant said. "Mouth, mouth, mouth and a stupid excuse. You'll find we don't like gents around here who make stupid excuses. Right, Sergeant?"

"Right, sir. They got twenty-five gigs already."

"They'll never make it by God. I'm going to load them down for disobeying a direct order. They're going to learn the hard way. You men follow me."

We picked up our equipment and trailed him in single file. We continued to salute everything along the street. The lieutenant was moving fast, and Yancey was hurrying to keep up. His fat hips were wagging like a marathon walker's. The lieutenant took us back to where we had first stepped on the grass.

"Get on your hands and knees," he said. "Find the grass you plundered, each individual blade, and straighten it out. As you work crawl backward toward the boardwalk. By so doing you succor the grass you bend succoring other grass. You get an extra gig for each blade I find that's not straight. When you finish, I shall inspect."

As he left us, we saluted. We got down on our knees. The assignment was diabolic. Each time we backed up we bent hundreds more blades. With great care we ran our fingers along them. Some of the grass just wouldn't straighten. Yancey licked his fingers and drew them along the blades. The window flew up.

"No spit!" the lieutenant shouted. "It's a filthy habit and you're vulgar and it will cost you five more gigs."

The window slammed down. As we worked, darkness was gathering around us. When we could no longer see what we were doing, Yancey and I dug into our duffel bags for flashlights. Finally we reached the boardwalk. I knocked timidly on the lieutenant's door. He came out, borrowed my flashlight, and examined the grass.

"Fair job. See only two blades in a bent condition. That's two gigs. Plus five for the spit makes seven. Then you have the gigs for not obeying my order in the first place. Forty for that. You report forty-seven gigs to the sergeant."

We staggered. Forty-seven added to the twenty-five we had would give us seventy-two gigs. That would mean we were not only leading all other candidates, but also were in a position where almost any series of small offenses could bust us out. Moreover we hadn't even reached the barracks yet. I was scared and so was Yancey.

"Please, sir," he said. "We didn't mean to do wrong."

"Please hell. You're lucky I don't scratch you for disobeying a direct order. Let me tell you this. If you ever bend another blade of Mississippi grass, you'll be kicked out so fast you'll be following your tail bone."

He left us in the dark. We saluted, picked up our equipment, and walked as fast as we could to headquarters. Shaken, we reported the new gigs to the master sergeant. He and the pfc's looked impressed. The sergeant wrote our new totals on the board. As we backed out, we saluted everything in the office.

It took us fifteen minutes to find the supply room. The corporal in charge was angry at our being late and threw our stuff on the counter. We asked him where barracks 820 was. He said he didn't know and locked us out. Yancey left me with our equipment, bedding, and rifles. Saluting as he went, he set off in the dark to find the barracks.

Luckily we were less than a hundred yards from it. He returned and we made alternate trips carrying our stuff. On the second floor of the barracks were two empty bunks across the aisle from each other. Candidates who had already cleaned up and prepared for inspection stared at us as we stumbled in with our equipment and rushed back for more.

Yancey and I worked fast to make our beds and arrange our footlockers according to the instructions tacked to the wall. No one around us offered to help. The men were afraid it might be against the rules. When Yancey and I were only about half finished, whistles shrilled downstairs. Everybody sprang to attention in front of his bunk.

The same lieutenant who had made us succor the grass came up the steps and into the room. He was followed by a sergeant carrying a pad and pencil. They moved along the line until they reached Yancey and me.

"These two men aren't ready for inspection," the lieutenant said. "They also have grass stains on their knees. Very sloppy characters. Ten gigs each."

14

Thus Yancey and I on our first evening at OCS had eighty-two gigs—only eighteen from busting out. We were reeling. When the inspection was over, we slunk down to the latrine like criminals. We were fearful that even talking might be against the rules. We sat on johns and whispered.

"We just got off on the wrong foot," Yancey said, wiping sweat from his face. "It'll be better tomorrow."

"It has to be better if there's going to be a tomorrow," I answered, my stomach leaden.

"From now on we'll show them some real soldiering."

I resented him for the fact we hadn't succored the grass in the first place, but I kept my mouth shut. That was past. The thing to do was to be ready for the future. We crept upstairs and lay on our bunks. In spite of our weariness, we were both so tense we couldn't sleep.

At six in the morning whistles blew. Even before breakfast we were marched to a cold, drab auditorium. In formation some of the cadre eyed Yancey and me. I had the feeling they had already singled us out and were sharpening their knives. Both Yancey and I strained to be alert for commands.

As we waited in the auditorium nobody spoke. Other candidates had not wanted to sit near Yancey or me. We were lepers. Men wouldn't even look our way. They were glad we were in trouble and not them.

Cadre called us to attention. A balding, severe full colonel strode upon stage. What he said was not reassuring.

"Fifty per cent of you will not be here six weeks from now," he told us. "We work on the quota system. If each of you had the ability of Stonewall Jackson, we'd still have to flunk out half of you. It's survival of the fittest and law of the jungle. You won't get any sympathy if you screw up. We love screwups. They fill the quota."

As he was talking, the men around Yancey and me must have been thinking we'd be the first to go. I was thinking it myself. I could imagine my mother's reaction.

We learned the quota system was indeed a terrible device. Its insatiable hunger destroyed any spirit of comradeship among candidates. It caused us to hope the unfortunate would bust out and feed the meat grinder. Overnight men became narrow of eye and calculating. Their movements were furtive.

Yancey and I, however, stuck together out of misery and desperation. We clutched at each other for help. We were like two poker players nursing our last dollars in a big game. By combining our meager resources, we might be able to survive.

Our tactics consisted of trying to anticipate everything before it happened. Each evening we huddled in the latrine in an attempt to foresee the hazards of the next day. When close or extended order drill was scheduled, we reviewed all trick commands, hand signals, and formations. If there were lectures, we crammed and asked each other questions we figured the instructor might use on a pop quiz. Before machine-gun drill, we studied stoppages and the proper manner of setting up perimeters.

In addition we policed one another. We bought a pair of scissors so we could trim our hair the prescribed two inches above the collar. We checked for the smallest details of neatness or dress which might bring on gigs. Before barracks inspections we concentrated on dust, lint, and wrinkles. We were as chicken to each other as we imagined officers could be.

For the first few days we lived on the knife's edge. As we suspected, the cadre already had the word on us. They, like the candidates, read the scoreboard at headquarters each day. They flew at Yancey and me as if they were a pack of mad dogs after sheep. We battled to keep our heads. Our greatest fear was being panicked into mistakes.

When we were not, the cadre was disappointed. They had believed we were going to be easy meat. They renewed their attacks with greater ferocity. They howled and snapped at our heels. They cursed us. They were furious because we made it through the first three days without gigs, which in turn lowered our totals.

We were men plotting for our lives. We studied training schedules for possible traps. If we wore the wrong uniform or were unprepared for a formation, we were finished. Our fear of busting out honed us to a terrible pitch of concentration. We put ourselves in the place of the cadre and anticipated how they would try to harass us. We lived in their world as well as our own.

For the entire first week they concentrated on us. In ranks they sneaked up behind us and shouted. At inspections they went over every inch of our areas as they sought a speck of dust or a pair of socks an eighth of an inch out of place in our footlockers. During recitations, Yancey and I were called on to answer the most difficult questions. We expected it and were ready.

After the first week, the pressures eased slightly. We had convinced the cadre we were not going to be pushovers. In addition each day we got through without gigs subtracted from our totals, which we sweated down to seventy-five. Seventy-five was nothing to feel secure about, but it was indicative of a trend.

Yancey and I were also helped by the fact other men were starting to pile up a significant number of gigs. Some who had believed we were going to be the first to bust out found themselves in jeopardy. Running scared, they attempted to join our nightly confabs in the latrine. Yancey and I wouldn't allow that. They hadn't aided us, and we closed ranks. Let them feed the meat grinder.

Nobody was getting much sleep. The cadre woke us early and kept us up late. One night the whistles shrieked for a fire drill. Yancey and I'd anticipated that and had sense enough to carry our rifles. Others, confused by the disorder, forgot. They were gigged. Hateful glances shot at us.

The cadre never allowed us to walk anywhere. On the way to classes or the drill field we double-timed. A person could look in any direction and see men running. The running had to be done at attention. The cadre barked out cadences. Our feet pounded into the dust.

Each morning after a skimpy, hurried breakfast we had a tough barracks inspection. Yancey's and my system of checking each other paid off there especially. We did not only the routine scrubbing, but also used damp cloths to dust everything we could reach. On our knees we cleaned out the cracks in the floor with nail files.

Yancey had an inspiration about bed springs. We removed our mattresses and wiped each spring carefully. At inspection the same morning a lieutenant came through wearing gloves. He turned back everybody's bed and ran his hand over the springs. Only Yancey and I escaped the flood of gigs.

The classroom was always dangerous. Instructors threw information at us so rapidly we couldn't write it all down. We had to sit at attention and were giggable for our facial expressions. The instructors spoke in lulling monotones. Tests were given without notice. Each night in the latrine Yancey and I compared notes on lectures in an attempt to make some sort of sense out of the scribbling we had done during the day.

Yancey was good on mathematics and coached me. On the other hand I was stronger on composition and reports. We became specialists in preparing our assignments. Furthermore Yancey had an instinct for guessing what instructors would ask on tests. More likely than not, he would be able to spot a large percentage of the questions which appeared. We'd have the answers memorized word for word.

During tests the instructors stood right over us. They called out the time every few minutes in a deliberate attempt to make us nervous. Candidates grew so excited they couldn't think. One boy even wet his pants. Pencil points snapped all over the room.

The first bust-outs were not long in coming. A high-strung, sensitive young schoolteacher from Connecticut misunderstood a command and plowed right into the rest of the platoon at close order drill, causing a melee. He was immediately given the boot and left the field weeping silently.

A second candidate, a broker from Florida, had been amassing gigs at the rate of five or ten a day since he arrived. He became confused by whistles and appeared for formation wearing the wrong uniform as well as without his rifle. He didn't even wait to be told. He merely walked off without a word, and later we saw him dressed in ODs carrying his duffel bag down the street. He continued to salute everything he passed in spite of the fact it was no longer required of him.

The instructors asked trick questions in the classrooms. What formation should a platoon use when advancing with flanks exposed? Of course a platoon should never advance with exposed flanks. Still some men fell for it and looked sick as they realized they had been suckered in.

One candidate's handwriting was bad. He was a big bear of a soldier from Oklahoma who'd been in the oil business. Instructors, discovering his weakness, harried him. They fussed, clucked their tongues, and subtracted points from his tests. Finally the big man who was drowning under his gig total became enraged and ordered an instructor to keep his goddamned mouth shut or get his head knocked off. The MPs came for the candidate. He was escorted from the area under guard.

The constant pressure and harassments made returning to straight duty seem a vacation. Naturally the cadre intended it that way. Straight duty was the Sirens' song to sap our wills. We'd heard the men we'd been in basic with had shipped out to Georgia where a new unit was being formed. Life in that outfit was supposed to be soft. There were Class A passes to town and a forty-five-hour week. It appeared a paradise.

The cadre encouraged us to drop out. They talked to us in a friendly fashion, telling us it was no disgrace for anybody to quit. Quitting was better than busting out. Once a person joined a unit he'd be free at night and could drink cold beer at the PX. A lot of men were swayed. They packed their bags and were never seen again.

Those of us left had to endure special hardships like being routed from bed during a heavy thunderstorm and being marched across fields of black, sucking mud. We stumbled through the dark, our shoes lead-heavy with muck. We were sent back to the barracks and given five minutes to prepare for inspection. The cadre gigged us for mud we had no fair chance of cleaning up.

The cadre stayed fresh. The school had two teams of the young animals to hurl at us. Each morning a rested team was sent in. They were judged and promoted on their effectiveness at making life miserable for the candidates. Possibly in the evenings they lounged around their quarters and laughed about how they had given calisthenics until we staggered or kept us standing at attention in the searing sun while candidates toppled over like trees cut by axes.

Though Yancey and I were high men in the classroom, he was beginning to have bad trouble outside of it, and there was little I could do to help. The reason was his physical condition. Because he had been pampered in basic, he was out of shape for the battle of OCS. The training schedule called for marches each Thursday. They were designed to destroy the weak, and every march was a test of will for Yancey. He burned will like a machine might gasoline.

As the marches lengthened, Yancey reached the point where his fat body simply would not obey the will part of him. His ruddy flesh sagged as if made of melting rubber. His mouth fell open, and he walked with his feet far apart. He would be unaware of what direction he was moving in. Shouts and threats from cadre momentarily straightened him. Red-faced, he bit at the air and wheezed frightfully.

Inevitably the time came when he had to drop out on a march. The cadre were waiting expectantly and circled him like vultures, each hoping to give the gigs. Yancey held on a lot longer than they or I believed possible. In that oily, rolypoly body was a hard core of strength which kept his fat legs dragging along after he was no longer conscious of what he was doing.

He finally collapsed on the side of the road. Doing so cost him fifteen gigs. By then he had worked his total down to sixty-one. The fifteen shot him up to seventy-six.

Though he did fine during the rest of the week, the marches began causing him to drop out with regularity. Thus assuming he didn't get gigged for anything else, his net was rising weekly by eight. There was no way he could beat the mathematics of it.

I advised him to try his medals as he had in basic. Something was required quick. He was losing weight, and his face was turning gray. His shoulders were bent as if carrying heavy burdens. He became very quiet, and at night he would lie on his bed groaning softly to himself as his muscles cramped painfully.

To my surprise he was reluctant to use the medals. He refused to do it until his gig total reached the high eighties. Then, just before retreat one Thursday, he dug into his footlocker and pinned the ribbons on his blouse.

In formation a corporal spotted the ribbons immediately. He hurried to Yancey to examine them closely. Without speaking, the corporal did an about-face, returned to the front of the platoon, and marched us to the parade ground where each evening we had to stand at attention so long in the flaming sun we had come to hate the sight of the American flag.

Yancey knew the corporal would inform the sergeant, and the sergeant our platoon officer, yet nothing happened until retreat formation the next day when both the sergeant and the lieutenant appeared. The lieutenant had a row of ribbons on his own blouse. He approached Yancey.

"You have a right to wear those," the lieutenant said. "If you're trying to impress anybody around here, however, it won't work. We're used to heroes."

What the lieutenant meant was that men who'd been in combat and won decorations were constantly being sent back to the States for OCS and cadre. Thus whereas in basic Yancey had been a personality and a celebrity, at OCS he was just fancy meat for the grinder.

He removed his ribbons after formation. Other candidates smiled, glad that he had been stomped for trying a trick. The cadre interpreted the lieutenant's reprimand as a signal to bear down even harder. They hounded Yancey in ranks and gave him special calisthenics until he was too exhausted to move. They took advantage of his weariness to try to trick him into making mistakes at drill. In the classroom if he as much as nodded, instructors were ready to pounce on him with gigs.

By the fourth week his total had passed ninety. That total was the highest of anyone in our section. Everybody was sure the weekly march would finish him. His eyes were hollow, and his shoulders bent. On the afternoon of the march he sat on the edge of his bunk, his head bowed, his hands lying limply across his thighs.

"They got me licked, Charley," he whispered.

"Hell no," I said without conviction. "You can stick it out."

"I've given it everything I've got. They've cut me up."

"You can't just quit."

"I've got one more chance," he told me, lowering his voice even further. "I'll probably end up in the stockade for it, but I have to try."

He stood slowly. Instead of dressing for the march like the rest of us, he began pulling on his ODs. Before buttoning his shirt, he unzipped the money belt he always wore around his fat waist and took out some bills, which he folded into his pocket.

"What you up to?" I whispered to him.

"I've been doing my homework and studying our company commander. He's no West Pointer. He came into the Army through the National Guard. In civilian life he owned a Plymouth agency in Michigan. I've never met an automobile dealer anywhere who didn't like the feel of green. Besides he has a wife and five children and's not selling any cars because of the war."

"You're going to try a bribe?" I was both shocked and afraid of what he was saying.

"I guess you could call it that. It's the only thing left."

"They'll court-martial you."

"Maybe. I don't give a damn. If I bust out of here, I just don't care."

Whistles started blowing. I had no more time to talk to him. Grabbing my rifle, I ran to formation, leaving Yancey putting on his clothes. When the roll was called and he didn't answer, the cadre smiled.

Because of the march, it would be evening before I saw Yancey—if I ever did see him again. Most probably he'd be gone by the time I returned. It occurred to me that I might be involved in any scandal. I didn't like the thought. I sweated more from anxiety than from the struggle of a forced march through the piney woods.

When we got back, Yancey wasn't in the barracks. His gear, however, had not been removed. At chow he slipped in to sit beside me. He was washed and looked rested. Because of others at the table we couldn't talk. Yancey winked.

"Well?" I asked as soon as we were outside, glancing behind to make certain nobody was close to us.

"I had it figured right," he answered. "I went to the chaplain. Everybody's been ignoring the chaplain. He was so happy to have somebody to help he personally took me to the company commander's office. I didn't even have to cool my heels."

Yancey stopped speaking as two men from the mess hall passed. He waited until they were out of hearing before continuing.

"I was nervous of course," Yancey said. "I can tell you I was plenty nervous. The CO was sitting behind his desk looking important as a general. He was mad at me for putting the chaplain on him. I'd already worked up the approach I was going to use. I let the chaplain get out. I didn't want to give the CO anything solid to hang onto. When we were alone, I told him my conscience was bothering me."

"Your conscience?" I asked, my head turning constantly as I wondered whether we were being observed. Yancey might still be in trouble, and some of that trouble could rub off on me.

"That's right. I told him my conscience was bothering me because I'd won five hundred dollars in a crap game. I said I believed gambling was morally wrong. I confessed the money had been worrying me ever since I'd won it."

" 'Did you win it here?' the captain asked me. He was frowning as if he was going to have me shot. 'You know the rules against gambling.'

" 'Not here, sir,' I answered him. 'I won it during basic.'

" 'If it had been here, I'd have to report you for disciplinary action. Needless to say you'd have been busted out. You might be busted out anyway for missing the march.'

" 'Yes, sir,' I told him. 'I understand you got to obey all the rules and regulations, and I came here to see you only because I got this money I don't know what to do with. I thought you could help me, sir.'

" 'Help you how?'

" 'Well, sir, you have a lot more experience about these things than I do. I tried to find the men I'd won it from and give it back, but they've all shipped out. I can't remember the amounts anyway. So to ease my conscience I thought I'd bring the money to somebody who could decide what ought to be done with it. I thought I'd leave it here with you, sir.'

"I began to count out the money slowly," Yancey said. "The captain was gaping at the fifty-dollar bills piling up on his desk. He was thinking of his five children and a wife clamoring for money. I left the stack of bills right in front of him.

" 'I want to thank you for helping me, sir,' I told him. 'You've taken a big load off my mind. I've been so worried I haven't said anything to anybody about this money, and I'm never going to either. I feel one hundred per cent better, and I want you to know I'll always appreciate your help.' "

"What did the captain do?" I asked.

"He didn't do anything. He just stared at all that new money sitting on the blotter in front of him. I was backing from the office. All the time I was saluting like mad."

"You really think you can get away with it?"

"I ought to find out pretty quick. I been out of his office over four hours and nobody's said anything to me about the march I missed."

I still didn't believe he was free. That an officer could be bribed was inconceivable. Yancey was attempting to treat the captain as he had cooks and KP pushers at the induction center. I was impressed by his nerve but convinced he had gone too far.

I didn't like being near him. I expected MPs to appear. They did not, however, come that night. At formation in the morning, cadre treated Yancey as if nothing had changed. They were still confident they'd have his carcass and smiled in anticipation.

During the week Yancey held on. The cadre didn't press. They figured to have him easily at the next march. They licked their chops.

Just before the march, Yancey was called from ranks. He was needed in personnel to complete information missing from his records. Yancey had looked desperate until he heard his name. He sighed and winked. The cadre were puzzled.

From then on Yancey was safe, and he knew it. He got out of enough marches to lower his point total and allow him to absorb gigs. If personnel didn't call for him, then the medics just happened to discover he needed another diphtheria shot or that his teeth required checking. Nothing was said to the cadre, but they understood.

Yancey now had a tremendous advantage over the rest of us. He possessed the knowledge that the quota couldn't devour him. While we lived in fear, he again became his old self. His skin glowed rosily, and he dispensed laughter and good cheer.

"It's all the same," he told me and smiled. "There's no difference between the military and anything else."

"What anything else?" I asked.

"You put money on the table and people pick it up."

"You're damned lucky," I said.

"I've always been lucky," he answered.

15

By the end of six weeks more than a third of our section had busted out. I, however, felt reasonably secure. I say "reasonably" because nobody except Yancey could feel comfortable. Still, my grades were high, and my gigs were down to the low sixties. A dozen men had more. I'd sized up the competition carefully and decided that after the initial bloody onslaught my chances of surviving were pretty fair.

On Tuesday of the seventh week we had a field problem. The platoon was on attack in the piney woods. As I ran, I tripped in a thicket of honeysuckle and sprawled to the ground. My rifle jarred loose from my hands.

The lieutenant saw me. He charged toward me blowing his whistle. He stopped the attack to chew me out. I stood at attention while he told me what sacrifices the taxpayers had made to buy the M-1 I had abused and ought to be shot with. At the end of his tirade he gave me twenty-five gigs.

Thus by one unexpected blow my total soared to eighty-seven. I still survived, but the difficulty about being in the high eighties was that I had no margin of error for situations I couldn't anticipate or control.

Of course I'd been through the whole experience before when Yancey and I first arrived at OCS. The difference was that now the grinder needed to be fed, and the men who turned the handle, the cadre, were finding it harder to get meat. Perhaps they'd been told they were falling down on the job. They hounded us like Furies.

They particularly assailed those who had high totals. High totals were like the scent of blood to sharks. Because of mine, the cadre slashed and ripped at me during every formation. They tried to rattle me by yelling, and my ears rang. Each was hoping he would receive credit for busting me out. On the way to classes, a button on my shirt worked loose as I ran. A sharp-eyed corporal spotted it, and I got five gigs. That brought my total to ninety-two.

Yancey was doing all he could to help. He was alarmed for me. Each night we sat late in the latrine discussing tactics with regard to the next day's training schedule.

"Stay alert for God's sake," he advised me. "You got to sweat those gigs down. If you can stay alive, the cadre will find somebody else to hop on."

I did work down my total. For the next three days the cadre were unable to find a reason to gig me. It was, however, a laborious, nerve-racking business. I'd never felt so tired and beaten in my life, yet I had to keep my head. I forced myself to check everything twice to be sure I made no errors.

I was able to bear the worst the cadre could inflict. With the agonizing slowness of a man lifting a huge weight, I got through

105

the day-by-day chamber of horrors and sweated my gigs down to a total of eighty-four. I sensed that in spite of the way the cadre attacked me, they respected me too. They understood the fight I was putting up.

For a while the pressure eased off me because of another's troubles. A young man who slept in the bunk next to mine forgot one of his general orders and shot above me in gigs. The cadre switched to him. As they were finishing him off, I could catch my breath a little. I didn't feel sorry for him. I was thankful his meat was saving mine.

By the time he busted out I had my gigs down to eighty. Yancey had helped me, especially at inspections. He worked harder on my area than he did on his own. At those inspections we stood at attention in front of our footlockers. The footlockers were open so that the officers could examine the contents. The officers entered on the first floor, inspected it, and climbed up to where we were.

We were able to hear the inspectors come in downstairs. We waited quietly, afraid to move because our footsteps might displease them. Yancey, who understood how nervous I was, winked confidently from across the aisle. I was so tense I felt brittle.

On our ninth Saturday in OCS we listened to the inspectors climbing the stairs. We stood at strained attention, our chests out and our hands pressed flat against our thighs. I just happened to glance down at Yancey's footlocker. Under one corner was a string from the mop. I should have seen it earlier while checking his area. I pointed.

"What?" he asked, bending over but not seeing.

"There!" I whispered.

"I don't get you."

The corners of his footlocker were beveled at the bottom, and from his angle he couldn't see the mop string. It was a certainty, however, the inspector would find it. He was close to the top of the steps. Believing I had time, I lunged from my place, crossed the aisle, and jerked out the string. I scrambled back just as the captain entered.

I stood trembling, not knowing whether he had seen me or not. He came down the line, stopping before each man, examining him and his equipment. He wiped his immaculate white gloves under beds and along baseboards. It was frightening how much tension could build up over the tightness of a blanket or the direction the creases in a person's underwear faced.

The captain was red hot. He found dust on a window, grease on a rifle, lint under a shoe. Scowling, he barked his gigs to the lieutenant and master sergeant who followed him.

He reached Yancey. Occasionally he would gig Yancey but never too hard. I believed that before the captain started on inspection he familiarized himself with Yancey's total.

"Rifle number," he snapped.

"35772915, sir," Yancey answered.

The captain grunted, got Yancey's rifle from a rack at the head of the bed, and inspected it. He always made a show of being severe around Yancey as if to impress the cadre he had no favorites. Probably he was not only ashamed, but also angered that there was one candidate he couldn't touch. Perhaps that anger was what fell on me when the captain turned to my area.

He glared as if I were an obscene sight. Behind him stood the lieutenant who had made us succor the grass and the master sergeant with his gig book. The captain's eyes went over me. He walked around my bed, and I heard him rubbing his gloved hand along the floor. I was hardly breathing. I told myself the inspection would soon be over and he gone. The captain, however, returned to stand in front of me.

"I'm waiting for your explanation," he said.

"Explanation, sir?" I asked, suddenly very fearful. I could see Yancey beyond the captain's shoulder. He too looked scared.

"You're not deaf are you? I said explanation. What the hell were you doing when I came in?"

"I wasn't doing anything, sir."

"Do you think me a fool? I saw you moving. Were you or were you not moving when I topped the stairs?"

"Yes, sir, I was."

"You don't have to tell me. I know you were. That little trick will cost you ten gigs."

I felt as if I'd been hit in the stomach. After the bloody battle I'd fought all these weeks, I was up to ninety again. The master sergeant made a note on his book. The lieutenant smiled. Sweat rolled down my body.

The captain passed on. I was thinking I was at least still alive. The lieutenant then whispered to the captain. The captain looked at my right hand where I held the mop string I had pulled from under Yancey's footlocker. I had balled the string and pressed it against my leg. A tip of the string hung below my index finger.

"Are you a pack rat?" the captain asked me.

"No, sir," I answered, terrified now. I thought I might wet my pants.

"It does appear you collect things."

He came to me, caught hold of the string, and pulled it from my hand as if it were a long, pale worm. He dangled it in front of my eyes. At the same time he smiled evilly at me.

"Where did you get this?"

"From the mop, sir."

"You were holding it. Did you perhaps think regulations stated that you should hold a mop string in your hand during barracks inspection?"

"No, sir."

"Then maybe you were trying to play the wag and make a little joke on the captain?"

"Oh no, sir."

"Aren't you the man who dropped his rifle?"

"Yes, sir."

"You're a screwup, mister. It's about time you learn what it takes to soldier in this outfit. Ten gigs, Sergeant."

I whimpered. Ten gigs sent me to a hundred. For the first time in my life I thought I might faint. I rocked on my feet and raised a hand to the captain who had already started away.

"Sir, I wish you'd reconsider," I pleaded.

"What's that?" he asked, frowning.

"I picked up that mop string in an attempt to help somebody else," I said, glancing in appeal at Yancey. I wanted him to speak up for me. After all I was in trouble because I'd helped him. He could take more gigs and survive. He stood at attention, avoiding my eyes.

"Very noble," the captain answered sarcastically. "You're not supposed to police another candidate's area. That's his responsibility. If you remember the colonel's speech, it's the law of the jungle here. Furthermore you shouldn't speak unless spoken to. That's ten more gigs."

The master sergeant whispered to the lieutenant and the lieutenant to the captain.

"Well, that's his tough luck," the captain said, walking on.

I was shaking. The discipline and training of the past weeks kept me at attention, but I wanted to run after the captain, grab his hand, and beg him. I thought I was going to be sick at my stomach. I tasted vomit in my throat. As the captain left the room, the master sergeant stopped by me.

"You know what to do," he told me.

As soon as they were gone down the steps, I rushed across the aisle to Yancey. Men in the room were watching me. They were looking at me in the same manner I had at others—glad it was me being fed to the grinder instead of them.

"Oh gosh, Charley, I'm sorry," Yancey said.

"You've got to help me," I whispered.

"Me? How?"

"Come on," I ordered and grabbed him by the arm. I led him down the steps. We went out back by the furnace room.

"You go to the captain and tell him what happened. I picked up that mop string for you."

"I know you did, and I want you to realize I fully appreciate it. You'll never know how much I appreciate it. It was a pure and selfless act. I don't think, however, it would do any good for me to go to the captain."

"I think it might do a whole lot of good," I told him, raising my voice.

"Wait a minute now," he answered, putting a hand on my arm in an attempt to calm me. "Let's be reasonable. You had a bad break, a real bad break, and I'm sorry. I'm so damn sorry I could cry. But you understand about bad breaks. They happen to everybody."

"Don't give me that. Any bad breaks I'm getting are your fault."

"Now look, Charley, I know you were trying to help me, and I'll always remember it. Maybe one of these days I'll even be able to make it up to you. But I can't do anything now."

"One of these days hell. You're going to the captain."

"It won't do any good," Yancey said, his pudgy hands upraised and his brown eyes outsized behind his glasses. "The captain's on edge so to speak. It bothers him he picked up money. Pressure him, he'll blow. He could turn on me. He's got the money after all, and he didn't exactly sign a receipt for it."

"Goddammit, Yancey, you owe me a try."

"Now, Charley, don't get excited. It stops you from thinking clearly. He's not going to back down. If he did it for you, he'd have to for others. Candidates would be lining up at his door. So you see even if he wanted to help he couldn't because of precedent."

"Yancey, either you go to the captain or I tell everybody how you bribed him."

"Charley, that's a foolish threat. It wouldn't do you a bit of good to tell people. There's no proof. I'd just have to deny it and naturally

109

the captain would too. People would think you were sour grapes. You can see that, can't you?"

"You sonofabitch," I told him.

"Please, Charley," he said, looking pious. "You got to take the bad with the good."

"You dirty lousy sonofabitch."

"Names like that aren't going to help anything. Tomorrow you'll be sorry you spoke to me this way."

Whistles started blowing out front. Yancey edged away from me. I went after him, catching at his sleeve. He began running. I called, but he kept going. Men were hurrying from the barracks to meet formation. I saw that my place in ranks had already been closed up. Cadre were taking reports, but my name wasn't even mentioned. I no longer existed. As I stood helpless, they marched off, leaving me alone.

Slowly I entered the barracks. It was spotless and without life. Upstairs at my bunk I packed. I was still dazed. I wished I could cry. I left my blankets, sheets, footlocker, and rifle where they were. Let supply send somebody for them. I shouldered my duffel bag and walked out of the barracks.

At headquarters I glanced at the score board. A line had been drawn through my name and following it was the number 110 with a circle around it and the date. The master sergeant who had acted so tough was now relaxed and considerate. He had one of his pfc's type my orders.

"Good luck," the sergeant said.

I left headquarters and carried my duffel bag along the boardwalk. A window banged up in one of the buildings. A cadreman leaned out.

"You're not saluting everything," he said.

"Go to hell," I told him.

He grinned, gave me a friendly wave, and shut the window.

I left the area and crossed the dusty, weed-strewn field. Stopping to rest, I looked back at the yellow buildings. I could hear the faint sounds of commands and cadences. For a moment I thought of what might have been. I lifted my duffel bag and walked on.

16

I had to report back to the company where I had taken my basic. The area was busy with a new shipment of draftees. The new men appeared naive and frightened.

At the orderly room the first sergeant, who no longer cowed me, told me I'd have to stick around a few days while new orders were cut. Until I shipped, I'd be kept off the duty rosters. I could sleep late and go to the service club when I wished.

I was left alone, and people had a special way of treating me. The draftees stared because to them I was mysterious. The cadre quieted down when I approached. After I passed, they whispered. I was not sure whether they were sorry for me or enjoying the downfall of the mighty. It was probably the latter.

I was badly shaken. I lay on my bed ignoring the covert looks of men milling through the hut in the ridiculous routines of basic. I was trying to pull myself together. I felt as if I'd been run over by a steam roller.

I slept late each morning, and I was allowed to eat in the kitchen with the cooks. Most of the day I remained on my bed. At night I sat by myself drinking beer at the PX. I had a place under the eaves in case of rain. I was sullen and other drinkers steered wide of me.

I couldn't seem to bounce back. Busting out of OCS was causing me to doubt myself. I was no longer the same person and felt as if some fundamental beam in my character had been jarred loose. Most of all, I was ashamed.

Furthermore, I was surrounded by the great amorphous shape of the Army. Anywhere else I might have picked myself up and been in there punching. The Army made such gameness seem without hope. I could batter myself bloody against the impersonal system. It was easier to lie full of bitterness on my bed and blame Yancey.

I hated him. I woke each day hating him, I lived with the hate all my conscious hours, and I hated him the last thing at night before going to sleep. I wanted to hit him. In the end I transferred the responsibility for failure from myself to him.

I had to write my mother. I went to the service club during the afternoon when I was the only man in the building. The Ping-pong balls were silent, and nobody played the boogie-woogie records. I didn't give her details. I said merely that I'd been dismissed from the school and was to be sent to another unit.

Approximately seventy-two hours later as I was sitting outside the PX drinking beer in my solitary spot under the eaves, a Red Cross lady wearing a gray uniform came looking for me. She was driving a jeep.

"You have a long-distance call," she told me. "The operator says it's an emergency."

At the very least I'd been expecting a call. I had been half afraid my mother might turn up in person. I rode with the Red Cross lady to the service club. She let me use her office. I picked up the telephone.

"I had an extremely difficult time locating you," my mother said. "The people at your camp were not at all polite. A man had the nerve to tell me there's a war on. If anyone knows there's a war on, I do. All right, I'm listening."

I leaned back in the chair, closed my eyes, and started talking. I hadn't thought out in advance what I was going to say, but I didn't need to. I just told her how Yancey had betrayed me on the mop string by not speaking up.

"I warned you about him," my mother said. "He isn't your kind. However, that's neither here nor there. What are your plans now?"

"Right at the moment I'm fresh out of plans."

"I don't like your tone. There are always things a person can do."

"Usually that's right, but not in the Army. You can't make plans because you're not in charge of yourself. Men you can't even see are pulling the strings."

"I definitely don't like your attitude. It isn't like you to give up so easily. There will be more opportunities."

"They have too many officers. At the school they wanted to bust us out."

"That's not important. Good men can always get ahead. There are never enough of them. You can succeed if you gird yourself up. I'd like to hear you say you will."

"All right, Mom."

"Say it."

"I'll gird myself up."

"That's better. I want you to think on those words constantly. Repeat them until they pound in your brain. Remember you're an Elgar. I expect you to become an officer."

There was a silence between us. I could hear buzzing on the line.

I imagined how she looked on the other end, her face creased in determination, her lips pulled in grimly.

"There's no need for anybody in Richmond to know you failed out," she told me. "I won't mention it to a soul. If they ask me questions, I'll explain you're undergoing special training."

"So now I'm a leper."

"You're definitely a leper. I've bragged too much about you to pretend this doesn't matter. It matters a great deal, and I'm deeply disappointed."

"Mom, try to understand there are some things a man can't control."

"I refuse to accept that. That's defeatism, and I detest it. It's sickness. You'll do all you can to get yourself a commission. In the meantime don't say a word, not a word, to anybody. You fight, do you understand me?"

I said I did, and she hung up without telling me good-by. I returned to the PX where I drank as many beers as I could before closing time. I didn't feel much like fighting. The hell with the family honor. Beer gurgled down my throat. I had never been drunk in my life, but that night I staggered along the company street like an old trooper. Guards helped me to my hut. I fell face down on the bunk.

Early the next morning the company clerk shook my shoulder to wake me. I moaned. He told me my orders had come in and that I was to get packed because I was going by train to Georgia. I shaved with trembling hands and carried my equipment to the orderly room. A weapons carrier picked me up. In the rear was a tall, lean man named Beanpost. He was from another company and had also busted out of OCS. He had tickets for our transportation and meals.

We traveled by coach, changing trains half a dozen times. I was silent, staring at the flat, snake-infested country. Beanpost was about my age and had been an undertaker in civilian life. He and his father owned the biggest funeral parlor in Pike County, Kentucky. Beanpost was in the process of convincing himself he didn't mind being kicked out of OCS.

"It's not the end of the world," he said. "Actually there are advantages in being an enlisted man. You don't have the heavy responsibilities. I'm going to look on the bright side of things."

There was no one to meet us at the small, rural station in Georgia. We waited by a track where weeds grew up among the ties. The agent was reluctant to allow us to use his telephone. It was not, he explained, a public facility, and acted as if he'd been put upon by many soldiers. Beanpost finally talked him into permitting us to call, but the agent watched us every second.

An hour passed before a truck came for us. We rode in the rear. Sere Spanish moss hung over the narrow road. The clay shoulders were as red as beefsteak. We saw a wild turkey flying among dark cypress trees.

The camp itself had just recently been built on the edge of a swamp. The lumber of the buildings smelled of resin and fresh paint. The truck stopped in front of an olive-drab structure. On the grass was a sign which said HEADQUARTERS, 606th REGIMENTAL COMBAT TEAM. I sat smoking while Beanpost carried our orders inside. From across the fields came the ferocious screaming of men going through bayonet drill.

A corporal came out with Beanpost. He talked to the truck driver. The driver took us up the road to an area marked 1st BATTALION. Again Beanpost carried orders in. He returned with a buck sergeant who pointed to a building across the street from battalion head-quarters. He said to ask for Captain Hanks.

We went to the building, which was a combination barracks and orderly room. A pfc was typing. He told us Captain Hanks wasn't in, checked our orders, and sent us to supply to draw our bedding, foot-lockers, and rifles.

Supply was an ill-lighted shed with racks of canteens, blankets, shoes, and gas masks. Around walls were crates of M-1's and carbines. Beanpost and I wandered about until we found a private counting out a pile of helmet liners. A radio was playing hillbilly music.

We signed for our stuff and carried it back to the barracks. The pfc helped us find bunks. We made our beds and transferred our clothes from duffel bags to footlockers. We lay resting until the pfc returned. He told us Captain Hanks wasn't going to be in but that Lieutenant Beady would speak to us. We went downstairs to the office.

Lieutenant Beady was sitting in Captain Hanks' chair. He was a good bit younger than I, and his uniform was new. He had probably graduated from OCS in the class just ahead of my own. I felt both envious and antagonistic. As Beanpost and I stood at attention be-fore the desk, the lieutenant leafed through our records.

"I know you men busted out of OCS," he said. "I hope you hold no grudges about it. The fact you lasted this long indicates you have better than average qualifications. We're going to need noncoms in this outfit. For men with drive, the TO is wide open on the enlisted level."

He stopped talking to light his pipe. Beanpost and I were still at attention because Beady had forgotten to put us at ease. The pipe was also new, and I had the impression the lieutenant had taken up smoking merely to appear more professional.

"Actually you're lucky," he continued. "We're just putting this unit together. It's going to be the best frigging outfit in the goddamned Army. We're forming a regimental combat team which under battle conditions can be shifted quickly and hit hard. We're a new concept of infantry, and our priority in Washington is A-1. We'll go where the fighting's the hottest, a self-sustained unit with its own transportation and command. We'll be a kind of army within an army, and when the history of this war is written the 606th will figure prominently on its rolls."

He had the speech memorized. Because the 606th had just been activated, he was undoubtedly the reception committee for a lot of replacements. We learned later Lieutenant Beady had worked for a travel agency before the war. He had developed his enthusiasm by selling tours. He now examined our records further, cleared his throat, and choked briefly on smoke from his pipe.

"Beanpost, you can help us out over in supply. They don't need an undertaker, but they do want a person who knows something about clothing sizes. As for you, Elgar, battalion headquarters has requested a clerk. With your business training and experience, you ought to fit into that routine. Plenty of good ratings available if you show your stuff. Lots of luck to both of you. Take the rest of the afternoon off. You report to work tomorrow morning at eight."

We left his office. Beanpost was cheerful.

"This place might not be so bad after all," he said. "What I see of it I like."

We showered, shaved, and dozed until men entered the barracks at five. I recognized a few people from basic. All had a clean, unused appearance which meant they were not on straight duty but office force. I saw Timberlake, the towheaded law student I'd beaten out for OCS. He was a pfc and obviously pleased I hadn't made it.

"Must be pretty much of a comedown to have to associate with the hoi polloi," he said, speaking loud enough for everybody on the second level of the barracks to hear.

"As a matter of fact you're right," I answered, angry enough not to care.

"We're not so bad," Timberlake continued, aware he was the center of attention. "We take baths and don't spit on the floor."

"I'm glad you in particular take baths because you stink," I answered him.

For a minute I thought I was going to have it out with him. I'd never been in a real fight in my life, and even as I faced him I was surprised I'd allowed myself to get into such a position. Fortunately Timberlake wanted trouble even less than I. Glaring, he took a towel from his footlocker and went to the latrine.

That evening at chow I saw more men from basic. Carter, the intense boy from South Carolina who was shot through with a sense of Civil War glory and a volunteer, sat beside Hatfield, the West Virginia coal miner who'd had syphilis. The latter hunched over his food and spoke to no one. Because of his dark, threatening nature and the knife he carried, he had acquired the name "Black" Hatfield.

Beanpost and I ate together. I was certain the story of our busting out of OCS was making the rounds. We were being talked over. After we cleaned our mess kits, we went to a movie. We sat apart from others. Already the outfit had formed cliques and alliances which shut us out. Beanpost was still optimistic. He liked what he had been able to learn about working in supply.

Both of us went to bed early and got up before the others. As soon as we'd eaten breakfast, he went to supply and I crossed the street to battalion headquarters. Just inside the door an overweight WAC was sitting at her desk. I introduced myself. She smiled and told me her name was Gabby. She led me to the office of WO Page.

WO Page was a prissy little CPA who looked as if his fingernails had been manicured. His office was antiseptically neat. Everything on his desk had an exact spot. He shook my hand as if touch were distasteful to him. He said I would be used in the payroll section. First I would have to speak with Colonel Box. All new men, WO Page explained, were interviewed by the colonel. I followed WO Page through the building where clerks were starting to work in cubicles.

I had to wait to see Colonel Box. WO Page left me sitting on a wooden bench outside the colonel's office. At a desk was his receptionist—a pretty WAC sergeant. She powdered her nose. She was a young, sandy-haired woman with an arrogant expression. She returned my look coldly. She put away her compact, lighted a cigarette which hung from pouting lips, and started typing rapidly. She cut me off completely.

On her desk a buzzer sounded. She went into the colonel's office and came back to tell me he would see me. I walked at attention. Actually Box was a lieutenant colonel—a bow-legged man with a white mustache and a choleric face. He paced the floor behind his desk, slapping a riding crop against his leg.

"We set examples here," he said, baring his teeth. "The entire battalion looks to this headquarters, and if we're sloppy, the line companies are going to be sloppy too. We work by the book. If the book says stand on heads and piss, we do it. Goof off and you'll be sent to straight duty quicker than an Indian going to crap. This is the best frigging battalion in the whole goddamned Army."

I knew where Lieutenant Beady had gotten at least part of his speech. Colonel Box dismissed me with a wave of his riding crop. I saluted, went past the typing WAC sergeant, and reported again to WO Page. He took me to a cubicle where four desks were placed close together. One was occupied by Carter, who stared distastefully at me. He was remembering how I hadn't backed him up the time he'd gone to the orderly room about Yancey. The other men were privates named Wilson and Gladstone.

"Payroll's already made up this month," WO Page said. "You can check figures though. Give you an idea of what's going on. Don't let the colonel see you using bad posture. He becomes excited about bad posture."

WO Page left me at the empty desk. He returned with payroll sheets which he put in front of me. The others watched. Wilson was in his thirties. He had a lined, cynical face. Gladstone was close to forty. He was losing his gray hair, wore glasses, and had bloodshot eyes. As soon as WO Page was gone, Gladstone opened the middle drawer of his desk and started reading a book which lay inside.

"Punch the keys a while," Wilson told me and smiled. "A little later we'll go down for a smoke. It's not allowed, but we can get away with it if we're careful."

I began using the adding machine as I scanned the meaningless figures on the payroll sheet.

"The drill around here is very simple," Wilson continued. "Just keep your posture straight and do something whether it's useful or not. Make those keys chatter. We're going to win this war with adding machines and typewriter ribbons. Our battle cry is up their giggies with ten-foot paper clips."

"Don't pay any attention to him," Gladstone said, not raising his eyes from his book. "He really loves it here."

117

I had learned to use an adding machine at the bank. In less than twenty minutes I had the column of figures totaled. The sums checked out.

"What'll I do now?" I asked.

"Add them again," Wilson told me. "The impression you want to create is frantic activity. A general might walk in here, see how busy we are, and award Colonel Box his eagles."

I did the figures a second time. Gladstone both read and used a hand on a typewriter. He didn't even glance at what he was typing. When the carriage rang the bell, he shifted and wrote on.

Wilson opened a drawer and brought out a small checkerboard which he slipped into a manila folder. His desk was pushed right against Carter's. They placed the folder midway between them and started a game. Each time they heard footsteps in the corridor, they closed the folder quickly. An officer passing our cubicle would have believed we were very busy, but in reality nobody was doing anything. Wilson nodded approvingly as I punched my adding machine. Carter won the checker game.

"We can have the smoke now," Wilson told me. "I'll go first. There's a door at the end of the hall which leads to the basement. Just look as official as you can. Everybody except the colonel will understand what you're doing, but nobody'll say anything if you act right."

"Keep your shoulders back," Gladstone said, still reading.

Wilson left. I waited a few moments before following. I saw the door and walked to it. The pretty WAC sergeant who was the colonel's secretary watched me. She was smoking and chewing gum. She appeared bored.

I faced a darkened staircase. I could find no light, but from below, Wilson's voice whispered for me to come on. I felt my way down the steps. At the bottom a hand grabbed my arm and steered me through the dark. A match flared. Wilson lighted a cigarette and offered me one. He had a Coke bottle to put ashes in.

"Of course smoking's not much fun in the dark, but it's better than not smoking at all," he said.

"She smokes," I told him, pointing to the ceiling where the WAC sergeant was. Now that my eyes had adjusted, I saw there was dim light in the basement from a small, dirty window at the rear. Around us were wooden shelves and storage space.

"She's a broad, and the colonel thinks he's going to lay her one of these days. He's afraid if he says anything to her she'll hold out on him. For everybody else he's wild against smoking. If he caught us down here, he'd send us to straight duty in a second."

"It might be easier."

"Don't kid yourself. This is a soft spot. Only crazy people try to get out. Like Carter. They discovered he had a typing course in high school and put him here. He's mad as hell. He wants to be a hero. Not me. I like being the white-collar type. As you probably noticed, we're overstaffed upstairs. Everybody's kidding Lighthorse Harry. He thinks we're working our tails off."

"Lighthorse Harry?"

"That's what the colonel was called at West Point. He believes he's a great tactician. He dreams of making an end run around the enemy the way Stonewall Jackson did at Chancellorsville. He likes a lot of zip and bustle. That makes him feel he's winning the war. If you want it easy, you're in the right place. All you have to do is learn to sleep at attention. Any man who can sleep at attention has a real future around here."

Our cigarettes glowed. I smelled mildew and the mustiness of paper. Wilson held the Coke bottle for me to dump my ashes in.

"It helps if you can turn olive drab too," he said. "When Lighthorse Harry goes on the rampage, you have to be able to turn olive drab. Then you can stand against a piece of Army equipment like a file cabinet or a water cooler and nobody can see you. If they can't see you, they can't chew you out either."

Each time he puffed on his cigarette, I could make out his face. It was cynically amused.

"We got good guys in our cubicle," he went on. "Of course you know Carter. He's humiliated at what's going on, but he's all right. He's so honorable he don't even catch me when I cheat at checkers. He thinks he's going to get out of here, but he isn't. Lighthorse Harry won't let him go. He likes Carter's posture."

"What about Gladstone?"

"He used to be a college teacher. We call him Professor, and he's got the highest IQ in the outfit. The only trouble is they can't make an officer of him. They tried, but he's always thinking of something else. I've seen him forget which hand he's supposed to salute with. Lighthorse Harry don't even bother to chew him out because he knows the Professor's hopeless. As long as he has books, he's happy."

Wilson sucked on his cigarette. He was shorter and heavier than I. He gave the impression of a strong man going soft.

"Now if you're wondering about me I don't mind telling you. In civilian life I started out a gut flusher. I bet you don't know what a gut flusher is. There's a place in a slaughterhouse where the guts come in wooden tubs on a conveyor belt. The flusher digs down in them with his bare hands until he finds a loose end. In the end he sticks the nozzle of a high-powered hose and turns on the pressure. The old guts straighten out stiff like the barrel of a long red rifle. Among the flushers I worked my way up to supervisor. I been ankle-deep in blood and slop. So you can see why I'm grateful to the Army for making me a white-collar type. I got a good deal and I know it. The hell with guts. I've found a home."

In the poor light I couldn't tell how serious he was. Everything he said sounded sarcastic. I cleared my throat.

"Are they allowing any enlisted men to become officers?" I asked.

"Nope. The TO on officers is frozen."

"Temporarily you mean?"

"You got me. All I know is they're not making officers. You think you got a chance after busting out of OCS?"

"Yes," I answered shortly.

"I hope you're not sensitive about me mentioning it. Around here everybody knows everything about everybody. You won't find it so bad once you get used to it. We got a good bunch, and we try to keep real friendly. We want people to be happy."

I wondered whether this were the real purpose of Wilson's talking to me. It might be a nice way of letting me know how I was supposed to act.

"Well, we better get upstairs," he said. "Lighthorse Harry might be snooping around. Help me get the smoke out."

He opened the small window at the rear of the basement, and we fanned the air. He hid the Coke bottle behind a box of payroll records. I left first. I went up the steps and returned to the cubicle. Carter treated me coolly, still thinking about how I had failed him at basic. Gladstone, reading, didn't look up. His one hand banged away on the typewriter. To keep from being caught, all he had to do was sit forward quickly. His body would knock the drawer shut, and he could type with both hands.

I again started adding the payroll figures. Wilson came in. He sat at his desk and flipped the manila folder open for another game of checkers. Throughout the building I heard activity, but I wondered whether anyone was really working.

WO Page entered, walking in dainty, precise steps. Wilson slapped the manila folder closed, and the Professor sat forward.

"Finished those figures yet?" WO Page asked me.

"I managed it somehow," I answered, smiling.

If I thought I was being funny, Wilson didn't. He glared as if I were betraying a trust. He didn't want any jokes about his set-up.

"Go to lunch then," WO Page told me. "I'll have something else for you later."

I walked to the mess hall. When I'd almost finished eating, Wilson joined me. His metal tray was heaped with food.

"Don't queer the deal," he said. "We got things organized in there. If you don't like it, ask for a transfer."

"Sorry."

"No hard feelings, but be careful. It's taken a long time to get things right. You're licking up the cream."

I smoked a cigarette while he ate noisily. The mess hall was a large building which reminded me of the induction center where I'd had to clean beams on KP. The beams caused me to think of Yancey a moment, and hate tightened my stomach.

The officers' section of the mess hall was separated from the enlisted men's by an oak railing. The officers ate from plates served by waiters. At the head of the first table was a full colonel. Wilson said that was Bone, the regimental commander.

"He's also West Point," Wilson explained. "Number one in his class. Lighthorse Harry was at the bottom. Bone was called the Fox at the Point. In case you don't remember, a fox is renowned for its cleverness."

"I know a little about foxes," I answered.

"Good for you. Anyway Lighthorse is trying to make everybody forget he was last in his class, and that's the reason he's such a heller."

Colonel Bone stood to leave the mess hall. He was a handsome, erect man who was pretty much my idea of what an officer should look like. Young and slightly gray at the temples, his face was long in an aristocratic manner. He walked with confidence and purpose.

As soon as Wilson and I returned to the office, Carter and the Professor went to lunch. I put a sheet of paper in a typewriter and practiced. When Carter and the Professor came back, the latter immediately resumed reading. He had on the same OD uniform as the rest of us, but it didn't appear to fit. His dry hair stuck up in rebellious shocks. His glasses needed cleaning. I was to learn he was never neat. He simply didn't care.

He lurched forward to slam his drawer and started typing rapidly. Wilson and Carter who were playing checkers slapped the manila folder. An instant later Lighthorse sneaked along the corridor. He was peering into cubicles. He nodded approvingly at us and continued on. He was carrying his riding crop as if it were a saber. Farther on, he was able to catch a corporal sitting with slumped shoulders.

"Do you realize what you're doing to your spine?" Lighthorse shouted. "This is a military establishment, and I expect my men to look like soldiers. Now straighten up and fly right or I'll bust your ass."

When Lighthorse stopped prowling, the Professor again opened his drawer to read while Wilson and Carter continued their game. They were interrupted by WO Page who ordered me to mimeograph some rosters for him. Glad to have something to do, I typed up stencils and turned the handle of the machine.

"Bring your knitting tomorrow," Wilson said after I finished. "That way you won't get bored."

I heard footsteps. I acted busy, but the others weren't alarmed. The WAC sergeant came in. She wore a tight skirt and had shapely legs. She was still chewing gum. The sergeant was common and gave the impression of being spoiled. Outnumbered by men several thousand to one, she was undoubtedly used to having her way. She left a paper for Wilson and walked out with an exaggerated hip motion.

"She's got the best-looking legs in the WAC detachment and likes to show them off," Wilson explained. "If you want on the good side of her, give her some stockings. Don't she brighten up the place though?"

"She belong to the colonel?" I asked.

"You have a dirty mind," the Professor said, not looking up.

"Not like that she don't, though it's not Lighthorse's fault," Wilson answered me. "She's engaged to a private in a line company. He's a Texan—a great stud and beauty. She does a little flirting around here and maybe allows Lighthorse to pat her on the butt now and then, but if anybody makes a serious pass she lets them know the Texan is all there is. It won't pay to get interested."

"I'm not interested."

"You're lucky. A lot of men, including me, pant after her. The officers try to snow her. She's too smart for them. She knows the Texan's going to marry her."

The afternoon dragged on. From three o'clock to five I had absolutely nothing to do. The warm office made me drowsy. All that kept me from nodding was the knowledge Lighthorse might creep up on me at any time.

That evening after chow I walked to the post library. It was a small, clapboard building with a few hundred books which had been donated by women's organizations. The next day I, like the Professor, kept reading material in my drawer. My hands played absently with the adding machine. Wilson smiled his blessing.

"Welcome to the club," he said.

The WAC sergeant spoke to me during the lunch hour when I was alone for a few minutes. She strode into the cubicle with a memorandum from Lighthorse Harry concerning saving paper and lightbulbs. She dropped the memo onto my desk. She couldn't have been much over twenty-one. She was wearing a strong, cheap perfume which smelled like honeysuckle. I thought that though she might be the prettiest of the WACs, in civilian life she would probably work at a ten-cent store.

"You don't appear happy in the service," she said to me, a hand on her hip. Her fingernails were cut short.

"I'm not overjoyed."

"That's tough," she told me. She started to leave but turned. I think she was expecting me to be looking at her legs. I wasn't. "I might as well tell you I don't think I'm going to like you."

"Why not?" I asked, surprised.

"You think you're better than the rest of us."

She left. Confused, I stared after her. Perhaps I felt that way, but I hadn't meant to show it.

I learned that she was an independent spirit around headquarters. Her name was Lou, and of all the personnel she was the only one who didn't play the game of pretending to be busy in front of Lighthorse. Her femaleness made her impervious to military regulations. Whenever she wished, she went to the PX for coffee or sat around buffing her nails. She never hurried.

Her posture was awful, but Lighthorse never mentioned it. She didn't hide the fact she had contempt for us men in the office. Her Texan was a machine gunner, thus to her a real warrior. She sometimes treated us as if we were doing women's work. We pretty much were.

She really did take a dislike to me, and she often attempted to administer the needle. Wilson, Carter, and the Professor enjoyed it. Maybe in a way she was speaking for them.

"Just because you've been to OCS doesn't make you a hotshot," was one of her favorite remarks.

"I'm sorry I give that impression."

"You're not really sorry. You did flunk out. Anybody can flunk out."

She walked off in her hippy style. Wilson, Carter, and the Professor were amused. I held my temper. I told myself that in a few years all that youth would be gone and she'd become a slattern.

Each afternoon when the line companies marched in, she stood at the front door in hope of seeing her Texan. Occasionally he was off duty before she was and called for her. He was a dark, rawboned pfc who had muscled shoulders and small hips. She'd rush across the thin grass to kiss him. In contrast to the arrogant manner she had around everybody else, she seemed submissive with the Texan.

I was returning from the service club one night and passed a darkened doorway in the post auditorium. Rustling sounds startled me. I had a glimpse of her white, strained face. I hurried on. The next morning she was indignant and caught me alone in the cubicle.

"You were spying," she accused me, balled hands on hips.

"You're mistaken. I don't care what you do in doorways."

"I know about men like you. They sometimes get in the WAC compound."

"I'm really not one of those."

"Listen, you better leave me alone. Roy'll knock your block off."

17

Working in battalion headquarters was indeed a soft life, and after a few weeks I felt myself sinking into the lotus-like routine. My mother would have reproved me for not advancing myself. Wilson, however, was correct about the officer TO being frozen. There were no opportunities to get ahead. I could do nothing except bide my time.

I caught up on my reading. Like Gladstone, I became absorbed in words. It made no difference whether the books were good or not. The act of reading was in itself a luxury after the privations of basic and OCS.

Of course I remained bitter about Yancey. At odd moments I brooded and fumed. I'd stand before a mirror in the latrine and wonder that my wounds didn't show more clearly. I appeared to be a perfectly healthy young soldier instead of a man who'd been deeply wronged.

I tried to make the best of things. I wrote my mother about the officer situation in the outfit and promised her I'd be alert for opportunities. I still believed I'd get a commission. I'd do my job as best I could, and I'd attempt to impress my superiors. I was quick to say "sir," and each day I studied the regimental bulletin board with an eye to finding an opening I could exploit.

Infrequently I went to town. All of us had Class A passes and were permitted to take the bus in whenever we were off duty. The town, however, wasn't much. Before the war, farmers had carried their cotton there to be ginned and had bought their feed and supplies. Now most of the civilians were trying to get rich off the Army. They were succeeding. Prices were high, and a dozen stores along the once sleepy street sold Army goods and junk. Red neon signs buzzed like insects.

The town was too small for the size of the camp. Soldiers filled the cafes, beer joints, and pool rooms. They overflowed onto the courthouse and post-office steps. They wandered down alleys and into back streets. They sat forlorn on curbs and fences.

At nights or on weekends when the crowds of soldiers were greatest, daughters of proper local people were not allowed downtown. Those daughters remained distant and pristine. Even the few battered hookers who worked the streets were particular whom they let pick them up. They acted like royalty.

Each time I went to town I promised myself I'd never return, but the stark, dismal sight of the post in winter was so depressing I had to get away once in a while. I sat in movies or stood in cafes drinking beer until I felt stupefied. I'd have a difficult time remembering I'd ever been a civilian with rights and privileges. I'd think that if it weren't for Yancey, I could have been enjoying myself in the civilized atmosphere of an officers' club instead of crowded, smelly roadhouses where glasses were not even served with the Jax beer.

Most often I went to town alone. If I had company, it was Beanpost who believed we had a bond since we'd both been kicked out of OCS and had joined the 606th together. Gradually I was losing even him. He was making friends with people in supply and moving increasingly among them. I don't believe men were actually avoiding me, but they were leery. I was growing used to being by myself.

On Christmas Day I telephoned my mother, slept all afternoon, and in spite of my promises decided to go into town. The post was almost deserted. I stood among the silent buildings as I waited for the bus, and I really began to feel sorry for myself.

The town itself was as crowded as I'd ever seen it. Sodden paper decorations hung from light poles and fluttered listlessly with the wind. The decorations had been ruined by rain. I walked dejectedly along the main street searching for a friendly face. I stopped to drink a beer in a cafe which had a single tattered holly wreath on the steamed mirror behind the counter. Soldiers jostled me for position.

What I needed was liquor. I'd heard there were bootleggers and started asking questions of soldiers around me. A corporal told me there was a man in the toilet room of the bus station. I went to the station. The bootlegger was elderly. He wore a long brown overcoat which had special pockets inside for bottles. He sold me a brand called Honey Bee for seven dollars a pint.

I went into another cafe, bought a Cola, and used it to chase the whisky. I kept the pint out of sight because of the MPs who patrolled the streets with their white nightsticks swinging. As I drank in a corner, Wilson and Carter slipped into a wooden booth four soldiers had just vacated. I walked to the booth.

"Happy holiday," I said as I sat beside Carter.

They drank their beer and talked while I quietly and methodically slugged myself with the liquor. Beanpost came in, caught sight of me, and joined us. As I drank, he watched.

"You're pretty thirsty, aren't you?" he asked.

"Help yourself," I answered, offering him the bottle.

"I don't want to die," he said.

Inevitably I thought of Yancey. He became the focus of my black mood. The situation I was in was his fault. He was responsible for my having to spend Christmas in a foul, smoke-filled cafe that thumped to the pounding of a jukebox. Because of him I was leading a degraded life. Right there as I sat in the booth I had a fantasy about beating him up. I had him backed into an alley and was sinking my fists into his soft, white belly. My arms jerked.

"He's got the twitches," Wilson said.

"Maybe we ought to put him on the bus for camp," Beanpost suggested, concerned.

"No camp," I told them. "I need more liquor."

"You definitely don't need more liquor," Beanpost said.

"Well, I'm getting it anyway."

I stood and left the cafe. I was having trouble walking straight. I went to the bus station where the bootlegger was still in the men's room. When he moved, his overcoat jangled with bottles of Honey Bee. I counted out another seven dollars and returned to the cafe.

Wilson, Carter, and Beanpost watched. They were drinking beer. They would take none of the liquor. I slopped it into my mouth without a chaser. They shook their heads.

The trouble was the more I drank, the more miserable I became. I was wallowing in self-pity. Yancey flashed in and out of my mind. I slumped lower and lower. The others were becoming alarmed that I might pass out.

Then Timberlake came in. He bought a bottle of beer before walking to the booth. He sat at the end of the table and looked at me in a supercilious manner.

"You're not particular about the company you keep," he said to Carter.

"You fool with me and I'll kick your ass," I told him, rising up a little.

Timberlake frowned. We'd come close to a fight the day I joined the outfit, and this time I believed it was going to be unavoidable. I had enough liquor in me that I didn't care much. Before Timberlake acted, however, there was a stir at the door.

Somebody whistled. A sergeant had come in with a local girl. Her skirt was short, and her sweater tight. Her little mouth was painted a flaming red. She was cheap and coarse looking. In normal times most men in the room would've paid only passing attention to her, but because of the abnormality of camp life her flesh had become hotly desirable.

She made the sergeant hold her chair and light her cigarettes. She repeatedly touched her hands to her wiry brown hair so that her breasts stuck out. Soldiers were gawking.

"You know what she needs," Wilson said longingly.

"She don't need it," Beanpost told him. "I'm the one who needs it."

"You all been out here too long," Timberlake advised them. "You're sick."

"You wouldn't?" Beanpost asked him.

"Oh sure. I'm sick too."

"You're all crazy," I put in. "I wouldn't touch her with a ten-foot pole."

They turned slowly to me. I shouldn't have opened my mouth.

By saying what I had, I'd put myself above them. Their faces were set. Even Beanpost's was.

"I guess it's beneath your station to associate with a girl like that," Timberlake taunted me.

"As a matter of fact it is," I answered, in deep and going deeper. "I can do better anytime."

They were staring at me. If I hadn't been drunk, I'd have shut up or gone back to camp, but I was plenty drunk and couldn't stop thinking of Yancey's wife who'd come into my bedroom wearing a white silk housecoat and furry slippers.

"Sure, you got a private supply in your fists," Timberlake said.

"I warned you," I told him and lunged. I turned over beer on the table. Wilson and Beanpost grabbed me just as two MPs came in the door. The MPs reputedly played rough. As they surveyed the room, they tapped the palms of their hands with nightsticks.

"None of that," Wilson said quietly.

At the sight of the MPs Timberlake and I sat down hurriedly. We watched the MPs leave. Beanpost's hand was still on my shoulder.

"Tell us about her," Timberlake said to me, refusing to leave it alone. "Where you keeping her hid?"

I shouldn't have answered him. I should have got up and walked off. I believed I'd come too far, however, and I was angry. I wasn't about to crawfish to Timberlake.

"She's something you wouldn't know about," I answered. "She's not only beautiful, but she's the kind of woman a peasant like you's never been in the same room with. Your kind of trash is allowed to look only from a distance."

He would have hit me had not Wilson thrust between us. Soldiers at other tables were eying us. A fat man in a greasy apron waddled toward the booth. He had his hand on a hip pocket where he carried a blackjack.

"Outside," he ordered. "And no backtalk."

We left. I walked with exaggerated care. My feet curved under me. Wilson was trying to calm Timberlake who was still outraged.

"He's drunk," Wilson said. "You can't hit a drunk."

"He ought to be hit. I ought to knock the bastard's block off."

I tried to get at him for calling me a bastard. Beanpost stopped me. Carter spoke warningly. We saw the white flash of MP helmets. We straightened and moved along the street. The big MPs glanced at us suspiciously.

128

"Trash he called me," Timberlake said. "Anybody can talk. You can bet he'll never produce."

"All I have to do is snap my fingers," I told him, refusing to quit.

"Snap them then," Timberlake snarled. "Everybody here is waiting to see. Give us trashy peons a break."

We'd reached the courthouse. I could feel them waiting for me to answer. Wilson, Carter, and Beanpost were expecting me to put up or eat crow. Even in my drunkenness I could see they figured I was lying.

"Well?" Timberlake asked. "I haven't heard a snap."

"I wouldn't want to show you up," I said.

"Oh hell no. You made your brag. You ain't going to get out of this without crawling. I got ten bucks here that says you're a liar."

He reached for his wallet and brought out the money. He waved it in front of my face. I was sobering up a little. If I did back down, stories of it would be all over the company by tomorrow. I could imagine the looks I'd get from Lou and men in the barracks and headquarters. I'd have the reputation of a blowhard.

"All right," I said recklessly, going for my own wallet.

I brought out ten dollars. Wilson held the money. I went down the street with the others following me. I climbed the steps to the town's only hotel—a three-story brick building with ivy on it. Inside was a public telephone. In front of the booth, a long line of soldiers waited to make Christmas calls.

I first got change from the willowy young desk clerk who was rumored to be a fairy. Some horny soldiers had been trying to get him to go out with them. My pockets heavy with coins, I joined the line. Wilson, Carter, Beanpost, and Timberlake stood along the wall. They had to stand because all the furniture had been removed from the hotel's lobby. I attempted to look surer of myself than I felt.

I waited twenty-eight minutes to reach the telephone, and by that time the liquor was failing me. As a result I was losing my nerve and cursing myself for getting involved. I hoped the others would grow tired enough to leave, but they did not. I had to go through with the call.

When I did get into the booth, I closed the door in the faces of men behind me. Wilson, Carter, Beanpost, and Timberlake gathered around so that they could watch me through the glass door. They wanted to be certain I wasn't bluffing, as I had once suspected Yancey of doing.

129

I put in the call, hoping Yancey would answer. If he were home, I'd hang up, saying in truth to the others that I couldn't be expected to deal with the woman's husband. They might swallow that. I really wanted him to be home. I was afraid that if I talked to Martha, she'd laugh in my face.

The operator sounded harried and peeved that I didn't know the number. I stood listening to the squeaks and squawks along the line as connections were made. All the operators were impatient with each other. Finally I recognized the voice of Bessie, the good-looking colored maid.

"Mr. Yancey's not here," Bessie said. "He's away in the war."

"Will you speak to anybody else?" the operator asked me.

I started to tell her no, but Timberlake and the others had their noses pushed right up against the glass door and were peering at me. They would never accept an alibi.

"Operator, I'll talk with Mrs. Yancey if she's available."

"Hold the line," Bessie said.

I was very nervous. I felt sweat. The operator told me to put in money. My hand was clumsy fitting coins into the slots. I realized how crazy this was. I was out of my mind. If Martha hung up on me, I'd keep talking and try to fool the men outside. I wasn't sure she'd even remember me.

"Yes?" she asked, cold and impersonal.

"This is Charles Elgar," I told her, and my voice slid around as if it couldn't find a register to settle in. "I hope you don't mind my calling."

She didn't answer immediately. I wilted in the silence. The booth was hot and the air stale. Dirty words had been written on the ragged telephone book. I waited for the click which would indicate the line had gone dead. I forced myself to grin in manly fashion at the men outside the glass.

"Are you in Richmond?" Martha said finally. She didn't sound particularly friendly.

"I'm in Georgia."

"I do declare."

"Have you ever been to Georgia?" I asked, afraid of the words as I spoke them.

"Are you being impudent?"

"I'm not meaning to be," I answered quickly, talking fast to keep her on the line. "I've wanted to call you for months. With one thing and another I haven't had the chance."

"What is it you're asking, Charles?"

I took a deep breath. I didn't know how to be subtle about it, not with time running out and the faces beyond the glass. Oh Jesus, I thought.

"I want you to come down here and see me," I said and stopped breathing.

For an instant I was sure she had hung up. The line buzzed. I felt like closing my eyes and slumping to my knees in the hot booth. I shouldn't have put it to her so crudely. Then to my relief and surprise she laughed.

"My, my, how you've changed," she told me.

"Will you come?" I said, daring to hope.

"Hardly."

"Why not?" I asked, desperate again.

"Even if I were interested in that sort of thing, which I'm not, Georgia is much too far."

"It's not so far," I told her, selling. "You could get a Pullman in the morning, sleep through the night, and be here the next evening."

"Why should I?"

"Because I need you."

I said the words with complete sincerity, and the answer was exactly right. To her my desperation must have come through.

"All right," she agreed matter-of-factly.

"You're coming?" I asked, not sure I'd understood her.

"Don't act so shocked."

"I'm not shocked, I'm happy. You've made me very happy."

"You'll have to get me a place to stay down there."

"I will. When are you coming?"

"In a day or two. Aren't you afraid of my husband?"

There was the note of mockery in her voice. She was teasing me for the way I had acted the time she had come into my bedroom.

"I'm not afraid. You'll need my telephone number. Call as soon as you reach town."

"Naturally."

"I promise you you won't be sorry for coming."

"Now you're boasting. Don't be so sure of yourself. Incidentally, Merry Christmas."

The line went dead. Excitedly I placed the receiver on the hook. Wilson, Beanpost, Carter, and Timberlake were watching me closely. I opened the door of the booth and stepped into the lobby.

131

"Well?" Timberlake asked.

"Made in the shade," I said, walking past him and the others to the street and down the sidewalk toward the bus stop.

18

In the morning, Sunday, I woke with a pounding headache from the sting of Honey Bee and with a guilty, shadowy realization of what I'd done the night before. I lay perfectly still, sending out mental probes to reconstruct exactly what had taken place. Groaning, I rubbed a hand over my face. The Professor was reading on his bunk.

"Did you see me come in last night?" I asked him.

"No," he answered, not turning his eyes from the book.

I got razor, toothbrush, and towel, and I went down the stairs to the latrine. Wilson was taking a shower. I lathered my face and shaved with trembling hands.

"Did I make a call at the hotel?" I asked him when he turned off the water.

"You sure did."

"That's what I thought," I said, staring at myself in the mirror. It wasn't a dream. Martha was coming.

"You were in excellent form," Wilson told me. "You insulted just about everybody. When does the lady get here?"

"I'm not exactly clear about that."

"Well, everybody's anxious to see her."

Even yet there was disbelief in his voice. The others would be the same. They would suspect I was attempting to trick them. I couldn't blame them. Obviously I was no great lover. Other than college forays to a Lynchburg whorehouse and one short, nervous affair with a pretty young saleslady, I'd had no intimate experiences with women.

I got under the shower. What the situation came down to was that I really didn't know enough about how a man went about being a lover. My lack of experience might cause me to make a complete fool of myself. I imagined Martha's scorn. I lifted my face to the water.

"You all right?" Beanpost asked, standing in the doorway.

"Why shouldn't I be all right?"

132

"Well, for one thing you been standing that way a long time without moving."

"I'm in the pink."

When I finished dressing, I went to the service club for a cup of coffee. I quickly understood I was already being talked about. Men had heard about the bet with Timberlake and were taking sides. I caught calculating glances wherever I walked.

I had three cups of black coffee and returned to my bunk. Lying with my eyes shut, I began to hope Martha wouldn't come. She would be too much trouble. Moreover if she didn't show up, she couldn't laugh at me.

I told myself there was an excellent chance she would remain at home. She'd have plenty of other men chasing her around. In truth I'd rather endure the humiliation of admitting to Timberlake she wasn't coming than have to go through the frightful ordeal of being a proficient lover. At the moment I didn't feel I could be a proficient anything. Timberlake would lord it over me for a while, but in time all would be forgotten.

I tried to work up my passion a little. I couldn't remember exactly what Martha looked like. She was small, delicate, dark. She was probably not as attractive as I'd originally believed the first time I saw her at Yancey's, yet it might be rewarding to make love to an experienced older woman, which she undoubtedly was. I found myself wanting her to come but afraid she would.

In the end wanting her not to come was stronger. The more I considered the question, the more I believed it best she be stopped. Some breath of scandal might get back to Richmond and put me in trouble with both my mother and the bank. I decided I'd call Martha and make up an elaborate lie about being assigned to special duty. Whether she believed me or not wasn't important as long as she didn't leave home.

I hurried to the service club. I got change from a hostess and put through a call on a pay telephone. Through the glass of the closed door I watched men playing Ping-pong under Christmas decorations. In a corner was a loblolly pine with a few sad ornaments and icicles hanging on it.

Bessie, the maid, answered the call. The operator asked for Mrs. Yancey.

"She's not here," Bessie said.

"Do you know when she'll be back?" the operator questioned her.

"Not for a few days. She's gone to visit a sick friend in Georgia."

At the mention of the word Georgia I closed my eyes. Martha was already on the way. She sure God hadn't wasted any time. I thought of meeting her at the station and telling her it was all a mistake. I could offer to pay her fare back to Virginia.

I imagined the contempt she would have for me if I tried that. I wouldn't be able to face it. Somehow or other I had to carry through what had started as a drunken blunder. At the most she'd remain only a few days. Even if she laughed at me, I could suffer anything over so short a period.

I had to find her a place to stay. I went to the orderly room to sign out, waited in the long line for the bus, and rode into town. At the hotel the clerk who was reported to be a fairy didn't bother to look up from the newspaper spread across his desk.

"We're booked six weeks in advance," he told me, turning a page. "Better tell your wife to stay at home."

I bought a copy of the newspaper and read the want-ads before I began making the rounds of the rooms for rent. I found dozens of other soldiers doing the same. All good accommodations had been taken. What were left were shabby and outrageously priced. Elderly Southern ladies who had surely once been kind and genteel had become weasel-eyed horse traders who bargained sharply for the Yankee dollar. By two o'clock in the afternoon I still hadn't found anything. My head ached, and my feet were sore.

I was back in the business district. I sat on the post-office steps to smoke a cigarette, my shoulders hunched against the cold, windy day. A rattling taxi pulled to the curb in front of me. An old Negro, wearing a billed cap, rolled down the window.

"If you're looking for a room, Captain, I just took a lady to the bus station. I'll show you her place."

I got into his taxi, and he drove me to a weed-grown field outside of town which had wheelless wooden trailers parked on it. Over them was a tangle of peeling electric wires. A surly, middle-aged man in a dirty sweater showed me the trailer just vacated. It was filthy and smelled of chitterlings.

The squalor gave me an idea. I could guess the elegant Martha's reaction on seeing such a place. She would flee. When she complained, I'd tell her it was the best I was able to do. Let her try to find her own room. After a couple of hours of what I'd been through, she'd gladly take the first train back to Virginia.

I paid the man ten dollars down as an advance on a week's rent and rode to camp feeling better. I was even able to eat a little turkey hash. Afterward I wrote to my mother and went to bed early. The next morning my headache was gone. I whistled as I crossed the street to go to work.

"He's acting smug," Wilson said to Carter. "Why do you suppose he's acting smug?"

"Maybe he knows something we don't."

I called the depot to learn about train schedules and figured Martha would arrive either during the late afternoon or early evening. People in headquarters were watching me because they all knew by now I had a woman coming. I was trying to think up a plan whereby I could have Martha seen briefly by Timberlake. I might be able to take his money and get her back on the train too.

I sat in headquarters until ten that night waiting for her to telephone. When she did not, I had new hope. Possibly she was not coming to see me at all and had used the Georgia story to cover a rendezvous with somebody else. I went to bed feeling both relief and regret at the adventure I was missing.

I woke with the CQ shaking my arm and telling me I was wanted on the phone. It was two-thirty in the morning. I pulled on my overcoat and hurried to headquarters. As I picked up the receiver, I was nervous. The corporal of the guard, a man named Leeds, watched me with interest.

"The train was late," Martha said. "Can you come in here?"

"Not right now," I answered. Even at the sound of her voice it was difficult for me to believe she was only a few miles away. "You take a taxi to the place I rented. I'll come in tomorrow."

"This isn't exactly a ticker-tape reception."

"The Army's fresh out of ticker tape. It's the best I can do."

"I'm not sure it's altogether the best. What's the address?"

I tilted the earpiece slightly to make sure the corporal heard. He was impressed. Now even if Martha left before Timberlake saw her, I'd have evidence that a woman had come. I gave her the address, and after she hung up, I sat down to wait. I borrowed a cigarette from Leeds. Fourteen minutes later the telephone rang. I answered it. Again I tilted the earpiece.

"Are you trying to be funny?" she asked, her voice hard and angry.

"Funny?" I said innocently.

"If you think I'm going to stay in that rathole you're crazy."

"It's all I could get. With a war on, people have to make do."

She didn't bother to answer. Instead the telephone clicked dead. I sat back and smoked another cigarette. Leeds was upset.

135

"You just going to let her go?" he asked. "You're not even going to try to stop her?"

"If she leaves, it's her hard luck," I told him and swaggered out as if I were the sort of man whose door women beat on everyday.

I returned to bed pleased. I might not be able to use Martha in front of Timberlake—she would probably be gone even before I saw her—but because of Leeds I was at least partially off the hook. I wouldn't insist on Timberlake's paying me the ten. I'd be generous with him. Though my conscience bothered me for my lack of gallantry toward Martha, I believed I had extricated myself from a dangerous situation. My life was still intact.

In the morning it was raining. Big drops came down noisily on the barracks roof. At breakfast I could tell by the way men were looking at me and whispering that Leeds was spreading his story. He would swear I had a woman in town and was indifferent as to whether she stayed or not.

"What you trying to pull?" Timberlake asked suspiciously. He had joined me on the way to work.

"Pull?"

"Don't play dumb. I'm not paying off on any phone call. Unless I see the goods, I don't pay."

"Maybe I'll let you see her one of these days."

"One of these days I'll be dead."

"The sooner the better," I told him, going on into headquarters building.

During the day I was watched. Each person who passed the cubicle glanced at me. I pretended to be bored and yawned frequently. By then I was certain Martha was headed back to Virginia. In truth I was delighted at the way things had worked out.

A few minutes after four o'clock the telephone on Lou's desk rang. She came down the hall and said it was for me. Her eyebrows were raised. Frightened, I followed her and picked up the receiver.

"I just woke," Martha told me, speaking slowly, lazily. She sighed. "I feel better. I've never been able to sleep on trains."

For an instant I was too confused to speak. Enlisted men and WACs had stopped working to stare at me. I cleared my throat.

"Where are you?" I asked.

"At the hotel. Room 303, or as the man says up three, down two, and knock once."

"I checked the hotel. It was full."

136

"It still is. I'm waiting for you to take me to dinner. Remember the number, 303."

She was gone. Dazed, I handed the receiver to Lou. With artificial sweetness she leaned forward to take it from my hand.

"Tell your sugar this phone's not for personal use," she said.

Without answering, I returned to my cubicle. Wilson who had been at the water cooler while I was talking made eyes at Carter and the Professor. I tried not to reveal how shaky I was. I made myself smile and wink.

At five o'clock I pretended to be eager to leave. I crossed to the barracks where I showered, shaved, and put on my blouse. I had an audience of men who sat around envying me. I attempted to appear confident. Timberlake remained stubbornly unbelieving.

"Going somewhere?" he asked.

"I'll be at the Dancing Pig," I told him. "The wraps come off tonight."

I buttoned my raincoat and left the barracks to go to the bus stop. It was six-thirty before I reached town. I went to the hotel, started for the elevator, and then remembering I was supposed to be a suave lover did a right flank into the drugstore to get equipped. I felt like a criminal.

The hotel elevator, operated by a Negro whose red uniform was threadbare, was a slow, creaking cage from which gilt paint flaked. I got off at the third floor. Carpets had been taken up, and the hall was dimly lighted. I heard rain beating against a window at the end of the corridor.

In front of room 303 I raised my hand to knock. I was sweating both from the airless raincoat and anxiety. I wished I were someplace else. My knock was timid.

"If it's you, come in," Martha called, her voice impatient.

I opened the door just a crack. Holding a perfume bottle in one hand and the glass stopper in the other, she was sitting at a dressing table. She had on a white silk slip, dark stockings, and high-heeled pumps. Her black hair touched the bareness of her shoulders.

My first impulse was to duck out because she wasn't dressed. She, however, was unconcerned. She dabbed at an ear with the glass stopper.

"I was giving you exactly five more minutes," she told me, her dark eyes narrowed. "If you weren't here by then, I was going without you."

I smelled the perfume she was putting on, and I was immobilized

137

by the actual flesh and blood of her. My memory of her had dulled to no real substance. As I stood there, however, I realized I confronted a striking and very desirable woman.

"Are you just going to gape?" she asked me peevishly.

Apologizing for being late, I took another step into the room and closed the door. I was trying to think of what I should do next. I felt I ought to play the bold lover, yet I was unsure how to.

"Let's get one thing straight right now," she told me, turning on the stool. Her slip stretched so tightly across her lap I could see the outline of her thighs and the slight curve of her stomach. "I'm not used to being kept waiting, and I don't like it. I don't like it at all."

She scowled, and her eyes moved over me. I suppose she was reassessing me just as I was her. I decided I should act. I hurried to her and put my hands on her shoulders. As I'd seen men do in the movies, I bent to kiss the side of her neck. She freed herself with a twist of her body.

"Don't mess me up," she commanded, reaching for a golden tube of lipstick on the dressing table.

I retreated. She painted her upper lip and rolled it onto the lower one. She rose to go to the closet. Though small, she carried herself like a long-legged woman. She removed a black dress from a hanger, raised her arms, and let the dress slip over her body. I thought that if she were a tramp, she was one no man would be ashamed to be seen with. I was hardly breathing.

She came to me to zip her up. I saw the powdered texture of her skin. Standing before the mirror, she straightened the seams of her stockings—pulling up her dress and running her fingers quickly along her calves. Her legs were well-bred to the point of thinness. Fascinated I watched. She put on a string of pearls.

I no longer wanted to be rid of her. On the contrary I desired her. I wished I could act with authority to show her that. Instead, like a rube, I rocked from foot to foot.

"Is something the matter with you?" she asked, frowning.

"You're wonderful," I said, and I meant it.

"You're going to have to sweet talk me," she answered, turning before the mirror to inspect herself. "You're going to have to make me forgive you. On probation is what you are."

The situation had changed completely. Instead of being scared of having her, I was frightened of losing her. I couldn't allow her to get away now. I waited humbly ready to serve her. She fastened on pearl earrings. She got out a raincoat and galoshes. They too were black, and her hat, which had a very wide brim, was of the same shiny material.

"All right," she said, hooking the belt of the raincoat so that her waist was pinched in. "I guess I'm ready."

I quickly opened the door for her. She locked it, and as we went down the hall to the elevator she dropped the key into her bag. She was not embarrassed at being seen with me, though I was a good bit younger. She walked out of the elevator with a sure stride. In the lobby sex-starved soldiers gawked at us. Men loafing along the street in doorways and under awnings shed their slouches as we passed. It was like being on parade. I was proud of having such a chic woman at my side.

We hurried through the light rain to the Dancing Pig, which was the best restaurant in town. That wasn't saying much. It was actually a roadhouse on the highway—one large, barnlike room lighted by neon tubes. Some of the tubes had burned out. The booths were scarred, and the tables covered with yellow oilcloth. Rosy pigs made of plywood were nailed to the walls.

When I opened the glass door for Martha, she entered with the certainty of a person who had been eating there all her life. Immediately I saw Timberlake, Wilson, and Beanpost. They were sitting in a booth drinking coffee. They goggled at Martha. She was both stylish and imperial. She removed her hat and shook out her hair.

I deliberately steered her past them. Timberlake's sullen mistrust was replaced by frank admiration. Beanpost smiled. Wilson rolled his eyes.

I chose a table at the center of the room so that everybody could see her and helped her off with her glistening raincoat. People had turned from other tables to watch. Martha was aware of the attention she was getting. She sat in an erect manner which pushed out her breasts, yet glanced around the room as if she were slumming. She reached to her pocketbook for a cigarette. I quickly lighted a match.

"What'd you do to land in this Siberia?" she asked, waving a hand. She meant both the restaurant and the section of Georgia. For a moment her eyes rested on Timberlake and the others.

"I tried to help your husband," I answered but was instantly sorry I'd mentioned Yancey. Bringing him up was not exactly an intelligent ploy for a lover. Her dark eyes swept to me.

"By the way you said that, I gather he wasn't grateful."

"He wasn't at all grateful."

"At the proper time you'll tell me. I'll want all the details."

A colored waiter came to the table. Martha leaned back and read the soiled menu with distaste.

"Are you absolutely sure the food's safe here?" she asked when the waiter left.

"You can always order fried eggs. They can't poison those."

"I don't like fried eggs. Besides I'm ravenous."

"Try the oysters."

"I don't need oysters," she said, and I blinked. I wasn't sure whether she meant the answer crudely or not. I decided not. She appeared cool and untouchable.

Timberlake and the others were watching. I tried to carry on a conversation with her. I wanted desperately to be entertaining. I could feel her holding back. Her face was emotionless. I was afraid she was sorry she had bothered to come to Georgia.

"How'd you get your room?" I asked. "The hotel was full."

"They always have rooms if you know how to go about it," she answered, exhaling smoke. "Marvin taught me that. I simply bribed the clerk with a ten-dollar bill." She covered a yawn with the back of her hand.

"You slept all day?"

"I did. I had them send me breakfast and went back to bed. The cleaning woman tried to get in. I made her wait. She thought she could get away with not putting clean sheets on my bed. They won't try that trick again."

"You're the only person I know who could get service there."

"I get it all right. I demand it. And don't try to flatter me."

"I can't help it. I'm very much impressed with you. Is it flattery if I mean every word I say?"

The mask cracked, and the corners of her perfectly made-up lips raised slightly. It wasn't much of a smile, but it held hope.

"Much better," I told her. I was really pleading. "The sun shines a little and warms my cold bones."

As we were eating, Captain Hanks passed the table. He stared at Martha. He was wearing his pinks, and in them he seemed dashing enough to sell war bonds. He had been on his way to join a group of officers at a table in the rear, but he changed course. When he approached, I stood. I realized that he and most everybody else would be making a play for Martha.

"Elgar," he said, hardly glancing at me.

"My wife, Captain," I told him, hoping he wouldn't remember I wasn't married. Martha hadn't removed the big diamond and the gold wedding band Yancey must have given her. The captain noticed the rings.

"Charmed," he said, bowing.

Martha looked at him with only faint interest. Her face had gone back to the mask, and under her unswerving gaze men had a way of crumbling. Even the knowledgeable Captain Hanks lost his composure. He was a little like a leaking balloon.

"Well, it's good to meet you, Mrs. Elgar," he said. "It's always a pleasure for me to speak with the families of my men."

"I can imagine," she answered.

Hanks touched a finger to his forehead in what was supposed to be a jaunty salute, but he ruined the effect by bumping into a chair and momentarily losing his balance. He retreated to the table where the officers were. They had been watching. As soon as he was seated, they questioned him. Martha crushed out her cigarette.

"He'll try to call me," she said.

"Do you want him to call you?" I asked, immediately suspicious.

"I don't think I like the tone of your voice," she said. Her face was threatening.

"I'm sorry," I told her quickly and humbly. "I didn't mean it that way, and it was stupid."

I'd meant it, but I didn't dare allow it to stick. She regarded me as if weighing me. I could imagine her flouncing out. I was relieved when she continued eating. I felt I'd had a very close call.

I kept worrying. She was so lovely and self-possessed I couldn't really believe that even if I pleased her I'd be permitted in her bed. She seemed too regal to give herself to anything as raw as intercourse.

All through the meal I was nervous. She might be so disappointed in me she wouldn't let me back in her room. I was miserable, but I couldn't show it. Timberlake, Wilson, and Beanpost were watching. So were others in the cafe. Women bristled with jealousy. Martha made them appear plain and tawdry. They resented her.

I was too upset to eat. I lighted one cigarette after the other. Martha, however, cleaned her plate and ordered dessert. She drank three cups of coffee.

"Doesn't coffee keep you awake?" I asked. I had to say something to ward off the silence.

"Perhaps I want to be kept awake," she answered.

As she spoke, a glimmer of the lascivious smile came out of the cool depths of her. There was no doubt how she meant the remark. I colored like a bumpkin. She laughed at me, raising a hand to the V of her dress. She had small, perfectly even teeth.

"If you could see yourself," she told me. "Perhaps I'll take you off probation."

She pushed back her chair. I jumped to hold it and help with her raincoat. We again passed Timberlake and the others. I saw Wilson purse his lips in a silent whistle of admiration.

It had stopped raining. As we walked along the street toward the hotel, Martha took hold of my arm in a proprietary manner which both surprised and made me extremely happy. She was humming. Occasionally she swayed against me. She stopped to look into shop windows.

Timberlake and the others had left the Dancing Pig also and were following at a discreet distance. I suppose he believed I still might try some trickery. Martha was unhurried. It occurred to me she must have done this many times before. I didn't like the idea.

"Maybe we ought to get a bottle," I suggested, thinking a drink might cut into the dryness of my throat.

"We won't need a bottle," Martha answered.

We entered the hotel and crossed to the elevator. Timberlake, Wilson, and Beanpost came into the lobby. I attempted to appear the conqueror and even managed to wink. The elevator door closed and cut them off.

In the dim light of the third-floor corridor Martha's face seemed to have a pale, spiritual quality about it which made what we were about to do appear both impossible and monstrous. She put her key in my hand. I felt the warm imprint on my arm where she had held it. I turned on the lights of the room and stepped aside for her to walk in. As soon as she was past me, I looked at her small waist and delicate ankles.

She went to the closet to hang up her raincoat. I was uncertain what to do next. To stall for time I lighted another cigarette. She came to me to unzip the back of her dress. Carefully she removed it, brushed it out, and put it on a hanger. She acted as if she had forgotten I was even with her.

She went into the bathroom and closed the door. When she came out, I was still standing in the center of the room. She had on her slip, but she was in her bare feet and carrying a small girdle with a satiny front. She folded it into a drawer. She examined herself before the mirror of the dressing table. Finally she turned to me as if she just happened to remember I was present.

"Now," she said, lifting her arms for me to come to her.

I hurried across the room and began kissing her clumsily. I was trembling and anxious about the mechanics of getting off her slip. She placed a hand on my chest to push me away.

"You are jumpy, aren't you? There's plenty of time."

She held both my hands in hers and allowed me to kiss her gently. I tasted her lipstick. I was shaking as if chilled. Like a young boy I was led back across the room to the bed.

"Turn out the lights," she told me. "And take off your uniform."

I snapped the light switch by the door and began tearing at my blouse, shirt, and pants. My fingers were sausages. There were knots in my shoelaces. The room was lighted red from a theater marquee on the street below. The red flashed off and on. When I was down to my underwear, I sat beside Martha on the edge of the bed.

I began tugging on her slip. She had to help me with that too. She shifted so I could pull it over her head. She removed her own brassiere and lay down. In the red glow of the room I could see her plainly. She had one leg bent over the other and an arm behind her head. I found it frightening to have such a woman at my disposal.

I wasn't quite prepared. I felt around for my pants. I couldn't remember which pocket the package was in. Martha was lying motionless on the bed, and I knew she must consider me a complete fool. How did famous lovers handle the terrible details of the act?

I fumbled, banged my shins on a chair, and limped to the bed. She put up her arms for me and tangled me in her small, strong legs. Her touch was too exciting. I was like a sixteen-year-old, and to my deep mortification I lost control. She started laughing. Her laughter made me want to run. I pulled away from her, but she immediately reached for and held me.

"Now don't get your feelings hurt," she told me.

"Sorry I was inadequate," I said, my voice as formal as if I were apologizing for failing to open a door or hold a chair for her.

"You weren't inadequate at all. In fact you're sweet. I knew you'd be sweet the first time I saw you."

She wouldn't let me go. Red flashed in the room. Though the window was closed, we could hear rain and the sound of hissing tires. Occasionally shooting from the war movie drifted up. She ran her nails lightly over my back. I wondered whether I was expected to repeat the fiasco. I didn't want to. I definitely did not.

143

"Why don't you have a shower?" she suggested. "That'll rejuvenate you."

Obedient and glad to be loose from her, I went into the bathroom. I closed the door and looked at myself in the mirror. I hardly resembled a Don Juan. I looked bewildered, disheveled, and scared of what I was involved in.

She was right, however, about the shower rejuvenating me. As I stood under the water, I got to thinking about her lying naked in there and to my surprise I was again ready. I dried quickly. I returned to the room with a towel wrapped around my waist.

The second time I was more successful. It was a matter of degree. My head knocked against the metal knobs of the old bed and ached as if it were being scraped along a washboard. Moreover I never quite lost the feeling she was controlling the whole act. Still I got through in a fashion which must have pleased her because in the blinking red I could see her face, and the teasing, patronizing expression was gone. Her eyes were closed, and her mouth was open slightly. For the first time in my life I understood something of why a man swelled his chest for making love to a woman.

She was breathing deeply, and I lay against her. She touched my temples with her long fingers. I could hear her heart beating.

I had another shower. This one was my idea. In the bathroom I flexed my muscles a little and strutted before the mirror. On the third go in bed I even managed to get an audible response from her. She gave a short, desperate sigh of pure pleasure which restored all my manhood and made me grin in the dark. She hadn't controlled things either.

Of course I was done in to the point that even a shower wouldn't help. Furthermore it was becoming late. I unwound myself from her arms and legs. As I dressed, she lay among the rumpled sheets like a lazy, sated courtesan.

"You'll have a sore back tomorrow," she said, speaking so low I could just hear her.

"Not me. I never felt better."

I was buttoning my shirt. I hadn't turned on the light. She reached to the table for a cigarette. When I finished dressing, I stood over the bed and looked down at her.

"What time will I see you?" she asked.

"As soon as I can get away."

I bent down to kiss her good night—a kiss chaste and without passion. For an instant she locked her fingers behind my neck and

144

wouldn't release me. I loosened her hands, straightened, and looked at her until she twisted voluptuously. I was pleased that I dominated her. Yet she wasn't ashamed of being naked. She didn't cover herself. It was a catlike movement, entirely female.

I left her, hurried downstairs, and ran to catch the last bus for camp. It was just leaving, and I slapped the metal sides to have it wait for me. I sat at the rear on a worn leather seat. There were only a few soldiers, and they all appeared tired. Maybe they were lovers like me. Technically I was a lover, and the realization elated me.

Yet my elation lasted but a short while. It withered as dark thoughts worked in. I couldn't stop myself from considering how little effort had been required for me to have her. Certainly I hadn't swept her off her feet. What it came down to was that in spite of her beauty and hauteur she was a tramp. God only knew how many men had played the same role I had.

I sat on the hard seat, swaying to the bucking of the bus, tired, my shoulders hunched, misery filling me up like a bottle held under a faucet.

19

When I signed in at battalion, the corporal of the guard, a man named Brooks, glanced at me admiringly, a fact which made me sure the news about Martha had traveled fast. I went to the latrine to brush my teeth. Timberlake, Carter, Wilson, and Beanpost were playing cards on a footlocker. Timberlake handed me a ten-dollar bill.

"I'm impressed," he said. "You smashed me."

"Thanks," I told him, liking him just a little for the first time. He seemed to hold no hard feelings.

"Frankly you had me fooled," he continued. "I personally thought you had qualifications for making chaplain's assistant."

"Still water do run deep," Wilson said.

"God Almighty, she's something," Beanpost exclaimed. "She could be a movie star."

"Include me in the applause," Carter said grudgingly.

"I guess I'll have to see her." It was the Professor behind me. He was holding a book. "When's the next showing?"

"I'll try to work it in tomorrow," I answered, pretending to be a lot more casual than I felt. After all I had a reputation to live up to. I was now a celebrity. I finished brushing my teeth.

"You don't have any old cast-off girl friends, do you?" Beanpost asked hopefully. "I'd be happy to take a couple off your hands."

"No surplus," I said on the way out. "They go only for me."

I was joking, but Beanpost and the others shook their heads as if they believed me. I went on up to bed. In the darkness, worry molded my face. I told myself it made no difference what Martha was. I was lucky to have her, and I should use her. The thing to do was not complicate the affair with emotions. Yet tired as I was, I had a difficult time falling to sleep.

In the morning I discovered Martha had been right about my back. It was sore, but not unpleasantly so. It was a reminder I liked. What I resented was her knowing about sore backs. Such knowledge was another sign of her professional experience.

As I walked the length of the barracks, men watched me. They not only watched, they made way for me too. In the latrine a path to a washbowl opened up as if I were Moses parting the waves.

At breakfast my bacon was crisp, and the two fried eggs which slid onto my tray were flawlessly white and round. Some of the officers looked in my direction while I ate. Rumor and gossip would make Martha more alluring than any woman could be. I realized I might become part of a legend.

Though I was full of concern and self-doubt, I tried to play my part. I acted as if adoration were an everyday affair. My lips twisted superciliously at men who couldn't command women to come running at the snap of fingers. I hoped to appear as if having Martha were so routine for me that I was somewhat bored.

I passed the orderly room on my way to work. Captain Hanks, lounging in the entrance to his office, called to me. He motioned me inside and shut the door.

"At ease, Elgar," he said, sitting on the edge of his desk. "I enjoyed meeting your wife last night."

Suspicious, I thanked him.

"Handsome woman," he continued. "Obviously has breeding. How come you're not sending her an allotment?"

So he had made a point of looking through my records.

"She doesn't need money, Captain. She has an income of her own."

"Nevertheless if you're married and have failed to declare the fact, you've falsified records."

I said nothing. He was smiling cannily. His shoulders were broad, his hips slim.

"Look, Captain, I guess you've got this figured."

"You don't mean you're not married?" he asked, feigning shock. "You're not living in a state of sin?"

"Well, sir," I said.

"I can keep you from getting a pass, you know. I can always find special reasons to do that for a man who's living in sin. I'd only be trying to protect his welfare."

I knew why he wanted to restrict me. He hoped to get at Martha himself. I thought of his climbing into her bed. The worst part was I wasn't at all certain she wouldn't desire him to.

"Captain, we're engaged."

"Well, it was thoughtful of you to give her the wedding ring she's wearing before the ceremony." He grinned. "That's all, Elgar."

I left his office and crossed the street to battalion headquarters. Silently I cursed the captain. WACs eyed me, attempting to figure out what other females could possibly find so interesting. I'd hardly reached my desk before Lou walked into the cubicle.

"Who would have thought it?" she asked, gazing at me.

"It's hard to tell about people," Wilson answered her. They were talking as if I weren't present.

"I'm not usually that wrong about people," Lou said. "He just doesn't strike me as a Casanova."

"I haven't turned it on for you girls," I told her. "Only when I feel challenged do I turn it on. Why waste it around here?"

She was properly insulted. She threw out her chest and walked away with hips swinging. She kept away, but she was the only one. The other WACs, the clerks, and officers peered at me when they passed as if I were on exhibit in a zoo.

"I think we ought to charge admission," Wilson said. "Maybe you could work up a juggling act."

I ignored the jibes. I was thinking of Captain Hanks. He could easily get into town during the day, and I started checking on him. He worked in his office all morning, but that afternoon he didn't come back from lunch. Evans, the company clerk, didn't know where Hanks had gone.

I knew, and I sweated out the hours. I had all sorts of filthy pictures in my mind. Twice I phoned Martha at the hotel, but she didn't answer. Maybe she didn't want to answer, or couldn't. I fidgeted at my desk. My fingers jammed among typewriter keys. The others watched warily.

At five I hurried from headquarters to the barracks to change my clothes. Men looked at me with the same interest they might have for a matador preparing for the bull ring. I went to the orderly room to sign out. When I reached for the pass list, Evans, sitting at his desk, dropped his hand across the paper.

"Sorry," he said.

"Sorry what?" I asked.

"Captain's put us on quota. Only ten per cent of the company allowed on pass today. Quota's already filled."

I whirled, rushed from the orderly room, and ran to the bus stop. I had to find somebody who'd already signed out. In line I saw Honeycutt, the Carolina farm boy. I talked fast to him, offering him five dollars to let me take his place. He folded the bill into his pocket, and we returned to the orderly room. Worried but having no grounds for refusal, Evans put my name down instead of Honeycutt's.

I ran for the bus where I shoved into the line and crowded to the door ahead of others. I punched with my elbows and threw the hip. I was out of breath, and I had to stand all the way to town.

At the hotel I didn't wait for the creaky elevator. I ran up the three flights of stairs. I pounded on her door and tried the knob.

"Charles?" Martha called from the other side.

"Me," I answered, wondering whether he was in there with her even now. Perhaps some mad scrambling for clothes was going on. I put my ear to the door. I wanted to kick it down.

Martha opened it. She wore a black-and-white striped dress. The stripes were vertical, making her appear slimmer and taller than she was. On an arm was a diamond bracelet. Her hair was fixed in precise black ringlets so firm they appeared breakable. I walked past her into the room. My eyes searched for evidence that Hanks had been present.

"What's wrong with you?" Martha asked, frowning. She was shutting the door.

"Nothing's wrong with me," I answered. "Have a good day?"

The room was neat. Not a wrinkle was on the bed. I looked into the bathroom. A pair of stockings hung over the shower curtain. I had an impulse to open the closet to see whether Hanks was hiding there. All the while she was watching me. She snatched a pack of cigarettes from her dressing table.

"Not particularly," she said. "I slept late and went to the hairdresser's."

"No recreation?"

"Now wait a minute," she told me, her face hard. "Maybe you better say what you mean."

"Sure," I said, my torment making me reckless. "Perhaps this particular hairdresser had silver bars on his shoulders."

Her dark eyes widened, and her painted mouth became small. She threw the unlighted cigarette back to the dressing table, strode to me, and slapped me hard. The skin of my cheek stung. She went to the door and opened it wide.

"Get out of here!" she ordered, her voice a whisper.

"Easy now."

"Just get out, you bastard."

I walked to the door and closed it. She tried to open it. Her eyes were flashing. I leaned against the door.

"Goddamn you, do I have to have you thrown out?" she demanded. Her fists were balled, and I believed she would attack me.

"Listen a minute," I told her, grabbing both her wrists.

"Why should I listen to you?" she asked, trying to wrench free of me.

"Because he gave me a bad time today," I answered and began to explain the conversation I'd had with Hanks that morning. I told her his reputation and about his being gone from the office all afternoon. As I talked, she gradually stopped struggling, but her face remained hard.

"You listen to me," she said, jerking her wrists loose. "I don't owe you explanations. Who do you think you are? I could crook my finger and a hundred better men would come running."

She paced in front of me. Her dark eyes were never still. It seemed impossible that such a small, feminine body could hold so much vibrant fury. I sank slowly into a straight chair by the door.

"Do you think I had to come all the way to Georgia to find a man who'd be nice to me? You better count your blessings."

"I'm sorry," I said, relieved and even happy at her anger. Its genuineness meant to me she was innocent of Hanks.

"I'm sorry," she mimicked, her voice becoming a nasal whine. "You just remember anything you get from me is a gift. You're not irresistible by one hell of a long shot."

Her anger cut me down. I sat like a young boy who was being disciplined. She paced in front of me, her arms crossed forbiddingly across her chest. She marched to the dressing table where she picked up a cigarette and lighted it. She inhaled deeply and shot smoke through her nose. Her nostrils flared. She was a thoroughbred, and as I watched her I knew I loved her.

"Don't ever get the idea I have to give you explanations," she continued, her fine, ladylike legs thrusting out. "If I do, it's because I choose to, not because I have to. Your Captain Hanks telephoned me today. I refused to see him. He then came up here and knocked on the door. I wouldn't open it. He begged me, but when I wouldn't let him in, he left. I went to the hairdresser in the basement where I spent the afternoon because I wanted to look nice for you. Apparently I wasted my time."

Her shoulders were squared, and each time she turned, her skirt spun around her calves. She was warlike. I wanted to go to her but was afraid to move. She crushed out her cigarette.

"We better get one thing straight," she said. "You have no right to question me. Anytime I wish I can walk away."

"Let me come over there and kiss you."

"Not on your life. I've got some thinking to do about you."

She meant it. She wouldn't allow me near her. I sat on the straight chair while she fumed and finished dressing. She put on a hat with a great floppy brim. It was large as a sombrero. Most women wouldn't have dared wear anything so big, but it made her all the more striking. She was royalty at a garden party.

Leaving the hotel, I hoped she would again take my arm, but she did not. We walked down the street as if we were strangers. Stares from soldiers and civilians alike gave me no pleasure. I was certain she was thinking of leaving.

At the Dancing Pig she chose the table. The Professor sat in a booth. He adjusted his glasses as if examining Martha under a microscope. I hoped he wouldn't notice how she was treating me.

"You're lovely tonight," I said, trying to soften her a little.

She shrugged. She knew how she looked and had undoubtedly been told so often she took compliments for granted.

"And you've absolutely smashed me," I continued.

"I couldn't care less."

"I feel honestly repentant. If I had ashes and sackcloth, I'd put them on."

"You weren't so repentant a short while ago."

"I admit it. In case you don't understand, I'm groveling now. I'm dying. Reprieve me."

She regarded me a moment. She didn't smile, but her face relaxed a degree—a slight easing of muscles.

"Much better," she said. "You just keep on groveling. It suits you."

"I will. I'll make a pilgrimage too. I'll eat locusts and wild honey and go to Rome."

"You don't have to do all that. Just be nice. I know it's difficult for you, but try."

"I'm not only going to try, I'm also going to succeed. I'm going to be humble and pleasing. You're going to enjoy me."

She didn't reprieve me all at once, but by the time we finished eating she was at least no longer stern. I continued to play the fool. I'd have jumped through hoops. I wasn't at all certain she was going to allow me to return to her room. My backache had disappeared. I, the cold fish, wanted her in bed.

She, however, stalled. She was still punishing me. She made me take her to the crowded movie—a war story about a jungle unit in the Pacific. She would not let me hold her hand. Afterward we went to the drugstore for a soda. She was acting like a teenager. I kept glancing at my watch but was afraid to hurry her.

Finally we went to the hotel. Without speaking, we rode up in the elevator. I was scared she was going to tell me good night and leave me standing in the hall. I was so relieved when she unlocked the door and left it ajar that my legs wobbled. I felt my blood pumping.

While she was in the bathroom, I snapped out the lights, removed my uniform, and lay on the bed. She came to me, but she still made me suffer a little. She held herself rigid. I had to work. After a time she wanted me as badly as I wanted her. I'd learned my lessons from the last night pretty well. By the end she was clutching at me. She who had been tyrannical and hard was now soft and clinging. I was bemused by what I'd done to her—by how much I had changed her.

She had wasted too much time punishing me, and as a result I had to hurry back to camp. While I dressed, she sat on the edge of the bed watching me.

"Do hurry back," she said when I went to the door.

I never hated the Army more than I did that night as I rode back to camp on the cold, dingy bus. I thought that instead of going to the Spartan barracks I could have spent the night in Martha's warm bed. Doing so seemed vastly more sensible than winning wars. It seemed more sensible than anything.

Yet from then on I was able to see her every day. I had no more trouble getting passes. Captain Hanks grinned as if he expected me to be a good sport. I eyed him coldly.

I had no idea how long Martha intended to stay. She was obviously in no rush to leave, a fact which pleased me. She had her hair fixed a second time and sent out dry cleaning. She bought two skirts from a department store. Each morning she ordered roses from the florist in the basement. The roses gave the hotel room a settled, permanent look.

In the evenings she called home to talk to Bessie. She and Bessie were in some sort of womanly cahoots. Bessie opened all the mail and read the important letters over the phone. She passed along messages. Martha gave instructions about the house and farm.

Our lovemaking was becoming progressively fancier. Martha directed that. She knew what she wanted. If I had read about what we were doing, I'd have called it pornography, but it never seemed that way while I was in bed with her. One night she might sit astraddle me and the next command me by subtle thrusts of her body to assume shocking positions. I was receiving an education in advanced bedroom techniques.

"I suppose I ought to leave," she told me as we lay smoking and watching the red reflection from the theater marquee blink on the ceiling after a particularly arduous session. We were both sweating.

"Not yet," I said, weary. I turned on my side to look at the red-tinted shape of her. I ran a hand over her stomach.

"I have to go sometime."

"Sometime's all right, but not now."

"You are nice. I haven't been bad for you, have I?"

"You couldn't be bad for anybody."

"You were pretty innocent about some things. You can never be that again."

"I don't want to be that again."

"It's a shame you've never known many women. It's good for a man to sleep around a little. It can be good for a woman, though most of them get their loving involved with tears and scenes. I've liked all the men I've slept with except one. I occasionally see old beaus on the street. They take off their hats for me and smile discreetly. The fact we've been to bed makes it all very friendly."

I didn't like what she was saying. I didn't even want to hear it. I wished her to be something special, something just for me. I hated the idea of becoming part of a crowd which took off hats in a friendly way.

"You have a remarkable philosophy," I told her, trying to control the anger in my voice. "Does Yancey know you've been in and out of bed with half the male population around town?"

A week earlier she wouldn't have permitted me to get away with talking to her like that. She'd have sent me packing. Now, however, she merely drew close and put a small arm around my waist.

"Oh, you're so moral and outraged," she said. "I can feel the righteousness boiling in you. I didn't intend to rouse you so. For your information there haven't been so many men. Hardly half a dozen. That isn't a great number for a pretty, loving woman my age who doesn't sleep with her husband."

I looked at her. The red glow was flashing off and on, illuminating her dreamy face.

"You don't sleep with Yancey?"

"I haven't let him touch me in years. I could have had a hundred lovers if I really let myself go. Actually I've been very selective."

I raised up on an elbow. I remembered all the bragging Yancey had done about her.

"Why not him?" I asked.

"I'm like you," she said. "In one respect I am at any rate. To put it simply, I detest him."

20

From that moment on it was as if Yancey were in the room with us. For a few days I had almost forgotten him while I lay in the arms of his wife, but now that he was back, he would not go away. He had to be exorcised by words.

"He bought me," Martha said. "He bought me just as he would buy one of his fine English shotguns or registered bulls."

We lay on the bed, and she reached across me to the night table for a cigarette. When she lighted the match, the flame flared, and her flesh was very white. She did not lie down but sat with her back against the knobbed headboard of the bed. As she smoked, she talked in a monotone.

"It's really funny," she continued. "You think I'm so immoral, but I'm the daughter of a Presbyterian preacher. My father was a gloomy man who saw Hell-fire in acts as innocent as a woman's wearing lipstick or a farmer's cursing a mule. 'You are a young female,' he told me when I was thirteen. 'As such you are particularly susceptible to the wiles and temptations of the Devil. Always sleep with your hands outside the covers.' Imagine a father telling his daughter that."

The cigarette glowed above me. I touched her leg and felt the tenseness in it.

"He died in the pulpit," she said. "He had become particularly enraged by the repeal of prohibition and was preaching a sermon condemning the politicians. His hand was raised in a fist, and his face was scarlet. Suddenly he looked surprised and sat down. The word 'doom' was still on his lips. He had knocked the big Bible to the floor. By the time the deacons reached him he was dead."

In the red glow her face appeared bitter.

"Of course my mother and I were poor while he was living. Without him we were destitute. As soon as the church had another minister we were forgotten. We moved into a tiny clapboard house in a part of town where we could hear screams from men fighting with knives. We locked all the doors and windows and sat trembling in the dark."

She leaned across me to spill her ashes.

"When Marvin arrived in town, he wasn't accepted. He talked too much, too fast, and too loud. In addition there were stories about the way he conducted his business. He supposedly took shortcuts on materials and had to be watched every minute. People claimed he was encouraging his partner, a local man named Scott, to drink. Scott was drunk the night he drove his car off a bridge into a river. He drowned in less than two feet of water.

"His widow was a white-haired lady who had put bluebird houses in all the trees around her home. A few days after her husband was in the ground, people began whispering angrily about Marvin. Talk had it that he had stolen practically the whole business from Scott.

"The town was outraged. Not only was Marvin a loud-talking outsider, he had also cheated a widow out of her inheritance. She had to sell her home and move in with a son at Richmond. From then on when Marvin walked down a street, nobody spoke to him. The younger men whispered about calling on him late some night with a strap.

"If he'd had to depend on the town for business, he would have gone bankrupt, but he was making a lot of money on Federal jobs. He drove a new car every year, and he went to the races at Charlestown. Everybody seemed to be caught in the Depression except him. He further upset the townspeople by buying the old Morton place. The property had been in the same family since the American Revolution, and he got it for almost nothing from two old maid sisters who were going blind. Nobody else had money to make an offer.

"All the while he was coming to church where I sang in the choir. I wouldn't even glance his way, but I could feel him watching me. I felt his eyes go over me inch by inch as if he were smoothing me with his fingers."

She shivered beside me and held her arms around herself as if cold.

"Next Marvin tried to pick me up on the street. He didn't know any better. He'd smile at me or follow me into a drugstore where he'd take the seat next to mine. I cut him dead. Like the other girls, I refused to see him. Even when he stood right in front of me, I stared through him.

"He began to telephone me. It didn't do any good for me to be rude. He kept calling even when I told him I didn't want to speak with him. I stopped answering the phone.

"He drove past me each afternoon as I walked home from work. I was a billing secretary at the electric company, and when I left the office he'd be waiting for me in his big car. He always had a big car. He'd drive down the street beside me and call to me. I finally complained to the police who ordered Marvin to stop.

"He then came to the house. He walked right up to the door on a Saturday afternoon. He had on a dark suit and a hat, yet he looked as if his skin had been shined with some sort of grease. Before I could do anything, he pushed right into the hall and introduced himself to my mother. He brought us a five-pound box of chocolates.

"I couldn't get rid of him. He was talking so fast I couldn't even interrupt. My mother just stared at him. He took over our kitchen to make lemonade. I followed him around helplessly.

"His visits became a weekly affair. My mother and I couldn't stop him. If we didn't answer the front door when he knocked, he went around to the back. If we latched the back door too, he looked in the windows and tapped on the glass.

"Each time he came he brought presents. At first they were for both my mother and me—candy, flowers, crates of oranges, bags of nuts. One Saturday, however, he handed me an expensive compact. The case was gold, and my initials were on it in pearl. It was beautiful, but of course I gave it back. I told him I couldn't possibly keep it. He wasn't insulted. You couldn't insult him. He just smiled and sat on the porch swing.

"Always he had presents. His pockets bulged with them. As fast as I returned them he gave me more. There were silk kerchiefs, pieces of costume jewelry, umbrellas, blankets, gloves, perfume, even kitchen utensils. When I wouldn't let him in the house, he'd leave them on the doorstep or send them through the mail.

"The trouble was I was weak. I wanted some of the things I had to give back. I owned so little. I'd never had anything really nice— anything luxurious and vain. On a Sunday night he came to the house and made me sit with him on the porch. My mother stayed inside. She had the radio turned up so she wouldn't have to listen to him. Marvin pulled a leather case from his pocket and snapped it open. Inside was a lady's wrist watch with diamonds around the face. It was lovely. He fastened it on my wrist before I could react.

" 'You'll have to return it,' I told him, but I was tingling with want of it. 'Nice as it is, I simply can't accept it.'

" 'If you don't, I'm going to throw it away.'

"And he did. He threw it right over the porch railing into the grass. I ran after it. I got down on my hands and knees to search. When I found the watch, I held it to my ear. It was still running. It cost more than I made in a month.

" 'You can't just throw it away,' I told him.

" 'Sure I can. I bought it for you. If you won't take it, it's no use to me.'

"I finally took it. I wanted it so badly I was hot, and he really would have thrown it away. As he put it on my wrist, he laughed. I unfastened it before entering the house so my mother wouldn't see it. I kept it hidden from her. I'd smuggle the watch out each morning and put it on while walking to work.

"Marvin knew how to play me. He sensed how starved I was for nice things. He found my weakness just as he finds everybody's. By accepting his presents, I no longer had the right to refuse to go out with him. He knew it.

"He began to insist on his rights. At first I went out with him only at night so nobody could see us in the car together. Then one Saturday afternoon he got me in his car and drove right through town where people looked at us. I wanted to bend over and hide my face. From then on he insisted I walk home with him after church. I lowered my eyes to keep from having to see the disapproving expressions on faces.

"I swore I'd throw him over, but I didn't have the strength. He was constantly undermining me. I who was used to cornbread and greens was eating lobster and pheasant. We sat in quiet, rich places which had thick rugs and French waiters. He started me drinking and smoking. One night when I asked him for a cigarette, he handed me a silver case with my name cut into it. He was always chipping away at me with presents.

"You have to understand what was happening to me," she said, her fingers brushing my arm. "I'd never had anything nice before, and now I owned this little hoard. I had to keep it hidden from my mother, but it was mine. I'd lock myself in the bathroom and play with the presents like a child. Moreover Marvin was always telling me how beautiful I was and treating me with elaborate politeness. Lastly I was just plain biologically ready for a man.

"At first he was physically repulsive to me. He had enough sense not to force himself on me that way. Instead he did things like take an interest in my clothes and hair. I was considered very plain then. I wore my hair straight back and people thought of me as being old-fashioned. He drove me to a Washington department store where he'd made an appointment for me to have some beauty treatments. When they finished with me, I couldn't believe what I saw in the mirror. I gaped at myself because for the first time in my life I realized I was pretty. I felt both glorious and grateful to him.

"On the next Sunday he persuaded me to go out to his house. He had been leading up to that. He had used his own men to restore the old Morton place. All the boxwoods were shaped and the fences painted. He had brought in an interior decorator from Washington to furnish the house with antiques. I fell in love with the place at first sight. I've never seen anything I wanted more. I could feel myself going weak with wanting.

"He kissed me in the master bedroom. I didn't push him away, but I stood perfectly rigid. He stepped back, held my hand, and led me downstairs where he had his library. From a desk drawer he removed two flat leather cases. Each contained a medal. One had the citation folded under it.

"He read it to me. When I understood the words, I was happy because they meant that no matter how he appeared, underneath he was decent and fine. He had to be or he couldn't have done all

157

the things written about in the citation. On top of that I was all fluttery about the house. As I held the medals, I knew it could be mine if I wanted it, and Marvin seemed to change from a fat, noisy man into a person worth loving. I let him kiss me and when he asked to marry me, I said yes."

She stopped speaking and moved across me to get off the bed. I could see the slim, lithe shape of her in the red glow of the room. She went to the closet where she pulled on a housecoat—not to hide from me, but to warm herself. She came back and sat on the edge of the bed. Holding the housecoat around herself, she looked at the floor. Again her voice was a monotone.

"He wanted a big wedding," she told me. "He bought me the most expensive wedding dress he could find and ordered a thousand engraved invitations. They were sent mostly to men directly or indirectly involved in the construction business. People from town came out of curiosity. After the ceremony in the church, Marvin gave a reception on the lawn of the house. He had professional caterers who put up a colored tent and served champagne from a fountain. To me it was more like a circus than a wedding.

"When we returned from the honeymoon, we went to the house— my house now. He let me change it anyway I wished. He set up a checking account for me and encouraged me to spend money. At first it was something I couldn't do easily because of the way I had been living for years.

"He particularly wanted me to buy clothes. He would give me a handful of money and send me into a store with instructions not to come out until I had spent every penny. He ordered all the fashion magazines for me. He liked me to put on new clothes and model them for him.

"He also encouraged me to give parties. As a result, we had guests in the house almost every weekend. After the townspeople's curiosity was satisfied, some of them would no longer come. Their snubbing Marvin made me furious. After all he had the medals. I saw to it that a piece about them appeared in the local paper. He didn't want me to, but I called the editor anyway. I had the medals mounted on black velvet and hung them on the living room wall. From then on I did the snubbing. I carried my head high and refused to speak to anybody who hadn't been nice to him."

She was silent a moment, as if thinking back to it. Her normally proud shoulders were hunched slightly. She seemed very small and alone sitting on the edge of the bed.

"I might actually have loved him if he hadn't insisted on confiding in me. At the beginning there were only hints, a word here or there, a slight twist of his face. Then he told me his name wasn't Yancey at all but Yankovitch. He had changed it after World War I. I wasn't too shocked. I could understand a man who was working to get ahead thinking his name might hurt him. Perhaps because I did accept it so easily, he believed he could tell me anything.

"The bad truth came out one evening while he was drunk. He was usually very careful not to drink too much, but it was our second anniversary party, and he forgot himself. He kept making toasts with champagne. After everybody had gone home, we went upstairs. He sat on my chaise to take off his shoes and socks. Suddenly he began to weep.

"I couldn't believe what I was seeing. I thought something must be terribly wrong and hurried to him. He grabbed me around the waist and pressed his face against me. He talked into me. At first I wasn't able to understand what he was trying to tell me, and when I did, I attempted to hush him. I didn't want to know. I didn't want to be his confessor."

"Didn't want to know what?" I asked.

She stood and walked halfway across the room. Her head was bowed. She turned slowly and came back toward me.

"About the medals," she said. "He shouldn't have gotten the medals."

"Why not?"

"He was a coward."

I sat up quickly. She paced the floor. From the movie below came the sound of shooting and galloping horses.

Marvin Yankovitch, I thought. Of course. Everything was falling into place now. I understood his actions on the infiltration course. What Martha had told me explained his reluctance to wear the medals at all. It had not been modesty but shame. He was phony to the marrow of his bones. I hated him not only for his lies and OCS, but also for the fact he had been able to touch Martha at all.

"I didn't get all the details," she continued. "He was sobbing, and his words ran together. I was too stunned to move. He was still holding onto me. When he looked up, he must have seen the horror on my face. He stopped talking, let go of me, and lurched into the bathroom. I heard him being sick.

"I was very confused. I tried to believe all he'd told me was just a part of his being drunk. Right at that moment it didn't even seem to make a great deal of difference. I shut it out of my mind. I pretended none of it had happened.

"Yet things were never exactly the same after that either. It wasn't my fault. He was the one who wouldn't let it alone. I'd catch him watching me with his big sad eyes. It was as if by telling me that awful thing about himself he had become crippled and dependent on me. He followed me around the house as if he expected me to reprieve him.

"There was nothing I could do. I couldn't wash away his sins. I just hoped he would act as he'd used to. I could sense, however, he wanted to say more. I wouldn't allow him to. I'd heard enough.

"He was the one who changed, and his doing so caused me to. He forced me to look at him differently. Against my will I began to see him differently. There were moments when he appeared weak and unsure to me. I'd shake my head to throw out the thoughts, but they kept coming back.

"Finally I started resenting him. I couldn't quite bury the feeling he had taken advantage of me. He had caught me while I was young and naive, and by using the medals he had got me under false pretenses. He had blinded me with money. I was another piece of furniture for his house—something he could dress up and show off to his friends. I felt I deserved better."

Her shoulders had straightened, and her head was higher. As she paced in her bare feet, her step quickened.

"He was still sleeping with me," she said. "We had beds next to each other. He would always cross to me hat in hand so to speak. I suppose I still liked that part of it, at least for a time. One night, however, it didn't work, and I realized I was merely putting up with him. I was suffering him.

"I'd been thinking of giving him a child. He wanted a son badly. He talked of all he could do for a boy. I, however, no longer liked his Yankovitch seed. I began to be very careful not to carry it.

"During the Christmas season we had parties at the house, and an architect friend of his was there. The architect wasn't beefy and coarse like the others. He was a well-bred, courtly man who caught me alone in the library late one night. I believed everybody was asleep and had come downstairs in my bathrobe for a book. I guess I was curious to find out whether I had become dead or another man could move me the way Marvin once had. I acted like an alley cat. The architect did it with me standing up against the door.

160

"He knew his way around. Worldly, suave, and a little jaded, he made Marvin seem a child. During the rest of the weekend, I met him all over the house. We used closets, the basement, the attic. After he left, I drove to Washington to see him. He rented a small apartment for me, and I'd tell Marvin I was going shopping.

"I wanted to marry the architect. I was sure I loved him because no one had ever shaken me as he had. I should have known better. He was a Catholic with a wife and children. Moreover he was tiring of me. We had no violent argument, but I could see—and oh how it hurt—that the relationship was boring him. I wept. I was still very innocent."

She came to the bed and sat on it. I put an arm around her hip. She was so tense she felt hard.

"After the architect I was pretty much in an emotional state for a while, and because of him I got into the mess with Marvin. We'd reached home late after a dinner party. Earlier in the evening I'd stood across the room watching him among a group of men. He'd been laughing and attempting to ingratiate himself with anybody who could possibly do him any good. He had seemed porcine and oily. I hadn't been able to escape his bootlicking laughter. At any rate he wanted in bed with me.

"'I'm very tired tonight,' I told him.

"'I need you,' he said, standing above me in the dark. He sounded mournful.

"'Not tonight. I really am washed out.'

"He didn't move for a long time. Then I heard him shuffle back to his own bed and lie down. I could feel him accusing me. He was quiet, but the accusation was thick in the room. I turned away from him and went to sleep. In the morning he got up early and left the house without waking me.

"I spent the day riding horses. I rode them through the woods and up into the mountains as if the Devil were chasing me. I slashed them with my crop until they were wild-eyed and frothy. I think I was a little bit out of my mind. When I finally returned to the house, I was exhausted and knew I would never allow Marvin to touch me again.

"At first he refused to believe it. I suppose he thought I was being merely female and temperamental. He bought me a cream-colored roadster and a diamond bracelet. It was his way of trying to bribe me. The rest of the country was struggling out of a depression, but he always had plenty to spend on me. One night he came to my bed and begged. He got right down on his knees. It was sickening. I moved to the room across the hall.

"It was a strange sort of life. We continued to live and go out together, but alone we rarely spoke and never about anything personal. I thought he might want a divorce, and for a price I was prepared to give him one. He wouldn't discuss it. I suppose he believed it was cheaper to keep me than let me go. I didn't really care as long as I had the house and my checking account. That sounds mercenary and heartless, but I had become used to money. He had made me used to it. I had no intention of ever being without it again.

"He got value out of me. After all I continued to entertain his friends and play the gracious hostess. I made him look good. He would have had difficulty replacing me and he realized it. No matter how high I ran the bills he never complained.

"I even got to like the way we were living. For the first time in my life I was free. I was still young, and there was nobody to tell me what I could or couldn't do. I was anxious to get my hands on a man —not to marry or become serious about—but just to act in freedom. I picked out a contractor who must have thought he had caught hold of a sex fiend."

I withdrew my hand from her. I wanted to hear what she had to say, but I didn't like hearing it. I especially didn't like the parts about other men. She turned a little on the bed and felt for me.

"Why shouldn't I have liked the way I was living?" she asked. "I had everything, including some damn fine men. I was always discreet. I never fooled around with townspeople, and I avoided complications. I'd sometimes go as long as a year without anybody, but I couldn't give that up completely. I was pretty, and my ego needed worship occasionally. It's unreasonable to expect me to give men up altogether. Besides I felt I'd been cheated and had a right to them.

"I'd always know when I saw the person I was going to have an affair with. It was as if a quiet little bell went off inside me. The little bell went off for you as you looked at me across the dinner table while Marvin was making a fool of himself. I was sure that you, like the others, would call me eventually. I wasn't in the least surprised you did. I'd have been more surprised if you hadn't."

She released my hand and stood to walk to the window. Red flashed around her. She talked with her back to me.

"When the war started, Marvin's business was better than ever. He was receiving all sorts of cost-plus contracts. He was making so much money that he kept bundles of it in a tin box. There was probably something illegal about that. Perhaps he was attempting to hide it from the tax collector or possibly it was his bribe money.

"One afternoon he came home early. For him that was rare because he was in his glory at his office where people rushed about at his command. I was upstairs reading on the chaise. He knocked on my door and asked to come into my bedroom. I was being careful. I didn't want to have to fight him off after all this time. He stood in front of me.

" 'I'm going to enlist,' he told me.

"I thought he was joking. I questioned him about being too old, but he was certain he could get around the rules. I then said he was being both romantic and foolish, that it was too late to try to prove anything. He answered he was going anyway.

"I still didn't take him seriously. I believed the impulse would be dissipated in a few days. The next morning, however, he left the house before daybreak and was gone for thirty-six hours. When he came back, we had dinner together, and he told me he had been in Washington looking into the matter of a commission. He said he could have worked it but at the last moment had decided not to. He would rather go in as a private and rise through the ranks.

"Apparently he was hoping to impress me by that. I wasn't impressed. On a Wednesday he drove down to the post office and stood in line like any farm boy. He didn't think I'd know he had taken money from his tin box, but I saw him stuffing bills into his pocket. Evidently he was able to find the right palm to grease, for he returned home that night proud of himself. He had three weeks to get his affairs in order.

"He was sure he'd become an officer. He was so sure in fact he left his measurements at a Washington tailor shop which specializes in uniforms. While waiting to report, he became a health addict. He bought a sweat suit and did road work around the farm, frightening the horses in the paddock. He had delusions of winning the war single-handedly and coming back the conquering warrior with a chest covered by medals. I suppose he even believed he was doing it for me. Well, it was too late for me, and if he could have seen how ridiculous he appeared, he'd have given up the whole idea.

"On the morning he left, I drove him into town. He'd asked me to come with him, and it was the least I could do. He made certain everybody on Main Street saw he was going. He strutted up and down in front of the stores. To be perfectly frank, I was amused. I didn't think there was a chance he'd stick it out for more than a week. I was amazed at his completing basic and even more so at his being chosen for OCS."

I broke in then. All my hate of Marvin Yankovitch Yancey rose in my throat. I told her how he'd gotten through basic by using his medals. I explained how he had bribed the captain at OCS. I described what Yancey had done to me after my helping him with the mop string. Martha came to sit by me. She watched my face and listened to every word.

"It sounds just like him," she said when I finished. "As well as I know him, how did he think he was going to impress me? His pathetic stab at a new life was corrupted before it could begin. Cheating is as natural to him as eating. His whole history's been a series of hidden tin boxes."

She stood, lighted a cigarette, and walked to her dressing table. I was still angry with my words about Yancey.

"I knew when he came home on furlough he'd want in my bed," she told me. "I was ready for him. I wouldn't undress. He went to his room, and I heard him close the door. Quietly I locked my own. During the night he tried the knob. I kept my door locked all the time he was home.

"You came to visit him. I was off men at that particular point. It'd been a long while since I'd had one anyway. Then Marvin was so awful that night. He was telling you the price of everything and slobbering drunk. You weren't the type he usually dragged in. As I sat across from you at the dinner table I saw you were concerned for me. The little bell went off inside me very clearly.

"That's the reason I came to your bedroom—that and the fact I undoubtedly wished to punish Marvin for the way he had acted. I never considered you might refuse me. I'd never been refused before. Actually you wanted me, but you were scared. Still I knew you'd call eventually, though I never suspected it would be from Georgia. I might say that at the moment I'm glad."

She returned to the bed, sat on it, and leaned to me. I put my arms around her back.

"Well you've heard my sordid little tale," she said. "What do you think?"

"I think I'm very much in love with you," I answered.

She looked at me seriously, her face only inches from mine.

"Ah love," she said and rested her face against my bare shoulder.

21

She stayed seventeen days, and I counted each of them. By then I was so completely wrapped up in her that nothing else mattered much to me. I could understand why Yancey had begged her. There were moments when I felt a terrible weakness in myself. I wanted to bow down before her.

She had to leave because of Yancey. She called Virginia and learned a letter had come from him. Bessie read it over the telephone. Yancey was about to get a leave and wanted her to spend a week with him at Sea Island.

"I won't go to Sea Island," she told me after she hung up. "I suppose, however, I better hurry home."

I protested. In the light of what she had told me, Yancey no longer had any right to her. I was jealous he was even going to be near her on his leave. I thought of him in the fancy uniform he had ordered. Martha smiled as if she were reading my mind.

"You don't have to worry," she said, patting my cheek. "I promise you you don't."

"You'll be in the same house with him."

"But that's all, and I'd much rather stay with you in our little room." She smiled. "My absence will do you good. It'll give you a chance to build yourself up."

"I thought I'd been manly enough," I said, my pride hurt at the hint I had been failing her.

"You have, idiot. Can you ever understand when I'm joking?"

It was difficult for me to do so. I was so absolutely committed to her now I couldn't joke. A frown from her absently sent in my direction alarmed me. Modulations of her voice expressing impatience or displeasure caused my stomach to tighten in anxiety. Knowing her was the most important thing in my life, and I certainly couldn't take it lightly.

The afternoon she packed I sat on the bed watching and feeling miserable. She was wearing a gray suit and hat. She appeared a chic matron. She called down to have her bill prepared, and I carried her bags.

We rode in a taxi from the hotel to the train station. I kissed her in the taxi. Though she wasn't the sort for that, she didn't stop me.

She merely got out her handkerchief and compact to repair the damage I had done to her make-up.

On short notice she had been able to talk the ticket agent into giving her a Pullman reservation. Some poor fellow had undoubtedly been done out of his. She and I waited at a lonely end of the concrete ramp. The day was cold, and gusts of wind blew up the track. Still we preferred being out there by ourselves than in the crowded, dirty depot. I held her gloved hand and asked whether I could write. She nodded but told me not to put the return address on the envelope.

When the train came in, I found her car and put her on. A last time I kissed her. People watched us. To hell with people. I stood outside the window of her Pullman, and we smiled at each other until the train pulled away. I ran alongside of the car as far as I could and watched it disappear among sooty buildings.

Riding back to camp, I was so glum I hung my head. I didn't return to the office as I should have. I lay on my bunk where I slept the rest of the afternoon and through the night. Men who lived around me were considerate. They spoke softly and held down curses from the inevitable poker game.

At reveille I dressed and drank two cups of coffee in the mess hall before walking to battalion headquarters. Wilson, Carter, and the Professor watched me when they believed I wasn't looking. Instead of working on the payroll, I wrote Martha a long, rambling letter. I was to write her every morning after that too.

Almost two weeks passed before I heard from her. By that time I was very nervous. I imagined all sorts of things. Maybe she was tired of me and was throwing me over. Or perhaps Yancey had used some trick. When I was on the point of telephoning, I received the letter.

Written on blue paper which was faintly scented with her perfume, the letter had been hastily scrawled. Her slanted handwriting was difficult to read. She apologized for not answering me sooner, but she said she hated to write people and I must not expect to hear from her often. "You'll have to put up with my slovenly ways."

She told me soldiers had tried to pick her up on the train and that snow was falling in Virginia. As I had asked her to do, she sent me a snapshot of herself. In the picture she was wearing jodhpurs, a tweed jacket, and a black cap with a long bill.

She said Yancey had come home for his leave. He had arrived wearing his tailored uniform and each day had walked up and down

Main Street so the townspeople could see him. He had acted as if he were a general of the Army.

He hadn't bothered her. She ate with him each evening, but that was all. In the mornings she remained in bed while he went hunting or to his office. He wouldn't come home until late afternoon at which time they had a drink together.

She wrote she asked him one evening what had become of me. They were at the dinner table.

"Charley Elgar?" Yancey said.

"Weren't you all such good friends?" she questioned him.

"Well, to be blunt about it, Charley just didn't have the stuff for OCS. He's a nice boy, but OCS takes qualities not everybody's born with. He didn't possess the necessary leadership ability."

As I read those lines in her letter my hands trembled with the hate I felt toward Yancey. I could picture him saying just that. I was so upset I breathed as if out of breath. Wilson, Carter, and the Professor eyed me.

The letter was the only word I had from Martha for another two weeks. Though I realized I'd be foolish to expect her to write regularly, each day I didn't hear from her made me morose. At the same time I longed for her, I resented her indifference.

My mood was black, and people avoided me. I was glad they did. It suited me to keep to myself. I'd go for days without speaking more than half a dozen words to anybody. A note from Martha was enough to lift me heavenward, but only temporarily. I wanted all of her—not just bits and pieces.

I hardly noticed what was going on around me. The regimental combat team went on with its training and was gradually hardening its shape. We had received our shoulder patches with orders to sew them on our blouses. The patches displayed a golden eagle striking with talons a red chain, symbolizing tyranny. Carter, the warrior, was pleased.

"Not bad," he said, holding the patch against his arm and examining it in the mirror. "Something a man can be proud of. People are going to hear from the old golden eagle."

He was still enthusiastic about the Army, though ashamed of being a clerk in battalion headquarters. He rationalized that his job was only a temporary condition. As soon as the outfit was overseas, he would demand a transfer into a line company. In the meantime there was no sense in giving up a good thing.

The regiment went on a series of bivouacking maneuvers. Line companies marched for miles through swamps. They shivered in pelting rains. Headquarters personnel rode in trucks and lived in dry tents. None of us understood much of what was going on in the simulated battles. Colonel Bone and Lighthorse Harry acted important as they rode around in jeeps. All the activity seemed to have little to do with war.

My thoughts were on how I could see Martha again as soon as possible. I pleaded with her to come back to Georgia now that Yancey's leave was over. She said she couldn't because there was work that needed doing around the house. She didn't trust the carpenters unless she was present to supervise them.

I sulked. She apparently thought more of the house than she did of me. I wrote to her that it was possible I might be shipped overseas at any time. I didn't really believe that. I hoped, however, it might have some effect on her. She answered she would come as soon as she could but that I must be patient with her a little longer.

I received a letter from my mother asking me what progress I had made toward becoming an officer. I couldn't tell her that a commission was no longer of prime importance to me. What mattered now, what I spent most of my time thinking about, was Martha. I wanted to marry her.

I'd come to that decision lying on my bunk during a long, lonely Sunday afternoon. I made up reveries of our spending our lives together. I would get on at the bank, and she would entertain graciously in our house.

I received another letter from her. She said the carpenters were almost finished and that she hoped to be able to come south again for a few days by the end of the month. I was joyful. For a while I spoke to people and attempted to be civil. Carter, Wilson, Beanpost, and the Professor acted suspicious. Lou believed I was making advances toward her and looked at me archly.

Almost immediately I was disappointed. Martha wrote me that her mother had become sick and was in the hospital. She herself couldn't leave the bedside. She was sorry but would come as soon as she was free.

To make matters worse, the outfit was alerted. The area became grim and purposeful as MPs were stationed at gates and all passes canceled. At headquarters we packed records in waterproof boxes. For once we honestly had more work than we could do. Lou who had been contemptuous of us for so long because of her Texan in the line company acted as if she might be sorry to have us leave.

She and I were in somewhat the same situation. She was unhappy because her Texan was to be taken away from her. I was thinking it might be years before I saw Martha. I couldn't even write and explain to her what was going on because our letters were censored and no long-distance calls were permitted. I was desperate enough to consider going AWOL.

The outfit swarmed in confusion. Moving, supplying, and bivouacking hundreds of men had to be worked out in detail. Nobody knew where we were going. Not even Lou had been able to get that information. The officers looked grave, but they were as ignorant as the enlisted men.

In the early spring we left on trucks. The WACs came down to tell us good-by. Lou kept kissing her Texan. The trucks pulled out in relays to keep from jamming the roads. Each mile we traveled made me more gloomy. We were moving north and headed, I figured, toward the POE in New York. The first night we bivouacked in a national forest.

We never reached New York. In South Carolina we turned west. A day later we arrived in Kentucky where we became part of war games involving armored units from Fort Knox. At the news he wasn't going overseas after all, Carter acted as if he'd been cheated. I felt I'd been pardoned.

The games turned out to be a regimental fiasco. Somehow a large part of our unit failed to position itself properly and was wiped out by our own artillery. Colonel Bone raged. He rushed about in his jeep. Officers slunk through the area with guilty looks.

We returned to Georgia where the WACs were happy to see us. I immediately wrote Martha what was going on, but I had to be extremely careful at the typewriter because Lighthorse was stalking battalion headquarters. As were all the brass, he was searching for scapegoats.

A lot of them were found. Noncoms were busted, and officers were shipped out. Both Colonel Bone and Lighthorse acted personally betrayed. We in headquarters kept the keys of our office machines chattering. Wilson and Carter played no checkers, and the Professor didn't read. We sat at attention in our chairs.

Of course Lighthorse was being chewed by Colonel Bone who in turn was receiving it from Corps Headquarters. Chewing was coming all down the line. Senior officers poured it on their juniors, the juniors on noncoms, and the noncoms on the rest of us. It wasn't unusual to have half a dozen chewing sessions going on in battalion simultaneously.

Enlisted men as well as officers were shipped out. A pfc switchboard operator got the boot for losing one of the colonel's long-distance calls. A line sergeant named Shep became so drunk he fell off his chair and puked into a wastebasket. Lighthorse transferred him the same day.

As if the purge weren't enough, the weather turned filthy. Cold rains drummed on the roof and frayed our nerves. Fights in line companies became common. They resulted in an unusually high percentage of court-martials. There were days when men snapped at each other like rabid dogs. I went to a supposedly funny movie on Sunday evening and though the theater was crowded, everybody was as quiet as if attending a funeral.

Rain fell four days in a row. It came down in flooding sheets. Red streams of mud ran in the gutters. Our clothes and bedding became damp. The soles peeled off our shoes.

On the last of those four days, the door to battalion headquarters opened. Carter, Wilson, the Professor, and I glanced up automatically. A new replacement came in, water dripping from his trench coat. As he passed the cubicle, my hands fell from the typewriter keys.

"You sick?" Wilson asked me, seeing my expression.

I didn't answer. Instead I stood and went to the doorway of the cubicle to look down the corridor after the replacement. He went to Lighthorse Harry's office. Fifteen minutes later he left. He was fat and rosy. Gold bars shone on his shoulders. He waddled. There could be no doubt. The new officer replacement was Lieutenant Marvin Yankovitch Yancey.

22

For a long time I sat at my desk without moving. I don't suppose I ever expected to see Yancey again. Certainly I didn't want to see him. When I recovered a little, my first thought was Martha might not be able to come now that he was in camp. I cursed him with a pure hate.

I didn't notify her about him in the hope he somehow might be put out of the way. Moreover I kept myself hidden from him. There was a chance I could get by without his discovering me. On the other hand not revealing myself would let him off easily. I owed him discomfort. Having somebody around who was wise to him would crowd him badly. I thought of all the things Martha had told me about him in the hotel room. He should be made to suffer.

By checking the battalion roster, I found that Lighthorse Harry had assigned Yancey to Apple Able Company as a platoon commander. The next day while the company marched out for drill, I stood at the window. Yancey moved by the side of his men. His short legs stretched out to keep the pace. He was scowling importantly, and his expression was pugnacious.

I spent a lot of time at the window watching for him. Wilson, Carter, and the Professor were, of course, aware I was acting peculiarly. They didn't like talking to me much, but they were curious.

"You know the lieutenant?" Wilson asked me.

"I know him."

"You seem awfully interested in his welfare."

"I couldn't be more interested."

They waited for me to elaborate, but I did not. I merely stared out the window. As much as I wanted to talk about Yancey, I couldn't. With Martha involved, the less they learned about him the better.

Yancey was quick to start browning Lighthorse Harry. He moved cautiously until he was certain Lighthorse liked to be browned and then poured it on. Not a day passed that Yancey didn't come to battalion headquarters to get in points. He entered with a bouncy step and smiled at both enlisted men and WACs as if he were dispensing alms. I always managed to have my back turned or to get a folder in front of my face so that he couldn't see me.

Yancey would spend fifteen or twenty minutes in the colonel's office. Out in the corridor we heard their laughter. Often they smoked cigars Yancey brought, though I remembered in basic he had advised me to give up cigarettes because they were bad for my wind. When he left the colonel's office, Yancey strutted with the cockiness of a man sure he was cementing his place high in Lighthorse's favor. I glared at Yancey's fat back.

Often he maneuvered to sit by Lighthorse in the mess hall. That was not easy because other junior officers were anxious to do the same. Yancey stationed himself by the door until Lighthorse entered and pushed up behind him as they walked to the tables. In effect he crowded out the others. During a meal his mouth poured out a flow of oily words. I watched Lighthorse Harry's face for some sign he was growing bored or disgusted. None appeared. He was obviously greatly pleased by Yancey.

We began to see Yancey riding around with Lighthorse in the colonel's olive-drab Chevrolet. The Chevrolet had a pfc chauffeur. Lighthorse sat hunched forward, sternly regarding his troops as he passed them. Yancey was on Lighthorse's left, constantly chatting and always jumping out to open doors before the pfc could.

I had to have more information about what was going on in the office when Yancey was with the colonel, and the only way I could get it was from Lou. I waited until she went to the service club for her morning coffee. I slipped out and joined her at the stand-up bar.

"I need your help," I told her. "I want to know what Lieutenant Yancey does in the colonel's office."

She arched a brow. It was a gesture she had practiced. All the men in the service club were looking at her legs. She cracked down on her gum.

"You know what he does. Everybody knows. He sucks around."

I tried not to wince at her words. I hated to hear women use Army expressions. Suck up, TS, the GIs—none of them in my opinion was meant for the female mouth.

"I thought Lighthorse was smarter than that."

"Our glorious leader has been waiting for a long time to make bird colonel. Your lieutenant binds his wounds. You a friend of Yancey?"

"No."

"Then why so concerned?" she asked, pulling down her blouse and stretching out her breasts—not for me particularly or even the other men in the service club, but for humanity.

"He fascinates me," I answered her.

"He fascinates me too—like a snake. I'll say one thing for him though. He's one of the few who doesn't look at my legs."

"He might when your back's turned."

"No, I'd get the vibrations. From him no vibrations." She frowned as if puzzled, finished her coffee, and started away. She turned to me. "Just because I'm talking to you doesn't mean you have privileges. To me you're no Don Juan."

I didn't want any privileges other than her keeping me informed, which she did. She told me Lighthorse was beginning to depend on Yancey. If Yancey was late dropping by headquarters, the colonel inquired for him. They bought each other drinks at the club. Other officers were worried about being cut out. They hated Yancey almost as much as I did. He smiled around as if he were popular and slapped them on their backs.

I had to call Martha. If I put it off any longer, she would hear from Yancey where he was. I hoped to have her come on a visit anyway. Yancey never went into town. She and I could find a place where she would not be seen.

It was lucky I did call. She'd received a letter from Yancey that morning.

"It's a small world, isn't it?" she said over the telephone.

"You can come here," I told her. "Nobody will find out."

"You're talking foolishly, Charles. I don't believe in being foolish. To come down there would be dangerous for me."

"You don't love him. What difference does it make?"

"In the hands of a smart lawyer it could make a great deal of difference. Whatever else Marvin is, he's not stupid. I'll not deliberately antagonize him. As long as he's there, I simply can't come."

I was angry at her because I felt she should have been willing to take chances if she loved me as much as I did her. I'd have gone through fire to be by her side. As I lay in bed later, however, I saw that she was right. There was no sense in her endangering a favorable divorce settlement, which she undoubtedly had in mind. Love did not rule out practicality.

I went back to hating Yancey for messing up my life. While thinking of him, I pounded typewriter keys as if trying to smash them. Wilson, Carter, and the Professor exchanged glances.

A week after I talked to Martha on the telephone, I allowed Yancey to see me. I figured I no longer had anything to lose. He was marching his platoon in from the obstacle course—a course he himself had never been able to run. I stood close to the window. Normally I stepped back from it, but not this time. He was counting cadence. He looked toward headquarters, perhaps hoping to see the colonel. Instead he saw me. His mouth remained open, and he missed a beat in the cadence. Then he was gone past the building.

Within five minutes he was back at headquarters. He peeked around the doorway to my cubicle as if afraid I might jump on him. I merely sat at my desk and stared. He straightened, smiled, and approached me with his hand extended. Carter, Wilson, and the Professor were observing.

"Well, my God, if it isn't Charley Elgar," Yancey said, thrusting his hand across the desk.

I didn't move. He pulled his hand back uncertainly, and his face reddened. He glanced uncomfortably at the others, but he held the grin.

"It's great to see you," he said to me. "I've been hoping we'd bump into each other."

"I bet you have, Marvin."

I used his first name purposely. He flinched because of Carter, Wilson, and the Professor hearing me do it. He licked his lips and wanted to escape.

"Well, listen, we ought to have a talk," he told me. "Maybe when you get off work you can meet me somewhere."

"Be glad to, Marvin."

"I tell you what," he said hastily. "You come on over to A Company orderly room tonight. I'll be there after chow."

"Sure, Marvin."

He smiled weakly, again glanced at the others, and hurried from the cubicle on his short, fat legs. For once he forgot about sucking up to Lighthorse. He couldn't get out of headquarters fast enough.

"You really routed him," Wilson said. "You acted more like an officer than he did."

They wanted me to explain, but I did not. I sat tight-lipped until five, washed up, and went to chow. I had no appetite. I drank coffee and smoked cigarettes. My stomach was too tense to accept food. I saw Yancey mouthing at the colonel's table and waited for him to leave the mess hall before doing so myself.

I walked down the street to A Company. In the orderly room a clerk was typing. I asked for Lieutenant Yancey, and the clerk pointed to a door. I didn't have to knock. The door opened immediately, and Yancey stepped out.

"Enter, Charley," he said, putting a hand on my shoulder and pulling me into the office. He closed the door quickly. He was afraid I'd call him Marvin in front of the clerk.

A large photograph of Martha was on a filing cabinet. It was in a silver frame, a picture showing her from the waist up. She was wearing black and no jewelry. Her black hair was pulled to the rear of her head. She could have been high-bred Spanish and looked very cold. I turned away quickly to keep Yancey from noticing my interest.

"I really can't tell you how good it is to see you," he was saying as he walked around his desk. "I mean it."

On his desk were an unarmed hand grenade used as a paperweight and an ashtray made from a brass 40-mm shell. A pipe rested in the ashtray. The pipe was new and, like Lieutenant Beady, Yancey had taken up smoking one to improve his military appearance.

"I know you're just tickled to death, Marvin," I answered.

His large, watery brown eyes darted about. They were shifty, horse-trader's eyes. He had on his tailored uniform, but his softness bulged against the expensive cloth. He was not wearing the ribbons which represented his phony medals. I supposed he saved them for dramatic effects. I remembered all Martha had told me about him, and my mouth wished to snarl.

"Sit down, Charley."

"No thanks."

"Now look, one thing I learned a long time ago is that a man gets absolutely nowhere holding a grudge. It's an unproductive attitude. I don't want to rehash affairs, but after all there was nothing I could have done at OCS. The captain wasn't going to back down no matter what I tried. He'd made up his mind to bust somebody that morning, and it just happened to be you."

Yancey had lowered his voice to prevent the clerk in the outer office from hearing. I had trouble not looking at the photograph of Martha. I hated him for having it. He sat down and leaned back in his chair.

"I was attempting to save your bacon, Marvin. I picked up that mop string to help you. I should be sitting where you are now."

"I know that's how it appears from your point of view and let me say again I'm sorry. I honestly believed, however, there was nothing I could do to help you. You were my best friend. How do you think it made me feel when you had to leave? I can tell you it wasn't easy for me. I wanted to write you a letter and explain. I wish you could know how much I've suffered about this whole thing. I've gone through hell."

He looked totally innocent, and his brow wrinkled in sincerity. I thought of what he had told Martha on his leave about my lacking leadership ability. I tasted bile.

"I mean it," he went on. "I valued your friendship. I consider you one of the finest people I've ever met. Now you got a bad break, Charley, and I'm the first to admit it. Because of it I want to help you. If you give me a chance, I can help you. After all I have some influence around here, and I don't mind saying I intend to have a good deal more. There's no reason I can't do you some good."

He was not only lying, but also attempting to bribe me.

"Influence, Marvin? You mean you have the colonel on the take?"

175

"Now that's not fair, Charley, and I wish you'd stop talking like that. I'm trying to make it up with you."

"No deal, Marvin."

"And listen, I don't mind you calling me Marvin here in the office—I want you to—but how about watching it outside?"

"You're pulling rank on me."

"It isn't a question of pulling rank. Calling me lieutenant is simple military courtesy. I've got an important job to do here. We'll be going overseas one of these days. There's no place in a combat outfit for sloppiness or hard feelings."

"I know you're anxious to get into combat," I said, thinking of his medals.

"You're damn right I am," he answered, not catching the tone of my voice. "As I told the colonel, that's what we came to this party for. The sooner the better I say."

He sat forward aggressively and picked up the unarmed grenade. He looked as if he might hurl it at an enemy beyond the door.

"Somehow I keep forgetting you're a hero," I said in spite of the fact that I had to watch my words. No matter how much I wished to, I couldn't reveal to him I knew what a fake he was. He would be able to figure out who'd told me.

"What?" he asked.

"I said I keep forgetting you're a hero. I have difficulty thinking of you as a mighty warrior."

"Now look here, Charley, I asked you to come over because I wanted to hold out the olive branch. I still want to. Let's bury the hard feelings and shake hands."

He stood and reached across the desk. I did not take his hand.

"I'll make it very plain, Marvin. I dislike you. You don't care about my friendship. You're just trying to con me so I won't cause you any trouble."

"If you don't like me, that's your business," he said, dropping his hand. "Nobody can stop you from taking an unproductive view. I just want you to remember I got a job around here and I intend to do it well. I hope you won't cause me any trouble, but don't get the idea I'm begging you. I can handle myself in the tight places."

I was backing toward the door as he talked. I put my hand on the knob. I looked one last time at Martha's photograph. Yancey caught the movement of my eyes.

"She asked about you," he said. "She wondered how you were."

"Give her my regards the next time you write," I answered.

176

"I'll do that."

"So long, Marvin."

"From now on it's Lieutenant Yancey."

"I hope you die."

I walked out past the clerk who'd heard me say the last and was astonished. I went to the barracks where I lay on my bunk. It was twenty minutes before I was calm enough to light a cigarette with a steady hand.

23

Yancey had no need to worry about my causing him trouble. If it hadn't been for Martha, I might have, but because of her all I wished was to get as far away from him as possible. In the morning I wrote out a formal request for transfer and handed it to WO Page. Page gave it to Captain Hanks who called me to his office a few hours later. He had his hands clasped behind his head.

"You don't like it here?" he asked and smiled. He always smiled at me. It was as if we had a bond because he had tried to get at Martha.

"This isn't a question of liking, Captain. I didn't expect to like the Army. There are personal reasons."

"Want to tell me?"

"No, sir, I don't."

"Trouble with your wife?" he asked, amused.

"I'm not married, sir."

"That's right. I guess I had you confused with somebody else. Well, let me give you my transfer lecture, Elgar. During a war there just isn't room for personal matters. You're disrupting the defense effort by even putting in for a transfer. Your request will have to be processed. It'll go through battalion, up to regiment, and eventually make its way to Washington. Think of the trouble it causes. What's more Colonel Box and Colonel Bone take very dim views of transfer requests. They think such requests indicate disloyalty to the outfit. So why don't you withdraw yours and save everybody trouble?"

"No."

"It's going to be denied. Furthermore, it won't help you."

"I want out, Captain. If I stay here, I'll keep putting in for transfer."

"You're a hardhead, Elgar. Get out of my office."

Three weeks later my request came back stamped DENIED.

I submitted a second one. This time Hanks didn't bother to talk to me. When we met, he looked the other way. The fact I was attempting to transfer from the outfit didn't do me any good with the other men either. There was *esprit* in the golden eagle, and I seemed to be scorning it. I couldn't very well explain why I wanted out. My exploits with a beautiful woman had dimmed in all memories except my own, and I was fast becoming a pariah. In the barracks, men stopped speaking and turned their backs on me.

As I waited for action on the second transfer application, I was able to watch Yancey boring into the outfit's command structure like a relentless termite. He daily made himself more indispensable to the colonel. Lighthorse Harry was reacting like a hound dog having its back scratched. Yancey sucked up to him so openly that enlisted personnel and officers had begun calling him "Lieutenant Brown." Lou made the mistake of saying it to his face, but Yancey pretended not to hear.

"Are you sure he understood?" Carter asked Lou.

"He understood," she said. "He's not exactly dumb. I could have dropped through the floor."

"He holds the record," Wilson said. "I've been keeping score. He's got all other officer brown-nosers beat three to one in intensity of effort. Only a captain in C Company can come close."

"I think he's a genius," the Professor said, looking up from his book. "Genius is an exquisite quality and should be appreciated. I mean here is an officer completely dedicated to his calling. Neither rain nor snow nor dark of night can keep this browner from his appointed rounds."

Everywhere I went I heard talk of Yancey. His reputation was growing like a snowball rolling downhill. In the barracks, at the service clubs, in the chow hall his name inevitably came up. He seemed to be ten men.

A lot of the talk originated in his own platoon. On assuming command, he had instituted the new procedure of wearing white gloves at inspections in the manner of OCS. He crawled under beds in his remorseless search for dirt. Moreover he insisted his men shine the brass on their uniforms and rifles with Blitz cloths. The platoon sparkled like doormen.

Of course an outfit is so inextricably joined to all its parts that other officers were forced to use white gloves and order their men to shine brass. From platoons it spread to companies, from companies to battalions, and from battalions to regiment. It even shot the gap by infecting an armored division which was temporarily stationed in camp. White gloves and brass cleaning became an epidemic.

Next Yancey gave his men secret practice in trick drill and put them on display one morning while Lighthorse Harry was passing. As the drill was well executed, the colonel beamed his pleasure. Other platoon leaders glared darkly. From that day on, all training schedules included trick drill.

When Yancey had been in the outfit only a little over a month, the captain who was his company commander had to report to the post hospital because of kidney stones. Other more senior officers in the company were passed over by Lighthorse Harry to put Yancey in charge. The officers resented it and stuck together like conspirators.

As an acting company commander, Yancey became even more chicken. He ordered his men to paint all the butt cans in his area green and made them rake the gravel of the walkways three times a day. Whenever his men were not busy following the training schedule, he had them whistled out of barracks for policing the grounds. They seemed eternally bent over, their hind ends skyward. Their shoulders sloped with what was called "Lieutenant Brown's crouch."

Yancey got the idea his company should bleach its leggings and web belting the way cadre had done in basic. Again he worked in secret so he could surprise. He had the bleached leggings and belting worn at battalion review where his company stood out as if they were wearing kilts. It was really a daring move, and the other officers were hoping Lighthorse Harry would become angry about it. Lighthorse, however, looked startled and then pleased. The next morning a directive was sent to all companies in the battalion ordering them to bleach their equipment.

That was the real trouble with what Yancey was doing. If he wanted to dress his men in lions' skins nobody cared except that such a move could not be isolated. Knock over the first domino in a row and the rest fall. His jockeying set up a whole series of reactions all down the line.

In other words he couldn't be ignored no matter how much he was detested. Other company commanders were compelled to have their butt cans painted green and the gravel raked three times daily. As competition increased among units, so did the work load. Free time was eaten up with the result that nobody had the opportunity any longer just to lie on his bunk and cool his feet.

Because Yancey was being imitated, he had to strive even harder to keep ahead of the pack. To do so he instituted an extra inspection. In addition to the normal full dress on Saturday mornings, he held one on Wednesday as well. His men had to get up two hours early to scrub floors and wash windows. Other company commanders followed. Midweek inspection became a permanent part of the regimental training schedule.

Usually those of us in headquarters were exempt from the activities of line companies, but no longer. Captain Hanks was being pressured by his environment. We had to bleach our leggings, shine our brass, and fall out for trick drill. Instead of walking to the PX for a cold beer at the end of the day, we stomped around a drill field and bumped into each other like recruits in our attempts to execute the complicated maneuvers Hanks thought up for us.

"This is an insult," Wilson complained as we hurried toward the barracks after being dismissed from formation at dark. "I'm a clerk."

"There must be something in the ARs against it," Timberlake said.

"I wish we were in the Navy," Beanpost put in. "Somebody could push Yancey overboard."

"You won't have to push him overboard," I told them. "Somewhere along the line he'll trip himself."

They all turned to look at me. We had reached the point where we rarely spoke, and they were out of the habit of hearing my voice. They didn't like talking to me now, but they wanted to know what I meant.

"You sound as if you have inside information," Wilson said.

I had it, though I couldn't reveal it. I did believe, however, that Yancey would eventually foul up badly. He couldn't fool the entire regiment forever. He would finally be judged for what he was, and when that happened, he would sink.

He continued to scheme. His own men grumbled about him constantly and spoke his name as if it were a filthy word, but he apparently cared nothing for what anybody of lower rank thought of him. He concentrated on buttering up those superiors who could do him some good. Chiefly he worked on Lighthorse Harry and Colonel Bone.

Officers of his own rank and even some above were becoming a little afraid of him. He was squeezing them out, and they didn't know how to stop him. Whether they wanted to or not, they found themselves being led by him. For example he was buying from his tailor every uniform the Army authorized, including the dress blues with the flaming red stripes down the trousers. He had all the hats and belts. He even wore a saber chain. His fellow officers had to do the same or appear shabby. They were going broke trying to keep up.

In the field Yancey was just as colorful. He wore paratrooper boots, and his helmet liner was coated with a shiny shellac. The holster of his .45 had been polished with oxblood. He had leather gloves, and he carried binoculars, though none as yet had been issued to him by supply.

It was his idea also to start using a swagger stick with a silver tip on each end. He held the stick under his right arm in the British manner and touched it to his hat instead of saluting. We hoped Lighthorse would reprimand him for it, but Lighthorse liked the idea so much he conferred with Colonel Bone at regiment from which came a directive that all officers should carry swagger sticks. The PX had to order them from the Marines.

Yancey had his jeep modified. Somewhere he acquired a large, chrome-plated combination siren and red light. The contraption, which looked as if it had been taken off an ambulance, was bolted to the right front fender. When Yancey's company was on the march, he'd roar up and down the column sounding the siren and making sweeping saberlike gestures with his swagger stick.

Some of us felt certain that Lighthorse Harry would not stand for the red-light siren. After all holes had been drilled in government property. Yancey, however, had evidently thought all that out. He bought two more of the red-light sirens and presented one to Lighthorse and one to Colonel Bone. They were so proud of the presents they drove around showing them off. Other officers began scurrying about to find red-light sirens for their jeeps. At times dozens of sirens wailed in the regimental area. A visitor would have believed the whole place on fire.

Yancey never let up. In his orderly room he had nameplates on the desk. A wall of his office was covered by a large map which kept up to date the deployment of American fighting troops throughout the world. On each side of the entrance to the orderly room was a guard—bleached and shined—who held a rifle and stood at parade rest. When an officer passed or approached, the guards snapped to attention with a loud click of heels.

Yancey got rid of the GI issue metal desk and bought himself a wooden executive model complete with a leather swivel chair and an inter-office squawk box. Behind his chair the company guidon was crossed with the regimental flag. In addition to his unarmed grenade and brass ashtray made from the 40-mm shell, he had a commando knife which he used as a letter opener. A dark spot on the blade was supposed to be Japanese blood.

Being in battalion headquarters, I saw Yancey every day. He rode up in his jeep with the air of a man concerned with the grand strategy of winning the war. He touched his swagger stick to his overseas cap in the fashion of a German field marshal. As he walked down the corridor, he never looked my way, but he spoke to all the other enlisted men and WACs. He was as patronizing as the old master greeting the darkies on his plantation.

The men in his company were hoping their former commanding officer would return from the hospital and put Yancey in his place. They hadn't really cared much for the former commander either, but in comparison he seemed a person of great charity. Hopes went unfulfilled. Surgeons in the post hospital decided the first lieutenant needed an operation. He was detached and sent to an Army general hospital in Atlanta.

Yancey's men were particularly bitter about the marches he required them to make. He'd bragged in the officers' club that he intended to push them farther and faster than any other company in the battalion. Instead of assuming his place at the head of the column, however, he rode in his fancy jeep. Driving by, he stirred up dust and shouted orders. He reprimanded soldiers for not closing ranks or for dropping out, while he sat in comfort. With the silver whistle he carried fastened to his shoulder strap, he was constantly signaling air attacks. His men had to run for the ditches and dive among palmettos and sand spurs. Yancey timed them against his watch.

Naturally his bragging about the marches caused other company commanders to enter the competition. The post went march crazy. Each evening ragged platoons staggered back into camp looking as if their members were survivors of disasters. Ambulances pulled in packed to the top. Men had fallen arches, blistered feet, and heat prostration. They were taking on the lean, hardened appearance of combat veterans, and their eyes were narrowed with resentment.

Lighthorse Harry loved all the frantic activity. He felt it made him look good to his superiors. Because he had graduated last in his class at West Point, he was afraid somebody might think he wasn't capable of command. Moreover he believed modern infantry a lark compared to the old cavalry. He didn't really think enlisted personnel had souls, and he relished calling junior officers onto the carpet and chewing until they were bloody.

He, of course, never chewed Yancey. They were chums. Yancey could walk right in to Lighthorse's office without even stopping at Lou's desk. He always had a Havana cigar for the colonel. In the officers' club where they spent a good deal of time together, Yancey was quick to pick up the tabs for drinks. There was a handball court on the post, and each Saturday after two o'clock Lighthorse and he would play. The colonel was always allowed to win the crucial games.

Yancey also worked on Lighthorse's thin, slightly frazzled wife who was considered a tyrant among the younger women just as her husband was among junior officers. If a wife failed to follow strictly military social procedures, Mrs. Box chewed her out. Many of the younger women were not familiar with the Army and were reduced to weeping.

Yancey discovered Mrs. Box was crazy about goldfish. He wrote a New York firm and ordered two dozen of their most exotic specimens. He also bought her a large aquarium complete with shells and seaweed. He presented the gifts to Lighthorse's wife on her birthday. After that he was asked to eat at the colonel's house every Sunday.

The enlisted men had only one pleasure in the whole shabby affair. It consisted of watching the discomfort of other battalion officers. Yancey's browning was so much more daring than theirs they didn't have a chance. They were jealous of his getting ahead of them but incapable of doing anything about it. Wilson, who sometimes tended bar at the officers' club, said half the talk at the club was caused by exasperation at Yancey. Behind the exasperation was envy at the originality of his browning technique.

For example he gave a party for the colonel and his wife on their anniversary. Yancey rented the banquet room of the hotel in town and hired a small orchestra. He had quail sent down from Virginia. Naturally Lighthorse turned out to be an old bird hunter but couldn't understand why none of the partridges had shot in them. The answer was the birds had been pen raised. Yancey had simply bought them and had them knocked in the head. The next week he was made a first lieutenant and given permanent command of A Company.

"He is a superior officer," the Professor argued. Yancey was about the only subject which could draw the Professor away from his books. "He works hard, is certainly conscientious, and he takes pride in his company. I think OCS can be proud of its product."

"He might be a superior officer, but he ain't no gentleman," Wilson said.

"Agreed. Our Lieutenant Brown is the result of a system which is basically unsound. You can't make a gentleman by an act of Congress. Eventually the machinery was bound to get out of whack and produce a monster."

"Monster or not he'll be a captain by June," Lou said. She was chewing gum and had a hand on hip.

"I'll be very much disappointed if he isn't a general by the end of the war," the Professor answered solemnly.

The normally stern Lighthorse always laughed when Yancey was around, but one afternoon I detected a change in the quality of that laughter. The Professor noticed also and glanced up. Instead of being gruff and hearty in the best military tradition, Lighthorse's voice had risen shrilly. The sound completely contradicted and belied the ferocious impression he attempted to create.

Yancey left the office that afternoon looking smug. The Professor could hardly wait to question Lou who was sitting at her desk. He signaled her to come to our cubicle.

"Dirty joke," she told us, making a face. "Lieutenant Brown's. About an Englishman and a horse."

"A magnificent ploy," the Professor said in admiration. "Who would have guessed our ascetic Lighthorse would go for that sort of thing?"

"I would," Lou answered, patting her pretty, girdled butt to indicate she'd had to swish it around to keep it safe.

"But it took real nerve to dare a dirty joke," the Professor went on. "And think of the possibilities. Why he could become a division commander by basing an entire browning campaign on stories of traveling salesmen and farmers' daughters."

Yancey was apparently trying something of the kind. At least he was on a definite mission. Each day he waddled into headquarters carrying his dirty joke like a squirrel a nut. As he entered the colonel's office, he smiled slyly. All we clerks would wait with hands suspended on typewriters or adding machines, pencils poised, breaths held, until the inevitable shrill, almost female laughter came from the colonel.

Of course Yancey had to have a constant supply of jokes. Wilson said that in the officers' club Yancey moved from group to group attempting to pick up fresh stories. We also heard he directed his platoon officers and noncoms to bring him any jokes they heard. Yancey supposedly wrote the jokes down and filed them for future use. Perhaps he even edited them for the best effect.

"A girl with big you know what," Lou said after a session where the colonel had been practically convulsed with laughter. She made a curving motion over her own big knockers. "The girl got caught in a revolving door." Lou walked out of the cubicle full of feminine disapproval.

"Just consider it," the Professor mused. "It's conceivable that this whole war could be won or lost because of command decisions made in response to the difficulties of a young lady with a tit caught in a wringer."

24

In the early spring we had field maneuvers. According to rumor, the purpose of the maneuvers was to show that the golden eagle was ready for combat. Lighthorse and Colonel Bone were very serious about proving that, especially after the fiasco with our own artillery in Kentucky.

Those of us in headquarters also had to take part in the maneuvers. We practiced putting up newly issued tents. We used folding desks and small, flimsy typewriters. We loaded our equipment into trucks, but this time, like the line companies, we marched to bivouac. Wilson complained about it. It was a further affront to his dignity as a clerk.

We trudged out under the Spanish moss. Yancey drove past in his jeep, stirring up dust, his red light flashing and siren sounding. A radio antenna whipped back and forth. To appear more dramatic, he drove with the windshield down. He was wearing goggles and a scarf made from a camouflaged silk parachute.

WO Page and Captain Hanks had picked a place for us to put up battalion headquarters. We were on a flat of sandy ground just above a dark river which if it flowed at all did it so slowly that no movement could be seen. In spite of our training we had trouble with the tents. The stakes would not hold in the sandy soil. Within an hour the tents were as swayback as old nags.

Lighthorse Harry had the main tent where he met with his aides and radioman. The radio was for keeping in touch with regimental headquarters and with company commanders who had walkie-talkies. In this particular field problem we were supposed to assist a division which was under attack by a spearhead of armored infantry. Lighthorse was excited because he believed he might have a chance to roll up the enemy's flank as Stonewall Jackson had done to the Yankees at Chancellorsville.

Near the radio was a large map board Captain Hanks kept up to date so that Lighthorse could have an instant picture of what each of his units was doing. Reports came in by radio, Hanks fixed the map, and Lighthorse, pacing before the board with his riding crop, made his decisions.

All battalion officers were called in for briefing. They sat on the ground while Lighthorse explained the tactical situation by using his riding crop as a pointer. Yancey, of course, was in the front row at the colonel's feet. He took notes on everything Lighthorse said. Yancey caught me watching him and looked away quickly.

When the officers returned to their units, Lighthorse got coordinated with regiment and began to put his part of the battle plan into effect. The infantry division we were to assist had already been pretty badly mauled. Regiment had assigned our battalion, code name Alert Airedale, to beef up the division's left flank.

Reports came in over the radio as units of the 606th moved into position, and Hanks stuck pins on the map. Lighthorse acted pleased. He and Colonel Bone talked cordially over the radio. At the same time Lighthorse was watching closely for an opening which would allow him to turn the enemy's flanks in the manner of Stonewall Jackson.

The attack by the 606th caused the armored infantry to halt its advance and pull back to regroup. According to regiment, there was a good chance of a breakthrough along the line if Alert Airedale pressed hard. Lighthorse used the radio to exhort his commanders to push forward with all the impetus they could muster.

I slipped out of the tent. There was nothing for me to do, and in the excitement I wouldn't be missed. I sat under a cypress tree to write Martha a letter. I hadn't heard from her in almost a month, and I was, as usual, miserable with apprehension. When I finished the letter, I returned to headquarters tent just in case anybody was looking for me.

I saw immediately something was wrong. Lighthorse was frowning and pacing rapidly in front of his map board. Wilson and Timberlake were whispering. Hanks', WO Page's, and Garnet's, the radioman's, expressions were serious. In the distance I could hear the faint sounds of M-1's and machine guns. I went to stand by Wilson. He told me all companies had reported in except Yancey's Apple Able. Garnet was attempting to make contact.

"Blue Leader to Apple Able," Garnet said and flipped a switch. He listened, but there was only static. He again made the call.

"Where the hell is he?" Lighthorse asked.

Garnet kept trying, but he had to sandwich his search for Apple Able between reports coming in from other companies and requests for information from regiment.

"Are you attacking?" Ron Regiment wanted to know.

"We are on the attack," Garnet answered, speaking for Lighthorse.

"We're getting pressure on the left. Where's it coming from?" Lighthorse took the microphone from Garnet.

"There might be a slight gap along there," Lighthorse confessed.

"If there's a gap, find it and close it," Colonel Bone answered.

Lighthorse had Garnet get a report from all companies in the battalion except Yancey's, which still couldn't be raised. Then Bonnie Baker Company came in with a second report.

"Sir, we've lost liaison with Apple Able."

Lighthorse Harry paled. At the same moment the radio spoke again, this time as if it had a life of its own.

"Alert Airedale, this is a referee," an authoritative voice said. "Your left flank is under attack by the Aggressor Enemy."

Lighthorse's mouth dropped open, and he sputtered. He grabbed the microphone.

"That's impossible. My left flank isn't exposed."

"I repeat your flank is under severe attack and is being rolled up."

"Bonnie Baker to Blue Leader," the radio said. "We're under heavy attack on our flank."

"How can you be under attack when you're on the attack?" Lighthorse demanded.

"I can't answer that, sir, but we're definitely under attack. Apple Able isn't covering us."

"Fall back and regroup."

"We're trying, sir, but we're being hit by tanks."

"Get me Cheerful Charley Company," Lighthorse told Garnet.

"Blue Leader to Cheerful Charley," Garnet said.

"Cheerful Charley command control," the radio answered.

"Are you under attack?" Lighthorse asked.

"We're on the attack, sir. Doing nicely."

"Bonnie Baker's in trouble. Slow your advance and pull left to help."

"Will do, sir. Over."

"Get me Dandy Dog," Lighthorse told Garnet. "How's the attack going, Dandy Dog?"

"So far right by the book, Colonel."

"You'll have to slow a bit. Keep a tight liaison with Cheerful Charley. Don't disengage your front, but don't get ahead of your flanks."

"Will comply, sir."

Lighthorse next called regimental headquarters. Colonel Bone sounded irritated.

"I've taken remedial action," Lighthorse explained and gave the details. "It ought to fix the gap."

"It damn well better," Bone answered and switched off.

"Now get me Lieutenant Yancey," Lighthorse ordered Garnet.

Again Garnet attempted to raise Yancey. He repeated the call signals. Everybody in the tent was watching the loudspeaker as if Yancey might spring from it. Lighthorse was again pacing. The radio came to life, but instead of Yancey, it was Colonel Bone.

"I thought your gap had been fixed," he complained. "We're still getting pressure."

"I'm working on it, Ben," Lighthorse told him. "One of our companies down here is a little out of position. I am rectifying."

"What's the strength of the enemy?"

"I'm waiting for confirmation. I'll shoot you that information as soon as I have it."

"Make it quick. Our attack's faltering."

"Sure, Ben."

Lighthorse was nervous. He had showed it by using Bone's first name and injecting friendship into the situation. He ordered Garnet to keep trying to contact Yancey. Garnet's calls were interrupted.

"This is a referee," the radio said. "Your Bonnie Baker Company has had its flanks rolled up and is wiped out. You can no longer use that unit in your plan of battle."

"Wiped out?" Lighthorse whispered and turned ashen. "That's impossible. How can they be wiped out?"

"That's something you should have learned in war college," the sarcastic voice of the referee answered. "I might remind the battalion commander that I'm a full colonel and as such rank the battalion commander. In the future it would be extremely unwise of the commander to question the decisions of the referee."

"Sorry, sir," Lighthorse said hastily. He began to sweat.

"Blue Leader from Bonnie Baker," the radio said. "We've just been informed we're wiped out."

"How in hell did you get wiped out?" Lighthorse demanded, his white mustache quivering.

"No flank protection, sir. They swept over us like Stonewall Jackson at Chancellorsville."

"Don't you mention Jackson at Chancellorsville to me. I'm an authority on Jackson at Chancellorsville. Where is Apple Able?"

"We've lost contact with Apple Able, sir."

"Send runners to find them."

"We can't send runners, sir. We've been wiped out."

"Do what I tell you, you idiot!" Lighthorse shouted.

"What's that?" Colonel Bone's voice asked.

"Sorry, Ben," Lighthorse apologized, wiping the sweat from his forehead. "I was speaking to one of my companies."

"We're getting severe pressure up here. Our attack is hardly moving."

"Sir, we're under attack here," Lighthorse said, obviously thinking fast and deciding there was no way he could avoid telling Bone the truth. "I've just lost my Bonnie Baker."

"Repeat."

"I've just lost my Bonnie Baker," Lighthorse said, speaking softly and in shame.

"An entire company gone?" Bone asked, his voice cold.

"Sir, my Apple Able didn't give us flank protection as per mission. Without flank protection the Aggressor Enemy has been able to roll up the line."

"We very much like to know up here at regiment when you lose companies," Bone said. "Perhaps you attach no importance to the matter, but up here we count companies of some consequence."

"Sir, I was just going to shoot you that information when you called."

"Have you found the company out of position?"

"Not yet, sir. We're attempting to do that now."

"You've had a company wiped out and you've misplaced a second. What the hell are you doing to me, Harry?"

"It isn't misplaced, sir. We'll find it and put it on line PDQ. I've got Cheerful Charley closing the gap."

"Do keep us informed," Bone said, switching off.

"Get me Apple Able!" Lighthorse yelled at Garnet.

Garnet called. There was no answer.

"Sir, is it possible that Apple Able's also been wiped out?" Captain Hanks asked.

Lighthorse looked horrified, and for a moment I believed he was going to have to sit down. He held onto a tent pole to steady himself. His voice was so low it was almost inaudible.

"Get me the chief referee," he told Garnet.

Garnet put in a call for the referee command post.

"General Parks, chief referee, here."

"Sir, this is Blue Leader, Alert Airedale Battalion," Lighthorse said. "Has my Apple Able been knocked out?"

"Can't tell you that," General Parks answered. "We haven't been able to locate your Apple Able."

"We are under attack," Cheerful Charley said, breaking in.

"What's your situation?" Lighthorse asked, frightened.

"We were redeploying as ordered and the Aggressor Enemy hit us on the flank. We're being shot at, and there's a lot of confusion."

"I'm surrounded by incompetents and fools," Lighthorse wailed, raising his eyes to heaven. He removed his helmet and ran a shaky hand over his face. He worked determination into his features. "Fall back and regroup," he said into the microphone. "I'll turn Dandy Dog to assist you."

Before he could get Dandy Dog, the radio squawked, and Yancey's voice came in loud and clear.

"Apple Able to Blue Leader. Apple Able is in position and ready to assume the attack."

"Ready?" Lighthorse shouted. "We've been attacking for hours, and we're getting the bejesus beat out of us. Where in the name of God are you?"

Static crackled over the radio. Garnet twisted his dials. A mournful, whining voice singing a hillbilly song blared forth.

" 'I'm up in the sassafras, thinking of you . . .' "

There was no accompaniment. The voice was nasal and high-pitched.

"Stop that immediately!" Lighthorse ordered the singer.

" 'I miss your sweet lips and blue eyes two . . .' "

"Stop that singing I tell you!"

"Apple Able here, Harry," Yancey said cheerfully. "Who's singing?"

"That singing," Lighthorse repeated, but the singing had stopped.

"I don't hear any singing, Harry."

"Somebody's singing a lousy hillbilly song down there."

"Sir, I'm standing right here listening, and I don't hear any singing. It must be the mosquitoes."

"Goddammit, I can tell the difference between a lousy hillbilly song and mosquitoes. Where are you?"

" 'You told me you wouldn't have nothin' to do . . .' "

"Stop that at once!" Lighthorse yelled, his face scarlet. "Whoever's doing that singing I give you a direct order to stop. I'll have you court-martialed."

" 'With no other man and that ain't true.' "

Lighthorse's mouth worked apoplectically. His feet were spread wide apart, and he was weaving slightly. The singing stopped.

"Lieutenant Yancey," Lighthorse said weakly to Garnet.

"I've lost him," Garnet answered, his shoulders hunched as if against a wind.

"Well, you can goddamn well find him or turn in your stripes." Garnet worked his dials frantically. Colonel Bone's voice came over the speaker.

"What's going on down there, Harry?"

"My Cheerful Charley's under attack, Ben. We're regrouping to try to stop this thing."

"Oh really?"

"I was about to inform you, sir, but I was in communication with the company I've been looking for."

"I know it's stuffy of us up here, but we are pretty much interested in what's going on. If you could see your way clear to keep us informed, we'd appreciate it."

"Sir, I'm attempting to stem the Aggressor Enemy, and I think I might have it done, especially when I get this Apple Able on line, but in case I need reinforcements—"

"Don't talk to me about reinforcements. What makes you think I have them to give? I strongly urge you not to request reinforcements. Are you aware you've stalled the impetus of our entire attack?"

"But I've got this company, sir, Apple Able, that hasn't even been in action. It's fresh and ready to go, and I'm attempting to get it on line."

"Please do," Bone said, switching out.

Garnet started calling Yancey again without waiting for orders. At the same moment a regimental staff captain drove a jeep up to the entrance of the tent. With him was a visiting British major. In all his agony Lighthorse had to pull himself together for polite introductions. The regimental captain explained the Englishman wished to observe American operations on a battalion level. Lighthorse quickly assigned Captain Hanks to brief the major. The young Englishman—slim and aristocratic—was smoking a pipe.

"Bit sticky eh?" he asked Hanks.

Lighthorse, his clothes wet from sweat, hurried back to the radio where Garnet was still trying to raise Yancey. The Englishman leaned against a tent pole and crossed one foot over the other. He seemed sleepy, but he was watching.

"Apple Able here," Yancey's voice came in over the radio.

"Let me have that microphone," Lighthorse said, grabbing it from Garnet. "Goddammit, where are you?"

The British major's eyes opened slightly, and he sucked at the pipe. Spit hissed in the stem.

"Harry, you know where I am."

"You idiot, if I knew where you are I wouldn't be asking."

"Well, sir, we're in position on the left flank of Bonnie Baker as per battle plan," Yancey replied.

"Bonnie Baker's wiped out," Lighthorse said. "How could Bonnie Baker be wiped out if you're on the flank?"

"They must be mixed up over there, Harry. We're not even under attack here. Unless you count mosquitoes. The mosquitoes are attacking like P-38s."

"I don't want to hear about mosquitoes. I need you on line to relieve pressure on Cheerful Charley."

" 'I'm up in the sassafras thinking of you. I miss your sweet lips and blue eyes two . . .' "

"I'll have that man shot!"

"Sir?" Yancey asked. "Are you under attack?"

"No I'm not under attack. I'm just trying to determine where in hell you are. Give me your co-ordinates."

"Harry, I'm in position along the river, co-ords down L, right 5. With your permission I'll push to the attack."

"Somebody's crazy around here," Lighthorse said, checking the map board. He remembered the British major and smiled sickly at him. The major smiled back. Lighthorse returned to the radio.

"You stay on tap," he ordered Yancey. "I want to question Bonnie Baker."

"Bonnie Baker's been wiped out," Garnet said.

"Don't tell me what they've been unless you want to lose your stripes. Get them on the horn."

Lighthorse glanced guiltily at the British major. The major, whose eyes were hooded, sucked on his pipe. Squirming, Lighthorse waited by the radio.

"Bonnie Baker here."

"Give me your co-ordinates," Lighthorse demanded.

"We've been wiped out, sir."

" 'You told me you wouldn't have nothin' to do, with no other man and that ain't true.' "

Lighthorse's neck swelled, and his eyes bulged. Like a man suffering extreme pain, he turned to Hanks.

"Find out who's doing that singing and place him under arrest."

"Yes, sir," Hanks answered, putting down his pins and hurrying from the tent. He drove away in a jeep.

"Are you there Bonnie Baker?" Lighthorse asked harshly.

"Sir, we've been wiped out," a new voice answered. It was Harris, the company commander.

"Captain, if anybody else over there tells me once more you've been wiped out, I'll have his hide. You understand?"

"Yes, sir."

"Then give me your goddamned co-ordinates."

Captain Harris gave the co-ordinates. The grid was the same as Yancey's. Lighthorse closed his eyes.

"Describe the terrain," he said.

"Not much terrain, sir. We're strung out along a dirt road by the edge of some swamps. They got mosquitoes around here big as turkeys."

"I don't give a goddamn about mosquitoes! Have you seen or heard anything from Apple Able?"

"No, sir. We sent out runners as you directed, but they were picked up by the Aggressor Enemy. The referee told us to stay put."

"Apple Able should be to your left. Send out more runners."

"Sir, I don't think we're supposed to take part in this after we're dead."

"Do as I tell you!" Lighthorse shouted.

"Yes, sir," Harris said.

193

The British major sucked on his pipe. Lighthorse had forgotten him and turned slowly.

"It really won't make any difference," Lighthorse explained. He laughed feebly. "After all, this is only a maneuver."

"I daresay you're right," the British major answered, but his wooden face indicated he believed all was not cricket.

By then just about everybody from headquarters section was standing in the tent. Even the cooks and the men who ran the motor pool were present. We were all watching Lighthorse and listening to the radio. Evidently the entire regimental battle plan was falling apart, and the keystone of the collapse was Yancey's company.

"This is Ron Regiment," Bone broke in. "My center's taking it hard. Have you found Apple Able?"

"I've got him standing by, Ben," Lighthorse answered, shining with sweat. He was undoubtedly thinking about his career and the fact everybody would remember he was last in his class at West Point. "I hope to get him on line any minute."

"I'm pulling back the center. That's your fault, Harry."

"Ben, I'm doing all I can."

"Don't you call me Ben. From now on I'm Colonel Bone to you. You get your situation fixed, and I mean damn quick."

Bone was gone, and the radio buzzed. Lighthorse was shaky. He ordered Garnet to contact Cheerful Charley.

"Are you still under attack?" Lighthorse asked.

"You can bet your sweet ass we are," the voice of the radioman answered.

"This is your battalion commander."

"Sorry, sir, but people are shooting at us all over the place. Here's Lieutenant Buglioni."

"Lieutenant Buglioni, sir."

"How long can you hold out?" Lighthorse asked.

" 'I'm up in the sassafras thinking of you. I miss your sweet lips and blue eyes two . . .' "

"Stop the singing, damn you!"

"I'm not singing, sir," Lieutenant Buglioni said.

"Somebody's singing out there and don't get smart with me or I'll have your bars. How long can you hold out?"

"I don't know, sir. The Aggressor Enemy is on all sides of us. They have tanks. Referees are snooping around."

"Can you fall back?"

"No, sir. We're pinned against the river."

"Now look here, Buglioni, don't you get wiped out on me. If you get wiped out before I have Apple Able on line the whole regiment's in trouble."

"I'll do my best, sir, but they're coming in."

"Who's coming in?"

"Paratroopers."

"Oh my God, they didn't tell me about paratroopers. Get me Dandy Dog."

Garnet called Dandy Dog.

"Are you under attack by paratroopers?" Lighthorse asked.

"Not yet, sir."

"What's your situation?"

"We have a lot of shooting around here, sir, but frankly nobody seems to know what's going on."

"Can you see the Aggressor Enemy?"

"No, sir, we're in the swamps and the brush is too thick."

"Dig in and hold."

"Can't do that, sir. Holes fill up with water."

"Then just hold goddammit." To Garnet. "Get Ron Regiment."

"You again?" Colonel Bone asked distastefully.

"Sir, they're attacking my Cheerful Charley with paratroopers. They weren't supposed to use paratroopers."

"Perhaps they didn't read the rule book. What do you want?"

"I need help bad, sir. I hate to ask you, but can you send me support?"

"What about Apple Able?"

"I haven't gotten Apple Able on line yet, but it should be moving in a matter of minutes."

"You understand of course the entire center of my line is being battered and I'll have to weaken it to send you support?"

"I wouldn't ask if I didn't believe this is imperative."

"You also understand that if there'd been no gap between your Apple Able and Bonnie Baker none of this would be happening."

"Ben, I mean, sir, it's not my fault. My companies failed to maintain proper liaison and protect their flanks."

"You're the battalion commander and you're responsible. I'll detach a company to send you, but that's it. There's no more money in the bank."

Bone switched off. Drawn and hoarse, Lighthorse asked for Apple Able. The British major was still smoking his pipe.

195

"Sticky, eh?" the major said to WO Page who kept glancing around as if he believed the Aggressor Enemy might be pouncing on him any moment.

"'I'm up in the sassafras thinking of you . . .'"

"Get off the goddamn air!" Lighthorse screamed at the radio.

"Sir?" Yancey asked. "You talking to me?"

"Not you, you idiot. Somebody was singing."

"This is no time for singing," Yancey said.

"Don't tell me that, you fool. I know what it's time for. Now shut up and listen. Have you seen runners from Bonnie Baker?"

"Sir, Bonnie Baker's been wiped out."

"Goddamn you, I know Bonnie Baker's been wiped out. You're damn well responsible for it."

"Sir, I object to that. I am hardly responsible for a company that is out of position and exposes its flanks. Shall I move to my right?"

"No, no. You stay right where you are until we know where that is." To Garnet: "Get me Bonnie Baker."

"Bonnie Baker here and speaking from the dead."

"No wisecracks! This is your battalion commander. What happened to your runners?"

"My runners never come back, sir. I think the Aggressor Enemy keeps picking them up."

"Oh God. Get me Apple Able."

"City dump," a voice said over the radio.

"What's that?" Lighthorse demanded. The British major blinked.

"Ooops, sir," the voice on the radio said.

Static crackled.

"Apple Able!" Lighthorse hollered.

"You're coming in loud and clear, Harry," Yancey said.

"Don't you Harry me, you sonofabitch. From now on I'm Colonel Box to you. I want the man who said city dump arrested."

"City dump, sir?"

"Somebody over there said city dump."

"Sir, I didn't hear it, but I'll institute an investigation immediately."

"No you won't. You get your company into action. Can your runners find Bonnie Baker?"

"Sir, how can they find Bonnie Baker when Bonnie Baker's been wiped out?"

"You sonofabitch, they haven't buried them. They're somewhere on your right. Have you heard shooting?"

"No, sir, but I can move out and find how Cheerful Charley got out of position."

"I don't want you to move yet. I don't trust you to move. Leave your command and report here to me on the double."

"Leave my company, sir?"

"At once."

"Yes, sir," Yancey said.

Lighthorse was so wrung out he sank heavily onto a canvas camp chair. His expression went completely slack. He ran a hand across his face like a man waking from a drunk.

"Get me Cheerful Charley," he told Garnet. Then to Cheerful Charley, "What's your situation down there?"

"There's a bunch of paratroopers caught up in the trees. They're hanging up there like Spanish moss. Boy can they cuss. Some airplanes been dropping paper sacks full of flour."

" 'I'm up in the sassafras thinking of you . . .' "

"I'll have him balled. So help me I'll have him balled. Get me Dandy Dog."

"Dandy Dog, sir."

"What's your situation, Dandy Dog?"

"Some airplanes just flew over and dropped flour."

"You have to hold on down there. I've got relief coming. If you can hold on another hour, we'll assume the attack."

"Yes, sir, but they sure are dropping flour. All the men are sneezing." The speaker sneezed.

A jeep drove up fast to the tent entrance. It was the captain of the relief company sent by regiment. The captain looked annoyed. He and Lighthorse went over the map. Lighthorse was sending the company in where Bonnie Baker had been wiped out. The captain left.

We were all waiting for Yancey. We stood about with solemn faces, but we relished his troubles. To our minds it was retribution. I most of all wanted him to suffer.

"He'll get it this time," I said.

"Don't be too sure," the Professor answered.

Yancey didn't come. Ten, twenty, thirty minutes passed and still he didn't appear. Lighthorse paced from the map board to the tent entrance. We listened to reports over the radio as the relief company got into position. From other parts of the regiment Garnet picked up chatter of units falling back. WO Page manned the pins on the map. To Lighthorse the tactical situation was beginning to resemble a rout.

"This is Russ Referee calling Alert Airedale."

"Alert Airedale here, sir," Garnet answered. Lighthorse stopped pacing, his eyes afraid.

"Inform your commander his Cheerful Charley's just been wiped out."

"Oh Jesus," Lighthorse said. "Get Ron Regiment."

"City dump."

"I'll have you balled too," Lighthorse yelled at the radio.

"What's that?" Colonel Bone asked.

"Somebody around here keeps saying city dump."

"I don't have time for lousy jokes."

"I know, sir, but I quite clearly heard somebody say city dump."

"What do you want?"

"Sir," Lighthorse said, swallowing, "Cheerful Charley's been wiped out."

"Isn't that goddamn delightful?"

"But Dandy Dog's in there pitching, sir, and the relief company is coming on line. I'm still hopeful about getting Apple Able into action. Apple Able could turn the tide."

Colonel Bone sneezed.

"This goddamn flour," he said. "You'd think with a food shortage they'd have better use for flour."

"Sir?"

"They're dropping flour all over the place and paratroopers are hanging in the trees like Spanish moss. I'm evacuating Regimental Command. You have to hold over there. No excuses. You hold."

Bone was gone. Lighthorse's shoulders slumped. In just a few hours he seemed to have grown old. He was probably envisioning those full-colonel eagles flapping away from him on their own wings.

"Where is Yancey?" he asked despairingly, not as if questioning us but the universe.

" 'I'm up in the sassafras, thinking of you. I miss your sweet lips and titties two. You told me—' "

There was a squawk as if somebody had grabbed the singer around the neck and was choking him.

"Find me Lieutenant Yancey," Lighthorse snarled at WO Page.

WO Page ran to the motor pool for a jeep. Dust rose up behind him as he sped from the area. Lighthorse glanced at the British major. The major was careful to seem occupied. The radio spoke.

"Alert Airedale, this is Russ Referee. Your Dandy Dog has been enveloped and wiped out."

"No!" Lighthorse protested.

"I wouldn't argue if I were you. I have you ranked."

"Get me the relief company," Lighthorse ordered. He was trembling.

"Roscoe Relief."

"Are you holding, Roscoe Relief?"

"I guess so, sir. They're dropping flour, and paratroopers are hanging up in the trees like—"

"Never mind what they're hanging like. You've got to hold. The fate of the entire regiment depends on your not giving up ground."

"We'll do our best, sir."

"Get me Ron Regiment," Lighthorse said, wiping off sweat.

"Me, sir?" the voice from Roscoe Relief asked.

"No not you. I have a radioman here."

"I figured you did, sir."

"Are you being smart?"

"City dump."

"Oh you dirty bastard," Lighthorse said, near tears.

"Now look here goddammit," Bone exclaimed indignantly.

"Not you, sir. It's that city dump again."

"I'm not interested in your sanitation problems. I'm trying to get my ass out of a sling."

"Sir, I find it optimistic that Roscoe Relief is holding in spite of heavy assaults by planes and paratroopers." Lighthorse paused before he spoke the rest. "But I'm afraid I have to report my Dandy Dog's gone."

"I don't want to hear any more of that. I've got enough troubles. You get that Apple Able on the goddamn line now."

Bone switched off. Lighthorse rushed out of the tent to look down the road for Yancey. He came back inside and ordered Garnet to call Apple Able. A Lieutenant Pegram answered.

"Where is he?" Lighthorse asked, speaking of Yancey.

"He left to report to you, sir."

"Well, he hasn't reported."

"Well, he told me he was going to report."

"Well, I don't give a goddamn what he told you, he hasn't reported. I want to know what's going on down there."

"Nothing's going on, sir. We're just waiting around and getting mosquito bites."

"Lieutenant, can you get that company into this fight?"

"Well, sir, I don't know exactly where the fight is."

"You have maps, don't you?"

"Sir, Lieutenant Yancey has the maps."

Lighthorse opened his mouth, closed it, and sat down on his canvas stool. He bent over and put his face in his hands. The British major looked embarrassed and went for a stroll.

Lighthorse raised his head slowly. He heard a jeep—faint at first, but coming fast. Hope worked into his face. He ran outside, believing it was Yancey and that Apple Able might yet salvage something.

Yancey, however, wasn't in the jeep. Instead it was Captain Hanks who'd been sent out to find the person singing "I'm Up in the Sassafras." The singer was Lou's Texas boy friend Roy. It was difficult to accept the fact that such a raw-boned stud could have the whiny voice we'd heard over the radio. He looked as if buckskins and a coonskin cap would have suited him better than Army fatigues.

"So you're the bastard who's been screwing up my radio?" Lighthorse yelled at him.

"I wasn't on no radio," Roy answered, sullen but not afraid of Lighthorse, whom he towered over by a foot.

"Don't alibi me. I heard you, and I'm having you court-martialed."

"It wasn't his fault," Hanks said. "He wasn't handling the radio. Somebody left the key open. This man just happened to be close."

"He was singing, wasn't he? I'd like to know what the hell there is to sing about. He probably said city dump."

"Sir?" Hanks asked, confused.

"Say city dump," Lighthorse commanded Roy.

"What?" Roy asked, squinting at Lighthorse.

"Don't you what me. Didn't they teach you how to address an officer? You're the bastard all right, and by God you're going to pay. You're under arrest. Take care of him, Hanks."

There was some question of how and where to put a man under arrest. Hanks decided to pass the responsibility on to others by driving Roy to regiment. They got in the jeep. Roy lighted a cigarette. He appeared unconcerned as Hanks carried him away.

We heard another jeep. Again Lighthorse rushed from the tent. This time it was Yancey. We could tell from a long distance because the siren was wailing and the red light flashing. Yancey wore goggles and was crouched behind the wheel. The jeep skidded to a stop. Lighthorse pulled him out of the driver's seat.

"You sonofabitch, where the hell have you been?"

"Got on the wrong road, sir. Asked directions from MPs, but they wouldn't tell me anything. Claimed they'd been wiped out."

"Do you realize you're making me the laughingstock of this whole goddamn command? Where's your company?"

"My company's right where I left it, sir. We're in position along the river as indicated on my map. My honest opinion is that Bonnie Baker, Cheerful Charley, and Dandy Dog are off line."

"You mean this whole bitch of a battalion is off line while you're on? Is that what you're saying?"

"Well, sir, I know we're where the map indicates."

"Show me," Lighthorse said and climbed into the jeep. Yancey pulled down his goggles, turned on the red-light siren, and they drove off fast.

The rest of us went back into the tent to listen to the radio. Garnet spun his dials and picked up reports. The regiment was falling to pieces. The end of our line had been flanked, and we heard Colonel Bone's angry voice as he desperately attempted to repair the damage by shifting a constantly diminishing force of men. The referees were having a field day.

"Russ Referee reporting your Artful Arty's been wiped out."

"Your Charley Chan's been enveloped."

"Your Dipsy Doodle's out of action."

It began to get funny to us. As each report came in, men laughed. Carter was sullen. He believed levity showed disloyalty and disrespect for the golden eagle. I was happy at thoughts of what was going to happen to Yancey.

An airplane flew over. We ran out to look up at it. It was a silver P-47 which had flour bags under its wings. Four of the bags arched down and exploded around us. We dived to the ground and lay flat until the plane was gone. Flour geysered around us. We were all powdered white and sneezing.

A motor pool mechanic named Ackers discovered a bag that had not completely busted. He threw a handful of flour at his dispatcher. The dispatcher scooped up flour and on throwing it back at Ackers hit Wilson by mistake. Wilson returned fire on the dispatcher and on the Professor who happened to be walking by. The Professor threw flour into the air. Everybody, including Carter and I, got into it. Laughing and hollering, we tossed flour as if it were snow.

The British major appeared. His uniform was immaculate. Perhaps American flour didn't dare settle on a representative of the Empire. He eyed us with lordly disdain. Sheepishly we stopped, dusted ourselves off, and filed into the tent.

"Alert Airedale, this is Russ Referee," the radio said. "Your headquarters has been wiped out."

"That's us," Wilson whispered.

"I'm dead, but I can inform you from experience it's not so bad," Timberlake said, keeping his voice low because of the British major.

"I'd say death is definitely overrated," Beanpost agreed.

"We can tell our children we were put out of action by a bag of Pillsbury's best," Carter remarked bitterly.

The British major stood by Garnet at the radio. Garnet twisted his dials. Yancey's voice squawked in clearly. He wasn't calling us but Lieutenant Pegram back at Apple Able. We glanced at one another.

"By God he's lost again," Wilson whispered.

"That means the colonel's lost too," Beanpost said.

"Lieutenant Pegram, come in for Apple Able," Yancey pleaded, his voice forlorn. There was no reply. "Come in Apple Able and Lieutenant Pegram."

"Retribution," I said.

"Not yet," the Professor answered. "Never underestimate a genius."

Garnet lost contact with Yancey. It was late afternoon, and we remembered we hadn't eaten. We went to the mess tent for hot rations. We carried our mess kits back to the radio so we wouldn't miss anything. Colonel Bone put in a call for Lighthorse.

"He ain't here, Colonel," Garnet said.

"Well, where the hell is he?"

"He's out trying to find Apple Able."

"Let me speak to the officer in charge."

Garnet looked trapped. With Lighthorse, Captain Hanks, and WO Page gone, there was no officer in charge. He glanced to the British major and thrust the microphone at him. The major accepted it reluctantly.

"Walton-Walton here, sir."

"Is this another goddamn joke?"

"Quite the contrary. Bit sticky, eh?"

"You're really British?"

"Quite."

"Well, I'll be damned."

"Rather."

"Do you happen to know where my battalion commander is?"

"Only generally. Perhaps he can be reached by wireless."

"By wireless. Quite."

We heard Bone's radioman trying to locate Lighthorse. The call was repeated without interruption for twenty minutes, but instead of an answer the only voices which came in were those of referees announcing the names of units that had been wiped out. Then as Ron Regiment continued to seek Alert Airedale Battalion Commander, we heard Lighthorse whisper clearly, "Don't speak to them for God's sake."

We waited until late that night, but Lighthorse never came back. Nor did we know what had happened to Apple Able. We slept in headquarters tent, waking occasionally to listen to reports from the radio. When the sun rose, we had breakfast and returned to the radio. Ron Regiment was still attempting to locate Alert Airedale Battalion Commander. None of our officers had come back. We heard the plaintive voice of Lieutenant Pegram with Apple Able.

"How come we're being left out here?" he asked. "We're hungry."

"They're looking for you," Garnet explained. He'd been up all night and was red-eyed.

"Well, they better hurry. We're being eaten alive by mosquitoes. There's not going to be anything left but the holes in us."

Lighthorse was apparently monitoring the conversation. His voice cut in.

"We must be close to you now, Pegram," Lighthorse said. "I'm going to fire my pistol. You listen for the sound. Perhaps we can take a bearing on each other."

Over the radio we heard the pistol.

"Well?" Lighthorse asked. "Did you hear anything?"

"No, sir," Pegram answered. "All we can hear out here are mosquitoes and bull alligators."

Wilson, Beanpost, and Timberlake were laughing. The British major had gone to Hanks' tent to shave. He came back looking fresh and smelling of lotion. He stopped the laughter with one sweep of his eyes.

"Where is he?" Colonel Bone demanded over the radio, speaking of Lighthorse.

"He should be returning shortly," the British major answered. "Have you been assigned to the American Army, Walton-Walton?"

"Not officially, sir."

"Then what the hell are you doing at Alert Airedale?"

"I suppose you could say I'm part of the Allied effort."

203

"All right, see if you can ally my lost battalion commander on the radio."

"On the wireless yes."

"You tell the dirty sonofabitch to report to me on the double."

Walton-Walton nodded to Garnet who started calling Lighthorse. Lighthorse had undoubtedly been able to hear Bone, for he came in over another frequency immediately.

"Shut up that yapping, Garnet. Tell him you can't find me."

"Sir, I know my outfit's around here somewhere," we heard Yancey say in the background.

"Do you now?" Lighthorse asked bitterly. "You mean as a commander you're assuring me your company hasn't disappeared from the face of the earth?"

"City dump."

"Oh God!" Lighthorse said, and the radio went silent.

We waited throughout the morning. By then the maneuver had almost ended, and not only the golden eagle but also the division it was supposed to assist had been mauled. Trying to total up losses was no longer even worth-while.

A line of jeeps came roaring down the road. Colonel Bone was driving the first one, and his aides followed. The colonel's West Point bearing was smashed. He hadn't shaved, and one pants' leg had pulled loose from a boot. He strode into headquarters tent breathing wrath. By contrast Major Walton-Walton could have been at a tea party he was so calm and contained.

"Is that bastard hiding around here?" Bone yelled, speaking of Lighthorse.

Before Walton-Walton could reply, we heard airplanes. Colonel Bone hurried out of the tent to stare up. Bags of flour were curving down. He dived back into the tent. White geysers were exploding around the area. More planes came over, this time dropping paratroopers. They came down very quickly, and some of them got tangled in cypress trees.

Bone let out a bleat of alarm, jumped up, and ran for his jeep. He was too late. Paratroopers were already jogging through the area and setting up roadblocks. Referees holding pieces of chalk came from the woods. One of them approached Bone and scratched a large, inglorious X on his helmet to signify he was dead. Bone looked as if he were about to cry.

"You've been wiped out," the referee told him and moved on.

Full of shame, Bone returned to the tent just as the radio came to life. We heard Lighthorse's voice as he continued his search for Apple Able. Bone snatched the microphone from the hand of Major Walton-Walton, whose arch expression indicated he considered such an action bad form indeed.

"Where are you, you dirty bastard?" Bone demanded of Lighthorse.

There was no answer.

"You better talk to me," Bone threatened. "I'll court-martial you if you don't talk to me."

"Sir, I'm inspecting my troops," Lighthorse answered.

"You don't have any troops. They're all dead. I'm dead too. You're in big trouble, Colonel. You have plenty to account for. Now you report to my headquarters on the double."

"What about my Apple Able?"

"The hell with your Apple Able."

With that Bone left the tent and went to his jeep. The seat was covered with flour, which he had to sweep out before he could sit down. He drove up the road past paratroopers. He was followed by his aides in other jeeps—all colored white from flour. They looked like ghosts.

At midafternoon Lighthorse reached us. He was in bad shape. He was unshaved, had been bitten by chiggers and mosquitoes, and had stood on the carpet for over an hour in front of a raging Colonel Bone.

Yancey, who sat in the back of the jeep, looked even worse. His puffy face was dirty, his eyes were watering, and his head hung low. Apple Able had not been found, and Lighthorse was chewing on him with profane viciousness. "You dirty, lousy sonofabitch. You stinking bastard." Without raising his head, Yancey went directly to Hanks' tent where he closed the flap.

Major Walton-Walton picked that moment to leave. He acted as if he had been paying a call and shook Lighthorse's hand formally. Lighthorse hardly saw him. He, Lighthorse, was still cussing Yancey.

"Toodleoo," Walton-Walton said and walked off sucking on his pipe.

Lighthorse requested division artillery to send out spotter planes to locate Apple Able. As he waited, he chewed on Yancey. Hanks' tent trembled with the violence of it. "You ignorant whore!" we heard Lighthorse yell.

"Alert Airedale Battalion," Russ Referee called over the radio.

"We can't seem to find your Apple Able. Are you holding it in reserve?"

"Turn that goddamn thing off!" Lighthorse screamed at Garnet.

"City dump," a voice on the radio said.

25

More than artillery spotting planes were required to find Apple Able. The region was so thick with moss-covered cypresses that large areas of the ground were entirely invisible from the air. What was necessary was a search by men on foot, and for that the entire regiment—filthy, hungry, worn-out—had to make a sweep. By then Yancey had been put under arrest.

The sweep took another day. The regiment lined up by companies and moved through the swamps. At times men were up to their necks in black water. They got caught in quicksand, and moccasins dropped from trees. All the while mosquitoes were attacking. A pfc stepped on a dozing alligator and howled in terror.

With Colonel Bone directing the search, Apple Able was found just at dusk. The company was seven miles from the position it should have taken. At no time had it apparently even been near the action. The dazed, hollow-eyed men were squatting with their feet in the water. Their faces were so misshapen by insect bites they looked like a different race. They had not eaten for thirty-six hours. A corporal had been snake bit in the rump.

Even after Apple Able was found, men were still missing—Captain Hanks, WO Page, and runners who'd been sent out from Cheerful Charley. The runners were picked up on a national highway some twenty miles distant. Hanks had been captured by the Aggressor Enemy. Fastidious little WO Page had driven his jeep into the river and become lost in the swamps. He had been found by a band of local Indians dressed for the tourist trade and had believed they were going to scalp him. He was carried back to camp so sick with fright he was immediately driven to the post hospital NP ward for observation.

Of course the story of the lost company and the regiment's defeat was all over camp. Our shoulder patches, which Carter was so proud of, were now a means of identifying us to other units for ridicule. Wherever we went on the post, soldiers pointed at us and hooted. Some of the men like Carter were too mortified to leave the regimental area.

The final report from the referees was that with the exception of one company—Apple Able which had never gotten into battle—the entire regiment had been wiped out or captured. The infantry division had been badly crippled. The Aggressor Enemy, though composed of lesser numbers, had won such a lopsided victory its members were given a commendation by the Corps general. Aggressor Enemy had followed a classic tactic used by Stonewall Jackson at Chancellorsville of splitting its forces and rolling up the flanks.

The purge was terrible. Proud Colonel Bone had to suffer intense chewing from division, and when he was finally released he naturally turned on those under him. Lighthorse received the greatest abuse. For a week he dutifully reported to regimental headquarters where he stood on the carpet for wild sessions of official chewing. Small to begin with, he appeared to shrink up even more after each session with Bone. Lighthorse's mustache drooped. He carried himself with the air of a man who believed he was soon to die.

All the regimental officers were frightened. The 606th was supposed to be a crack outfit, but for the second time in war games it had fouled up badly. The officers realized the purge would reach out for them. They moved about cautiously and wore long faces, sad for the promotions they had been hoping for but would no longer receive.

The chewing was continuous and violent. A person could walk through headquarters at any time of day and hear a trio or quartet of recriminations. It was not uncommon to see men being chewed from all sides. The unit was going through a convulsion of self-inflicted pain which was something like a snake swallowing its own tail.

All officers were angry toward their equals and underlings. They growled at each other, their juniors, and the enlisted men. Lighthorse was preferring charges against Lou's Texan for the singing. She interpreted that as a personal insult and strode about stiff-legged, her hips wagging aggressively. Her typewriter chattered with the rapidity of a machine gun. The other WACs displayed their sympathy for her by being generally outraged.

Naturally, Yancey was in the deepest soup. He was universally blamed and hated. The other officers wished him cut down because of the manner in which he'd previously sucked up to Lighthorse. Yancey's own men hoped he was permanently removed from com-

207

mand of his company for the chicken way he'd treated them. I myself wanted him busted and kicked out of camp. My desire was not altogether revenge. Once he was gone, Martha could come.

Yancey was catching hell chiefly from two directions. In the mornings Colonel Bone worked him over at regimental headquarters, and during the afternoons Lighthorse continued the flaying at battalion. In our cubicle we were able to hear the louder outbursts.

"You imbecile," Lighthorse shouted at Yancey. "You stupid crapper. Only an idiot could lose an entire company. Only a fool could have caused a campaign planned with infinite care to fall to pieces. If we were on line, I'd have you shot. If I had it in my power now, I'd have you shot anyway. How did I ever get mixed up with you? I've been in the Army twenty-seven years and seen stupid officers, but you win the grand prize. You're a disgrace to your outfit. You've made it a laughingstock and put in serious doubt its combat efficiency. You've damned near ruined us, goddamn you."

The news that a company had been lost during maneuvers got out of camp and reached the ears of reporters for a wire service. The reporters drove down from Atlanta to ask questions. Colonel Bone called all regimental officers together and swore them to secrecy. Lighthorse himself had to face the reporters at a press conference.

"But what about the lost company?" a reporter insisted.

"Lost company?" Lighthorse answered and laughed. "Do you honestly believe that I or any of my officers could lose an entire company of over a hundred and fifty men?"

The reporters looked as if they could indeed believe it and left acting as if they had been tricked. A few of them attempted to get information from enlisted men, but enlisted men were afraid to open their mouths. We had been warned not to talk. As long as reporters were still in camp, officers patrolled the streets.

I waited anxiously to learn what was going to happen to Yancey. I had already written Martha that there was a good chance he would soon be leaving Georgia. I hung around the filing cabinets near Lighthorse's office in the hope of hearing something and pestered Lou for information.

The wave of terror stayed on for Yancey. When it wasn't Colonel Bone or Lighthorse chewing on him, other regimental officers took their turn. Everybody down to the senior lieutenants had a whack at him. Though confined to quarters, he was allowed out to eat. He sat by himself at one end of a long table where he looked exposed and miserable. Officers passing curved around him as if he had some terrible contagious disease. He ate with a bowed head.

From Lou we learned Colonel Bone and Lighthorse were going through with a court-martial. They were holding daily meetings to discuss the matter. Usually there was a major from the Judge Advocate's office sitting in to advise them. They were studying the ARs in an attempt to put down all the charges against Yancey they could find. Knowing they were so determined made me feel good. I found myself whistling around the office.

"Don't be so sure," the Professor told Carter when Carter said Yancey might be sent to prison at Leavenworth.

"He can't get out of this one," Carter answered, expressing my feeling.

"He's a genius," the Professor maintained. "They do things us ordinary mortals can't."

"He's no genius," Wilson said. "He's a screwup like the rest of us."

"I'll have to see him down before I believe that."

"He's down now," Timberlake argued.

"He's temporarily down," the Professor said.

For the most part, Yancey remained alone in his hut. When he had to come out, he acted furtive. Where previously he had strutted about arrogantly, he now slunk. He moved like a man fearful of being seized. He was seen mostly after dark and stuck to the shadows along streets.

Lou was keeping us informed on decisions made at regimental headquarters. She found out from WAC talk in her barracks. Colonel Bone and Lighthorse were pushing for the limit, though the representatives from the Judge Advocate's office were advising them to modify charges somewhat. The less severe the charges, the more easily they could be proved. Bone and Lighthorse prevailed, however, and started the machinery for a special court-martial—the most severe of all. They accused Yancey of destroying government property and of gross disregard for the safety of his men.

"What you think now?" Wilson asked the Professor.

"I think the verdict's not in," the Professor answered.

I believed the court-martial board would roll right over Yancey. Like a cornered animal, however, he had reserves of strength. When officially notified of the charges against him, he informed the Judge Advocate's office that he had hired a lawyer to defend himself.

The lawyer wasn't an officer of the post. Rather he turned out to be a full colonel from Washington who'd done work for Yancey before the war. He came to camp by plane—a smooth, portly man who dropped the names of generals and politicians as if they were old friends. He passed out expensive cigars and good Scotch. When he spoke at all of the case, he called it "the little trouble my friend Marvin Yancey's in."

The fact Yancey had access to such counsel caused Bone and Lighthorse concern. Being professional soldiers, they automatically respected rank and influence. Furthermore, they were uncertain as to just how high the lawyer's connections went. He might be able to do them harm. They had to weigh possibilities. Lou reported that Bone and Lighthorse huddled together like old women and spoke in whispers.

"He's got them on the run already," the Professor said smugly. "This is going to be a pushover."

"Don't bet all your money on it," Lou answered. "If there's any way to get him without exposing themselves, they'll do it."

"They're out of their class," the Professor told her.

The second move Yancey made—and I had been waiting for it— was to bring out his medals. He pinned the ribbons over the pocket of his blouse, and officers who normally would have jumped him on sight were put on the defensive. They couldn't very well keep chewing the tail of a hero. The same officers hurried to battalion headquarters to check Yancey's service record. Upon leaving, they looked both angry and baffled.

I wanted to talk. I needed to tell everybody what Yancey really was, but to do so would necessarily expose my relationship to Martha. I had to clamp my teeth as he maneuvered under the protective umbrella of medals he'd never deserved to win.

Yancey now had not only a first-class lawyer with connections, but also a modicum of leverage under the court-martial board because of his past record. The Army went out of its way not to punish men it had rewarded. There could be lots of bad publicity if a former hero were given severe treatment. Lawyers from the Judge Advocate's office visited Bone and Lighthorse, and the two of them began to look grave.

Yancey was working from within as well. He still had the ear of Lighthorse's wife. He ordered her more seaweed and tropical fish. She in turn sent him a pan of beaten biscuits, and each night as soon as Lighthorse reached his house she worked on him. According to the colonel's orderly, she refused to believe a nice man like Yancey could be entirely at fault for what happened during the field problem, and she wasn't just going to stand by and allow him to be pilloried without speaking her piece.

Next Yancey's lawyer let it be known that he intended to bring countercharges against Lieutenant Pegram who, the lawyer claimed, was really responsible for Apple Able's being out of position. It had been Pegram's duty to maintain proper liaison with Bonnie Baker and notify his company commander if a gap existed.

Lieutenant Pegram was a pleasant, friendly young man of twenty-two. He had been a track star at the University of Alabama. He was the officer the men of Apple Able hoped would become their company commander. He answered the charges against him by saying that not only had he informed Yancey of the gap, but had also attempted to explain to Yancey the company was out of position. He had been ignored. As legal representative he was assigned a captain of artillery who was not even a lawyer.

"It's reasonable," the Professor said, nodding like an owl. "Yancey understands the system has to be fed, so he's feeding it Pegram."

"Pegram can defend himself, can't he?" Beanpost asked.

"Doubtful. He doesn't have a big-city lawyer working for him, and technically he was liaison man."

"How could he keep liaison when the company was seven miles out of position to begin with?" Wilson wanted to know.

"You're splitting hairs. How far one is out of position has nothing to do with the responsibility for liaison."

Daily we saw Yancey's lawyer driving around the post. He had been assigned a limousine and a chauffeur. The colonel was an imposing figure with a paunch and the general mien of a person used to being treated with deference. He spent a great deal of time in consultation with Bone and Lighthorse.

"I can't hear everything they say," Lou told us. "They keep the door closed. What I get is that the lawyer is trying to talk Bone and Lighthorse out of a court-martial. He's arguing it won't help anybody. He says that because Yancey has medals, the affair will look bad in the newspapers. The reporters might even attack the Army for ingratitude. Such a situation would be bad for either Bone or Lighthorse. He tells them it's the sort of contest in which nobody can win."

"That's putting the pressure on," the Professor mused. "Actually, it's a polite threat. They'll fold."

"I don't know," Lou said. "Lighthorse is still furious. It won't be easy to convince him."

I was growing uneasy at the thought there was even a possibility that Yancey might get out of the mess he was in. I both wanted my revenge and longed for Martha. As soon as Yancey was gone I intended to hurry to town and engage the hotel room.

On Tuesday morning Lou came into the cubicle to tell us that in spite of the pressure from the lawyer, Bone and Lighthorse had decided to continue with court-martial proceedings against Yancey.

"It was Bone who wouldn't let go," Lou explained. "Lighthorse wavered."

"Colonel Bone is making a mistake," the Professor said.

"How?" I snapped, irritated by his omniscient attitude.

"I have faith in Yancey's strength of purpose. He will overcome."

"He'll be busted out of camp by the end of the month."

"Do you believe that strongly?" the Professor asked, adjusting his glasses to peer at me. The others were watching.

"I do."

"Enough to give me some odds? I mean if you're convinced, you can afford to give me odds."

"I'll give whatever odds you like," I answered, knowing I was being foolish but desiring Yancey's conviction so badly I couldn't admit to the slightest chance of being wrong.

"I don't wish to be greedy. Eight to five will be satisfactory. I'll put up a ten spot. It'll cost you sixteen to play."

"Done."

"I hate to take money from a colleague," the Professor apologized. "It's just that this is going to be a pushover for Lieutenant Brown."

The court-martial papers were not withdrawn. Furthermore the brigadier general from division had agreed to sit on the board as presiding officer. After the battering his outfit had taken in maneuvers, the general was not sympathetic toward Yancey. The general's star outweighed the eagle of the lawyer colonel Yancey had brought from Washington.

Yancey wasn't finished. He still had many connections in northern Virginia where his business was. Probably he had made large contributions to political campaigns in the area. Colonel Bone received a special-delivery letter announcing that the congressman from Yancey's district was flying south for an inspection of the regiment. He wished to speak with all men from his constituency.

The letter, written on official stationery, was impressive. It had been signed by the congressman and countersigned by an undersecretary of war. In the last paragraph, according to Lou, the congressman stated he particularly wanted to meet with his old and esteemed friend Lieutenant Marvin Yancey who was such a patriotic American.

The congressman was a member of an important committee on military appropriations. Not only was it possible for him to control strings on Army requests for money, but he was also in a position to block promotions. Thus Bone and Lighthorse's move with the brigadier general had been more than effectively neutralized. Not even a general was going to buck an influential congressman.

Reluctantly Bone decided to put the court-martial in abeyance until after the congressman's visit. In addition while the congressman was on the post, something had to be done about Yancey. At the very least he must be notified. Lighthorse summoned him to battalion headquarters and informed him the congressman was coming.

"So Old Bob's paying us a call," Yancey said. "It'll be good to see him again."

"Old Bob?" Lighthorse asked, his distaste held in check by the intimation of familiarity. Though he'd been in government service all his life, he knew no congressmen he could call by their first names.

"Sure, Old Bob. That's what all his friends call him. He used to come by my place to hunt birds."

"Yes," Lighthorse said glumly. "Well, keep yourself available. He might ask for you."

"I'll be darned disappointed if he doesn't," Yancey answered, and as he left headquarters that afternoon his face was no longer that of a cornered man. Rather it was once again sly.

"You want to pay me your money now?" the Professor asked.

"But a man can't con the whole Army," I protested.

"A genius can do anything in his field. Yancey is a great artist at the manipulation of men."

Old Bob arrived on an Army bomber. A band and an honor guard was lined up to greet him. Yancey, however, wasn't present. The brigadier general, Bone, and Lighthorse were going to try to get away with not producing him.

Old Bob himself was beaming and jolly. He waved his hat from the door of the bomber and shook hands with everybody he could reach. The brigadier and Bone immediately carried him on a tour of the post in an open car. Soldiers along the street saluted.

When the general and Bone were beginning to believe they

had succeeded in keeping Yancey under wraps, the congressman turned and asked to see him. Scowling, Bone sent his own runner to 1st Battalion where Yancey waited alone in his hut. He was driven back in a jeep. Yancey climbed out, saluted, and then he and Old Bob put their arms around each other. The brigadier and Bone looked gloomy.

There was a full-dress review. The day was hot, and the enlisted men cursed. The few from the congressman's district vowed they would never vote for any sonofabitch who made them march for his pleasure. During the review Yancey stood right up on the platform with the congressman, the brigadier, and Bone. Yancey saluted smartly each time a unit passed, acting as if he were commander of the Army.

Later the press came in, and Old Bob had a special Army photographer assigned to him whose job it was to send glossy prints back to local newspapers showing the congressman with sons of constituents. In one shot he posed with the brigadier, Bone, and Yancey. By that time the brigadier had begun chatting with Yancey. It seemed he too was an old bird hunter, and they were discussing dogs.

They finished off the day by going to the officers' club for drinks and dinner. All officers and their wives were ordered to be present. A small orchestra had been hired, we learned later, by Yancey. He danced not only with Lighthorse's wife, but also Bone's and the general's. According to Wilson, who was tending bar, Yancey discovered the brigadier's wife was interested in roses and promised to send her some unusual varieties that a friend of his in Washington, a senator, grew.

By then both Lighthorse and Bone acted like men dazed. After all, each had made his career in the Army and had to live by its rules. Those rules told them they had been outflanked and outgunned. They looked befuddled, as if they still weren't sure just what it was that had rolled over them.

The congressman spent two hours the next morning holding conferences with what he called "the boys from my district." Because of the dress parade, none wanted to see him, but they were ordered to. During the conferences Yancey stood at the congressman's side and performed the introductions.

After lunch Old Bob was ready to leave on his bomber. Yancey rode with him to the airstrip. The congressman shook hands with Bone and the brigadier. He saved his last and warmest good-by for

Yancey. As the plane took off, Yancey waved. The same night he was invited to eat dinner with the brigadier and his wife.

The court-martial charges were never officially dropped. They were just allowed to wither. To the disgust of his men, Yancey quietly assumed command of his company. His first act was to order an intensive review of map reading—as if the fact of his company's being seven miles out of position had been the fault of his subordinates rather than himself.

Furthermore he again began calling on Lighthorse. At first Yancey was extremely cautious about it. He poked his head into battalion headquarters as if afraid of being shot at and was ready to duck out quickly. Lighthorse, however, was now fearful of rebuffing him. Sensing it, Yancey grew bolder. Dirty jokes were reinstituted, and Lighthorse's shrill, unmanly laughter rose with a note of sycophancy because Yancey, having become chummy with the brigadier and his wife, was in a position to influence Lighthorse's promotion to full colonel. Lighthorse, moving by the sure instinct of the career Army man, was actually browning Yancey.

"They're calling each other by first names again," Lou told us. She was full of anger. Her Texan had undergone two weeks' company punishment for the radio incident. She'd had to endure without him.

"If at first you don't succeed, brown, brown, brown again," Carter said, his warrior's soul repelled.

I counted out the money I owed the Professor, laying the bills on his desk.

"Don't feel bad about it," he advised me. "Our Lieutenant Brown's an indestructible force. Instead of resenting him, you should admire him like any of nature's miraculous phenomena."

The only hope I had left was that Yancey might bungle Apple Able on the next maneuvers. He didn't. He'd evidently studied up on his own map reading, as well as grasped the advantages of relying on his fellow officers. Apple Able punched a hole into a weak sector of the Aggressor Enemy's line and swept up an artillery battery. The move made regiment look pretty good. Colonel Bone smiled upon Yancey.

"A beautiful thrust," Bone told him. "The Aggressor Enemy was in a panic. You should have heard them on the radio."

"Thank you, sir," Yancey answered, acting modest. "I don't really deserve much of the credit. It's one of Harry's favorite tactics, and he taught me everything I know about it."

"I shouldn't be surprised if you don't get a little present out of this," Lighthorse Harry said after Bone was gone. He beamed on Yancey like a son.

The little present came in late spring. Yancey, who only a short time before had been in disgrace and danger of losing his commission, was made captain. Pegram, the young lieutenant Yancey had blamed for failure to maintain liaison with Bonnie Baker during the fiasco, was transferred out to a truck battalion in Oklahoma.

26

That spring I was living to get to Virginia. Because the golden eagle had done well on the last maneuvers, talk was going around of our shipping overseas. That talk made me very nervous. The thought that it might be years before I again saw Martha caused me to sweat.

Yancey and I had nothing to do with each other. When he entered battalion headquarters, he wouldn't look my way. If I passed him on the street, he had to return my mocking salutes, but his eyes never focused on me. Sometimes we met in corridors. We moved around one another without speaking.

On a Thursday a directive outlining furlough procedures came in from regiment. The furloughs were to be allotted by a rotation basis starting the next Saturday. The news rolled through the outfit like a comber, and men who'd been resigned to never seeing home had to learn to smile all over again. Even Black Hatfield acted as if he might enjoy getting back to his West Virginia coal camp. Lou was primping. Her boy friend Roy was planning to take her to Texas to meet his parents.

I had complications. I could not put my own name down for furlough until I knew for sure when Yancey was taking his leave. He on the other hand was manipulating to be gone at the same time as the brigadier and Bone. I watched the officers' roster. Yancey finally chose the third week in May. I then put myself down for seven days later and wrote Martha to be ready to meet me in Richmond.

Waiting was painful. Because so many men were gone, there was even less to do in battalion headquarters than usual. The heat of the building made me drowsy and each day seemingly endless. Outside the sweet, languid spring was giving way to a blazing summer.

I found myself indulging in sexual fantasies. I became so excited thinking of Martha that I had to walk around the area or hurry to the barracks for a shower.

All the week Yancey was on his leave I was particularly upset. The knowledge that he was with Martha made me twist and roll in my bed. I knew she wouldn't allow him to touch her, but I didn't want him even near her.

I'd made up my mind Martha and I would have to get our future straightened out. There was no question of what had to be done. She would divorce Yancey and marry me.

Yancey came back from his leave acting pleased and happy. He wasn't wearing his ribbons. Lou reported he had invited the brigadier and Colonel Bone to his farm for a quail shoot. They had returned to camp with a bushel basket full of birds. The brigadier and Bone had the birds prepared in the officers' club and gave a dinner for ranks of field grade and above. Yancey was toasted with champagne.

On the Saturday my furlough began, I rode a taxi into town. From regiment I had gotten a priority to fly. On the plane was a group of wounded Air Corps officers. I felt guilty sitting among them, but not enough so to consider giving up my seat. The closer we got to Virginia, the tighter my loins squeezed.

My mother was at the airport. Though the weather was balmy, she had not changed her clothes from the winter. She wore the same black coat and black hat with a veil. She was carrying her long-handled umbrella. She leaned forward to allow me to kiss her cheek, but she was anxious to hurry me from the terminal.

Her actions irritated me. She was still worried about my not being an officer, and though I understood she was merely attempting to protect my reputation down at the bank, my being in the Army wasn't exactly shameful.

We rode home. My mother sat like a *grande dame*. She was absolutely erect and clasped her hands on her umbrella. She fussed at the driver for going too fast. She complained to me that my plane had been seven minutes late and asked why the airlines printed schedules if they weren't going to be governed by them. She kept glancing through the rear window as if she suspected we might be followed.

At the house I shook hands with Sam and Lucy before going to my room to unpack my bag and wash. I wanted to get away to call

Martha without arousing my mother's suspicions. I went to the parlor where she sat regally in her Victorian chair.

"Now I'm ready to listen to you," she said, her eyes going over me critically. "I trust you've made some progress toward a commission."

"Not very much," I admitted. In the past months I had hardly thought about becoming an officer. My longing for Martha had crowded out everything else. "To be honest, there's no chance of getting one in the present outfit."

"Then transfer out," she told me.

"I've tried," I answered truthfully, though my reason for trying was not what she thought. "It's not easy."

"Whether it's easy or not doesn't interest me. If transferring is necessary, I'm disappointed you haven't found the means to do so."

"The pipes have clogged up, Mom. There's a surplus of officers. The Army overdid it."

"You make it sound like a plumbing problem. Are you telling me you don't believe you'll get a commission?"

She was squinting, and I smelled the cologne on her. I didn't look directly into her eyes.

"I'm just saying it's very difficult at the moment."

"I dislike your lack of resolve. I refuse even to consider the possibility you can't get a commission."

I sat quietly. I was thinking I had just come home from the wars and should be receiving a soldier's welcome instead of being grilled. I also thought of Martha.

"You can avoid the bank," my mother continued. "What they don't know won't hurt them. I've told no one you're coming. You won't have to visit the family."

"Maybe I ought to hide in the basement."

"No smart talk," she said, frowning. "You don't have to go downtown and around here you can wear civilian clothes."

We were angry at each other and ate dinner in silence. I felt I was being harassed, and she believed I was letting down the Elgar family honor. As soon as I finished eating, I told her I was going to walk around the block. She shot me a glance which meant I was to be careful not to be recognized.

I went to a drugstore where I got change for the pay phone. My plan was to install Martha in a hotel room and visit her each day. Naturally I hoped to do it without arousing my mother's suspicions.

Martha herself answered the telephone.

"I've been waiting for you to call," she said.

"When can you get here? And I mean the sooner the better."

She was silent a moment. Oh God, I thought, more complications.

"Why don't you come here?" she asked.

I hadn't even considered that. There was the problem of getting away from my mother, and after all it was Yancey's house.

"I might have some trouble," I told her. "Obligations I'll need to break."

"You can manage I expect."

"You'll have to help me. I want you to call me tomorrow and pretend you're the long-distance operator. I'll act as if you're a friend who's inviting me to spend a few days."

"One would think you're an expert at this business," Martha said. "Give me your number."

I returned to the house, smoking along the way. I'd never lied to my mother, but I didn't feel particularly guilty about what I was doing. Lying didn't bother me nearly so much as losing precious hours I could be spending with Martha.

The next morning I worked around the flower garden at the rear of the house. I nervously waited for the call. I wore a long face in an attempt to condition my mother to the fact I wasn't exactly happy on my furlough. By four in the afternoon I still hadn't heard from Martha and had become jumpy. I thought perhaps she had not understood my directions. I considered going to the drugstore again. Then, just before five, the telephone rang. I pretended to be busy spraying roses so my mother would have to answer it. She came to the back door for me.

"Long distance," she said.

I put down my sprayer, wiped my hands, and went to the front hall where the telephone was. My mother was in the parlor. She could hear easily.

"Your favorite operator," Martha said and laughed.

I went through an act of greeting a friend. I named him after Wilson and the Professor—Eddy Gladstone. I asked how he was enjoying his furlough and so on. I then made believe he was doing the talking, merely adding an "Uh-huh" from time to time. Martha was amused. Finally I put down the telephone and went to my mother in the parlor.

"A friend of mine in Washington," I told her. "He wants me to spend a few days up there. Since I more or less have to hide, I'm inclined to accept his invitation."

She regarded me a moment, her eyes narrowed in calculation. "Your going might not be a bad idea. Of course I'm assuming you will spend a few days around here. In spite of conditions, I do enjoy seeing you."

"I'll spend the last part of the furlough here."

"All right. I suppose you deserve some fun. At any rate you'll be out of sight for a while."

I was relieved. I had pulled it off easier than I'd expected. I returned to the telephone.

"Very well acted," Martha told me before hanging up. "Call me when you arrive."

I could hardly wait to be gone, yet I didn't want to show it for fear of hurting my mother. Throughout the rest of the evening I attempted to act as normal as I could. We played cards. I wanted to get to bed, but she kept me up until late. When I did lie down, I couldn't sleep. By morning I was bleary-eyed. I smoked a pack of cigarettes during the night.

After breakfast I packed a small bag, and my mother came to the door with me. As I walked away from the house, I felt her watching my back. I was glad when I was out of her sight behind the box-woods. At the corner I caught a streetcar to go downtown to the bus station.

The bus itself was crowded—mostly by servicemen and their wives—and I had to stand up most of the way. Toward the end of the trip I got a seat from which I saw the mountains. They were a light green with spring growth. I was still smoking one cigarette after the other.

When the bus reached the town, I hurried to a telephone booth in the waiting room and dialed. Bessie, the maid, answered. To my disappointment she told me Mrs. Yancey wasn't in but was expected shortly. I left the number and sat on the closest bench to the booth. I was annoyed that Martha had not been waiting for me. I resented each person who used the telephone and glared at them. When it rang almost an hour later, I sprang for it.

"Here's what you do," Martha told me, strictly business. "Take a taxi out of town. Start walking toward my place. I'll pick you up along the way."

I found a taxi in front of the bus station and gave the driver instructions. An unshaven white man, he stared at me with curiosity. I explained to him I was going to hitchhike up the valley. That satisfied him. He let me out by the sign which marked the western entrance to the town.

I walked less than a hundred yards along the highway before I saw the powder-blue convertible with the white top speeding toward me. Because there was a second car not too far behind her, Martha passed without a glance, her head high. I kept walking. She returned a few minutes later. She stopped the convertible and leaned across a leather seat to open the door.

"Ride, soldier?"

"Thank you, mam. How far you going?"

"You can just never tell about that."

She was wearing brown jodhpurs, a white shirt, and a blue sweater. Her black hair was tied at the nape of her neck with a blue ribbon. I wanted to kiss her right there, but as soon as I closed the door, she sped off. I could smell horse and an expensive perfume. She kept glancing in the rear-view mirror.

She drove fast, even recklessly. In spite of the rubber shortage, her tires squealed on curves—most of which she rounded on the wrong side of the road. I couldn't stop looking at the lines of her patrician face, the thrust of her sweater, and the outline of her legs under the jodhpurs.

She turned into the drive to the house. Magnolia leaves were shiny, and the grass seemed too green to be real. Both the fences and the perfectly proportioned Georgian house had been freshly painted. Martha parked in the garage and told me I'd have to carry in my own bag because Yancey's man had gone to get a defense job at the Norfolk shipyards.

Light-skinned Bessie opened the kitchen door. She looked at me in what seemed a conspiratorial fashion as I followed Martha into the house. She had undoubtedly figured what Martha and I were up to. I felt heat in my face.

"Your room's the same," Martha said, stopping by the front steps. "Why don't you go up and get comfortable."

I didn't want to get comfortable. I wanted to put my arms around her, but when I tried, she slipped away. She walked to the kitchen.

Disappointed I went on up to my room which I found just as I'd left it the time I'd visited Yancey. I touched the bed where Martha had sat that night in her negligee. Quickly I washed, put on a cashmere sweater instead of my blouse, and went downstairs. I found her in the den. She had mixed a drink which she handed me.

"Make yourself at home while I change."

She again escaped me. I paced the den. In addition to the pretentious oil painting of Yancey over the fireplace, there was a large photograph of him on the mantel. It'd been made so recently that the captain's bars were on his shoulders. He must have brought the picture home on his leave. I was immediately jealous.

I heard Martha coming down the steps and went to the hall to meet her. She was wearing a white blouse, a dark skirt, and walking shoes. Her black hair was tied by a black ribbon. She led me back to the den.

"Now let's have a look at you," she said.

"Why don't we go upstairs?"

"Does the Army do this to all the boys?"

"I don't know about all the boys. It does it for me."

"I think we'd better have dinner and wait till Bessie leaves. I bought you some beautiful roast beef on the black market. We'll build a fire afterward and drink brandy. How does that sound?"

"I want to get in bed with you."

"We'll see about that."

It seemed she was avoiding me, but perhaps she was worried about Bessie's being so close. Bessie came to the doorway to tell us dinner was ready. Martha walked ahead of me into the dining room where old silver had been laid out at ends of the antique table. I held her chair for her. While sitting across from her, I found myself pretending we were already married and thinking it could be like this every evening of our lives.

When we finished dinner, a coolness slid down off the mountains. Martha asked me to light a fire in the den, and she poured brandy. As we sat on the sofa in front of the fire, I reached for her hand. Though the kitchen door was closed, she shook her head and stood. She was definitely avoiding me.

"Is something wrong with me?" I asked.

"Of course not," she answered, going to the coffee table for a cigarette. She held her fingers stiffly because of her long, painted nails.

"I thought maybe I have a malady that's keeping you away from me."

I meant the remark as a joke, but her face became serious. She returned to the sofa and sat at the other end of it, half-facing me, her knees drawn together primly, her hands in her lap.

"I think this is the time to have a little talk," she said.

"What's there to talk about?"

"I've never wished to be unkind to you."

I stared at her and filled up with fear. I understood where this conversation was going. Martha's dark eyes were lowered, and in spite of the cigarette she held on an ashtray in her lap, she seemed Puritanical across from me. My voice was shaky when I asked the next question.

"Is this a Dear John situation?"

"You're making it difficult," she said, frowning. She stood and walked to the fireplace where she kept her back to me.

"It's a little difficult for me too."

"I never meant it to go this far," she said, turning. "I didn't think it would."

"I bet you thought it would be a lark."

"Don't talk like that."

"It's the only way I know how to talk. I been thinking of marrying you."

"I know you have, and I'm very much complimented. I really am."

"Thanks a lot."

"But I'm too old for you. I'm ten years older, and it wouldn't work. It couldn't work. I'm terribly sorry. I should have stopped you somehow. It's my fault, and I take all the blame."

"Your taking the blame really makes me feel better," I said.

She threw her cigarette into the fire. Her skirt fitted tightly against the girlish flatness of her stomach, and her legs were slim and ladylike in silk stockings. Through my sickness and fear, I still wanted her.

"I am sorry," she said, folding her arms. "I'm completely miserable."

"Why you telling me now?" I asked. "You could have played me along for a while. We could have had fun and games in the bed and maybe I would have grown tired of you."

She came back to the sofa. She sat on the edge of it and put her palms flat down on a cushion.

"I want to tell you that too," she said. "I've met a man."

"I thought maybe you had. That's why you wrote me your mother was sick."

"He's an admiral," she hurried on. "I met him at a cocktail party in Washington. I've never had a man affect me the way he does. He's the most forceful person I've ever known, and he makes me feel like a little girl. I'm very much in love with him, Charles. Please try to understand. I want to marry him."

I closed my eyes. I was thinking of all I had expected from my furlough. I felt tired.

"I assume you're going to divorce Yancey," I said.

"Of course."

"Have you told him?"

"Not yet. I'll tell him but not yet."

Neither of us spoke. The fire crackled. I couldn't just keep on sitting there, so I pushed myself up. Martha's head was bowed, and her hands lay in her lap. I guess I needed to hurt her a little.

"I'd like to thank you for not marrying me," I told her. "It's the luckiest thing that ever happened. You'd have probably ruined me. You'll probably ruin any man you marry."

She didn't look up or say a word. Her shoulders were hunched, and she appeared small. I knew I'd better get out before I started feeling sorry for her.

"I'm leaving," I said. I walked toward the steps. "It's been fun. A million thanks for everything."

27

I climbed the stairs to my room, packed my small bag, and walked down to the door. Martha wanted to drive me into town, but I'd have none of that. It would spoil my dramatic exit. I left the house without a glance at her and slammed the door. My shoes crunched on the gravel drive. Like Lot's wife, I had to take one last look. In the black shadows of the trees I didn't turn to salt, though I did see Martha shading her eyes to peer from a lighted window after me.

I had to walk all the way into town. With gas rationing, no traffic was on the road. One automobile passed but speeded up when its headlights swept me, the people in the car thinking I was some sort of predatory night creature. I trudged along the curving pavement and allowed the pain to fill me a little at a time, like a person lowering himself slowly into icy water.

The town itself was deserted. Even the depot was closed. I stood outside of it, shivering a little from the coldness of the air and smoking cigarettes which I flipped into the street. When I heard a bus,

I flagged it down and got on. It was going to Washington. I slumped so low in my seat the passengers believed I was drunk.

We reached Washington in the early morning while it was still dark. I walked the streets looking for a place to sleep. All the hotels were full. A policeman and MP stopped me, asked to see my furlough papers, and examined them under a street light. They then referred me to a service organization which got me a bed in a rooming house—an old brownstone lighted by globular lamps. I had to share the room with another soldier. He was a sergeant who played trombone in a military band. He was in Washington to take part in war bond drives.

I went through the business of adjusting to my grief. Each day I lay on my narrow bed until the cleaning women ran me out to the bars where I attempted to drink forgetfulness in the traditional manner of men who have lost women. I was, however, simply no good with alcohol. Instead of dulling the pain, it caused me to feel gloomily sorry for myself and to sniffle in self-pity. It tricked me too, for in a surge of unhappiness I put in a call for Martha. At the last moment, when the call was actually going through, I hung the receiver on the hook. The operator rang the bell and fussed at me.

In playing the part of the jilted male, I appeared ridiculous to myself. I don't mean I wasn't suffering—I really was—but at the same time I had a sense of going through a ritual. No matter how miserable I felt, I wasn't the type to spend my life mourning a lost love. Some men might thrive on that sort of situation, milking it all their days, but I was tired of bars, my postage-stamp room, and the trombone player practicing his J. P. Sousa.

I returned to Richmond. From the bus station I rode the streetcar to the house. A light rain was falling and caused my shoes to become damp. In the house I found my mother at her library desk, the month's stack of bills before her. She always went through them suspiciously, glaring at each as if it were an attempt by tradesman or grocer to cheat her. She totaled every item in tiny handwriting on the backs of envelopes. She enjoyed doing it, especially when she was able to find an error. Errors made her triumphant.

"Did you have a good time?" she asked, peering over the tops of the silver-rimmed glasses she wore when reading.

"Very nice," I answered.

"I expect you're hungry. I'll have Lucy fix you a little something."

I ate a chicken sandwich and chatted with my mother about the non-existent friend in Washington. That afternoon and for the rest of my furlough I was careful not to show her how broken I was. In my bed I groaned softly. My only balm was the knowledge that Yancey was going to lose Martha too.

On Saturday my mother and I went to the airport. She didn't give me another lecture on becoming an officer as I expected. Instead she was quiet.

"There's some chance you'll be going overseas, isn't there?" she asked when the plane's departure was announced. She held her umbrella.

"I guess so."

She was silent a moment. Then she came to me and reached her thin, strong arms around my neck.

"Don't let anything happen to you," she said and kissed me. "Please don't let anything happen."

She began to cry, and I knew she was thinking both of me and my father whom she had loved very much. I hugged her, feeling her smallness. She wasn't nearly so severe as she acted.

I flew back to Georgia. In the plane I thought that each droning mile was carrying me farther from Martha and had relapses into sorrow. I arrived at the post just three minutes before my furlough officially expired. A sleepy corporal of the guard signed me in. I walked down the dark, empty company street to the barracks where I undressed among snoring men. As I sank to my hard bunk, I felt old, tired, and without hope.

In the morning whistles blew. After breakfast I crossed to battalion headquarters. Nothing had changed. Wilson and Carter played checkers. The Professor read a book lying in his desk drawer. WO Page brought me a sheet of payroll deductions to work on.

Lou came by the cubicle. She was, as usual, chewing gum and wearing a tight skirt.

"How were your in-laws?" Wilson asked, referring to the Texan's parents whom she'd visited.

"They were crazy about me. Of course I was on my best behavior. I knew I was in when one of the old men, an uncle with a beard, pinched me you know where." She patted a buttock and smiled proudly.

During the afternoon I saw Yancey. He strutted down the corridor, his fat bouncing. He'd come to visit Lighthorse. They sat in Lighthorse's office talking and laughing. I wanted to see his pain when he learned Martha was leaving him. Obviously he didn't know yet or he wouldn't have been so jaunty.

In the outfit itself, there were rumors we were shipping out. As soon as all furloughs were over, we were put on alert. MPs guarded gates, and our mail was censored.

At battalion we were ordered to pack up headquarters. We put all records in waterproof boxes and numbered the boxes. The WACs, especially Lou, were depressed at the prospect of losing their men. Yancey, full of self-importance, bustled in and out of headquarters. He wore his oxblood .45 and cut the air with his swagger stick. I smiled in anticipation of the hurt which was coming to him from Martha.

The morning we left, the WACs told us good-by as they had the time we went to Kentucky. We rode loaded trucks into town where we transferred equipment onto boxcars at a siding. We worked stripped to the waist and were covered with sweat.

The train carried us north. Men believed that meant we were going to England. On the second day the tracks changed directions by curving west. That created talk of Pacific jungles. On the third day we headed south. Questions were asked about the Panama Canal.

We ended up in Arizona where the temperature was over a hundred. We weren't being shipped across at all but taking part in desert maneuvers which were supposed to prepare us for fighting in Africa. Censorship was lifted, and we could go to town for beer.

The maneuvers were not a success for the 606th. Neither Yancey nor 1st Battalion was involved, but a part of the regiment got turned around in a sandstorm and assaulted its own flanks. Bone started another purge of officers and noncoms. The golden eagle was again transformed into a snake swallowing its tail.

We moved. This time we went to North Dakota to join war games in progress. We were assigned the roll of Aggressor Enemy. I was still praying Yancey would get into more trouble, but he didn't. He was leaning heavily on his platoon officers in order to avoid making mistakes. By riding their backs and picking their brains, he was fairly safe from error. Each evening he drank with Bone and Box in their tents.

We remained in North Dakota playing Aggressor Enemy for any unit which wished to sharpen its teeth on us. There was talk the high brass was not pleased with the 606th. Because of the purges, an air of discontent and frustration hung about the golden eagle.

"This is a hard-luck outfit," Wilson said. "It's never going to amount to anything."

"We'd be all right if they'd just quit fooling with us and ship us overseas," Carter, always a defender, argued. "They're not giving us a chance to show our stuff."

Colonel Bone and battalion commanders were constantly shifting personnel in an attempt to shore up unit weaknesses. The pressure was on from above to get the kinks out. Tempers were short. Lighthorse, touchy because of Bone and the fact he himself was still a lieutenant colonel, snooped around headquarters in attempts to find soldiers goofing off. He almost caught me reading a novel. I shoved the drawer of my desk in so quickly I banged a finger.

"Ouch!" I cried as I sprang to attention.

"What?" he asked, scowling. "What's that you said?"

"I was calling attention, sir."

"You said ouch."

"I meant attention, sir."

"You must be crazy," Lighthorse told me and prowled on.

In spite of all the doctoring, by the end of the summer the outfit was going through its role as Aggressor Enemy with the élan of sleepwalkers. None of the enlisted men except Carter could work up any enthusiasm about the repetitious war games. Officers threatened and raged, but entire platoons dozed in sunny meadows while waiting for the word to advance. Each week the number of AWOLs increased. Bone's frown deepened and became habitual.

On a Sunday morning the 606th was put on alert. It'd happened so often nobody took it seriously except the MPs who wouldn't let us out of the area. The rumor was we were returning to Georgia for more training. The WACs would be glad to see us. Unenthusiastically we packed our equipment.

The rumor was completely wrong. We went directly to a staging area in New Jersey. It was a grim-looking camp with barbed wire around it and burly guards at the gates. This one time the golden eagle was not going to be left at the altar.

We boarded ship at night. Trucks transported us to docks, and ferries carried us across the Hudson. The water was black. Hulls of rusty troop ships soared above us in the dark. Numbers had been chalked upon our helmets, and as we went up a gangplank transportation officers checked their lists.

We were hurried below into crowded compartments furnished with tiers of iron bunks from floor to ceiling. Lying down, each man had only a few inches clearance above his face. The air was foul. During the night as we waited uneasily and silently, we heard vibrations from the engine. In the morning when we were allowed on deck for twenty minutes, we looked back and the land was gone.

28

For the first few days I remained on my bunk as long as possible. My compartment was below the water line, but I tried not to think what would happen if a torpedo hit us and the cold North Atlantic came rushing in.

The food was so awful I, like many others, lived mostly off Coca-Cola and Hershey bars we could buy at a PX. For the greatest part of the day and night we were kept penned in our compartments by officers stationed at the exits. Other than a daily visit to the PX, we were permitted to go out only for meals and twenty minutes exercise each morning and afternoon on deck.

The outside air was hurting cold. Its freshness after the fetidness of the compartment was painful to the lungs. We watched a silver blimp slide over us on submarine patrol and the blinker lights flashing from ship to ship among the lumbering convoy. The ocean was a dark gray.

Naturally a lot of men were seasick. In just a few hours the entire ship smelled of vomit. Of those suffering, Beanpost was the worst. He couldn't go below even for a minute without retching.

As a result he was given special permission by a medical officer to remain topside. Bundled in overcoat, scarf, and gloves, he slumped in a corner of the promenade deck which afforded some shelter from the wind—a pitiful heap of a man who rolled his eyes heavenward as if praying for death. Each day he seemed to grow smaller. If we didn't reach England soon, nothing would be left of him except a soiled pile of clothing and an empty pair of shoes.

All of us hated going below. The air gagged us, and we had no room to stretch in. There was a limit to how much sleep we could get. We lay on canvas bunks which rubbed our skins raw and snapped at each other. Tempers flashed in a poker game which was played in an aisle hardly a foot wide. Crumpled dollar bills littered the floor.

Black Hatfield had his guitar out and moodily strummed atonal chords that were dark with feuding and coal mining, the making of liquor, and death. The chords got on everybody's nerves, but no one said anything to Black Hatfield who had bought himself a long knife which he wore on his belt and sharpened lovingly on a boot.

At chow time I went to the mess hall for coffee and to get out of the compartment a few minutes. Each section of the ship was numbered. When our numbers were called over loudspeakers, we formed a line which snaked through dirty passageways. The big dining room pitched from side to side so badly that even if a person had managed to work up an appetite for the food, he lost it quickly. We dumped most of what we were served into GI cans and carried only the coffee back to our bunks.

I had a piece of good luck. Men from other units on the ship who had been assigned to gun detail wore special green brassards which allowed them to pass freely around the decks. I found one of the brassards in a forward head and stuffed it into my pocket.

By wearing the brassard, I discovered I could move unchallenged just about anywhere I wished. I spent long hours on the deck. All I had to do was look official when I passed officers guarding exits. I promenaded like a tourist and was able to enter the kitchen for hot coffee and sandwiches.

Still I was not entirely satisfied because to sleep I had to return to the stink of the compartment. What I wanted was a place out of the wind which was private, clean, and quiet. I began to explore all parts of the ship. I ran into naval officers and a general, but I assumed the stern mien of a soldier going about his duty and was never questioned.

On the afternoon of our fifth day out I opened a door near a smokestack at the midsection of the ship. Inside was a paint locker. Technically it was on the officers' part of the deck, but I was breaking so many regulations anyway one more made no difference. Because of the smokestack, the small space was warm. The locker had a porthole which had been painted over, and a ceiling light that burned only when the door was closed. The whole area was hardly bigger than a closet, but compared to the crowded conditions on the ship the locker appeared a stateroom.

I rearranged things a bit—pushing cans and gear out of the way. On the steel floor I spread a thick tarpaulin. I returned to the compartment for my blankets, one of which I lay over the tarp and the other I used for a pillow. I wedged an empty Coca-Cola bottle into a corner for an ashtray. I had books to read. I was snug and content.

Almost immediately I was discovered. During the night a sailor came in for block and tackle. He was surprised to see me but didn't order me out. I wasn't sure whether he would report me or not. I decided to wait instead of running. After twenty minutes passed and no officer appeared, I knew I was safe. When the sailor returned the block and tackle, he winked at me. I settled down for a comfortable voyage.

I developed a gentlemanly routine. I slept late each morning, put on my green brassard, and shaved in the best head amidship. About eleven I had coffee and cigarettes. Later I took a leisurely stroll around the uncrowded boat deck where ranking officers had their quarters. Lastly, feeling invigorated by the salt air, I went to my hideout for a nap and to read.

Wilson, Carter, and the others missed me. They hadn't seen my green brassard and couldn't understand how I was able to get out of the compartment until they caught me one morning while they were on deck for their twenty minutes. They stood on the other side of a locked iron gate which was to prevent them from stepping onto officer territory.

"I figured he had a deal," Wilson said.

"We thought perhaps something had happened to you," the Professor told me. "We didn't know whether to report it or not."

"Not," I answered.

"How about cutting us in?" Timberlake asked, sallow from being forced to live in the stench below.

I had no way of cutting them in. The paint locker was simply not big enough for them and me. Moreover they didn't have brassards, and I didn't want to risk my own. I told them I would try to think of something, but after that morning I avoided coming out when their section was on deck.

Occasionally I saw or heard Yancey. He had somehow manipulated to get himself quarters on the boat deck with field-grade officers. He shared a stateroom which had real beds and a bath. Envy burned among my hate.

The officers played bridge or poker every day. Strolling past their luxurious quarters, I heard cards slapping tables and the jangle of coins. In the evenings at five they drank cocktails, each group of officers being expected to have a party for others along the deck. They served canapés made by their cooks who raided the kitchen under orders.

Though we met now and then, Yancey and I had not spoken to each other since the night I had gone to Apple Able to confront him in his office. He avoided me as much as I did him, a fact that suited me fine. I wanted absolutely nothing to do with him. I just wished he would move once and for all out of my life.

Still I was watching him too, trying to determine whether Martha had told him she was leaving. My guess was she had not because Yancey seemed too elated. He moved along the deck visiting officers, his fingers snapping, a bounce to his step. I heard his laughter, subservient and oily, rise up over the din of other men talking.

On the seventh night at sea, while I was reading, the light in my hideout snapped off because somebody opened the door. It was an automatic device to prevent detection by submarines. I thought at first a sailor must have come in for tools or tackle. When the light flashed on again, however, there was Yancey.

"Well, well, well," he said, grinning down at me. He had an unlit cigar in his mouth, and he wobbled a little. I believed it was the roll of the ship. "You got yourself a snug little harbor here, don't you?"

"You come to chase me out?" I asked, sitting up and looking at my watch. It was almost midnight.

He stopped smiling. He put a hand against the bulkhead to steady himself. He was wearing ODs, a field jacket, and his oxblood .45. His tie was loosened. His overseas cap which had captain's bars pinned on it was tilted forward, and his eyes were watery and flat. Again he staggered. I realized he must be drunk. He reached to his hip pocket and brought out a pint of bourbon.

"That's a lousy thing to say," he told me. "Why would I want to ruin it in here for you?" He laughed. "I been seeing you sneak in here all right. I knew what you were doing, and I don't blame you for it. A soldier has to look out for himself. It's a crime the way the enlisted men are packed below. I got sympathy for them."

He was very drunk. His words slurred, and his feet shuffled to stay under him. He smacked his tongue as if trying to work up spit.

"I been to a little party for Ben Bone," he continued. "It's the colonel's birthday, and a bunch of the regimental officers got together to give him a little surprise reception. The cooks made us a cake. I mean to tell you we have a sweet colonel and a sweet outfit. An outfit like this is no place for hard feelings. We're all in this thing together."

"Get out of here, Yancey."

"Now wait a minute," he answered, frowning and swaying. "Don't talk that way to me. I came in here to offer you a little drink and say now that we're on the ocean we ought to let bygones be bygones. I'm ready to offer you my hand in friendship. I don't have to. If I was chicken, I could really get you in trouble. You're not supposed to be in this part of the ship, and you're not supposed to have that green brassard either."

"You going to report me, Marvin?"

"No, I'm not going to report you. I'm going to offer you a little drink of good liquor. I want you to take a swig and shake my hand. Now go on and grab the bottle. I don't have any social diseases."

He pushed the bottle toward me. I still sat on the deck, my back against a bulkhead. The bottle circled in front of my face. I shoved it away.

"All right, goddammit, be like that," Yancey said angrily. "I ain't going to beg anybody to drink my good liquor or shake my hand either. I was trying to be generous. Sometimes it just don't pay to be nice to people. But I got a couple of things to say. You're going to listen to me whether you want to or not. I'm ordering you to listen to me."

He was glowering and weaving as he sought to keep his balance against the roll of the ship. He drank from the bottle and stuffed it back into his hip pocket. Whisky spilled from his mouth, ran down his chin, and dripped onto his field jacket.

"All right," he said. "What I want to tell you is this. We're going into combat soon. No matter what you think of me, you have to re- member the golden eagle. The eagle's a lot more important than our personal differences. Let's bury the hatchet in the Krauts in- stead of each other."

He sounded like a high school coach giving a pep talk except the words were thick from liquor and fell half articulated from his lips. His hypocrisy infuriated me. I despised him not only because he'd used both Martha and me badly, but also because I knew what he really was underneath the bluster.

"Stop it," I told him, pushing myself up. "You don't want combat. If anybody in this outfit doesn't want it, it's you."

"What's that?" he asked, the unlit cigar clamped in his teeth.

"You know what you are."

"I don't know what the hell you're talking about. You got some- thing on your mind, spit it out."

"Okay," I told him, trembling with the fury I'd built up over the months. "You're a fake. You're yellow all the way."

"Me yellow? You're crazy. It's on my record what I am. Anybody can read what I am."

"How'd you get it on your records. You bribe somebody to put it there?"

"Now you listen here—"

"You listen," I told him. I no longer had a duty to protect Martha, and I was full up with Marvin Yankovitch Yancey. "I saw you on the infiltration course. As for your medals, you're not fooling me with them. You never earned them. You know it and so do I."

He stared at me, and the cigar dropped from his mouth. He reached to the bulkhead to steady himself. He licked his lips.

"Who told you that?" he whispered.

"You figure it out."

"I got it figured out. There's only one person who could of. You been seeing my wife, Charley?"

His eyes were bulging at me behind his glasses, and he reeled. Instead of answering, I smiled. Yancey's face reddened, and he made fists as if he would come at me.

I hoped he did attack. I'd have liked nothing better than the pleasure of pounding him—of sinking my fists into his soft flesh just as I had dreamed about in Georgia. I wanted to see him bloody. I waited, ready to swing on him. His cheeks puffed up like a blowfish.

He didn't, however, attack. He staggered, ran his palms across his face, and reached for his pint. As he raised it to his lips, he closed his eyes, and his glasses reflected the light. Carefully, laboriously, he put the cap onto the bottle, twisting it with his fat fingers. A heavy foot mashed the cigar. When he spoke, he sounded not angry but weary.

"The trouble is, Charley, you don't know a goddamn thing," he said.

The ship rolled, and he fell against the bulkhead. He attempted to put the bottle back into his hip pocket but was unable to manage it. He held it in a dangling arm. A slackness came over him, and when he raised his watery eyes they seemed to be looking beyond me. Very slowly he collapsed, his back sliding down the bulkhead until he was sitting on the steel deck. He closed his eyes, and I thought for an instant he had passed out.

"You ever been in a coal camp, Charley?" he asked in a choked voice. "Hell no, you never have. You're a Virginia aristocrat, and Virginia aristocrats don't go into coal camps. Well, they're wonderful places. The one I lived in sat in the crotch of two narrow valleys. All the trees on the mountains around it were dead because slag

234

piles burned continuously and filled the valley with bitter, blue smoke. Everybody coughed from the smoke.

"The house I grew up in had a tarpaper roof and a privy out back. In winter men would leave home before the sun came up and not get out of the mines until the sun was down. There was a creek through the middle of camp where the women threw trash and cans. Sometimes the creek would flood and wash houses away. I didn't think it was unusual for dozens of men I saw daily not to have arms or legs."

He stopped talking to remove the cap from the bottle and drink. His legs were spread in front of him, and he had slobbered on his chin.

"I had two brothers, and like them I quit school and lied about my age to work in the mines. I was fifteen. Both my brothers got killed—one by a slate fall, the other by a rock about the size of a pea which was squeezed out of a column of coal by the weight on top it. The rock went through him like a bullet. Each time my mother sat up all night by the coffin. She didn't look as if she expected anything but for us to get killed.

"When I went to work I was scared, but I thought being scared was normal. Lots of time I loaded coal in water up to my knees— water so cold my legs would go numb and stay that way an hour after I left the mine. I had all the hair burned off me by fire damp. A room where I'd been loading collapsed ten seconds after I left it. I was once buried a couple of hours by coal. I thought it was all a part of living.

"When my second brother was killed, my mother took all my clothes to the front yard of the house and poured kerosene over them to burn them. She told me I had to leave camp because she wanted one son who didn't give his life to the mountain. I didn't leave though. There was no place to leave to. I just bought myself another outfit at the commissary and walked to work the next morning as always.

"My mother died that winter. She got skinnier each day, and she kept her face toward the window as if accusing the mountain. A neighbor woman sat with her and ran errands. When my mother stopped breathing, nobody came to tell my father and me. We finished our shift before we found out.

"The mines in those days were mostly non-union and had no standard safety regulations. Funerals were as normal as rain. The miners had a saying, 'Kill a mule, buy another one; kill a man, hire another one.' That was the truth of it. There were no pensions when you got crippled or old. There was nothing.

"On Sundays some of the miners used to go into the woods for snake-handling religious services. They'd wrap snakes around their arms and necks. The supers tried to keep them from doing it because even if a man didn't die when bit, he wasn't good for work for a couple of days. The super's house was painted white, and we tipped our hats to his daughters who were sent off to Virginia to school and as soon as they got married never came back.

"I didn't understand anything about the outside world. Compared to what I was, Black Hatfield's cosmopolitan. We didn't even have roads out of camp. Salesmen and anybody else with business came in on coal trains. There were no radios or newspapers. When the war started in 1914 we didn't understand who it was that was fighting. Even after the U.S. became involved nothing changed except there was plenty of work in camp for everybody.

"A friend talked me into going with him. He made it sound exciting. I was living with my father who since my mother died had become a sullen, drinking man. I put on my one suit of clothes and walked into the kitchen where he sat in his undershirt at the table.

" 'I guess I'll go along,' I told him.

" 'Go along where?' he asked. His eyes were dark with bug dust, and black hair grew out from under his arms.

" 'To fight the Heinies.'

" 'You better stay here. That war don't have nothing to do with you.'

" 'I'm going anyway.'

"I walked from the house and down the street, which was nothing but cinders. My father came to the doorway to watch. He never called or waved. He just stood seeing me go. At the end of the street I looked back, and he was still standing there.

"My friend and me rode out of camp on a hopper car full of coal. At the county seat we jumped off and went to the post office to sign up. The Army sent us to Arkansas which then was a kind of wilderness covered with pine trees and kudzu vines. We weren't issued uniforms or rifles. Instead we were handed axes and went to work clearing land to make room for barracks. It was hot, sweating labor, but it was ten times easier than mining. I was already thinking of staying in the Army.

"Some of the recruits fainted because of the heat, and those of us used to hard work would drag them into the shade. I know what

236

people think of me now. They laugh at me because I'm soft and fat, but back then I wasn't. I was all muscle from loading coal. I could lift twice my weight."

He stopped talking. His head had lolled forward, and his eyes were almost closed. He shook his head as if trying to remember how his sagging flesh had once been young and strong. He raised the bottle for another drink, wiped his mouth, and again began talking. He spoke as if I weren't there, as if the words were driven out of him rather than voluntarily coming forth.

"At the end of six weeks we started getting bits and pieces of uniforms—a hat, pair of shoes, a khaki shirt. We were finally issued rifles, Springfields, though there weren't enough cartridges for target practice. Occasionally we ran through close-order drill among the bleeding pine stumps. We were a sorry-looking bunch of soldiers.

"Me and the other boy from the coal camp had split up because he wanted to go to cooks and bakers school. It didn't matter much because I'd made another friend, this time a fellow eighteen from Winston-Salem. He bunked next to me. He didn't seem old enough to be in the Army, and he wasn't cut out for manual work. Light of build, he didn't know how to handle an ax or sledge. His white hands blistered easily. I guess we became buddies because I helped him all I could, doing not only my work but part of his too.

"Of course I realized he was different from me. His name was Beverley Pendleton, and mine was Marvin Yankovitch. He was educated. I guess he was the first person I'd ever known who could speak good English. He always had plenty of money, and he wrote to a pretty girl every week whose picture he carried in his wallet. He showed me the picture. The girl was holding a tennis racket and standing in front of a country club, though I didn't even know what a country club was.

"By the time basic was over, Beverley and I had become pretty close. We always sat together in the mess hall or walked to the PX together. If there was guard duty to be pulled, we tried to get on the same shifts so we could jaw while making tours. We were a sort of working combination.

"He and all the rest of the company got excited when the CO announced furloughs. I wasn't so excited, and I had no intention of taking mine. By then my father was dead too. I got a telegram from the super's wife. A dust explosion had killed him. The Red Cross arranged for me to take an emergency leave to the coal camp. I stood by my father's grave a while, and after I left, I knew I'd never come back.

"I asked the first sergeant if it'd be all right for me to spend my furlough around the barracks. He told me I could help out in the supply room. When Beverley heard I wasn't going anywhere, he couldn't believe it.

" 'You're staying here?' he asked.

" 'I'll catch up on my sleep.'

" 'You're coming with me if I have to carry you.'

"He was so thin he couldn't have carried me twenty yards, but he really did want me to come. I didn't have any idea what I was getting into. As we rode the train up to Winston-Salem, Beverley kept peering out of the window like a little boy going to a party.

"We took a taxi to his house. Of course I was sure he didn't live in any coal camp, but I thought he must be fooling when we turned into a circular drive leading to a white mansion. The drive was lined with elm trees, and there were white columns. I'd never seen anything like it before. I didn't believe real people could live in such a place.

"Beverley had to shove me into the house. His mother came down steps to meet us. She was a tall, aristocratic lady in a lace dress who must have sized me up with one glance, but she never showed it. She was bred gracious and would have cut her throat rather than make a guest in her house feel bad. I could hardly untwist my tongue to talk to her.

" 'They would have kicked me out of the Army a long time ago if it hadn't been for Marvin,' Beverley told his mother when introducing me.

" 'Beverley's always needed someone,' she said, taking my rough hand in her long fingers.

"I was still gawking. The house was full of silver and old furniture. A chandelier like diamonds hung over the curving stairs. All my Yankovitch instincts told me to bolt and I probably would have if Beverley's mother hadn't held my arm as she guided me around the house.

"Later Beverley showed me to my room. It had so much expensive stuff in it I was afraid to sit down or touch anything. Out a window I could see a garden and a collie dog sleeping on the grass. The bathroom was big enough to live in. A colored servant unpacked my cheap little canvas bag.

"As soon as I'd washed up, I went down the corridor searching for Beverley. I was still scared and thinking of running. I wasn't sure how to get out of the house. I found him lying in his bathtub.

" 'Maybe I better move on,' I told him.

" 'What you talking about?' he asked, sitting up.

" 'I don't belong here. I better go back to camp.'

" 'You'll have to fight me to do it.'

"In the end I stayed. I did have on a uniform which made me look a little like Beverley even if I wasn't. I figured that if I didn't open my mouth too much I might be able to bluff my way past anything really embarrassing.

"I had to admit to myself that in spite of being afraid I didn't want to leave. For the first time in my life I had rich things around me, and I liked the feel of them. I believed greatness could happen to a person who lived in such a fine house and had a lady like Beverley's mother for a wife. I believed that those in themselves could make a man great.

"Later in the afternoon I met Beverley's father—a tall and distinguished gentleman with gray hair and blue eyes. He owned a kennel full of highbred dogs. He had a cabinet of fine guns which he took out one at a time to show me. He treated me as nice as he would have the governor.

"I guess I must have made a fool of myself at least a dozen times at the dinner table. I didn't know what fork to use or even what to eat. Beverley and his parents were very careful to look the other way rather than shame me. To tell you the truth I felt I was in church."

He stopped talking and drank from the bottle. He stared at the steel deck between his legs as if he were seeing the memory right in front of him. He closed his eyes, licked his lips, and continued.

"Beverley insisted we go out. He had his girl—the one he intended to marry—and she got me a date with a friend. Both girls were beautiful and sophisticated. We went to a country-club dance. I didn't say ten words the whole night to my date, and she must have thought I couldn't talk. I sat gaping at all the fluffy, perfumed beauty around me. If any of the girls had tried to make me dance, I'd have jumped out the window."

Again he drank. He tilted his head back to do it and blinked at the light on the ceiling.

"That furlough was the great time of my life," he said. "Everybody has one period he can look back on when things were just right, and that was mine. It was the golden age of Marvin Yankovitch. If I think of happiness, I remember the visit I had with Beverley in Winston-Salem.

"The day we left for camp, pretty girls came down to the station to smile and hand us presents. Beverley's mother took me aside and said, 'Look out for my son.' I promised her I would. I carried the glow of the visit with me long after the train pulled off. I kept thanking Beverley, and he kept telling me he hadn't done anything.

"At camp, orders came through to send us overseas. It wasn't like today. Today nobody seems to want to fight much. Back then we were all fired up. We were in a hurry to get into the war. While marching, we sang songs, and getting the Heinies seemed a picnic.

"I made corporal. I didn't buy it if that's what you're thinking. When I got the rating, I was the most surprised man in the platoon. I'd figured somebody with a better education would be picked. I found out the rest of the squad wanted me. They gathered around to slap me on the back. They believed I deserved the rating, and I was proud.

"We shipped over in the spring as part of an infantry division. In France we formed up like a huge snake which uncoiled and wiggled toward the front. At times we rode on French trains and sat in the doors with our legs dangling out. We whistled at French girls who waved at us. The country was pretty and green as we traveled toward the Argonne where we were to relieve another division which had been on line a couple of months. The front had been established for years, with only minor changes taking place.

"We'd actually had very little combat training. We'd done more lumberjacking and latrine duty than preparing for trench warfare. One thing, the trenches had already been dug for us. There was a complete system of them, crisscrossing and interlocking. Back of each trench were more trenches in case we had to retreat. We lived in bunkers reinforced with timbers and sandbags. There was a coal stove, straw mattresses, and a lantern. The men we'd relieved had nailed up pictures. The bunkers were almost cozy.

"At first, war seemed a kind of holiday. We took our places on line, positioned our machine guns, and then had nothing to do. We could peep across the desolate stretch of land in front of us but not observe anything happening. In the daytime we wrote home—not me, but the others—or played cards. There was rarely any firing, and that was always farther down the line.

"To kill time, Beverley was helping me with my English. I'd

asked him to, and he'd sent home for the grammar book he'd used in prep school. He'd sit around with me working on verbs and sentences. Some of the days were warm as summer. We'd take our shirts off to soak up the sun. It was hard to believe anybody could really get hurt.

"We were on line more than a month before the Germans massed for an attack. None of us had been under fire previously, not even our officers. We cleaned our rifles and checked our grenades, each of us trying to act more sure of himself than he felt. We filled sandbags to strengthen the bunker.

"I wasn't particularly afraid. I was a little, but not worse than any of the others. I believed I was more prepared than the rest of the squad because they were mostly city boys who until coming to the war had been kept under a mother's wing. I figured I'd be a good influence by acting calm and knowledgeable.

"When the German barrage started, we waited in the bunker. Some members of the squad lay on their bunks and others sat with their backs against a wall. We knew that as long as shells were falling the Heinies couldn't get too close. We had our rifles lined up at the entry so we could run into the trenches and start shooting as soon as officers blew their whistles.

"At first the barrage was way down the line. It wasn't too bad—like a thunderstorm coming over the mountain. Gradually the pattern of shells began moving down the trench toward our bunker. The explosions became louder, and the earth rocked. The guns were traversing like a watering hose—only instead of water, death was coming out.

"I sat looking at the roof of the bunker. I had the feeling I was back in a coal mine. I used to be afraid of all that mountain coming in on me. I couldn't stop myself from remembering it and my dead brothers—how each was lying in the ground. At the same time I was trying to watch over my squad, checking them for any signs of panic as shells dropped closer. In particular I kept glancing at Beverley who lay in his bunk. He was white as lard.

"A big shell landed close. It must have been fired from one of the German railroad guns. The concussion bounced us off the floor, and dirt fell from the top of the bunker. A sandbag split. Sand poured into a pile. Clods of dirt rattled against our helmets and mess kits.

"A second big shell exploded, this one even closer. Our rifles were knocked over, and the lantern went out. Beverley got up to light it. The timbers holding up the roof had buckled and were popping. I had to push dirt off my face.

"Beverley came toward me. I didn't realize the whimpering was from my own mouth. I saw scared faces turned in my direction. I was shaking and gasping for air. All I could think was that I was going to die under the mountain.

"I ran for the entry. I didn't will it. My body was acting without me directing it. Beverley grabbed for me. He caught my arm, and I fought. I hit him. He was the best friend I had in the world, but I hit him right in the face. He fell away. I pushed up through the blackout curtain into the trench. As I ran, I heard Beverley shouting after me.

"Shells were exploding close. I ran with my eyes clenched, my hands over my head. I was bumping against the sides of the trench and weeping. I fell, got up, and fell again. A shell hit so near me it flung me head over heels. The concussion blacked me out.

"When I opened my eyes, I was lying on my back in a pool of muddy water. Maybe it was the shell blast or the chill of the water, but as I staggered to my feet, I began to get hold of myself. As I stumbled back toward the bunker, I was still shaking. I was slimy with mud. My helmet had been knocked off. I had a back full of shrapnel too, though at the time I didn't even feel it.

"I went past the bunker without realizing it. One of the big shells from the railroad gun had hit on top of it. The shell must have landed dead center. The stink of cordite was strong, and split timbers stuck up through the earth like fractured bones.

"I crouched there, staring stupidly at the mound, not understanding. Then as I did understand I went crazy. With shells still falling, I started digging. I had no shovel. I clawed and threw dirt between my legs like a dog. I was howling.

"That's the way the others found me after the barrage stopped and whistles blew. They came out to take their places in the trench. I was bloody and half-buried in the dirt and screaming. They had to pull me off. It took half a dozen of them to do it, and they were careful with me—as if I were something precious."

29

Yancey stopped speaking and was covered with sweat. His shoulders were hunched, his head bowed, and his hands trembling so badly the pint bottle he held tapped against the metal deck like a telegraph key. His moist, brown eyes had the terror in them of a man looking into Hell.

He drank quickly from the bottle. He closed his eyes and cried without a sound. I stood over him. He was as repulsive to me as a great wet slug. He drew up a knee and let his head fall onto a forearm. When he spoke again, his voice rasped.

"They didn't understand," he said. "The men who dragged me away from the bunker believed I'd dug myself out and was trying to save my squad. They thought I was a hero.

"Medics shuttled me back through evacuation trenches to an aid station. Though there was a lot of blood on me, I wasn't badly wounded. The small pieces of metal in my back hadn't gone deep. A doctor picked them out. Before I was sent on, I saw the squad lying stiff on the ground in a row. Dirt was still on them. I went berserk. Medics had to hold me down and give me morphine.

"I was put into an ambulance and driven back to a general hospital. The doctors assigned me to a special area which was screened off from other enlisted men. Nurses and orderlies treated me like a king. I kept thinking of Beverley and the others shoveled under the ground.

"I didn't know anybody had put in for medals. I was afraid they'd start investigating and court-martial me for running. Nobody even questioned me. When I was released from the hospital, they gave me a job in division headquarters instead of sending me back to the line. The idea was to keep me away from fighting so nothing would happen to me.

"My medals came through, and a battalion was pulled off line for a formal presentation ceremony. I had to march out front to let a general pin them on me. I wanted to hide my head, but I stood at attention before all those men. The general shook my hand and embraced me. That night I got drunk. People around me didn't understand that either. They believed I was crying because I'd been touched.

"I never had to return to the trenches. Instead I lived like a privileged character. There was little for me to do, and I drank. I had to have liquor around to keep from choking on memory. The first thing each morning I had a drink. I drank through the day, and at night I went to bed with a bottle. Nobody reprimanded me. Men covered for me. I was a hero.

"Yet as much as I drank I could never let myself go either. I was afraid I'd give myself away. I drank quietly and alone. I sat in the dark to drink.

"At the end of the war I didn't want to go back to the States. There was nothing for me in the States. There was nothing for me anywhere. I put in for occupation duty. Later, after most American troops went home, I was transferred to a Graves Registration unit in Paris. I worked with colored troops who laid out cemeteries and exhumed bodies. I was where I belonged—among the dead.

"My drinking required a lot of money. I was a sergeant by then, and each month after my pay was gone, I'd steal Army blankets from supply or cans of food from the kitchen to sell on the black market. A lot of people knew what I was doing, but nobody turns in a hero. Because of the medals, I could even steal with approval.

"Our unit was billeted in a small hotel, and I had an unimportant clerk's job. None of us had to work more than a couple of hours a day. I'd made up my mind never to go back home. When the Army had no more use for me, I'd take my discharge in France. I could always find something. I'd have pimped if nothing else. That's how low I'd sunk.

"One afternoon I was lying on my bed. I lived on the top floor of the hotel in a room to myself. I spent a lot of time on the bed and would go for days without letting the *femme de chambre* come in to clean up. That afternoon a guard pounded on my locked door. He said somebody wanted to see me. I told him I didn't want to see anybody. He left, but then the captain came up and ordered me to go down.

"I thought it would be somebody I owed money to. I owed a lot of money. Standing in the lobby, however, were a man and woman. As soon as I recognized them, I started backing off. They were Beverley's parents.

"The mother, wearing a hat and fur coat, came toward me. I believed she was going to accuse me, but she put her arms around me, and the man—tall and distinguished—patted my shoulder. They treated me as if I were the person who needed comforting.

244

"They had come to see Beverley's grave and wanted me to drive out with them. I tried to make excuses. I'd never even gone near the cemeteries. Beverley's parents wouldn't let me refuse. I had to sit between them in the rear of the big chauffeur-driven car and at the cemetery lead them down between rows of crosses. They'd brought flowers which the mother laid on the grave.

"On the way back to Paris we stopped for lunch in a small country town. All I was thinking of was getting rid of them and to a bottle. They wouldn't let me escape. They drove me on into Paris to the Crillon where they were staying. The room was full of gilt furniture and mirrors. They sat me on a sofa.

" 'We've talked to your commanding officer,' Beverley's father said. 'He explained everything to us. I hope you understand how deeply we appreciate your efforts to help Beverley.'

"I sat looking from one to the other of them. I was going to pieces inside. The woman was next to me and put her hand on mine in a gesture of sympathy.

" 'He also told us you were ruining yourself,' she said.

"They were watching me with concern. They couldn't have understood in a million years the kind of person I was.

" 'We weren't attempting to pry,' the man said. 'We wish only to help you. We realize you've had a terrible experience. We'd like to do some small thing for you in return for what you did for Beverley.'

"I was staring at them in horror. That I had deserted a man and friend was bad enough, but that I would now be rewarded for it by his parents was so awful I was almost sick at my stomach.

" 'It would give us a great deal of satisfaction to be able to help you,' the woman said, still holding my hand. 'Your commanding officer told us you scored well on your intelligence tests. With an education you'd have a real future. You're still young and strong. You have a duty to make something of yourself. Please don't let us lose you too.'

"They wouldn't let go. They stayed in Paris and haunted me. Each day they came to my hotel. I got stinking drunk and was thrown into jail by the *gendarmes*. Beverley's parents learned where I was and brought a French lawyer to fix it so I could leave. Even in the gutter the parents wouldn't turn me loose.

"The night I was released from jail I tried to kill myself. I loaded a .45 and held it to my head. At the last second I moved the gun just enough so the bullet grooved my scalp and burned my hair. Men broke down the door of my room and carried me to a hospital.

"The doctors put me under sedation and kept me at the hospital—a bright, sunny place on the outskirts of Paris. I couldn't get anything to drink because the orderlies watched me. Even when I went for a short walk, an orderly followed. The doctors gave me shots to make me eat. Each morning and afternoon Beverley's parents came to see me. They brought flowers and sat by my bed. The woman read to me from the Bible.

"Beverley's father fixed it with his congressman to get me out of the Army. By then I no longer had charge of my own life. They made me go back with them on the ship. I stood at the stern of the big luxury liner and watched the muddy wake trailing toward France. Beverley's father had hired a male nurse to stay close to me in case I tried to jump off or hurt myself in some way. The nurse gripped my arm.

"On the way I sometimes stood in my stateroom and looked at myself in the mirror. I figured I should have changed after what I'd been through, but I didn't look ravaged. Though older and heavier, I didn't resemble a man who'd been living in Hell.

"Beverley's parents took me to Winston-Salem where I stayed with them in the same fine house under the elm trees. Beverley's room had been closed up. His mother showed it to me. Nothing had been changed. It was as if he were coming back any day. Silver cups were on the mantel and dog pictures on the walls. His clothes were still hanging in the closets. I'd have run had not the male nurse glanced at me warningly.

"In September Beverley's father drove me to Virginia where he had gone to college. Again it was the fact I was supposedly a hero which paved the way for me to get in. Beverley's father talked to the dean and made it sound as if the college had a patriotic duty to admit me. The dean was honored to shake my hand. I was given special entrance examinations I don't think were even graded.

"I was glad to get to college because it at last provided an escape from Beverley's parents and all the kindness they'd been pouring over me. I could be alone. I found also that work kept my mind off myself. A man can hide in work just as he can in liquor or dope. That's what I did. I got high on work.

"I began to come to terms with myself a little too. I was trying to understand. It seemed to me I'd been given my life back. It wasn't much of a life, but if I was going to live, I figured I ought to do the best I could. I owed that to Beverley's parents. I couldn't cheat them twice.

"Of course a lot of times I thought of what'd happened in France. I might be sitting in class or walking down a street and I'd get shaky hot at remembering. Yet I tried to be reasonable too. After all I hadn't killed Beverley. He'd have died whether I ran or not. I told myself a man could accept the fact he was a coward just as easily as he could the color of his hair or having ten toes. Cowardice wasn't a thing a person willed on himself.

"Work was the best thing for me. It was something to hang onto when everything else was shifting. I'd always had a flair for figures. I guess I liked them because there were no loose ends. Each mathematical problem comes out the neat way it's supposed to. At first I was at the bottom of the class, but I became stronger every year. By the time I was a senior I was on the honor roll. Other students who'd been to fancy prep schools came to me for help with their projects.

"Occasionally I had to go to Winston-Salem. I did it as seldom as possible. I lied to them on vacations. I told them I was going to visit relatives in the coal fields, which I never did. During the summers I found jobs which kept me from being able to visit. Beverley's mother was always sending me money as well as shirts, socks, and an overcoat.

"The summer jobs were with a construction company based in Roanoke. The boss liked me well enough to promise me a permanent position after I graduated. Naturally Beverley's parents came to that graduation. They wanted me to go back to Winston-Salem, but I told them I'd already signed a contract. They were both disappointed and happy about me. They gave me a Ford for a graduation present.

"I lived in rented rooms and worked. The Roanoke firm was building maintenance barns for the N&W railroad. I'd stay at the office sixteen hours a day sweating over cost figures. I liked tiredness because tiredness kept ghosts out. I could become so involved with cost problems I forgot everything else. Figures were my religion.

"I worked for the company eight years, and in the eighth year Beverley's parents drowned in a boat wreck off the Carolina coast. I went to Winston-Salem for the funeral. I was asked to sit in the family section of the church during the service.

"Beverley's parents left me twenty thousand dollars. That nearly drove me crazy. I went out and got falling-down drunk. Then I wrote the lawyer and told him I didn't want the money. I asked him to give it to somebody who needed it. He wrote back I had to do that. I did give it away. I sent it to every charity I could find,

247

mailing out the envelopes with no return address so nobody'd know who I was."

He stopped talking. His tongue worked shakily around the edges of his lips. He lifted the bottle but lowered it again without drinking. His face shone with sweat.

"I went back to work," he said. "All I did was work. I slept maybe two or three hours a night. People were always telling me to slow down, yet I couldn't because I thought about myself when I did.

"I'd reached my ceiling with the Roanoke construction company. It was a family-owned firm, and the sons and cousins were taking all the top positions. I decided what I needed was something of my own. Even though I'd given away all the money Beverley's parents left me, I had plenty in the bank. Living alone in small rooms, I'd spent next to nothing of my salary.

"While I was looking for a business, I met Dabney Scott. I'd been sent to his town to submit a bid on the construction of a municipal building. Scott, a slow-talking country man in his fifties, had put in a bid of his own. It was unrealistically low, and he was obviously going to lose money on the job. He was bound to have made mistakes in his estimate.

"I liked the town. Though small and old, it was near enough to Washington that a construction company ought to be able to get plenty of business in the capital. Moreover the town was already beginning to catch an overflow of people across the Potomac from Washington itself. Real estate would rise in value. Lastly the cost of labor in Virginia was lower which would help when it came to bidding the Washington jobs.

"Through a local lawyer I did some checking on Scott. I learned he had a good reputation, but he was staying just about one jump ahead of bankruptcy. It was the figures which were killing him. His work was sound, and his crews were the best in the area. I thought his outfit could be the nucleus of a really fine small company.

"I never considered doing it without him because I needed him as much as he needed me. I was essentially a cost man, not a builder. Furthermore the people in the town stuck close together and were hostile to strangers. He was from an old family and could call the bankers by their first names. I hoped we'd be able to get enough local jobs to meet our payrolls until I could land us something big.

"Before approaching him, I decided to change my name. I'd been thinking of doing that for a long time. There were a couple of reasons. The first was that Yankovitch didn't go too good in Virginia.

People eyed me as if I were a refugee from Poland. It was a name that hurt not only in business but in any kind of social life as well.

"Secondly I was trying to be a new man. A new man needs a new name. I thought by shedding the old one, some of the bad would go with it. I chose Yancey because it was Beverley's middle name and it sounded aristocratic to me. I went with a lawyer to a Roanoke court where the judge ordered the change.

"I drove to see Scott on a Saturday and made him a partnership offer. I expected him to dicker for terms, but he didn't. He was relieved somebody was going to bail him out of the financial mess he was in. We had papers drawn up, and they stipulated that in event of death the surviving partner had a right to buy the company at its book value.

"My first job was to straighten out the books. I took them over and turned Scott loose with the work crews. We had a disagreement right at the start. I intended to chop all deadwood from our payrolls, but he made excuses for carpenters or bricklayers who could no longer carry their weight. He kept them on because he'd known them for years or been a friend of their fathers. I told him we couldn't stay in business on a sentimental basis. The firings hurt me in town because the men who lost their jobs talked about me.

"I was after a big bid and decided to shoot for a large school building which was planned on the outskirts of Washington. I figured we could handle the job. I worked on estimates for six weeks, checking and double-checking every specification. I sent Scott to sweet-talk subcontractors into lowering their quotes to us.

"I carried the bid to the school board. In the room were representatives from some of the biggest construction outfits in the East— two of them with listings on stock exchanges. Those representatives smiled patronizingly at me. They acted as if I were a country cousin who'd got into the place by mistake.

"They didn't smile long. I was low by twenty-five thousand dollars. Of course the job was a big gamble for Scott and me because we couldn't afford to lose money. It was feast or famine. Scott was scared, but I had confidence. I knew my figures. Given an even break, we'd be all right.

"We didn't get the even break. No sooner did we put a steam shovel in to start on the foundation than we discovered a narrow stratum of limestone running only a few feet below the topsoil. That limestone had to be blasted out yard by yard, not only costing time and money but also bringing suits from homeowners in the area who claimed their plaster was being cracked and their windows broken by detonations.

"That was only the beginning. We started work in the early spring, and the rains that year were heavy. For weeks at a time we could pour no concrete. The place became a sea of mud. Trucks bogged down and required expensive maintenance. When men could work at all, it went slow. Our labor gang had to be paid rain or shine to hold them together.

"All the while I was watching the books. I gave up sleep. I lived in the office or on the job. Scott was so afraid he began drinking. Half of the time I was doing his work as well as my own. There was no longer any question of profit. I was just trying to keep the whole company from going down the drain.

"I had to take a long shot. I didn't want to do anything dishonest, but I was cornered and fighting for my life. The original specifications for the building called for the best door, window, and railing hardware which could be bought. You'd be surprised how much hardware there is in a school. I knew I could purchase a second line just as serviceable and nobody would notice the difference. In addition the heating system could be modified to knock off another chunk of money. The spread would be enough to save Scott and me —providing the architect and inspector went along.

"They went along. It was easy. I put the money down, and they picked it up. It didn't involve much risk for them. They both told me that if there was trouble, they'd howl for my hide. I'd have to take all the blame.

"I hurried back to the office and began putting in orders for the new hardware and canceling the old. I had a talk with the heating contractor who agreed to make certain changes rather than chance getting nothing at all out of the job.

"Scott knew what I was doing. He sat across the desk from me while I telephoned and looked as if he were going to cry. He tried to act innocent, but he was just as involved as I was. He didn't want to know the messy details. He never tried to stop me either.

"We got by with it. When the building was finished, the inspection went off without a hitch. I turned over the key to the school board chairman. By the time payoffs were made, Scott and I had a net profit of a little over a hundred dollars."

Yancey raised his bottle and drank. His eyes were closed, and liquor ran from the corners of his mouth. His head fell back against the steel bulkhead of the paint locker.

"I'm not proud of what I did on that building," he said. "I didn't want to be crooked, but it was better to be crooked than to be ruined. The trouble is once you start you can't get away. The next time it was the architect who came to see me.

"He had a nice little deal worked out. I was to bid so low on government work that nobody could beat me, then he through his connections would see to it that there were changes in the specifications. The changes would be very expensive since they weren't covered by the original bid, and they would furnish the profit.

"We made a lot of money that way. The big outfits who'd once treated me like a poor relation flinched every time I walked in the room with a bid. Old Scott with his fine gentleman's feelings never said a word because he was building himself a new house and driving around in a big car.

"Each job we bid increased our business because it brought us into contact with more people of influence. I was discovering just how many men there were who'd pick up money if it was laid down in the right way. Mostly getting them to take it was a matter of technique, and I never found one yet who wouldn't reach for his bundle when the technique was good. That includes you, Charley boy."

As I stood over him, he blinked and smiled contemptuously.

"So don't act superior," he said. "The payoff doesn't have to come only in money. Sometimes you put down other currency. Like if a person thinks you might help him into OCS. You were willing to do just about anything I wanted when you thought I could help you. You were browning me, Charley."

God how I hated him at that moment. I'd have loved to kick his fat, round face until it was bloody and roll him into the ocean. I was hot with blood pumping in me. Yet he'd spoken the truth. I had tried to use him, and I was more ashamed of it than anything I'd done in my life.

"Of course Scott who loved the money wouldn't condescend to get his own hands dirty with the dealing," Yancey continued, watching me with his watery, cynical eyes. "He left that for me to do. I had to wade through all the crap.

"He was hitting the bottle. He didn't show it much because he was a quiet drinker. I walked into his office looking for some papers and opened a drawer of his desk. The drawer was full of empty pint bottles. He sucked them like a baby. He'd start out light in the mornings and increase the feeding hourly until by dark he was pretty far gone.

"He died on a Sunday. He was sitting on the front porch of his new house taking an after-dinner snooze. He never woke up. At the funeral more than two hundred people came because he was popular and related to all the old families.

"By the terms of our partnership agreement, I had the right to buy him out on the book value of the company. Well, a construction outfit isn't worth much in itself. There aren't a lot of fixed assets and a big inventory. The real value of the firm was the management, and that's not on a balance sheet.

"I paid Scott's widow more than the company was actually appraised for, but a lot of townspeople believed I'd cheated her, even though her lawyers and accountants went over the books. People acted as if I were hiding money someplace. They didn't really care for the facts. They were thinking about me being an outsider who'd come in, fired local workers, and now owned a company which had belonged to one of their own. Everything would have been dandy if Scott had outlived me, but they wouldn't accept it the other way around.

"The widow wasn't too bad off. She just didn't know how to handle the money she had. I'd have been glad to help her, but she had no use for me. She thought her husband was better than me and hadn't liked him going into business with me in the first place. She let a son play the stock market with her capital. It took him two years to run through most of it. She had to sell her big house, and of course I got blamed for that too.

"I was treated like the town whore. I liked the community and had worked hard to become a part of it. I gave to charity, churches, and civic clubs. I used my own equipment to turtle-back the football field. Instead of thanking me, people acted as if I were trying to put something over on them.

"They condemned me for buying the old Morton place. Nobody else wanted it. There were chickens and goats in the living room. I was trying to do the best I could with my life. Even being involved in all the crookedness, I still wanted to be better than I was. All the time I was struggling to be better.

"The people in the town wouldn't let me be better. They said I'd cheated some elderly sisters out of the place. They called me new rich and wouldn't look at me on the streets. I spent thousands of dollars restoring the house to the way it was back in Revolutionary times, but they would have rather seen it burnt to the ground than for me to own it.

"It was a bad time. Nobody would come out to see me. I sat alone among the antiques. I had trouble finding servants. They even had the niggers looking down on me."

He was very drunk. Each roll of the ship caused his head to bump softly against the bulkhead. He sighed and had to wait for a counter roll to right himself. He kept blowing out air as if surrounded by water threatening to rise above his face.

He took another drink. It was the last in the bottle, and after all the liquor was drained, he ran his tongue into the glass neck. When he lowered the bottle, he peered at me as if he didn't understand where he was or why I was with him. His chin sank slowly to his chest.

"I'd already seen Martha," he said. "She sang in the choir of the Presbyterian church. Her family had been around there for years, and she wouldn't have anything to do with me. I had to force myself on her. I made more in a week than she and her mother lived on in a year, but the first time I went to their house they treated me like white trash. They were insulted I'd come to the front door. I didn't give them the chance to kick me out. I was a high-pressure salesman selling the goods, and the goods were me.

"It took me one date to discover Martha wasn't as angelic as she looked up in the choir loft. She had an itching for the worldly. Her eyes lighted up at pretty clothes or an expensive piece of jewelry. Her fingers stroked fine materials the way a cat licks itself. She purred in the presence of money."

I wanted to stop his mouth. Martha had thrown me over, but I still had love and loyalty for her. She had left vestiges in me which would require years to obliterate. At moments I could even believe I might have her again. I glared at Yancey.

"I finally got her to my house," he said. "It took a lot of scheming and bribing. Out there was where I really felt her change about me. She went from room to room touching things and moaning. She could imagine it all belonging to her, and she kept biting her lip.

"I followed her around. She got so sexed up over things she let me kiss her. She was confused because she was thinking about all the worldly goods I could give her while at the same time remembering what people in town thought of me. She was weighing my pocketbook.

"When I saw her weakening, I got out the medals. I didn't want to. I hated doing it. I had to show them to her because it was the only way I could push her over the line. She held the medals and read the citation. They did the trick. I got her to marry me.

"Even after she did, I didn't fool myself into believing she was in love with me. I didn't require that. I was happy with the part of her I had. I hoped maybe in time I could bring her around to where she loved me, but I meant to be patient.

"I couldn't look at her enough. The shape of her hands and the way she touched her hair drove me crazy. I'd sit on the bed and watch her primp before a mirror. I liked to take her shopping and see her excitement at being able to buy all the clothes she wanted. In the office I'd sometimes get the impulse to drive home just to look at her. I'd want to get her face in mind so I could have it with me the rest of the day.

"She was learning how to spend my money and be a hostess. She liked to give parties to show off in front of the people in town. She read all the books on etiquette and stood at the front door greeting guests as if she were a queen. After six months of entertaining, she could have held her own with royalty.

"I guess I was too happy with her, and that made me lose my sense of judgment. At any rate I was trying to change my ways. I was untangling myself from the crooks I was involved with. It was costing me money, but I wanted to be clean for her. As the Boy Scouts say, I wanted to be worthy.

"I attempted to change my personality. I knew people thought I talked too much and too loud. I worked at being dignified so she could be as proud of me as I was of her. When I spoke, I wouldn't let my hands move, and I made myself pause before answering questions to give weight to what I said. I was striving to be somebody she could admire.

"My big mistake was loving her too much. I loved her so much I was trying to make everything absolutely perfect. I couldn't forget how I'd used the medals to trick her into marrying me. She had them mounted on velvet and hung on the wall. Each day I passed them they reminded me of the lie between us.

"I needed to wipe that out, and the only way I could do it was by telling her the truth. I tried to tell her a dozen times but could never get the words out. Then one evening I had a little too much to drink. We'd been on an anniversary party, and she was wearing a blue silk dress which shimmered as she walked.

"I caught hold of her and held my face against her. I confessed with my eyes closed. I told her about the medals and felt the stiffness come in her. I should have stopped, but I didn't until I looked up and saw her face. She pulled away from me. I kept waiting for her to say she understood—that the medals didn't make any difference. She went to bed without a word. I got sick in the bathroom and later lay in the dark not knowing what to do.

"She never mentioned what I'd told her. It was hard for me to believe I had. I was sorry I'd opened my mouth and hoped it wouldn't make any difference. It did make a difference though. Not all at once but gradually she began to change. I'd catch her looking at me as if she was wondering. One evening I came home to find the medals gone. She'd taken them off the wall and put them in the attic.

"The same night I tried to be a husband to her. She made excuses. I retreated to my own bed afraid. I told myself I should grab her and make her do it with me. I should have gotten rough. I couldn't. It was as if her coldness had frozen the balls right off me."

"I don't want to hear any more filth from you," I said to Yancey, stepping across him to get out of the paint locker.

Yancey, however, caught one of my legs, and I almost fell. I stumbled back to the bulkhead. He pushed up to his feet and staggered. I tried to get around him. He reeled in front of me. I smelled liquor on his breath, and his eyes were glazed. The roll of the ship threw him from side to side.

"You're going to listen whether you want to or not," he answered, blowing his breath into my face. "By God, you have to listen."

"Out of the way," I warned him.

He shoved me, and before I could catch hold of him he fumbled his .45 from the oxblood holster. The big pistol waved at me—the dark hole pointing at my stomach. He lowered his aim a little, as a jealous husband might, and my hands wanted to clasp themselves over that part of me.

"You're going to listen," he said. "I'm going to make you listen or kill you. For your information she didn't cut me off completely after that. When she wanted it, she'd invite me to her bed. She didn't give a damn about me, but she didn't mind using me. I was a handy dildo when she got the urge."

If it hadn't been for the pistol, I'd have gone for him. I'd have beat hell out of him too. The .45, however, circled at me. He was just drunk and crazy enough to use it. I couldn't rush him.

"I guessed she was going to try another man before she did it," he continued, swaying from side to side. "That was just a matter of time. She'd learned to flirt, you see, and I'd watch her in a crowd of men using her eyes and touching them with her long fingers. She'd been so innocent when I first knew her, but she wasn't any longer. She was anything but innocent.

"I don't know how many men she had, but I caught her with one. I just happened to see her car on a side street in Washington. I thought she must be shopping. I parked my own car, hoping to surprise her and maybe help with her packages.

"It was after five when she came out of an apartment building. She looked beautiful and slim in a dark suit and a big hat. She didn't appear at all as if she'd been rolling in the hay. With her was the architect—the great architect who was a bigger crook than I could ever be, yet who she thought was better than me.

"Would you be interested in how I felt? I felt as if somebody had taken an ax and chopped into my stomach. I drove out of town, parked my car beside the road, and cried like a baby.

"I didn't know whether to accuse Martha or not. That's how mixed up she had me. My anger wasn't as big as the fear of losing her. When I got home, she was in her room. On the bed were her packages. She acted so cool and poised it seemed impossible she had been doing God knows what with a man in that apartment."

I watched Yancey's gun. It had dropped slightly, and I might yet have a chance to jump him. He leaned against the door. He shook his head.

"I couldn't say anything right then," he continued. "She was so sure of herself I couldn't break through. I thought also she might stop with the architect. I wanted to give her plenty of chance to come back on her own. Every time she went out after that it killed me, but I never opened my mouth. She didn't make explanations. She was sure she could do anything she wanted with me.

"One evening she was leaving just as I was coming in, and I asked her to stay. She told me she had to play bridge. After she was gone, I called a member of her club. The woman said there was no game that evening. I waited up for Martha. She didn't come in until after midnight, and I asked her about the architect.

"She didn't act guilty. She took off her hat without hurrying and lighted a cigarette.

" 'All right, what are you going to do?' she said.

" 'I ought to beat hell out of you.'

256

"'As the old song goes, "You Made Me What I Am Today."'"

"'Don't try to blame me, you slut.'"

"'You did. A wife ought to respect her husband. I have no respect for you. If I've changed, you're the reason.'"

"Her saying that really scared me—I mean the fact I might have corrupted her and driven her to what she was doing. I remembered her young and innocent. I started out accusing her and ended up feeling guilty myself.

"'If you want a divorce, you can have it, but it's going to cost you money,' she said.

"'Why should I pay anything? I'm the person who's been kicked in the teeth, not you.'"

"'There are lots of reasons, but the main one is that all I know about you will come up in court. Don't think it won't.'"

"'Get out of my house!'"

"She shrugged, put down her cigarette, and packed a suitcase. She drove to her mother's. I supported the mother too, yet whenever I was around the old lady she acted as if the sewer were leaking.

"With Martha gone, my place was a tomb. After twenty-four hours alone in those quiet rooms, I knew I'd rather take her on her terms than not have her at all. I went to her hat in hand. It was noon, but she was still sleeping. Her mother called her. Martha came down in a yellow bathrobe I'd bought her, her black hair let out and falling on the yellow. I told her I wanted her back. It's a joke. She had me begging her.

"'I won't change,' she said. 'If I come back, you'll have to accept me the way I am. I'll entertain for you and keep your house, but I won't let you touch me and I'll have a man once in a while.'

"I took her home. She meant what she'd said and never let me near her after that. She was very reasonable about it. She told me to find a shopgirl. I couldn't believe any of it was happening to me. I kept thinking things somehow had to get better, but they never did. They just got kind of dead.

"At the parties I'd stand watching her and wondering which men in the room she'd slept with. There must have been a lot because the word was around about her. She was the subject of the gossip, not me. She blamed me that people wouldn't come to the house, yet it was her fault. The only ones we got were the second-rate—the kind that drink your liquor, tell dirty jokes, and trade wives driving home."

"You're lying," I said to Yancey. I was watching the gun wobble, waiting for it to sink far enough so I could rush him.

"I'm no liar and you suffer, you sonofabitch. You go through a little of what I did. It'll be good for a bastard like you. You're just one of a long line she played with."

He raised the pistol. His face was twisted into a mask of rubbery, sweating fury. He was crazy drunk enough to pull the trigger of the .45. I pressed back against the bulkhead.

"I kept her bank account full for her," he said. "I never asked her how she spent her money but always knew some of it would be going on a man. Because of her I tried another woman—a young girl just out of high school who came to my office looking for a job. I drove her to a tourist court and was so sorry afterward I gave her a hundred dollars. I never tried anything with her again or any other woman either.

"I wanted a son. I was making lots of money and no longer had to do business with the crooks. I figured I could give a son a lot. At first Martha didn't want to ruin her figure. Later, after finding out about me, she refused to have a baby. How do you think that makes you feel to have a wife who detests you so much she won't even bear you a son?

"When the war started, I didn't get the idea of joining the Army all at once. I was busy with government work. The cost-plus contracts being handed out made it pushover for anybody to make money. A man could pick his jobs. I was expanding my firm and becoming one of the biggest contractors in the state. I could be home right now counting my money instead of here with a sonofabitch like you.

"I decided to go because of an accident during the winter. I was driving on an icy road and skidded around a curve. My car spun right in front of a truck. I saw the driver's face and heard his horn. I felt the air swoosh past me. My car smashed into a snowdrift.

"The truck ran off the road, turned over going down a bank, and crashed into a tree. As I stepped out of my car, I saw smoke. I ran toward the truck. The smoke was becoming thick, and I smelled gasoline. The truck driver was lying in the cab, blood on his face, his eyes closed. I yelled at him, but he didn't move. Any second I expected things to explode.

"I thought of going back to my car and driving like hell to a phone where I'd call the fire department. I knew if I did, the man would be dead by the time I got back. I had to do something quick. I tried to open the truck door. It was jammed. I got my tire iron from the car trunk. All the while smoke was coming out so bad it was like night. I was coughing. I felt heat in the truck. It was getting hotter and hotter.

"I pried open the door. The poor guy was all broken up and bleeding. I pulled him out. I had to be rough. I just dragged him across the snow fast as I could. His blood left a trail. Just as I got him to the top of the bank, the truck went up. The explosion and heat knocked me down. The blast rattled windows of houses a mile away.

"I staggered up and jerked the driver to my car. I took him to the doctor in town. After I found out he was going to live, I started home. I began to think I could have easily been killed. Except for a few seconds, I might have been burnt bacon. Yet I hadn't been afraid. I should have been shaking, but I was as calm as if I'd just climbed from my bed.

"Up to then I'd accepted the fact I was a coward. I'd lived with the knowledge so long I no longer even thought about it. Because of the truck, though, I seemed changed. I'd just missed being killed, but my heart was beating regularly and my hands were steady. I wondered whether it was possible that over the years I'd developed some sort of courage. Maybe a man could change.

"I wasn't able to get the idea out of my head, and because of it I began to consider going back into the service. I saw a chance to recoup a bad part of my life. If I found pride in myself, I might win my wife back too. It wasn't a question of being a hero and getting real medals. All I wanted was to come out with honor and make her see I was no longer what she thought."

The pistol sank a little, but Yancey no longer acted as drunk. His forehead was wrinkled as if he were puzzling out a problem. The fat of his face had firmed. He staggered against the roll of the ship.

"When I told Martha I was volunteering, she thought I was being funny. I'd gone physically soft a long time ago and was over the draft age. My hair was turning gray. Maybe her believing the idea was ridiculous was what clinched it for me. She made me have to do it. I dyed my hair before going downtown to enlist. I still dye it.

"I could have got myself a direct commission. I had the connections and would only have had to drop the word in the right place. I didn't because she was watching me, and for her I wanted to keep it pure.

"But things happen. Things always happen. I'd forgotten how

tough the Army can be for a man not in shape. Once I was in, I had to stay at all costs or I'd be worse off in her eyes than before I'd joined up. I could see myself busting out because of a stupid wall on the obstacle course or because of a bunch of goddamn marches. The only way I could survive basic was by using those medals. I hated doing it, but I had no choice.

"If you think I enjoy going around pulling strings and bribing people you're crazy. OCS was just like when I went into business with Scott—I was fighting for survival. If I flunked out, Martha would be sure she was right about me all the time. I did wrong putting that money on the captain's desk, but as long as I held on I still had hope. I had to bribe and brown and use those medals because if I failed I'd never have a chance with Martha again."

"You don't have a chance with her again," I told him.

"Maybe not," he answered, raising the pistol. "But then maybe I do too. When this outfit gets into action I might get clean, and when I'm clean I'll try. I just might talk her into starting over with no cheating or lying between us. We'll bury all the bad. That's what I want—to bury the bad."

"She's leaving you."

"Sure she's leaving me."

"She told you about him?"

"She didn't tell me. Whoever he is, he's just one more man to me, and I've been waiting and expecting her to leave for years. Only she won't for a while yet, no matter with who. She's too greedy. She likes the money, the house, and the stable full of blooded horses. She loves her closets full of dresses and racks of shoes too much. She wants a bank account so full she don't have to keep the stubs of her checkbook. She might be thinking of leaving, but she won't while there's a war on because no judge is going to award her much for running out on her husband while he's fighting for his country."

He was weaving and seemed to be staring behind me again—as if he could look through the steel plates of the bulkhead to the ocean itself where he saw Martha and him living out some two-bit romantic solution to the mess he'd made of his life. His eyes refocused on me, and hardness set his face.

"But you, you sonofabitch, you got no right to treat me like garbage every time we meet," he said. "I might be pretty bad. I might be just about the worst there is, yet I'm not as bad as you, Charley. No matter what I am, you had no right to lay my wife. You're ten times the bastard I am."

A wave caused the ship to pitch, and Yancey lost his balance. He slumped into a corner by the door, steadied himself, and reached for the knob. Spit bubbled on his lips. The light went out. His dumpy, sagging shape merged with the dark.

30

After Yancey was gone, I lay awake a long time thinking of what he'd said. In spite of the hate I had for him, his story had affected me. It was not only the new picture of Martha he had furnished, but also the one of himself. There now appeared depths and shadings to him I hadn't imagined—a sorrowful, Pagliacci-like quality that bespoke tragedy beneath a flabby and comic façade.

Yet I was troubled only a short while. I made myself remember that Yancey was a sly, unscrupulous man. Dealing and manipulating were a way of life for him. There were undoubtedly bits of truth in what he'd told me, but he had been living a lie so long he was unable to sift the true from the false. He believed anything he wanted.

I saw him the next morning as I took my stroll around deck. He looked terrible. His eyes were bloodshot, and a dark stubble sprouted from his pale skin. He acted furtive. At the sight of me, he hurried away on his fat legs.

He never came back to the paint locker, and for the rest of the trip he avoided me. When I met him on deck, he'd change directions or turn into a companionway. His watery eyes never looked into mine. He was a waddling definition of guilt and deceit.

On the fifteenth day at sea, we smelled land. The odor was like mown alfalfa hay. Those of us on deck searched for a shoreline. Everybody was sure it would be Africa where American troops had been engaged in battle since the fight at Kasserine Pass.

Unlike me, most of the enlisted men were in a sorry condition. They had been living like prisoners for two weeks in the steaming squalor below deck. Their eyes had the dazed, uncomprehending stare of men who had already been in combat. Only the officers showed zip. They hurried around full of plans and self-importance. Colonel Bone and Lighthorse scowled with the weight of command. Yancey too acted the part of the warrior except when he caught me watching him. Then he seemed to wilt.

At the first sight of land, men cheered. Loudspeakers announced we were off Morocco. Our convoy anchored in the Casablanca harbor which resembled a resort town in Florida. LCIs came to shuttle us ashore. Trucks were waiting at the docks to carry us to a tent area outside the city.

The tent area was supposedly for transients, but as things turned out we sat in it for months. The Red Cross issued radios. We listened to what little of the fighting was left, which wasn't much because Rommel had flown to Germany and the Afrika Korps was crumbling. There were so many prisoners no one knew what to do with them. They trudged aimlessly about the desert.

All the officers at regiment started wearing pith helmets. We learned Yancey was responsible for those. In searching for souvenirs, he had discovered an Italian supply depot and requisitioned the helmets. As he was still bucking for major, he gave Colonel Bone and Lighthorse the first ones out of the crate.

Bone, instead of allowing us to recuperate from the ship, immediately put us through a schedule of desert training. There was no value in it because all the fighting was petering out. Still we stumbled around among the sand dunes playing soldier. Arabs squatted in the shade of palm trees and watched. They sometimes ate live grasshoppers, holding them by the head and thrusting them into their stained mouths.

In May we heard rumors about an approaching invasion of Sicily. Carter, still hungry for glory, believed the regiment had been selected to go in with the first wave. He heard Bone had received a promise of that assignment from the corps commander.

"Then what are we doing training in the desert?" Wilson wanted to know. "Do they have deserts in Sicily?"

"It's to confuse the enemy," Beanpost answered. "The enemy will believe we're going to attack Outer Mongolia and leave Sicily open."

"Are there Germans in Outer Mongolia too?" Carter asked.

We were alerted on a Sunday evening. We loaded our equipment onto trucks and drove through the night to a staging area near Oran. The harbor was full of gray ships. We were issued new gas masks and life preservers. Men's faces became sober at the thought that the rumor about our being in the first wave might be true. Lighthorse rushed around and was undoubtedly dreaming of making his end run like Stonewall Jackson at Chancellorsville. Yancey was never far behind, his jeep siren wailing.

After being given Italian currency, we were certain we were on the way to Sicily. Each morning we looked out over the storybook harbor, waiting to be loaded onto ships wallowing in the blue water. We sat watching other troops in the area shuttling out by LCIs.

Carter was excited. The young blond believed that at last the golden eagle was going to soar to glory. Black Hatfield sharpened his knife. The Professor had an extra supply of books in his pack. They would last him a while in case he wasn't able to find a library.

We, however, never got to the ships—at least not with the others we didn't. We remained on a promontory overlooking the harbor and saw troops sail away. Over our Red Cross radios we heard reports of invasion. We raised our eyes to airplanes flying over. Men of the golden eagle began to act sheepish. Carter was shamed past consolation.

"We're destined to be spinsters," Wilson said. "We've been bridesmaids too often."

Ten days later ships returned to pick us up. By that time the invasion was already a success and what fighting was left was disorganized. We went to Palermo where we bivouacked in ancient, yellowish houses which had neither running water nor johns. Battalion headquarters was set up in a shop that had belonged to the Fascist party. Emblems and slogans were painted on the flaking walls. Beanpost found some blackjacks which were supposedly used on political prisoners.

Nobody knew exactly what our mission was, but the colonel immediately ordered us onto a new training schedule. Inevitably the rumor arose that the 606th had been promised the first wave invading Italy. Only the real believers like Carter took it seriously. The line companies hiked around the scabby Sicilian countryside to the amusement of the Italians. All troops were followed by bands of children who shrilled for chewing gum and cigarettes. The children stole everything not under guard.

Off duty there were vino and women. An evacuation hospital was busy treating VD. The USO provided a movie star wearing a low-cut dress. She sang and shook her knockers in such fashion that even men who'd sworn chastity were driven to the whores for relief. The cheap vino was responsible for epidemics of dysentery.

The officers were gloomy. Bone and Lighthorse acted cheated because they'd been denied a part in the fighting. They were beginning to believe they were persecuted. Their attitude filtered down through the outfit.

Yancey continued to avoid me and to carry on his campaign for a majority. He was always busy. For example he found a huge red

Persian rug which had belonged to a German general. Yancey spread it in Lighthorse's office. The office looked like a harem, but Lighthorse was pleased. He removed his shoes to walk on the rug.

"When do you think Captain Brown will procure a woman for the colonel?" Timberlake asked disgustedly.

"That's about all that's left," Wilson said.

Though Yancey didn't go so far as to pimp for the colonel, there was no doubt he had the inside track at both battalion and regiment. He was telling Lighthorse and Bone dirty jokes. He played poker with them in the hotel which had been designated as the officers' club. Wilson, still bartending, claimed Yancey lost on purpose to please Bone and Lighthorse.

The Professor was taking bets on how long it would require Yancey to become a major. What made the problem interesting to him was the fact no opening for major existed in the battalion. Thus the challenge for Yancey was even greater because he would have to create the rank.

"He can't be stopped," the Professor said confidently. "It's just a matter of time. He's an irresistible force."

Events broke right for Yancey when Colonel Bone had his semi-annual physical. At the evacuation hospital it was discovered he suffered from a perforated ulcer. Against Ben Bone's wishes the head surgeon ordered him to the States for treatment. Colonel Bone pleaded with tears in his eyes, but in the end he had to climb aboard a silver C-47. He had a wooden chest full of pistols, swords, and Nazi belt buckles. The regiment was drawn up in formation. As the plane took off into the sunset, we saluted.

With Bone gone, Lighthorse was put in charge of regiment and Yancey given temporary command of battalion. He sat in the big office with his red Persian rug and sent out directives as if he were a general. Chicken orders to paint butt cans and shellac our helmets came down. WO Page learned Lighthorse had already put through for Yancey's majority. The Professor smiled.

Suddenly, however, the situation was complicated. While Lighthorse Harry was out on a field problem with the line companies and speeding down a narrow country road, his driver lost control of the jeep. It crashed into an olive tree. Lighthorse sailed over the windshield and banged headfirst into the hood. At the hospital where he was X-rayed the doctors reported he had a concussion and broken collarbone. He too had to be evacuated. Again the entire regiment stood in formation at the Sicilian airport pocked with shell craters. Lighthorse's orderlies struggled to lift his chest of souvenirs aboard. Lying on a litter, he shook Yancey's hand fondly. The plane flew away.

"Maybe Captain Brown won't make major after all," Wilson said, meaning now Yancey had neither Bone nor Box to look out for him and was hated by the other officers.

"A pushover," the Professor maintained.

Yancey knew better than to try to butter up the acting regimental commander—a lieutenant colonel named Peters. Peters openly showed his feelings about Yancey and was trying to bump him from battalion command. Yancey fought a rearguard delaying action and bided his time. He was saving his stuff for the full colonel we'd heard was on his way from Africa. Yancey gave orders he wanted to be notified the instant the new colonel arrived.

Colonel Oxam reached the outfit on a Monday morning. He was an elderly, grizzled-looking man who'd been to West Point and came from Maine. He walked with an absolutely straight back. Yancey and all the other officers hurried to the airport to meet him, but Yancey elbowed to the front so he could be the first to shake Oxam's hand.

Oxam was astonished at the sight of Yancey who was wearing paratrooper boots, a yellow scarf, an oxblood .45, black gloves, and a pith helmet. He was also carrying a swagger stick.

"Who are you?" Oxam asked, staring.

"Captain Marvin Yancey, sir, acting commander Airedale Battalion. May I say to the colonel I consider it an honor to serve under his authority."

"Where'd you get that uniform?"

"Sir?" Yancey replied, still smiling but unsure.

"Are you a paratrooper?"

"No, sir."

"Then take off those goddamn boots. Who told you you could put that red crap on your holster. Scrub it off."

"Yes, sir," Yancey answered, at attention in front of the other officers who were glancing at each other with hope reborn.

"You're not British, are you?" the colonel demanded.

"No, sir."

"Get rid of the pith helmet. Do you hold a commission in the Marines?"

"No, sir."

"Then flush the goddamn swagger stick."

With that the colonel strode past Yancey and shook hands with the other officers. Yancey was momentarily immobilized. He had meant to ride with the colonel around the area to show him the sights, but now his timing was off. Colonel Peters beat him to it.

The word was quickly passed that Oxam was not a man who could be browned or manipulated. The Professor didn't believe it. He laughed.

"He's never been subjected to Yancey before," the Professor said.

It was true Yancey was subdued only a short time. He retired to battalion to lick his wounds and consider. Within twenty-four hours he made his next move which was to have the red Persian rug from his office rolled up and carried by truck to regimental headquarters. At night, while Oxam wasn't in his office, the rug was spread on the floor. The next morning when Oxam arrived, he stopped in the door-way.

"Who's responsible for this?" he asked.

Colonel Peters was happy to tell him, and Oxam immediately sent for Yancey. Yancey believed he was going to be thanked. Instead Oxam shouted at him so loudly that it could be heard in the street.

"Is this place a whorehouse?" Oxam yelled.

"The colonel doesn't like the rug?" Yancey said, frightened.

"The colonel definitely doesn't like the rug. Now get it off my goddamn floor."

The rug was taken out immediately, and Yancey again fled to battalion where he shut himself in his office.

"Well, well," Carter said.

"Well, well indeed," Wilson seconded him.

"The millennium has arrived," Beanpost put in.

"There's balm in Gilead," Timberlake, who had been reading one of the Professor's books, said.

"Captain Brown hasn't warmed up yet," the Professor maintained. "He'll rise to the challenge. Adversity brings out the best in genius."

We all were watching to see what Yancey would try next. Compared to Ben Bone and Lighthorse, Colonel Oxam was a Puritan. He had come not only from Maine but the backwoods. He could neither be told dirty jokes nor offered bourbon at the officers' club. He had no use for idle conversation. When Yancey went to regimental headquarters, Oxam frowned impatiently.

"What is it you want here?" he asked.

"Well, sir, I have a few minutes and thought I could fill in the colonel on regimental affairs," Yancey answered nervously. He was wearing the authorized uniform. "I was very close to both Colonel Bone and Colonel Box."

"A battalion commander shouldn't have time on his hands. I'll see if I can't find more for you to do."

"I have plenty to do, sir. I just thought there might be some way I could assist the colonel."

"The day I need assistance from a captain I'll retire. Now get the hell out of here and stop wasting my time."

At regiment, officers and men loved it. Under Bone and Lighthorse, Yancey had become universally despised. His browning had cut others out of favor and promotions. Now he was receiving retribution.

Within the week Yancey was bloodied again. He maneuvered before chow one evening to offer the colonel a lift to the mess hall. Oxam spotted the chrome-plated red-light siren on Yancey's jeep.

"What's that thing for?" Oxam demanded.

"Well, sir, I find it handy on these crowded Italian roads. Essentially it's a safety measure, and I've always believed these lights should be standard equipment. I've been considering drafting a letter to the War Department on the subject. If the colonel would permit me, I'd be happy to have one installed—"

"Get that goddamn thing off," Oxam said and walked away.

The combination red-light siren was removed in the motor pool, and holes were left in the fender. By then Yancey was beginning to act defensive. All his plans were bouncing off Oxam. Yancey was so unsure of himself he began to avoid regimental headquarters. He stayed at battalion with the door shut.

Colonel Oxam had apparently been sent to work the slackness out of the golden eagle. He ordered a series of inspections which were as chicken as any back in the States. He scheduled long marches, the only consolation of which was that Yancey was no longer allowed to ride. He was caught by Oxam doing so and chewed out. Afterward Yancey had to hoof it through the hot, muggy air like the rest of his men. He staggered around covered with sweat and dust.

Oxam assembled the regiment for a speech. He spoke from a command car on which a public address system had been mounted. We stood at attention in a field outside Palermo. The farmer who owned the field later complained to the military government about damage to his crops which were trampled.

"There's talk going around that this is a hard-luck outfit," Oxam said, his voice stern as an Old Testament prophet's. "Well, I'm going to spike those rumors right now. I don't believe in luck. I believe in soldiering and hard work. When the history of this campaign is written, the 606th will—I repeat will—share in the glory of those pages."

Although the speech was about what we expected, a lot of the men approved of it. They were mostly people like Carter who felt they had been left out of the war. There was no doubt the majority of us considered the golden eagle defective or it wouldn't have been held so long out of action. Oxam brought the outfit heart.

He introduced a tough training schedule and cut down on vino drinking by announcing it would be a court-martial offense for a soldier to have alcoholic beverages in his possession. Early one Wednesday morning he pulled a surprise inspection. We had to empty our duffel bags. Illegal bottles thumped to the floor. The men caught were ordered to dig holes six by six feet in size and fill them again. The Sicilians watched in amazement as hundreds of soldiers tore up the countryside to no purpose.

Yancey remained quiet for almost ten days. He was plotting his next move in his brownie campaign. The move turned out to be one of his old tricks from the Georgia days—fancy close-order drill. He met secretly with his company commanders to work up complex patterns. At regimental review, he sprung his surprise. Oxam watched with a stone face.

"Very pretty but it won't impress the Krauts," he said. "You'd be better off using drill time in the field."

As soon as the review was over, Yancey retreated to his office and again shut the door.

"It's exhilarating," Timberlake said. "The whole thing's what you might call a heady experience."

"He isn't beaten yet," the Professor answered. "Captain Brown's at his best when cornered."

"Like a rat," Wilson said.

Next Yancey put on the ribbons which represented his phony medals. I had been expecting that. It was a shameless act which destroyed any shred of sympathy I had for what he'd told me in the paint locker of the ship. The medals, however, did him no good.

"Old stuff," Oxam said. "We don't run on memories in this outfit. From now on we wear only what we earn."

Yancey hastily removed his ribbons.

"I believe he's washed up," Wilson remarked.

"Not yet," the Professor said. "He's just being put to the test."

He was wrong. Yancey was becoming desperate. There was talk of reorganization in the regiment, and he was scared he was going to lose both the battalion and the rating which went with it.

He got hold of a Mercedes convertible sedan which had belonged to the German General Staff. It was the kind of car Hitler stood in to salute from as he rode past cheering crowds. Yancey traded food for it. The Mercedes had reportedly run out of gas and been abandoned. Italian farmers were hiding it in a barn. Yancey brought it into Palermo on a wagon covered by canvas.

At battalion motor pool he had it worked on. Men cleaned the fine leather with English saddle soap. Official olive drab was sprayed over the black paint. The fenders and great chrome headlights were shined. The engine was tuned by a master mechanic. When the job was finished, the car was in perfect condition and sparkled.

Yancey didn't consult Oxam. Instead he involved the colonel's chauffeur, a pfc who was delighted to sit behind the wheel of a Mercedes instead of a jeep. He and Yancey arranged it so the car would be driven for Oxam when the latter left regimental headquarters in the evening. The word spread, and a lot of enlisted men loitered around the street or peeked from windows.

The colonel walked from headquarters and saw the car waiting for him. He stopped. Then, without speaking, he circled the Mercedes slowly.

"Who's responsible for this?" he asked his driver.

"Captain Yancey, sir," the pfc answered. He was standing at attention and holding open a door.

"Where'd he find it?"

"I don't know, sir."

"Well, get the goddamn thing away from here and bring my jeep," the cussing Puritan said, red in the face.

The chauffeur saluted and drove off fast. He hurried back with the dusty old jeep. Meanwhile Oxam had returned to headquarters where he sent for Yancey who waited expectantly at battalion. Yancey waddled quickly up the street, uncertain whether he was going to be rewarded or shot.

"Do I look like a fool?" the colonel shouted at him.

"No, sir," Yancey answered, hunching his shoulders.

"Don't you think I know what you're trying to do by giving me that car?"

"I hoped the colonel would be pleased."

"I know what you hoped. You thought you could brown me, and I'd make you a major. Well, by God, you might not even be a captain when I'm through with you. Now get out of my sight."

Shocked and battered, Yancey backed out of headquarters. When he reached the street, he rushed to battalion.

"Finished," Wilson said. "Washed up."

"No," answered the Professor.

For almost a month, Yancey was a recluse. He came out of his office only when he was forced to. We guessed he was working on something really ambitious.

He was indeed. He planned to throw a reception, dance, and buffet for Oxam at the Officers' Club. Yancey began negotiating with the mess personnel of other units as well as Navy ships in the harbor—trading guns, captured from the Italians, for flour, sugar, and good red meat. Without Oxam's knowledge the regimental radio was kept busy as Yancey dickered with supply officers around the island. He put battalion cooks to work preparing a feast while the rest of us ate out of cans.

He next went after women. Except for local whores, they were hard to find. He invited the nurses from the evacuation hospital. There were WAC officers in Africa for whom he arranged transportation by plane. He consulted the mayor of Palermo to draw up a list of Sicilian women of good family and social standing. Those ladies were notified by special messengers. He persuaded a USO unit in Casablanca to send its females.

Enlisted men of Airedale Battalion were ordered to help prepare the ballroom of the hotel. We had to wash down walls and build a bandstand for the five Sicilians in moth-eaten tuxedos who played Neapolitan music. We made tables on which to serve the buffet, waxed the floors with flattened K-ration boxes, and hung the ceiling with flowers.

On the night of the party, enlisted men and Sicilians gathered around the front of the hotel like peasantry at the entrance to a palace ball. The marquee was lighted in spite of air-raid precautions. From inside the hotel came the sound of tinny, off-key music.

Officers arrived in jeeps, command cars, and limousines. Their women, painted and girdled, stepped out showing knees and thighs. The Italian ladies wore silver, red, and yellow gowns which, though old-fashioned, caused hostile looks from the nurses and WACs who had only their uniforms.

The party started at nine, but by ten Oxam still hadn't arrived. He was, it was reported, working in regimental headquarters. Yancey waited nervously for him at the entrance to the hotel. He had WO Page watching Oxam's office. At ten-thirty, WO Page reported that Oxam had called for his car and driven out of the area.

"He's not coming?" Yancey asked, his rubbery face disappointed.

"Doubtful, sir," WO Page answered. "Perhaps he forgot."

"He didn't forget," Yancey said, thinking himself spurned.

He returned to the ballroom where enlisted-men waiters carried trays of food. Near the door was a dark, slinky Italian countess in a golden dress who put her arm through Yancey's. Yancey had been saving her for the colonel.

"So he finally got to the pimping after all," Wilson, who was tending bar, said.

The fact that Oxam wasn't coming spread quickly through the crowd, which had been on its best behavior. People immediately became more relaxed and moved toward the bar as if a signal had been given. There was nothing to drink except a sickly grapefruit punch, but some of the doctors spiked it with a quart can of medical alcohol.

Soon the dancing became livelier. Because of the threat of Old Puritan, couples had been constrained, moving around the floor in a formal, stiff-backed manner. Now a major went to the bandstand and thumped on the bass drum with his fist in an attempt to increase the tempo. The thin, ragged musicians fiddled away as they tried to follow the beat. A pretty little WAC lieutenant started jitterbugging with a dentist.

The Sicilian girls sat in straight chairs pushed against the wall. They had a ferociously ugly duenna with them who scowled at the dancing and the officers who wished to approach her charges. The girls were plump and giggly. The Sicilian countess was different. She had been to New York, she said, and when Yancey wouldn't dance with her, she took a fancy to a young, wholesome lieutenant. She sat with him, her legs crossed, whispering in his ear and running her long fingers down his neck.

Captain Hanks was after her. He pulled his rank on the virginal young lieutenant and himself sat by the countess. Though she didn't care for Hanks, she smiled. They danced. She was an older but very striking woman, and as she kicked out small feet, her golden dress shimmered. She kept looking over Hanks' shoulder for the lieutenant.

Because of the countess, the duenna allowed some of the Sicilian girls to dance the slow numbers. She, however, watched every movement, and they had to return to their chairs against the wall as soon as the music stopped. Officers were teaching them American steps. Sicilian flesh bounced under colored dresses. The duenna glared whenever a man stood too close to a girl.

"I feel I just reached puberty and am back in dancing school," a captain from New York said.

The musicians were doing a little better. The major had brought them all cups of the spiked punch, and as they played, they sweated. The music grew faster, though the only number they could handle at the pace was "Casey Would Waltz with the Strawberry Blonde," which they believed was the latest hit in the U.S. They repeated it until the wooden rhythm pounded into the dancers' heads. There was laughter each time the number started.

Yancey bustled about the room. He continued to look up the street for Oxam in spite of what Page had told him. Again he sent Page to check. Oxam's office was still dark. Refusing to quit, Yancey decided to go see for himself.

A captain was working on the ferocious duenna with the spiked grapefruit punch and the ugly old lady smacked her thick lips. The medical alcohol was insidious stuff. In fruit punch it was tasteless, yet caused a quick, crazy kind of highness. The stags took a cunning delight in carrying cups to the Sicilian girls who giggled more loudly and sipped daintily.

A band of Sicilian boys, barefooted and dirty-faced, slipped into the kitchen through a window and stole food. Wilson and the enlisted-men cooks and waiters chased them through the ballroom. Within minutes the children were back—through another window. They were adult in expression and rapacious as hawks, making a swooping raid across the dance floor to swipe armfuls of sandwiches from a table.

The first sign that things were getting out of hand was in the dancing. The pretty WAC lieutenant did a particularly high kick which flipped her skirt up to her garter belt. Her foot slid out from under her, and she bounced on her buttocks. Men helped her up. She hobbled to the bar where she called for another drink. The duenna, nose in the punch, hadn't noticed.

"*Meraviglioso il frutto*," she told her girls, and they nodded enthusiastically.

The girls had warmed up considerably. They were attempting to jitterbug. Though heavy and awkward, stag officers cut around and showed off for them as if they were raving beauties.

A first lieutenant who had really been at the punch got caught up in the frenzy of the dance, stood on his hands, and walked on them around his astonished partner. His change fell from his pockets. Some of the Americans applauded. His left arm collapsed, and he hit the floor on his head. He had to be carried to the sidelines, but was quickly replaced by another eager officer. The Sicilian girls, at first shocked, giggled. The duenna hadn't noticed.

The band of urchins was back. This time they galloped in at the front entrance and swarmed into the cloak room. They ran off with officers' coats. The hotel *padrone* chased after them, waving his arms.

Captain Hanks, dashing in his immaculate pinks, dogged the countess. He gave her no opportunity to be with her wholesome, virginal lieutenant. He was maneuvering her toward a balcony at the rear of the ballroom. She wished to be free of him, but she held her smile. His hand was pressed hard against her bare back.

A crap game started in a corner. Officers squatted and rolled dice against the wall.

A new element appeared—a dusky, painted, brightly dressed girl who had a room upstairs and was a believer in free enterprise. She walked down the steps, across the dance floor, and stopped at the bar. A short time later she left with an officer. Fifteen minutes later she was back for another man.

The American women resented her. They said something ought to be done, though nothing was. Some of the American women were being coaxed up the steps anyway by officers with rooms. Even coming down again, the American women stared haughtily at the whore, who was indifferent.

There was excitement at the entrance. A fat, small-time comedian from the USO had gone out for fresh air and found a Sicilian mule hitched before a *trattoria*. He had bought the mule with a pile of lira and now rode it right up the stone steps into the hotel and the ballroom.

"I am Sancho Pancha," he proclaimed and fell off.

The *padrone*, a small, nervous man with a black mustache, complained about what hoofs would do to the dance floor, but he was given the conqueror's smirk. An aggressive medical major told him the hotel belonged to the Allied Military Government who could blow it up if they wanted to. The fat comedian offered rides to the guests. Women hitched up their skirts to climb on. They squealed and waved their arms as the comedian led them around the room.

One lieutenant from Information & Education fed the mule spiked punch in a cup. Getting the mule loaded then became the thing to do. A captain went to the kitchen for a large pot and filled it with punch. The mule slurped the juice. The crowd cheered, including the Sicilian ladies who were also being watered, or punched, and who were beginning to appear a little dazed and unsteady.

It required three pots to affect the mule. Even after the third the animal seemed all right until he attempted to take a step. When his foot was out, he realized how dangerous moving was. He looked startled, rolled his eyes, and drew back the hoof slowly. Each mulish move brought more cheers from the crowd circled around him.

Cautiously, like a drunk taking the white-line test, he took a step, weaved, and tottered. His front legs went in different directions from the rear ones. He was trying to get out the entrance, yet he swayed off course as if a strong wind were blowing against his flanks.

All the while the music continued. For a moment the mule's hoofs actually moved in time with "Casey Would Waltz with the Strawberry Blonde." That caused more cheering. The mule looked astonished as his legs became tangled and his hoofs slid out from under him, making deep scratches on the polished floor. The mule's rump settled first, and he rolled to his side. Closing his eyes, he whinnied.

There were applause and shouts of victory. As the music never stopped, dancers joined again, stepping around the passed-out mule as if there were one on every ballroom floor. Some of the dancers, burning the spiked punch, were bolder. Their feet didn't move, though their bellies did.

Hanks was pressing the countess toward the balcony. He was bent over her as if he would break her back. Suddenly he looked surprised, stepped away, and hunched himself. His hands fluttered in front of himself like a modest maiden. He rushed from the ballroom. The countess smiled and touched her black hair. Immediately she headed for her wholesome lieutenant, who appeared frightened at her approach.

Now a number of whores were working the party. They came right in off the street. They were snitching men so rapidly that nurses, WACs, and USO girls found themselves without escorts. The whores haggled over men like goods in the bazaar until this began to have its side effects.

"No wop can outhustle me," a nurse from St. Paul said belligerantly. She hooked onto her date, a captain from the MPs, and led him up the steps.

The steps were crowded with the traffic up and down. People jostled each other. The line going to rooms moved considerably faster than the line returning to the ballroom.

The whores were relentless. One soiled little streetwalker went right up to WO Page who stood against the wall and grabbed him between his legs. Page was so shocked he dropped his cup. His face rapt, the prissy man followed her docilely up the steps.

The musicians kept on with Casey and the strawberry blonde, and their bows faltered and squeaked. The drummer only sporadically hit his snare. He took a wild swing at his dented cymbal, missed it, and toppled backward off the platform. He never reappeared.

The band of dirty urchins returned. They raided the ladies' room, causing shrieks and screams. They came out with lamps, toilet paper, and cushions. One small boy was inside a moth-eaten fur coat. The coat, ghostly and headless, scampered out into the night.

The Sicilian girls were being coaxed up the steps. They giggled, talked to each other in rapid Italian, and glanced at the duenna who still drank punch. Her filmy old eyes were glazed. She blinked as if surrounded by a dense fog.

Enlisted men were coming to the party, invited by officers who in the good feeling caused by the medical alcohol lowered the barriers. The officers generously served the enlisted men at the punchbowl, which had been kept refilled by the medical major who had been making frequent trips to the hospital for more alcohol.

The whores were happy to see the enlisted men, many of whom they knew by name. Prices were cut a little.

A dance ought to have balloons, said the USO comedian. He solved the shortage with the help of a tired, pimpled lieutenant from the Signal Corps who had twice been up the steps with the whores. The fat comedian and the lieutenant went to the mezzanine around the ballroom where they blew up condums and let them float down on the dancers.

"I used to be an artistic dancer," said a USO girl. She was a stout, muscular brunette billed as a blues singer, and she was piqued that her date had slipped off to go upstairs. Grunting, she climbed onto the table being used as a bar. She put her hands behind her head and bumped her pelvis. A crap player hollered for her to take it off.

Another member of the orchestra retired. As the cellist, he sawed away in a slumped position, the slump became too much, and he tumbled forward out of his chair. He rolled off the platform to the dance floor. His instinct for his instrument, however, was intact, for during the fall he protected the cello, which when he came to rest lay on him like a lover.

Captain Hanks returned, his trousers changed. The countess was moving the wholesome young lieutenant toward the balcony. Hanks again pulled rank on the lieutenant, who seemed glad to escape. The countess was annoyed as she put up her arms for Hanks. He steered her to the balcony.

The stout brunette dancer was taking off clothes. She hung each piece on a painted, wooden coat-of-arms nailed to the wall of the ballroom—the coat-of-arms displaying bears and arrows. The brunette wasn't getting much attention because with the whores and the free-lancers the men had been seeing one kind of show or another all evening. They were not only drunk, but also jaded. The tough audience challenged the brunette to be bolder, and she stepped out of her skirt and slip. She was wearing gunmetal-colored stockings attached to a girdle.

The game in the corner was getting wild. Players, drinking as they rolled the dice, piled lira all over the floor. A lieutenant stuffing money into his shirt front, was pregnant with winnings. The band of urchins ran through the room and grabbed up a lot of the money. The lieutenant was knocked to his back, and the urchins trampled him in escaping. Lira burst from him like sawdust from a rag doll. He howled after them.

"Look at me!" the USO brunette kept calling. She threw bumps which snapped her head, but only a few enlisted men watched.

Captain Hanks came hurrying from the balcony. He looked sheepish and again held his hands in front of him. The countess leered after him and crooked her finger at the virginal young lieutenant.

The USO brunette dancing on the table allowed one rosy breast to bump out over her GI brassiere.

An artillery captain and a medical major who worked in X ray were Indian rassling. Each had been bragging, and they were taking the contest seriously. They strained against one another on the dance floor. They were red-faced, and their eyes bulged. The medical major won, throwing the captain to the floor. The artillery captain was mortified and insisted on another match.

276

Indian rassling became the thing. Between the dancers, combatants went at it. The ladies got into it too, a nurse throwing a WAC captain. Dancers tripped over the fallen.

All over the room men and women were running down. They collapsed in chairs and sat tilted, their faces dazed. Several officers lay under a table, neatly stacked there by enlisted-men waiters, themselves so drunk that when they tried to carry trays they staggered and had to run to keep up with their load. Trays fell, causing glasses to crash across the floor. The dancers hardly noticed the crunching under their feet.

A couple sat on the mule to smoke and drink as if it were a divan. The mule occasionally clicked his teeth like castanets.

A little whore came running down the steps in her slip. She was being chased by a surgeon who held a great bologna in front of him menacingly. His expression was like a satyr's. The little whore was screaming and laughing. She ran around the room pointing behind her and smiting her head. The surgeon chased her into the kitchen.

A lieutenant who had played second-string guard for Michigan State found the football in the clubroom's recreation box, along with a badminton set and some rubber horseshoes. The game was supposed to be touch, but as the officers were playing the enlisted men, it was rough immediately. A cook who wandered out of the kitchen threw a block on the Michigan State lieutenant and laid him out cold.

Two captains tossed rubber horseshoes at the chandelier. Delicate strips of glass fell and broke musically.

Desperate now to attract attention, the USO brunette finally wiggled out of her girdle. She was completely undressed except for a paper napkin which she held in front of herself like a fig leaf. She kicked and bounced, but the few enlisted men who were watching might have been looking at a bridge being constructed their faces were so expressionless. The brunette lost her footing and would have fallen from the table had not an enlisted man caught her.

"I'm Laverne Kelly," she said, stretching a hand above her head. "I used to be an artistic dancer." She dropped the paper napkin and Yancey walked in with Colonel Oxam.

Yancey had gone to Oxam's quarters and told the Old Puritan everybody was waiting for him. Reluctantly Oxam had agreed to come.

He was angry even before he entered because the marquee lights

277

were burning in disregard of air-raid regulations. His mouth fell open at the sight of the ballroom.

Colonel Oxam's presence was felt like a wave sweeping through the room. The football players froze in a flying wedge, sweating and bloody.

The USO brunette stumbled and because the enlisted men were at attention had nobody to catch her. She fell to the floor with a fleshy thump and started blubbering.

The crap game died, dice clicking once against the baseboards. Lira fluttered to the floor.

The surgeon came from the kitchen, still chasing the little whore. She ran shrieking up the steps. The surgeon was surprised at seeing Oxam but kept after her.

WO Page came down the steps wrapped in a sheet. The band of urchins had jumped him in the upper hallways and stripped him of his clothes. In the sheet he looked like a Roman citizen.

The last musician fell from his chair, taking two metal music stands with him. Only one violinist remained, and he played on two strings. The other strings were curled under his nose. He kept sneezing.

"Whee!" the fat USO comedian and the pimply lieutenant shouted from the mezzanine where they released more freshly blown-up condoms, which floated down gaily, one of them passing close to Oxam's outraged face.

The ugly old duenna belched.

Captain Hanks ran in from the balcony, again looking both defeated and weary. He stared at the colonel, and, saluting on the run, left by the front entrance before Oxam could find his voice.

Adjusting her dress, the slinky countess came from the balcony. She was searching for her virginal lieutenant, but when she saw Oxam, she headed for him. She put her bare arm through his.

"*Balcone?*" she asked, and touched her upper lip with a wickedly pointed tongue.

Sicilians girls came down the steps giggling and disheveled. Seeing the colonel, they put hands over their mouths and went back upstairs.

Oxam tried to free himself from the countess. She wouldn't turn loose of his arm.

He shook her off roughly and glowered. Guests stood at swaying attention. The mule whinnied. The Old Puritan turned on Yancey whose mouth worked like a fish's.

"A whorehouse!" the colonel shouted. "A goddamn whorehouse."

278

"Sir," Yancey said, his lips quivering.

"A stinking whorehouse and you brought me over here?"

"Colonel, honest none of this was supposed to happen."

"You close up this whorehouse right this goddamn minute and get your ass to my office first thing in the morning."

"Sir, I'm not responsible."

But Oxam was already striding out. The countess made one final attempt to get hold of him, but the Old Puritan flung her away so hard it spun her around. She shrugged, straightened a golden shoulder strap, and spotted her wholesome young lieutenant. She went for him.

"*Balcone, caro?*" she asked.

"Oh, my God!" Yancey said and wiped his face. The room was silent.

From the balcony came the countess' laughter.

The duenna hiccuped. "*Meraviglioso frutto,*" she muttered.

31

The next morning Oxam, cussing with Puritanical rage and righteousness, busted Yancey from command of the battalion and sent him back to Apple Able. A lieutenant colonel from a repple depple took over Airedale.

Colonel Oxam chewed Yancey daily for a week. As a result of the party, furious Sicilian fathers were making threats because of their daughters who had been driven home with their clothes half off. Sicilian doctors had made examinations. There was wailing and the sound of blows behind studded doors and shuttered windows. Oxam was taking the trouble caused his office out of Yancey's hide.

That wasn't all. When Yancey's fellow officers were certain he'd lost his suck, they no longer hid their feelings. At the club they turned their backs on him. No places opened up in the poker or bridge games. During mess, seats on both sides of him were vacant. Only a lonely chaplain talked to Yancey, and the chaplain was reluctant.

It was no better for Yancey in his company. The platoon officers who'd done his work lost their fear of him. They obeyed direct orders because he possessed the power to make them, but they no longer performed in a manner which would make Apple Able look slick. They did what was required, nothing more. As a result, on marches and field problems the company resembled a unit of raw recruits. Men straggled or arrived late at missions. During regimental review, somebody was always out of step.

Yancey attempted to hold things together by increasing discipline. He had a third of his company working extra KP, and throughout the night, soldiers' feet shuffled Sicilian dust as they walked duty tours with full-field packs. He chewed out his officers and placed entire platoons on restriction.

It was a rearguard action. No one person could do anything about the amorphous lassitude which hung about Apple Able. Men sneaked vino into the area, got drunk, and fought. The morning after a fight in which two corporals knifed each other, Colonel Oxam transferred Yancey out of the company.

I hoped the colonel would drive him from the regiment, but as Puritanical as Oxam was, he still lived by the Army caste system. Instead of being broken and exiled, Yancey was made motor pool officer—a job usually held by a lieutenant. There was no chance for advancement, and the mechanics were a surly, bullying lot.

"It's the fall of the gods," the Professor said, mock sadness pinching his sensitive, scholarly face. "We all lose our heroes."

For the first time in months, I smiled.

We could not completely enjoy Yancey's disgrace because within the week the regiment was alerted. Everyone, including the Germans, knew the next invasion had to be of the Italian mainland. Even I believed the golden eagle would have its feathers ruffled this time. We had escaped combat too often.

Then, to our bewilderment, the third battalion was detached. It was simply lopped off by the butchers in Corps and sent to beef up an infantry unit at a staging area. The amputation sent a host of new rumors through the outfit. One was that the regiment would be split up and assigned to other units. A second argued that we were going to be used as replacements for the invasion.

The loss of the battalion had a bad effect on the remaining line companies. Where before they had been taut with the possibility of action, they now went slack with their old inferiority. In lovers' terms, they felt rejected. Everybody sensed disgrace.

"They're making hamburger out of us," Carter said. "They're cutting us up like sausage."

"Maybe it's a good thing," Wilson answered. "This outfit would've been a disaster in combat."

"Don't you have any red blood in you?" Carter asked.

"I don't care about the color as long as it stays in me," Wilson said, but even he was subdued.

In September, right after the invasion of Italy, we were hit by a second alert. The rumor spread we were going to join our lost battalion which had been merely an advance party to the mainland. Men perked up. We were getting reports of the fighting over our Red Cross radios. Supply issued us new ammunition and grenades.

We were ordered to board ships at anchor in Palermo harbor. In the best swashbuckling style, we climbed the landing nets. Some of the men had blackened their faces. Others wore sheath knives strapped to their legs. I saw Yancey as trucks were swung aboard. He didn't have on paratrooper boots or a yellow scarf, but he was wearing jungle netting on his helmet. He scurried below, afraid of the colonel's wrath.

As we left Palermo, dusky Sicilian maidens who had taken up with our men cried and waved their handkerchiefs. It was a golden sunny day which seemed especially beautiful because we were going into battle. Gulls soared about the ships. We had no escort, and there was talk about submarines.

"They won't sink us," Wilson, our cynic, said. "This outfit is an asset to the Krauts. In particular they won't sink bureaucrats, and that's what this bunch is."

"Can they tell I'm a bureaucrat just by looking at me?" Beanpost wanted to know.

"Sure they can. They have special periscopes on their subs for spotting bureaucrats. They've also got built-in non-synchronizers on their shells and torpedoes. You don't have to worry about a thing."

We were all waiting for some sort of briefing. We expected the officers to have a meeting and then come down to the decks to explain our mission to us. As men stayed close to squawk boxes in case of announcements, they cleaned their rifles and attempted to appear belligerent.

No squawks came from the boxes, and our ships never turned toward Italy. By the sun we could tell we were moving west. Timberlake, always professing to know more than the rest of us, said it was a maneuver to avoid German patrol planes. After a while that explanation began to seem ridiculous.

"Maybe we're going to Italy a different way," Carter suggested forlornly, clinging to a last shred of hope.

"Sure by way of China," Wilson said. "That's a brilliant idea because we can take care of the Japs too."

At dark the ships still hadn't turned. Rather than go below, most of us lay on deck listening to the water slap the hull and watching the black sky. During the night Carter got one of the sailors to talk. The sailor said we were going to the Atlantic to join a convoy coming up from Africa.

In the next few days rumors built upon that fact became absurd, but men wanted to believe anything.

"We're going to be a special force," Carter said excitedly. "We'll undergo jump training and be sent to Germany by parachute."

"We're landing in France for an end run," Timberlake announced authoritatively.

"There's a special mission for us in Norway," Beanpost said. "The Germans don't expect anything in Norway."

"We could be going to the States for cadre," Wilson said, in spite of his cynicism caught up in the madness. "I read in the paper they need cadre in the States."

"We're sailing for merry old England," the Professor told us without looking up from his book. "Land of roast beef and the stiff upper lip."

Nobody paid any attention to the Professor, but he was right. On the fifth day out the squawk boxes announced the UK was our destination. At first men were dejected because they had believed the rumors they themselves had manufactured. After a while they revived somewhat. England was a place none of us had ever been, and there was curiosity about it.

The afternoon we pulled into Southampton the weather was gray and dirty. Until a train arrived, we were left standing on the docks in the rain. Stevedores went about their work as if they didn't see us. Tired, wet, and hungry we boarded the train which carried us northwest to a grimy industrial town. The section was nothing like the Shakespeare or Lake country I had in my mind when I pictured England. We could have been in Pittsburgh.

We were billeted near the coast in abandoned British barracks which needed paint. Immediately we put up lines to dry our clothes. I had to go to work to help set up battalion headquarters in an old stone house with a red tile roof. In the cellar were rats as big as groundhogs. Our new battalion commander, a lieutenant colonel named Cavanaugh, shot a dozen of them with his carbine. Wilson,

Carter, Timberlake, and I buried them. Even the rats appeared downcast.

As always the regiment was put on a training schedule. The disgruntled line companies marched out daily to the rocky coast where they bobbed around in landing crafts and made simulated attacks. Lines were shot to cliffs for men to haul themselves up by.

We had a casualty. A mortarman slipped from a rope and fell to the rocks. He lay screaming. We carried him to a hospital and men from his company visited him daily. They felt a certain pride at his broken leg. He was the first member of the golden eagle to be bloodied in what might be called an honorable manner.

Yancey almost drowned. Since we'd reached England, he had been staying out of the way as much as possible. He sneaked around by side streets or under cover of night. He had given up the officers' club altogether. More often than not he ate his meals with his dispatcher at the motor pool, though neither the dispatcher nor the mechanics had any use for Yancey.

During one of the exercises off the coast Yancey misjudged the step from ship to shore and did a Charlie Chaplin right into the foaming water. He was wearing a full-field pack, helmet, and combat boots. With the weight he sank like a stone. My heart jumped into my mouth as I believed him surely dead. I wanted him to be.

The Navy, however, had lifeguards on the landing crafts for just such emergencies. They dived into the cold surf and were under for perhaps five seconds. When they came up, they were holding Yancey who was spouting water. They pulled him onto a boat, pumped him dry, and took him to the hospital. Although he was away for a week, nobody went to see him.

We had hardly settled in England before the golden eagle received two more hard jolts. The first was the information we weren't going to rejoin our battalion in Italy. It had been permanently detached. The second jolt, related to the first, was that Colonel Oxam's attempts to draw replacements were unsuccessful—in spite of the fact that at the time England was bulging with repple depples.

Sniffing the wind, officers began to get out. They had strings they could pull and were able to see that their own requests for transfer reached the right hands. Field grade and above were first to go because they had the most influence. As a result large segments of the regiment were being run by officers of junior rank.

A few enlisted men in line companies and romantics like Carter still had hope as long as Old Puritan was in command. Rough as

Oxam was, he nevertheless had a big following because he was strictly business. His admirers felt he would somehow hold the outfit together and get it to combat strength.

They misplaced their faith, for the Old Puritan himself left us. Without speech or announcement, he was gone. He received command of a paratrooper regiment. Later we saw his picture in YANK magazine. He had grenades attached to his lapels and was scowling. He could have been Uncle Sam on a recruiting poster.

His going pulled the plug. Officers began to jostle each other to escape. Sometimes they were able both to submit and approve their own transfers. Nobody was quite sure any longer who had responsibility for what. The training schedule was frequently ignored. Men lay in their beds all morning, knowing nobody would punish them. Drunkenness and fights became common. The golden eagle looked like a picked crow.

A sort of deadly indifference crept into the cogs and joints of the unit. Because men were no longer inspected, they developed sloppy, slouching habits. They stopped doing their washing or pressing their uniforms. Some of them grew beards and got away with it.

In battalion Lieutenant Colonel Cavanaugh transferred out. He was followed by a succession of majors, captains, and lieutenants. WO Page was really running things. He was an orderly man and near crying at the chaos.

The golden eagle was further decimated because of a directive from Corps stating that while it might be useful for units of regimental size to take support positions in a battle plan, commanders were within their rights to utilize such units as they felt was best in bringing their line divisions up to battle strength.

Interpreted, the directive meant we could be officially plundered. Division commanders considered themselves understrength no matter how many men they had. They were misers. As soon as the directive was out, they came for us, taking the personnel in our line companies. Our own trucks carried the men away.

Everybody got in on the raiding. When the combat units were finished, the special services came for booty. They wanted our mechanics, radio technicians, and medics. The official word put on their records was "detached," but we all knew they would never come back.

The outfit was shrinking at such an alarming rate nobody was sure who was left. The remaining officers were not important enough to stop the pillage. Besides they were trying to get out themselves.

Six weeks after the directive was issued, about all that was left of the golden eagle were a few tailfeathers.

The tailfeathers consisted mostly of men in the various headquarter sections and the cooks. The headquarters weren't bothered because somebody had to preside over the demise of the unit. Cooks were left because they were a glut on the market. During combat everybody wanted to be in the kitchen.

At battalion we had a mountain of paper work to complete. WO Page, struggling against anarchy, insisted records be kept in perfect order. He worked us eighteen hours a day.

When the job was done, however, we had nothing whatsoever to do. There was really no reason for us to be in existence. We slept all day and played cards all night. Men drank with the silent despondency of the unemployed. Carter, who to the very end had maintained faith in the ultimate glory of the golden eagle, acted like a person betrayed.

"You think I'm going to stay here?" he howled in his hurt. "They don't deserve me."

But he couldn't get out. Channels being hopelessly jumbled, nobody was around any longer for him to submit transfer papers to. He went from headquarters to headquarters only to learn he was traveling in circles.

The area was growing deserted. At dark a few lights shone from isolated buildings where lonely dogfaces sat huddled around stoves. The place was like a Western ghost town. Loose tin banged on roofs, and all that we needed was tumbleweed blowing before the chill wind.

One of the lights in the officers' section belonged to Yancey who lived by himself. Naturally he was still with us. He'd also been trying to get a transfer, but his reputation prevented that. By attrition he had become senior officer first in the battalion and then the regiment. The position required nothing of him. He rarely left his quarters.

Ironically Black Hatfield had not been taken from us. Though a natural killer, he was left because he'd been temporarily attached to regiment as a runner. He sat around strumming dark coal-mining chords on his guitar. He had discontinued sharpening his long knife.

Being left in the outfit had one bright side. Since we were still drawing supplies for a regiment, there was a superabundance of food. We gorged ourselves. We also received PX supplies for ten times as many men as were left. Each of us had all the cigars, after-shave lotion, and cigarettes he wanted. The few remaining officers could not drink the whisky ration and sold most of it to enlisted men. We were getting drunk on the best bourbon at a dollar and a half the bottle.

We told ourselves it couldn't go on. Somebody was eventually bound to find out about us. We, however, shamefully played the game as best we could. Soft and spoiled, we didn't want to be discovered.

We went through winter and into spring. Perhaps we could have made it to the end of the war had not on a March day a lieutenant colonel of infantry stumbled on us. He was looking for a bomb demolition unit. Needing information, he asked to see the officer in charge. WO Page sent for Yancey. He came out of his hut rubbing his eyes and buttoning his uniform. He and the colonel talked while the rest of us peeked from windows.

The colonel didn't return, but by the end of the week we were sure we were under observation because our food and supplies were suddenly cut down. People somewhere were concerned with us.

Then Yancey and the remaining officers—three lieutenants and WO Page—were summoned by special messenger to Corps Headquarters in the industrial town. We enlisted men sat around drinking and wondering what was going to happen to us.

Yancey and the officers didn't drive in until dark. Carter questioned WO Page. The orderly little bookkeeper had been extremely nervous ever since men started leaving the outfit. He had grown thin to the point of emaciation.

"I can't tell you much," he said. "We are to have an outfit, however, and it'll involve some training."

"Now you're talking," Carter said. He was excited. "Special mission, huh?"

"You'll see," WO Page answered him.

The rest of us perked up, especially when the officers spent the next few days in conference working out a table of organization. Word had it that new equipment was on the way. Yancey, in command, was straightening up and again acting impressed with himself. He wore the expression of a man facing great decisions. He became pompous.

Lying on our bunks one afternoon, we heard the roar of engines. We hurried outside. A dozen huge trucks pulling lumbering trailers came through the gate. The drivers were helmeted Negroes. A jeep led them to our almost empty motor pool. Air brakes hissed.

"Rockets," Carter whispered. "Stuff the regular artillery has never used before."

As soon as the white officer who'd been driving the jeep went into headquarters, we approached the trucks cautiously, not sure whether it was allowed or not. The drivers were lighting cigarettes. Carter questioned a big sergeant who was wearing a white scarf.

"What's in the trailers?" Carter asked.

"You'll find out," the sergeant answered, winking at the other drivers who nodded and grinned.

"Secret, huh?"

"You bet it's secret. If I told you, I might be shot."

When Yancey and the officer came from headquarters, they acted serious. I'd never stopped hating Yancey, not even in his disgrace, and now he had landed on his feet again I felt that hate lick through me like fire. I found it unbelievable the Army, aware of his record, would place him in charge of anything, yet here he was bustling with importance.

He gave orders to assemble all men left in the regiment. The orders were unnecessary because everybody had already gathered around—some seventy of us not including the officers. We lined up in two unwieldy platoons.

"All right, at ease," Yancey said, standing with his hands on his fat hips. His flesh was an unhealthy toadstool color. "Tomorrow early we get started on special training. That means all of you. Your clerking days are over. Have a good night's sleep and be ready to go to work in the morning. Any questions?"

"What's in the trailers, Captain?" Carter asked.

"You'll find out soon enough. I want guards on those trucks tonight. Each section can furnish a shift."

Guarding the trailers increased our curiosity about what was inside them. While making tours, each of us tapped the metal sides and attempted to find some chink to peer through. Carter even crawled underneath with a flashlight. We could discover nothing.

At breakfast everybody was tense. We learned Yancey intended to consolidate the remnants of the regiment into four permanent platoons served by one orderly room. We were told to move into adjacent barracks. We still didn't know what was in the trailers, and Carter was about to go crazy.

After we shifted our gear, whistles blew. We ran out carrying our rifles. Yancey and all the officers were present. He made our lieutenants and WO Page platoon commanders. The lieutenant who had come in with the trailers stood beside Yancey.

"You can return your rifles," Yancey said. "You won't need them."

We carried them back in. The fact we didn't need them made Carter all the more certain we were going to be made technicians. When we were again in formation, Yancey called us to attention and marched us to the motor pool, counting cadence in his high-pitched voice. We stopped in front of the trailers. The colored troops had just finished breakfast and were standing around watching.

Yancey talked with the lieutenant who had come with the trailers. We'd tried to find what sort of unit he was from by looking for collar insignia and braid on his overseas cap. He wore neither. He was a swarthy, heavy-set man with hairy hands. He spoke to the colored sergeant. The sergeant climbed into a tractor cab and pulled one of the trailers away from the others. The lieutenant drew a key from his pocket to unlock the rear of the trailer. Everybody was straining to see.

At first we believed Carter was right—that it was some sort of secret weapon. When the tailgate was lowered and the big doors opened, we saw gleaming metal tubes, toggle switches, stainless steel drums, and machinery which looked as if it belonged in the laboratory of the mad scientist. The lieutenant stood on the tailgate.

"Gentlemen, you see before you the insides of a Model 42740B high-speed, selfsustained mobile laundry unit."

"Laundry unit?" Carter asked, suddenly pale.

The colored drivers were giggling and punching each other.

"Laundry," the lieutenant repeated. "Four of these units properly put on line can easily handle the soiled clothing from an entire division and its supporting elements, including both field and evacuation hospitals."

We gaped. Carter looked sick. Black Hatfield spat. Wilson smiled cynically, as if he had expected nothing else. Beanpost was ashamed. Timberlake was insulted. The Professor appeared academically interested. The colored troops held their hands over their mouths as they laughed.

"No," Carter said.

"What?" the Quartermaster lieutenant asked, for even though we couldn't see his insignia or braid, we knew laundry was a part of the Quartermaster. "Somebody have a question?"

Carter didn't answer. He sagged among us. I glanced at our officers. They too appeared humiliated with the exception of Yancey. He was swollen with the pride of a new command. Our eyes locked, and he smiled at me. I turned away.

"These units are brand new," the Quartermaster lieutenant said. "They just came over from the States and are as fine equipment as the U. S. Government can buy. Don't be disappointed. Laundry is an area of warfare which until recently has been neglected in servicing theaters of operations. Don't think it's not an important job. The morale of an entire battle group might hang on whether or not infantrymen have clean underwear. Your part in the war effort will be just as great as any other soldier's."

"Shit," Black Hatfield said, his West Virginia pronunciation making the word sound as if it were two syllables.

"Now look here," the Quartermaster lieutenant said angrily. "I won't stand for that."

"We were trained for infantry," Carter protested.

"What you were trained for doesn't apply here. What you're needed for is the determinant, and that's to learn how to operate these mobile units. We hope to have you ready in two weeks, which will require very intensive effort on your part. I know when you realize just how essential this work is you'll give it your best."

"The hell I will," Carter whispered. "I'll desert before I serve in a lousy outfit like this."

The lieutenant started lecturing us that morning. His name was Godoy, and he owned a steam laundry in Boston. He opened an entire side of the trailer so he could point out and explain various pieces of equipment. Most of us were too numb to hear what he said as he demonstrated how to hook up the water pump, light the boilers, regulate the agitators, and control the drying machines.

While that was going on, Yancey and the other officers held a meeting to assign jobs. Only a few men would be needed for the paper work. Yancey turned that over to WO Page and a company clerk named Doggins. The rest of us were to be used in or around the trailers.

I found out what Yancey's smile had meant. He saw that I was given a job on the big kettles, easily the worst work of all. Heat from scalding water was suffocating, and clothes had to be lifted high by wooden pitchforks. Even stripped to the waist I was soon covered with sweat which mingled and stuck in a greasy film of soap. While we trained, I cursed him, plunging my pitchfork into bundles as if they were his soft body.

During the first week we practiced on our own uniforms. Lieutenant Godoy showed us how to tag and pile them on the tailgate at the rear of the trailer. The clothes moved through the machines toward the front. Into kettles we poured gallons of oily chemical soap from cans. We switched on electricity supplied by our own portable generators. The machinery moaned, shook, and rattled. We toiled on the slippery metal floor among billows of steam like creatures from Hell.

In each trailer was a timing gong which sounded like those bells used at boxing matches. When the gong rang, the clothes were put into a new phase. We transferred them from foaming kettles into rinsers and from rinsers into driers that shot out blasts of hot air. At the front of the trailer clothes were sorted, tied, and loaded. Nothing was pressed.

Not everybody worked inside the trailers. Men had to learn to drive the big tractor trucks. Black Hatfield was one of those. Others took care of the generators and boilers. Carter was assigned to the latter. He slammed doors and twisted valves as if he would break them off.

In the trailers we had to swallow salt tablets to prevent heat exhaustion. Our skins wrinkled in the steamy air and began to take on a pale, shriveled appearance. We couldn't wear watches or metal of any sort because it soon became corroded from our sweat. Our hair became straight—all wave steamed out of it—and hugged the contours of our skulls. We stank of the bitter chemical soap.

Each night there was a lot of drinking in the barracks, though the officer whisky ration had been cut off. Hard cider became the staple. Carter, who previously had left liquor alone, got roaring drunk.

"I'm leaving," he shouted, reeling among the bunks. "I'm getting out of here and finding me a combat outfit."

He ran from the barracks before we could stop him. We chased him among the abandoned buildings of the area. He climbed onto the roof of a hut, hung over it, and passed out. We carried him to bed. The next morning he was more shamefaced than ever, but he was also drunk again that night.

We went about training as if attending an execution. Lieutenant Godoy, a worshiper of efficiency, was becoming impatient with us. We refused to hurry. We allowed rinsers and driers to get out of phase. The lieutenant complained angrily. Yancey finally lined us up for a speech.

"I know some of you are po'd," he said, unable to look directly into our accusing faces. "I feel the same way myself. We have, however, to do the best we can. I say let's be the best laundry unit in the ETO."

Men snorted. The speech only made them more resentful. They might not hate Yancey as much as I did, but they had no respect for him. He realized it. He returned quickly to his office and shut the door.

We were shunted to one end of the area so British troops could have the rest of it. They were combat engineers and inevitably remarks were made about our being laundry women. Those remarks led to fights. We couldn't go into a pub without trouble. Though we wore no insignia, the British had no difficulty spotting us because they could always smell the soap. Carter had a tooth knocked out. MPs came looking for one of our men who'd stuck a knife into a lance corporal. We hid Black Hatfield until they were gone.

Lieutenant Godoy predicted we would fail the examination we had to pass before being certified and put on line. The examination consisted of taking in laundry from a division down the road. Godoy attempted to make the event sound grave and even hazardous. We couldn't have cared less.

The examination was scheduled on a Monday. Trucks from the infantry division started arriving early. None of us was prepared for just how much laundry a division put out. Bundles of clothes grew over our heads into a fair-sized hill. Godoy had placed us on a per-hour quota which aimed at finishing the entire batch in two days.

At first we went about our jobs properly. We fired the boilers, and hot water surged through rubber pipes from pumps to kettles. We flipped switches, poured in soap, and like Devil's helpers pitchforked clothes. Even with the sides of the trailers propped up, the temperature was soon over a hundred degrees.

There was no preconceived plan about screwing up the job. Action and reaction developed naturally and instinctively in a sort of mass protest against what was happening to us.

The first thing was Godoy's leaving us a few minutes to go to the kitchen for a cup of coffee. Next Beanpost who was supposed to keep a close watch on the hose which brought water into the boilers was careless. The hose lay in a pond, and he didn't notice the mouth had started to suck mud off the bottom.

When, however, the hose thrashed a bit and the laundry water turned a rich brown, we in the trailers immediately became aware of it. Instead of notifying Beanpost to change the position of his hose, we pretended nothing was wrong. The dark water churned into hot kettles and rinsers.

Even then any of us could have stopped further damage by reaching over the door to pull an emergency master switch. Nobody did. We continued to load clothes and phase them to the sound of the gong. T.ie water, infused with soap suds, resembled hot chocolate.

Smooth and Timberlake began to use too much soap. Without words the idea swept all four trailers. We poured five-gallon cans of the chemicals into the kettles. Great swarms of bubbles rose up and slurped to the floor. The suds trembled around our shoes, and the deck became so slippery we had to hold on to braces to keep from falling.

Carter fiendishly built up the pressure on his boiler. The safety valve shrieked in complaint. The kettles were growing so hot we couldn't approach them. All the while soap was foaming up higher. We threw puffs of it at each other like snowballs. The suds were dripping off the trailers to the ground. As they fell over ramps and tailgates, they caused a Niagara Falls effect. A crowd of awed British soldiers gathered to watch.

Clothes which had come in one end of the trailers OD color were going out brown—the mud cooked into them. They looked as if they had been dyed. Furthermore the men collecting and tying were unable to perform their assignments because they could no longer read laundry marks. They gave up attempting to match pieces and merely threw clothes haphazardly from the driers into a heap. They bound unmatched bundles and tossed them onto a canvas where they would be picked up by trucks from the infantry.

The amount of soap suds was becoming alarming. They were oozing all around the trailers and over the ground like a live thing. They were rising from steam exhaust pipes and electrical circuits. The boiler continued to shriek. The trailers were rocking from the motion of the agitators which had been turned on full speed to cause more suds. Suds drove us from the trailers. The crowd of British had grown.

Lieutenant Godoy and Yancey came from the kitchen. When they saw what was happening, they stopped in disbelief and fright. Then Godoy hollered and ran toward the trailers waving his arms. Just before he reached the nearest one, Carter's boiler blew.

There was a glorious explosion of pipes and iron. Debris fell around us like shrapnel. All the British hit the ground. Our skins were stung with scalding drops of water. Lieutenant Godoy, still running, reached the advancing, amoeba-like soap. He went into a long skid and disappeared yelling, sliding on his back into a billowing, foaming rainbow of sparkling suds.

32

First of all the entire unit was put under arrest. Secondly the uniforms which had turned brown and gone back to the division had almost caused a riot. Infantrymen were unable to find clothes which fitted them and were seen marching along resembling refugees in pants too short and jackets too large. Because of the chocolate color, the uniforms looked as if they were from some other army.

The division general chewed out a colonel of Quartermaster who was in charge of all laundry sections. The colonel in turn sent his special representative to us. That man, a major, spent the entire morning working Yancey and our other officers over while we waited in the barracks.

After the major left, Yancey called us out. He was furious and paced in front of us.

"You ought to be in the stockade, and if you think you're going to get away with that kind of stuff you're crazy as hell," he said. "You might not like being laundry, but I'm not taking it in the tail because of your sensitive feelings. Any man who screws off from now on gets a court-martial."

We had no doubt Yancey meant what he threatened. Because of us, he was in jeopardy. He might not care about us, but he did about himself. He would court-martial the whole unit to save his own flabby skin.

The same day a representative from the Judge Advocate came to examine us. A solemn lieutenant colonel, he questioned us under oath. Those who were guilty admitted it. That involved practically everybody, thus no ringleaders could be found. We were scared though. I could imagine what my mother and people back home would think if I were locked up. A story might even appear in the Richmond newspapers.

Nobody had to go to the stockade. Instead we were given a probationary reprieve. As punishment we again were to wash the division's clothes. Before we could do it, however, we had to clean our equipment. We took all pipes apart and chipped at the caked mud. We scoured the kettles and agitators. Godoy kept us at it until water ran pure as a mountain stream through the system.

When we were ready to operate, the division trucks came in with another mountain of laundry. We were watched constantly by Godoy, Yancey, and other officers. We washed each bundle by the book, working twenty-four hours straight through to complete the job. By the time we finished, we were limp and bleary eyed. Godoy gave us his grudging okay.

As if to rub salt into our wounds, Yancey ordered us to turn in our crossed muskets and pick up Quartermaster insignia for the lapels of our blouses. We also had to cut the golden eagle from our shoulders and replace it with a sickly special services emblem. Carter hung his head.

"You can truthfully say you gave your all for your country," Wilson consoled him. "You can claim you were put out of action by dishpan hands."

After Godoy's approval, we went on line and operated regularly for troops in the area. Like civilian washer women, we put in a twelve-hour day. Clothes were constantly coming in and going out. We became so trustworthy that Yancey and the other officers stopped checking on us.

Because we felt degraded and had taken so much abuse from the British, we stuck to ourselves. Instead of being able to go to the warmth and light of a pub, we remained in the barracks. We lay on our bunks or shivered around our small coal stoves.

There was talk about an invasion of France, but none of us believed it would happen anytime soon. Even Carter could work up no excitement. For one thing we knew so little of what was going on, invasion seemed an impossible undertaking. The Army was becoming a life without end. We would always be at war.

Orders came down for us to waterproof our equipment, but we thought it was only a part of our training. When the British pulled out, we surmised they were going to war games down the coast. We had finally learned not to hope for anything.

Yancey, though, had come to life once more. Now that he was in command of his own unit, he reverted to his old ways. He again shellacked his helmet, put on his paratrooper boots, and wore a silk scarf. He strapped on his oxblood .45. Somewhere he got hold of a leather map case and binoculars. The combination chrome-red-light was back on his jeep. He raced about the area as if he were being consulted by Supreme Allied Headquarters.

During the early hours of the invasion, we were asleep. Carter, the first to learn, woke us. We gathered around the radio to listen to the unemotional voice of the British announcer. We wondered whether we'd stay in England. We guessed we wouldn't get to France until most of the fighting was over.

On the evening of the next day, however, a special courier roared in on a motorcycle. He had our orders in a sealed packet. Yancey announced we were to move our equipment to a staging area. He held an inspection to check our weapons because he believed we might have to defend ourselves. By then he was also wearing a commando knife.

We remained in the staging area eleven days before going to Southampton to board ship. We had been issued life preservers, chocolate bars, and fancy French money. Our trailers were swung up by huge cranes. On the ship with us were other units—mostly medics, Chemical Warfare, and Ordnance men. When they learned we were laundry, they acted superior.

The ships, eight of them in line, left early on a sunny morning. The voyage across was leisurely, with no sign of war. At France more ships were at anchor, and although we went over the sides by means of nets, we walked ashore from landing craft as easily as we could have at Miami Beach.

Steel ramps had been laid on the sand. Through the dunes bulldozers had smashed roadways. Gas masks and deflated life preservers were strewn about. Men worked at unloading equipment and supplies, but nobody hurried or seemed much concerned. Carter who had been holding his rifle at the ready lowered it disgustedly. Yancey kept surveying the beach with his binoculars as if he expected the Germans to pop up beyond the dunes. Colored stevedores snickered at him.

We marched away from the shore, leaving only our drivers to bring the trucks and trailers after they were floated ashore on rafts. A few miles inland an area had already been assigned to us in a meadow near an evacuation hospital. At the area we found piles of bloody clothing and blankets. Nearby was a small, clear stream where we could draw water. As we waited, we heard no shooting and wondered where the war was.

"It's just a lull," Carter said. "The Krauts are bound to attack sometime. I'm digging a foxhole."

If the Germans attacked, we didn't know about it. With the exception of Carter we snoozed in the sun until our equipment arrived. We immediately put all four vans on line and began operation. Though at first we had more laundry than we could handle and ran the machinery on twenty-four hour shifts, the work went well. There was no goofing because being in France made even laundry seem pretty serious. Lieutenant Godoy would have been proud of us.

Yancey was the only man not carrying his weight. Instead of doing a job, he was off souvenir hunting. When he returned each evening, his jeep was loaded with German rifles, pistols, and flags. His pyramidal tent was soon full of booty. He horsetraded it with officers from the evacuation hospital. He had Honeycutt make him crates to mail souvenirs home in.

Yancey had got hold of a yellow parachute and made himself some new scarfs. His commando knife also had a fancy Plexiglas handle. On some days his tent was like an Arab bazaar as doctors and nurses haggled with him over the prices of swastikas, ceremonial daggers, and Lugers.

Nobody within the unit bothered to hide his contempt for Yancey. Our three lieutenants and WO Page had as little to do with him as possible. He in turn avoided us. We'd go for weeks hardly seeing him. He became so useless to the outfit he could have disappeared and it would have made no difference at all to operations.

He had one setback. In searching for souvenirs, he drove through a small French town where American paratroopers were billeted. They stopped him and at gunpoint made him remove both his scarf and his boots. Yancey returned to the outfit barefooted. He was too embarrassed to report the incident to the MPs. Within a day, however, he had another pair of boots and a new yellow scarf.

Besides trading in souvenirs, he played at war. He kept a Red Cross radio in his tent as well as a large map board into which he stuck pins. He made notations on the map with colored pencils. When he was in the area, he never missed a news broadcast. Napoleon-like, he sat before the map as he studied the Normandy campaign. His face was somber, like a general's about to give orders to mount the attack.

He hadn't given up brownie sorties for a majority. At least once a week he drove to Quartermaster Command to suck around the big brass. To ingratiate himself, he carried them souvenirs, wine, and cigars. He brought their laundry back, and it had to be given special consideration. Not trusting us, he never left us alone while we were doing it.

He spent a lot of time searching for fresh food—especially eggs. He'd drive around the countryside looking for farmers to trade with. He took bags of sugar from the enlisted men's mess to use for barter. He cooked his eggs in his tent and sold the overflow to medical officers at the evacuation hospital. He never offered any to us.

He threw us off balance by throwing a party for children in the vicinity on a Sunday afternoon. He had the kitchen cook up some fancy cake and make lemonade. He ordered the rest of us to help with the entertainment, which consisted of American picnic games like sack races and relays. The children's faces, suspicious at first, bloomed like flowers as they relaxed and became happy.

"How do you figure it?" Timberlake asked, confused by Yancey's apparent charitableness.

"He's probably starting a whorehouse," Wilson said. "Ten to one he wants the kids' older sisters to lay for him."

Toward the end of the summer, the war moved away, and for a time we had so little laundry we kept only one trailer in operation. We listened to announcements over the radio describing how American and British troops were nearing Germany itself. It seemed the fighting would be over by Christmas.

When our orders came, they sent us to a field on the outskirts of Versailles. Instead of uniforms and bloody blankets, we received whole truckloads of women's clothing. The clothes belonged to WACs who had been sent into Paris to take over administrative jobs. Carter held up a dainty OD slip and stared at it as if it were a mass of snakes.

"What am I going to tell my goddamn children?" he asked. He wasn't married, but like most Southerners he sincerely worried about his posterity.

"Tell them you got your foot caught in a wringer," Wilson suggested.

"Or that you were spun dry," Timberlake said.

"Say you were balled by a flying brassiere hook," Smooth added.

We were now serving non-combat organizations altogether, a fact which made doing laundry shameful. The organizations had hurried into Paris to get themselves the best billets and the prettiest women. While our work had seemed of some value to fighting men and wounded, we felt humiliated to become the lackeys of people who were having a good time out of the war.

Carter could stand it no longer and made up his mind to leave. He shook our hands and crept out in the dark of night with his pack and rifle. The MPs brought him back the next morning. They had caught him hitchhiking toward Germany. Yancey chewed him out and threatened him with a court-martial.

Our lives became insidiously easier. We were in the Quartermaster Corps, and the Corps took care of its own. We had an abundance of food, chocolate, and cigarettes as well as hundreds of old blankets and cast-off uniforms. These items drew hungry Frenchwomen in need of material to make clothes. They began to take over our duties. Nobody was actually aware of the exact moment they started firing boilers or swinging laundry into the kettles. The metamorphosis was so unplanned the officers didn't have a chance to object.

Within a few weeks all work had practically ceased for us. It was a case of getting two for one if a person wanted because the small, chirping mademoiselles willingly shared their perfumed sheets. They sapped our strength with luxury and indolence. Others might be suffering and dying, but we slept in the mornings, had breakfast in bed, and were even shaved. Our food was cooked in the French manner—the ladies had taken over the mess too—and transformed magically into high cuisine. They made our beds, cleaned our tents, and giggled musically when pinched.

Smooth went on an orgy with the girls. He was a slow-talking Italian boy from Baltimore with slicked black hair. He was so active he grew thinner before our eyes. His olive cheeks sunk, and his back became bent. Still he couldn't stop chasing not only the laundry girls, but also women in Paris. He propositioned them right on the street. A surprising number accepted. Bug-eyed and weak, he tried to explain how he felt.

"You ever stop to think how much of that stuff there is?" he asked in wonder. "I mean every woman in the world's got one of them fuzzy things and they were put here to be used. They're around a man all the time. I go crazy thinking of them around me all the time."

At camp we were suddenly surrounded by Germans—not the enemy attacking but prisoners assigned to work in hospitals and service units. The French girls were enraged because the Germans put them out of jobs. The mademoiselles waved their hands, cursed, and spat. The pretty ones were well enough established in other ways not to lose their source of food, but their plain sisters were definitely out. They shook their fists.

The Germans were even better than women at doing our work. They had a talent for cleanliness and machinery. They quickly learned operating details and ran the laundry with precision-like Teutonic efficiency. They served us breakfast in bed and shaved us without acting as if they owned us. They developed a proprietary attitude toward the trailers, treating us as if we had no right to meddle with their work.

There was so little for us to do we were getting paunches. An endless supply of food and lack of exercise kept us comatose. The weather was balmy. We sank into torpor.

One warm afternoon while I was in Paris, I saw a *poule* who reminded me of Martha. She had the same dark hair and small, delicate features. Of course it was just an impression that flashed through the *fine* I was drinking, an impression filtered through longing.

We went up to her hotel room, which was sunny and clean. She tried to please, showing some pretty inventive stuff, but even with her French lore she could never touch Martha. For me nobody would ever be able to touch Martha.

I wondered whether she had yet informed Yancey of her new love. On the boat he had told me he had been expecting it. I saw so little of him I couldn't figure what he was thinking. When I did see him, my hate no longer flared up but burned with an even heat.

With the start of cold weather we left Versailles to go to a general hospital near Liège. During the Christmas season a lot of bloody clothes had to be washed because of the German breakthrough at the Bulge, but the added work caused us no hardship. Our POWs ran the equipment with beautiful mastery.

Yancey had traded souvenirs for a Thompson submachine gun which he carried in his jeep. He'd also wired two hand grenades to his field jacket in the manner of a paratrooper. None of us ever saluted him. He drove past without looking at us.

By spring the war was almost over. Long convoys of POWs were being sent back as Allied units punched deeper into Germany. At the laundry we lay around on the new grass to sunbathe. We had plenty of wine and beer. I slept fifteen hours a day.

In April we were alerted for a move into Germany. Combat outfits had advanced so far they were sucking service units after them. We had to leave our prisoners in Belgium. They were gloomy, and we were unhappy about losing them. Their being detached meant we would again have to do some work.

Our unit split into two sections. Yancey and WO Page were to take the first section to the rear of an infantry division which had been pushing toward the Elbe River. Lieutenants Pringle and Eberhard were in charge of the second, positioning it to support an armored corps in the vicinity of Stuttgart. Yancey and the officers conferred about routes and convoy procedures.

The Germans loaded our trucks for us, and as we pulled out, they stood waving like faithful wives. For an hour or so the convoy traveled in line, but at a crossroad the two sections separated. We didn't know when we'd see the other trailers again, but nobody cared much.

Yancey was leading our group. He had on his full battle array of paratrooper boots, oxblood .45, lacquered helmet, and jungle netting. On his helmet also was a pair of goggles of the kind the Afrika Korps had used. Around his neck were binoculars and a map case. He was so loaded down he rattled when he walked. Just before leaving, he had made us a speech.

"Men, we're going to Germany," he had said pompously. "They have snipers up there, and we're always in danger of being caught in a counterattack. Keep your eyes and ears open."

Because nobody would ride with him, he was alone in his jeep. At the rear of our convoy of two trailers and five six-by-sixes was WO Page. I was sitting in the cab of a big tractor with Black Hatfield. In the trailers themselves some of the men put down bedding so they could sleep along the way.

From where I sat I could watch Yancey. He drove at exactly thirty-five miles an hour. That was the speed he had chosen for the convoy, but it was too slow on the good roads. The truck drivers had difficulty keeping proper interval. Black Hatfield was constantly using his air brakes. He cursed steadily and filthily. The big trailer lumbered like an elephant.

We crossed the Rhine on a pontoon bridge, the metal webbing of which caused our tires to hum. The sky was overcast, but the weather remained warm. Though we were all curious about Germany, it appeared no different from France except more towns had been bombed. There were few civilians.

I cocked a foot on the dashboard and smoked. At crossroads Yancey threw up his hand like a cavalry leader to stop the convoy while he consulted his maps. Every fifty minutes he halted us for relief calls. At lunch we were allowed thirty minutes to eat K rations.

Black Hatfield and I had little to say to each other. He was a loner who lived by the silent code of his West Virginia mountains. Rough and unshaved, he chewed tobacco and spat from the side of the truck without turning his head. He continued to curse Yancey.

"He thinks he's a great warrior," I said. "He believes he's the commanding general leading victorious troops into Berlin."

"Huh?" Black Hatfield asked, glancing suspiciously at me.

"Just look at him. He's not being followed by a laundry unit but by a column of tanks. Defeated Germans are throwing rose petals and palm leaves in front of his jeep."

"He's just a shit," Black Hatfield said.

It was midafternoon before we realized Yancey had us lost. We should have guessed when he speeded up a little and stopped more often to read his maps. His actions were those of a man becoming increasingly nervous. I remembered the maneuvers in Georgia and looked at Black Hatfield. He spat a particularly large blob of juice. Yancey halted us to read a road sign in German which was attached to a concrete post.

"The dumb sonofabitch," Black Hatfield said. "Can't even follow a map."

"Don't help him. Let him sweat."

"I ain't about to help the sonofabitch. I'd like to ball him."

Putting his jeep in gear, Yancey motioned us forward in the best General Custer style. The road was good and ran straight through the green countryside. Only he could have become lost on it. I wished I had a map. Because of the overcast, getting a bearing on the sun was impossible.

We passed a stone house. A German farmer herding a cow stared at us. Yancey should have halted the convoy to ask questions. Asking questions, however, meant admitting he was lost. He would never do that. He kept on.

In Black Hatfield's trailer was a small panel which could be opened. Wilson, who had been sleeping, called out to ask what was going on.

"Yancey's lost," I answered him.

"We'll end up in Bulgaria," Wilson said.

The later it became, the faster Yancey drove. Just before dark we were moving down the road at a dangerous speed. I suspected we were traveling in circles. Rain began to fall lightly. Men on trucks rolled down their canvases, and Yancey put up his top. He wouldn't quit, though, until it was completely dark. He parked beside a meadow, pulled on his slicker, and walked down the line.

"We'll have to bivouac," he said. "Better dig yourself foxholes in case of planes."

"It's wet out there," Smooth, our Sybarite, complained from a truck.

"I know how wet it is," Yancey snapped.

We hadn't planned to bivouac, and there were no rations for doing so. Luckily the cooks found some powdered pea soup which they mixed with water from a creek and heated on a field range. Rain continued to fall. Instead of putting up pup tents, we slept in the trucks where we were crowded and uncomfortable. Nobody dug a hole.

Yancey and WO Page sat in a truck cab going over maps by flashlight. Yancey was attempting to get little Page to help find where we were and plot the next day's route. Page, however, had been at the end of the convoy and had no idea at what point Yancey had gone wrong.

Rain drummed against the metal sides of the trailer I slept in. I was lying by a kettle and smelled the sour encrustment of soap which had been built up over the months. The steel floor hurt my head and back.

At dawn the next morning Yancey blew his whistle. We had nothing for breakfast except soluble coffee and odds and ends from our K rations like fruit bars and sticks of hard chocolate. We filled our canteens from the creek.

Yancey ordered us to mount up. Again he led the convoy while WO Page was stationed at the rear of the column. Though the rain had stopped, the road was still wet and the sky murky. Black Hatfield cut himself off a new chaw of tobacco. He continued to curse Yancey's driving. The road narrowed and became crooked. We swept along among low hills covered by forests. Yancey drove so fast around a curve he almost ran into one of the slow, ungainly German tractors which burned wood smoke and made an ungodly racket. The old farmer was so rattled he drove off the road into a field. The convoy bunched up. Black Hatfield sent Yancey to everlasting Hell in a hissing, deadly voice.

By eleven o'clock we were all very hungry. We passed two young German girls walking along the road. Nobody except Smooth even whistled at them. I saw a stone farmhouse which looked familiar. I was all the more convinced we were traveling in circles. We had used up most of our reserve gasoline which we carried in cans strapped to the sides of the trucks.

"I think we passed that place before," I told Black Hatfield.

"The dumb sonofabitch," Black Hatfield said.

When we came to a junction, Yancey bore left where he had previously gone to the right. For a few miles the road was level, but it then began climbing a long, gently sloping hill. At the crest we looked down over trees to the pointed top of a church steeple.

The sight of the steeple caused Yancey to drive even faster. In the town would be either MPs or an Army unit. That meant food, information, and more gasoline. The road dipped like a roller coaster. We rose up again, and for a moment we had a clear view of the town.

It had evidently been a resort—one of the innumerable German *Bads* throughout the country. The pink and red houses appeared quaint and medieval. They were bunched together picturesquely, their fronts decorated with flower boxes. The town looked untouched by war.

Farther on, just at the outskirts on the other side, was a large hotel built like a castle. Beside it was a lake surrounded by dense, dark woods. The view was pretty enough for a post card, but it had an unreal air about it too—as if we had suddenly come upon another land.

The road dipped, and we could not see the town for the forest. Yancey was still speeding. At the bottom of the hill the pavement gave way to old-fashioned cobblestones. We saw no people down the street.

Yancey slowed but continued on. The street was so narrow the big laundry trailers cleared the houses only by inches on each side. Tires rolled on the sidewalks. Our engines roared in the canyon created by the buildings. Shutters were drawn across windows. We were barely moving.

"Wait a goddamn minute," Black Hatfield said, jerking around to look over his left shoulder.

"What's the matter?" I asked.

"I thought I saw somebody." He drove and tried to look back at the same time. I turned but could not see his side of the street for the bulk of the trailer.

"It's a town," I told him. "You're supposed to see people."

"This people had a uniform. It weren't American either."

My hand instinctively reached for my carbine, which I had not thought of in months. I couldn't even remember the last time I'd cleaned it and was not sure it would fire. The rear sight was bent where I had dropped it on concrete. Rust splotched the barrel. The bullets had been in the clip since the invasion of Sicily and were gummed together. I had to hit the bolt with the butt of my palm to make it operate.

I was thinking it was entirely possible we were under enemy observation. During the past weeks our armies had been moving so fast whole units of Germans had been bypassed. Many of those units were merely waiting for somebody to surrender to. Others, however, were holding out and expecting to fight. Certainly it had been a long while since we passed any friendly faces. I held my carbine ready.

Of course Black Hatfield could have been mistaken. Chances were his eyes had tricked him. Furthermore even if he had sighted a German we weren't necessarily in trouble. A lot of Krauts had been cut off from their outfits or were deserting. What Black Hatfield could have seen was one of those or perhaps a man home on sick leave.

Still I could imagine all those dark shutters flying open and guns thrusting out. I decided Yancey ought to be notified even if he wouldn't know what to do. Unconcerned, he was driving his jeep on down the street. I didn't want to stop among the houses. I waited until we were through the town and out on the other side.

"Blow your horn at him," I told Black Hatfield.

At the sound of the horn, Yancey looked back. I signaled for him to wait for me. I jumped down from the high cab of the truck and ran to the jeep.

"Get moving," I ordered Yancey as I climbed in.

"Who you think you're telling what to do?" he asked.

"Listen, Black Hatfield thinks he saw a Kraut back there."

"Back where?" Yancey said, adjusting his glasses and blinking.

"It doesn't make any difference where. Unless you know this is an occupied town we better get out fast."

"It's possible I took the wrong fork somewhere. These maps aren't up to date."

"For God's sake get going!"

He glared at me, but he bucked the jeep forward. Black Hatfield had been alerting the men in the trucks behind us. They were all scrambling around in an attempt to find their weapons and ammunition.

The road was too narrow for the trailers to turn without sinking into the wet dirt. We drove on past the lake, which had swans on it. In front of the castle-like hotel was a circular drive. We curved around it fast. For an instant I could see my own reflection in a glass door. I looked scared.

We went back through the town. Watching windows, we snaked along the narrow streets. I believed we were going to be all right. At the last curve, just before we would have been free, Yancey's foot hit the brake pedal. Blocking the street was a German personnel carrier. Truck tires squealed on the cobblestones as the convoy skidded together like an accordion.

At the same time shutters banged open, and a burp gun fired. Even as I heard the sound, I couldn't understand bullets were actually flying around me. I jumped from the jeep and ran back among trucks. Some of them had crashed into each other. Men were yelling and climbing down. A grenade exploded. I felt the hot deadly force of it, and concussion knocked me against the wall of a house. Somebody screamed like a woman.

I ran in a crouch. Men were tumbling from trucks and crawling beneath them. A bullet hit a can of gasoline, which exploded. Flames drove us back, and smoke choked us. Bullets ricocheted among the buildings. I dived under a trailer. I saw Black Hatfield on his knees in a doorway. He was hammering at the lock with the steel butt of his M-1.

I ran to him. I threw my shoulder against the heavy oak door. It wouldn't give. Another grenade exploded. I heard the rapid *tap-tap-tap* of the burp gun. Black Hatfield shot the lock on the door. We both kicked, and the door swung open. We lunged in and fell to the floor, our guns ready.

Nobody was in the darkened hallway. Men were pitching in behind us and sprawling to the floor. All of us were terrified—our eyes bugging, our mouths agape. Carter trembled so badly he knocked against the boards. Black Hatfield had spewed tobacco over his face. In our shock we were unable to move.

We had to move. Germans could be in other rooms of the house. I looked for Yancey. He was lying on the floor like the rest of us, but his head was covered by his arms. He wasn't about to take charge, and somebody had to before we got killed. Shaking, I forced myself to my knees.

"Watch the door," I told Black Hatfield. He stared at me. "Some of the rest of you help me search the house."

I crawled toward the steps at the end of the hall. I could just see in the dim, rosy light from a small, stained-glass window set in the door. Honeycutt, Batten, and Smooth followed me. Their eyes rolled, and their shoulders were hunched.

I signaled for Honeycutt and Smooth to go on up the stairs. They didn't want to and shook their heads. I motioned again. Honeycutt started up slowly, ready to dive back in case he was shot at. Smooth, covered with sweat, followed on his tiptoes like a man trying not to wake the sleeping.

Batten came with me. To the right of the hall was a living room or parlor. I reached a shaky hand to a switch. To my surprise the lights came on. The room was furnished with black Teutonic pieces. We crawled past a piano to the dining room. Again I turned on a light. Batten and I lay quivering, at any moment expecting to be shot.

Breathing noisily, we inched on into the kitchen off which was a pantry. The door at the back was latched with a strong wooden beam. There were windows on either side of the door, but they were covered by shutters. We turned on more lights.

Upstairs Honeycutt hollered. Batten and I threw ourselves flat and waited for shooting. When none came, I pushed up and ran crouched to the steps. Men were still lying in the hall. Black Hatfield was facing the closed door. Yancey's head was covered by his arms. I ran up the steps.

At the top were bedrooms on both the front and back of the house. The lights were on. Each bedroom had overstuffed furniture with tassels. On a table was a photograph of a young soldier in the uniform of the Luftwaffe. The windows had lace curtains, but the shutters were bolted.

Honeycutt and Smooth stood in front of a closet. They were pointing their rifles inside. My carbine ready, I looked. On their knees among clothes were an elderly man, his wife, and a fat girl who was wearing the apron of a servant. They were whimpering and holding out their hands as if to ward off bullets.

"Do they speak English?" I asked Smooth and Honeycutt.

"We ain't had a conversation with them," Honeycutt answered, his rifle half raised to his shoulder.

"Speak English?" I asked the Germans.

They didn't understand. They continued to hold out their arms and started babbling. There was more shooting in the street at the front of the house. Smooth, Honeycutt, and I all lay on the floor.

"What do we do?" Honeycutt asked.

"Watch them a minute," I said.

I crawled across the floor to the stairs. At the landing I stood and ran down to the first floor. Some of the others had gotten up nerve enough to move a little farther into the house, but Yancey was in the same place. Black Hatfield was peeping out the door.

"Anybody there?" I whispered to him.

"Can't see nobody."

"Barricade it."

Black Hatfield got to his knees and crawled among the others. He shook their shoulders roughly to make them obey him. Carter lay by the piano, and Wilson was under a table. Black Hatfield cursed them until they began to help him stack furniture at the entrance. They pushed the furniture along the floor, ready to release it and flatten themselves at the first shot.

I went to the kitchen where Batten was. We searched until we found a trap door in the pantry. At the same instant we both realized Germans might be down there. I flung the door open and rolled back. Nothing happened. We raised a little to look at the dark hole.

The smell of earth rose up. If Germans were hiding in the basement, the elderly couple and servant girl could find out for us. I crawled to the steps and called for Honeycutt and Smooth to bring them. Honeycutt herded them down the stairs. The old woman was weeping and pressing her hands against her face.

In the pantry they wouldn't climb down the ladder into the basement. Honeycutt punched at them with his rifle until they did. The dark closed over them. We kicked the trap door shut and latched it.

A burst of shots hit the front of the house as Batten and I reached the parlor. Bullets chewed up shutters and glass splattered. A truck exploded in the street, causing the house to rock and plaster to fall. We pressed to the floor until the firing stopped. Except for a crackling of flames, all was quiet. We lifted our heads slowly to look at each other with the stupid, terrified expressions of men touched by death.

33

We sucked at the dusty air. Besides terror, our filthy faces showed disbelief. Everything had happened so rapidly it was difficult for us to comprehend that people were seriously trying to kill us. We lay motionless—as if digesting the fact.

We had to do something before the Germans attempted to finish us off. Again I made myself get up. Others watched me.

"Let's take a count," I said. "Let's find out who's here and what we're doing."

"That's my responsibility," Yancey said.

He crawled from the hall to the entrance of the parlor. He blinked his large brown eyes. Though his face was bloodless, he had partially gotten hold of himself. He came a little farther into the room. His fat body was shaking. He kept licking his lips.

"I'm in charge here," he said. "I'm the one who has to make the decisions."

He was still wearing all his ridiculous equipment, including the map case and binoculars. One of his pants legs had pulled loose from a shined paratrooper boot. A cheek was smudged with dirt.

He took the count. In various rooms on the first floor were Yancey, myself, Beanpost, Honeycutt, Timberlake, the Professor, Carter, Wilson, Smooth, Batten, and Black Hatfield. That meant along the street somewhere were another twenty-five or thirty men. They had probably found cover as we had. Some of them, however, might be wounded.

"They got to a house," Timberlake suggested, his eyes cutting about as if he expected Krauts to come pouring in the windows.

"We'll assume that," Yancey said, frowning. Moving about had helped him. He no longer was quite so pale and was definitely pulling himself together. "I'd like to get one thing straight. I'm not responsible for this snafu. My maps were defective."

He was lying by the piano in the parlor. The rest of us exchanged glances. Nobody cared who was responsible. We were concerned about how we were going to live.

"Maybe we ought to be thinking of something to do," Wilson said. Fear had made him appear old. All of us looked as if we had been in combat for days instead of under fire only a few seconds.

"I've got plans," Yancey snapped at him. "I'm thinking right now. You fellows won't get the blame for this foul-up. I will. Well, I refuse to be crucified because of defective maps."

We had just escaped being killed, but he was more concerned with cooking up an alibi for himself than trying to get us out of the trouble we were in. It was as if he were already on the carpet before a superior.

Another burst of gunfire pressed us to the floor. The shooting was coming from directly across the street. Splinters of wood and glass flew about. A bullet dug a pockmark in the plaster wall. A second one smashed into the upright piano which twanged off-key. A lamp was knocked over and broken.

The firing stopped. We waited fearfully, wondering whether the Germans were coming for us. There was no sound of running feet. I looked at Yancey. He was as he had been on first entering the house —on his belly, immobile except for shaking, his hands over his head. When he did uncover himself, his expression was bemused—like a man who couldn't remember where he was.

He still had his submachine gun. As he drew himself up, his finger touched the trigger. The gun exploded out of control. Bullets were flying around the room, smashing into walls and furniture. Men hurled themselves about to escape. The gun jerked like a live thing. Yancey's mouth was open in astonishment. Black Hatfield dived on the gun and tore it from Yancey.

"You dumb sonofabitch," Black Hatfield said, snapping the safety and crawling back toward the dining room.

Yancey, on his knees, followed.

"I'll forget you called me that," Yancey told him. "Now give me my Thompson."

"Captain, you sure you know how to use that thing?" Timberlake asked.

"Of course I know how to use it. I've qualified with it on the range. Now return it to me."

Black Hatfield had crawled to his cover under the dining-room table. He lay with the gun. Yancey held out a trembling hand to him. Black Hatfield didn't move.

"You could have killed somebody," Batten said to Yancey.

"Nobody's been killed have they? Give me my Thompson. That's an order."

For a moment I believed Black Hatfield was going to refuse. Then slowly, reluctantly, he pushed the submachine gun across the floor. Yancey took hold of it. We were all eying the weapon as if it might again go off. Yancey crawled back into the parlor and licked his lips.

"All right," he said. "We're wasting time. We ought to be assessing the situation. As a start let's get guards on the windows. We'll also check our ammo supply. After that we decide what to do."

He was at least making sense. Moreover, his voice carried enough authority to penetrate the fear of men lying about and to get them up. He assigned them to different rooms. On the first floor front he stationed Wilson and Beanpost. At the door itself was Carter, who,

309

though attempting to hide it, was still bumping gently against the floor. Black Hatfield and the Professor were put in the kitchen. Upstairs at the windows in the two bedrooms were Timberlake, Smooth, Honeycutt, and Batten. Because the house was sandwiched in between others and windowless on the sides, only the front and back needed guards.

The ammunition situation was serious. Not only were our cartridges old and discolored, but we also had less than fifteen rounds per man. Most of us carried carbines with one clip stuck in the rifle itself. We had thrown away the spares we were supposed to wear on our belts, believing we'd never have use for them. Black Hatfield carried the infantry M-1 he had never turned in to supply and half a bandoleer. Smooth shamefacedly admitted he was without a rifle. He had left it in a truck.

We cleaned the ammunition to keep it from jamming our guns. Wilson's carbine was so gummed up he couldn't see light through it. He worked to fix it. I sighted along mine. The crooked rear peep caused me to aim left. I thought we had about as much chance of repelling a serious attack as the Keystone Kops.

Yancey had assigned me no post. I wasn't sure whether he was refusing to speak to me or expected me to stay with him. I followed him around the house and back to the parlor. He sat by the piano.

"Does anybody have any idea how many Heinies we're up against?" he asked.

Nobody did. None of us had even seen a German in the few wild moments we had been scrambling through the streets. Nor was it possible to tell from the shooting. A few men with automatic weapons could sound like a platoon. We argued among ourselves, our voices hissing through the house. The talk gave us hope.

"There's at least the possibility we might not be facing too many of them," Yancey reasoned. "They could have the advantage of surprise and nothing more."

He sounded like an instructor at OCS or a candidate who had been given a problem. I guessed he was trying to remember what the officers' manual said. He squinted as if attempting to see the appropriate pages before his face.

"We shouldn't panic," he who'd panicked worse than anybody continued. "After all we don't even have a casualty, and we're not under attack. The thing to do now is to sit tight."

We turned off the lights. I crawled to the window where Wilson was. Pressing my cheek against the wall, I peeped through a crack in one of the shutters. The street was full of black oily smoke from the burning trucks. I could see the rear of a trailer and the front of a six-by-six.

Across the street was a house very much like the one we were in. I drew my head back quickly, thinking there were undoubtedly Germans in it. The fact they hadn't pressed their advantage while we were stunned with shock and fright did seem to indicate they lacked numbers. They would, however, need only a few men to keep us holed up. They might have more troops in the area and merely require time to deploy them. We'd surprised them almost as much as they had surprised us.

"Here's my assessment of the situation," Yancey announced, growing more sure of himself all the time. "It's just a freak accident we met them here. They'll probably pull out quietly and leave us alone. The war's practically over. They don't want a fight any more than we do. In addition it's entirely possible Allied units are on the way. It's more than a possibility if they're using the same maps I have."

In the dim light I watched him closely. He could go off his nut any moment. If he did, somebody would have to take charge. He caught me looking at him. He must have known what I was thinking, and he stared back defiantly.

Again I peeped from the window. There had been no shooting for some time. The shutters of the house across the street were open and the windows up, but I could see nothing except blackness beyond them.

Yancey's assessment had pleased the others. By whispers it had swept through the house. He had told them what they needed to hear. He was offering an easy salvation. It helped them conquer their fear.

"Now what about rations?" Yancey asked. "We might have to stay here a while. Maybe there's food. Elgar can search. He's not doing anything else."

He smirked at me. I wanted to tell him to go to hell, but I crawled to the kitchen where Black Hatfield and the Professor were sitting in the dark. I turned on the light. The Professor's glasses were low on his nose.

They helped me go through the kitchen and pantry. We found nothing to eat. The cellar was next. I hesitated to go down there. Black Hatfield, perhaps drawn by some miner's instinct for a hole, climbed into the dark. The German couple jabbered. He reappeared carrying potatoes in his helmet. Yancey ordered us to divide them equally.

"Not caviar but they'll fill an empty belly," he said. "There's plenty of water in the kitchen. We can be snug here."

His confidence was taking hold on the men. Furthermore his so-called assessment of the situation appeared to be correct. As much as I hated him, I still wanted him to be right.

He spread his maps by the piano. Enough light came in from broken shutters for him to see. He looked up, his face creased in thought.

"We ought to try to make contact with the others," he said. "If they're down the street, they'll be able to hear us."

It was a good suggestion. Yancey was definitely growing stronger. He crawled to the stairs where he called for Honeycutt. Honeycutt, a big farm boy, crept down the steps and at Yancey's instructions lay on his back under one of the front windows.

"What say golden eagle?" he shouted in the slow, drawling voice which would be instantly recognized by anybody who knew him.

Guns banged at us from across the street and bullets smashed into shutters. One was torn half off and swung by a single hinge. The room was lighter. Until the shooting stopped, we cowered on the floor.

"Can hear you," the voice of WO Page answered. The little accountant's terror was in his wavering words.

"Are you right?" Honeycutt asked after another short burst of gunfire.

"We have a man who is not ambulatory. Is there a drill?"

Honeycutt turned to Yancey for instructions.

"Tell them to sit tight but keep using the mixed-up language so the Heinies won't understand," Yancey said.

"Should I ask how many there are?"

"No. That information might help the Heinies."

"Use your cans a while," Honeycutt yelled. "We'll be talking at you."

No more shots came from across the street, and we sat up slowly. Yancey removed his netted helmet and wiped his brow with the sleeve of his field jacket. The others were accepting his leadership completely.

"I wish we could join up," he said, frowning. "A classic military axiom is that an inferior force should not be split in the face of the enemy."

312

We were a mere piece of a laundry unit, but he was calling us a force. I knew what he was thinking. He hoped to use us to better himself. If he were able to get us out of this, there would be publicity and perhaps even the promotion to major. The brass at Quartermaster Command were always very self-conscious about being noncombatants. They would play us up good because it would show them off to advantage.

As Yancey fooled with his maps, firing started across the street. It sounded like a single automatic weapon. Bullets chipped at a window near Beanpost and sent him diving to the floor among clouds of plaster. Yancey crawled about warning us to be prepared for an attack. We crouched by the windows, our rifles ready. A picture of a severe, white-haired German lady which was hanging on the wall of the dining room fell with a crash. The sun broke through. We heard birds singing.

34

We waited by the windows. No attack came. Trucks in the street continued to burn, and the stench of black rubber was thick in the air. I kept looking at my watch. It was early afternoon, and more than twenty minutes had passed since the Germans stopped shooting at us.

The silence made the sound of a cork being pulled from a bottle seem extraordinarily loud. Yancey raised from his maps. Holding his submachine gun, he crawled to the kitchen. He caught Black Hatfield drinking wine in the pantry.

"None of that," Yancey ordered.

"None of what?" Black Hatfield asked, having another swig. His dark, brooding face was twisted with insolence.

"Put down the bottle."

"That's what I'm doing," Black Hatfield answered. He drank again and wiped his stained lips with the back of his hand.

"You lift that bottle once more and I'll see you're court-martialed," Yancey warned him.

"How you going to go about it, Captain? The Krauts won't let us out just so you can court-martial me."

"We'll get out of here," Yancey said. "When we do, you'll be accountable. Now hand me that bottle."

Black Hatfield wasn't afraid of Yancey and had never liked him, but Black Hatfield was convinced Yancey could back up his threat. Sullenly he handed over the bottle.

"I ain't drunk or anything," he said, lowering his eyes. He had lost face.

"You're not going to be drunk either," Yancey told him. "You go take Smooth's post. He can replace you here."

Humiliated, Black Hatfield picked up his M-1 and went to the second floor. Smooth came down to the kitchen. Yancey poured the bottle of wine into the sink. As he started away, there was pounding on the trap door over the cellar. Yancey motioned for Smooth and the Professor to open it.

"What's the matter?" Yancey demanded, looking into the dark.

The elderly German couple and the servant girl were talking at the same time. The old man tried to get up the ladder. Yancey kicked at him to force him back.

"Can anybody here speak German?" Yancey asked.

"They want to go out under a white flag," the Professor explained.

"We can't let them out. They know too much about us. The Heinies might want information."

The Professor spoke softly to the Germans as he and Smooth pushed the trap door shut. For a while the Germans continued to pound.

Yancey returned to the living room where he studied his maps. I alternated with Wilson and Beanpost at windows. An hour had passed since any shooting across the street. Yancey was apparently correct about the Germans. They wished no fight and had probably pulled out.

Yancey himself appeared relaxed. Perhaps he dreamed of being awarded an honest medal for this action and presenting himself to Martha an authentic hero. Whatever his thoughts, his influence on the others was good. Their features flowed from the contortion of fear into normal shapes. I lit a cigarette. Wilson was chewing noisily on his potato.

"They had the Battling Bastards of Bastogne," he said. "Maybe we'll be known as the Aborting Ablutionists of Allemande."

"We've been in combat now," Beanpost added. "If you're in combat, don't they have to give you the combat infantryman's badge?"

"The laundryman's combat badge is a cake of brown soap rampant upon a washboard," the Professor called from the kitchen.

I waited for Carter to join in. He didn't speak. He was lying in the

314

hallway near the door. He'd been badly frightened when we first entered the house, and he couldn't forget it. Up to now he'd thought of himself as a warrior, but no longer. He was having to face himself, and he was ashamed.

It was fine to be talking. Men were seizing at words as if they were life. Even Beanpost who had been so scared he rattled like a tin lizzie was speaking excitedly. He, like the rest of us, was thinking it wouldn't be much longer before we could leave. Once back we'd have something to brag about. We'd have to be reequipped as well. The war in Europe ought to be over before we could again go on line.

"Captain!" Smooth said from the kitchen. His voice was frightened.

Yancey crawled quickly through the dining room, and I followed. Both Smooth and the Professor were staring at the back door.

"I think there's somebody out there," Smooth whispered.

A German could have slipped along the line of houses. Because the shutters were closed, however, we could not see out to make certain. Yancey hurried to the steps. Upstairs the shutters on the rear had been cracked slightly by Timberlake and Honeycutt. Yancey told them to take a look. They couldn't without sticking their heads way out, and they were afraid of that. Yancey crawled back. He was unsure.

"Use a grenade," I told him.

"What?" he asked, staring at me.

"One of your grenades," I said, pointing to those he had wired to his field jacket.

He continued to stare, but he unfastened a grenade and handed it to Smooth.

"Take it upstairs," Yancey ordered. "On my signal drop it out a window but not right in front of the door. We don't want to blow the door in."

Smooth ran for the steps. I'd moved closer to the door. I put my ear against the wood. At the same moment I touched the knob. To my horror I felt the pressure of a hand turning it from the other side.

I shouted and threw myself away from the door. Shooting started outside. Small splintered holes appeared in the thick oak door. Bullets from a gun held against it were not coming all the way through. Those of us in the kitchen were scrambling to escape. "Drop it! Drop it!" I was screaming at Smooth.

Smooth had already dropped it. The grenade clanged on the cobblestones and exploded. The house rocked. Plaster and rubble fell. We clawed at the floor as if to get under it.

The shooting had stopped. We lay motionless among the dust. Coughing, I made myself crawl to the steps and go up. In the rear bedroom Smooth, Black Hatfield, and Timberlake were pressing to the wall in an attempt to see down to the street without exposing themselves.

"There!" Timberlake said and pointed.

We couldn't see all of the German soldier. The sill of the window cut off the lower part of him. The grenade must have gone off within a few feet of him. He was sprawled on his back among ruptured cobblestones. His bloody, unbelieving face was turned up to the sky, and his mouth was open. One arm was flung out. For a few minutes he twitched.

We were fascinated by the body. The German soldier was the first dead man any of us had seen in the war. Word spread quickly through the house, and others came to look. Solemnly they took their turns at the window. Laundry outfit or not, the tattered remnants of the golden eagle had finally made a kill.

"I just pulled the pin and let the grenade roll out," Smooth kept explaining. He looked proud, awed, guilty. "Anybody could have done it."

Yancey stopped the macabre sightseeing. He believed the Germans might attack and ordered us back to our posts. We were funereal in our movements because death was with us. We kept glancing at each other to be sure what we had seen was genuine. We had actually ended a life.

Fear was again upon us. As we waited, the streets on both sides of our house remained quiet. The German lay out there, and Black Hatfield reported that flies were collecting on the bloody places.

Yancey motioned to me. I left the window and followed his fat buttocks into the dimness of the dining room. We were on our knees in a corner.

"I'd like to remind you I'm in charge here," he whispered to me. His lower lip stuck out petulantly.

"So?" I asked, not understanding.

"It was up to me to decide about that grenade. It was also my job to give the command to drop it. You were usurping my authority."

He was serious.

"I'm not trying to usurp anything. There wasn't time for formalities."

"Well, you just better remember I'm in charge here and give the orders. I was about to issue those commands when you anticipated me. I'll remind you that anybody who doesn't obey me around here can expect a court-martial when we get back. I personally guarantee it."

He crawled away from me. I wanted to grab him and call him the liar he was. He hadn't thought of using the grenade, and he'd been too scared to give the command to drop it. Furious, I returned to the window. Wilson and Beanpost were watching me.

Yancey made the rounds to be certain each man was at his post. There was no further shooting, and our hopes revived a little. I peeked at the house across the street. It appeared deserted. The sun was again covered by clouds. Yancey came back and studied his maps by the piano.

I was tired. Like the others, I had been burning adrenalin ever since entering the house. Now the letdown was hitting me. I couldn't stop yawning. I looked at Wilson and Beanpost. Their dirty faces were strained and weary. Their eyelids drooped.

A single shot was fired from across the street at the rear of the house. An instant later somebody upstairs yelled. Yancey crawled to the steps, and I followed him up. In the back bedroom Batten, our mail clerk, lay on the floor. Blood was squirting from his face. He had been peeping out the window at the dead German and exposed too much of himself.

We could do nothing as the blood pumped out of him. When life stopped, we pulled him to the wall and Timberlake covered him with a blanket from the bed. Smooth got Batten's carbine. We crouched around the body. The blanket was soaking up blood, and the flies sought it out.

35

We were all badly shaken. Batten was one of our own, and seeing him dead made us know for sure it could happen to any of us. We felt pity for him and dread for ourselves. Vomit flakes formed in the back of my throat.

Only Black Hatfield acted unmoved. Perhaps as a coal miner he was used to death. He stayed at his window, methodically chewing tobacco and spitting it onto the wall. The rest of us crept back to our posts as if we'd seen something shameful.

I couldn't quit thinking of Batten up there under the blanket. He was just a few years older than I was, and I tried to imagine myself dead like him. I was unable to do so. Even with my fear I couldn't. I wasn't going to die. Dying was ridiculous. Yet Batten had and was already turning stiff.

As I sat by the window I attempted to put myself in the place of the Germans. The fact they hadn't attacked in force made it seem likely they weren't going to. The killing of their man with the grenade might have discouraged that. Probably they intended to keep us under siege by taking occasional shots at us. We would have a long wait.

Covertly I watched Yancey. He was still fooling with his maps. He had become very pale at the sight of Batten, but he now seemed recovered. He was making marks on the margin of the maps with a pencil.

"Look at these," he said to Wilson, indicating Wilson was to leave the window. Wilson obediently crawled across the floor. "I defy anybody to have done a better job than I did with maps as poor as these."

Wilson pretended to examine the maps, but he also turned his eyes questioningly to me. Beanpost and I looked at each other. Instead of worrying about us, Yancey was still thinking how he was going to alibi himself.

"I suppose the infantry's issued the best maps," Yancey continued. "Quartermaster gets the hind tit. Just wait till I get back. I'm going to raise some hell."

"You really think we'll get back, Captain?" Beanpost asked. The skinny, Pike County, Kentucky, undertaker was sitting Yogi style with his carbine on his lap. His face was darkened by beard.

"I have no doubt of it," Yancey answered. "I admit I must change my assessment slightly. As yet the Heinies haven't pulled out, but they will. They were just testing our resolution, and that grenade fixed their wagon. For all they know we have hundreds of grenades."

He spoke with certainty. He could have been making a speech. His goggles were awry on his helmet, and his clothes, like everybody's, were powdered white from plaster. As he studied his maps, what he'd said was whispered through the house.

318

"Hey, I think something's going on down the street," Timberlake hollered from upstairs.

I stood against the front wall of the parlor, but I could neither see nor hear anything. My field of vision was restricted by the angle of the window. Without waiting for Yancey, I ran to the steps. He crowded past me, glancing at me angrily. I followed him up to the front bedroom where Timberlake, Honeycutt, and Black Hatfield were. Timberlake squatted by a window.

"I thought I heard men running," he said.

We all listened.

"You must have been mistaken," Yancey told him.

"I don't think so."

"Occasionally soldiers hear what they're most afraid of," Yancey pronounced, his voice assuming the lecturer's tone. "It's a form of self-hypnosis. Those feet were running in your mind."

As he finished speaking, shooting started. We pressed to the floor, but no bullets were aimed at our house. Rather the firing was up the street. It was sustained as if covering an assault.

"They're attacking the other group," Yancey explained unnecessarily.

"I must have been hypnotized pretty good," Timberlake said.

We lay listening. The shooting stopped. We heard a distant voice, but we couldn't tell whether it was English or German. We raised to our elbows.

"Ask them if they're okay down there," Yancey ordered Honeycutt.

"You golden eagles in the pink?" Honeycutt shouted, cupping his hands.

A heavy burst of firing came from the house across the street. Bullets chipped into the walls and tore apart a window frame. One of the shutters fell off and crashed to the cobblestones. We covered our heads as plaster dust swirled around us.

The shooting stopped. Yancey had thrown himself down so forcibly his glasses were knocked off. When he put them on with shaking fingers, a lens was cracked. They were chalky white from the plaster. His lips were quivering, and he was very frightened.

"Call them again," he said weakly to Honeycutt.

Honeycutt did. His voice caused shooting a second time, though not as much. When the street became quiet, we heard the bass voice of Boomer, a cook.

"In the pink," he answered.

319

There was more gunfire at that end of the street.

"Ask if WO Page is all right," Yancey told Honeycutt.

"What about Page?" Honeycutt yelled.

"I'm his hog caller," Boomer answered. "He's got a loose stool."

We heard one last flurry of shooting before the street became quiet. Yancey crawled to the landing and down the steps. He was waiting for me at the bottom.

"From now on you stay at your post," he said. "That's an order."

He turned his back on me and crawled into the parlor. Carter was watching us. I slid along the floor to the window where Wilson was. Yancey sat by the piano.

"I'm optimistic," he said to Wilson and Beanpost. Yancey was smiling, but he still looked scared. "I figure if we were outnumbered, the Krauts would have tried something decisive by now. We've been here almost three hours, and they haven't. They don't have the strength to overpower us, and as soon as they tire of the game they'll pull out."

"They could have a plan," Wilson said. "Maybe they're just waiting to put it into gear."

"Highly unlikely," Yancey answered, his voice patronizing. "I'm quite sure they'll be gone by dark. We'll leave shortly after that. As soon as we get back, I'm going to send a hell-raising letter through channels to Washington about these maps."

Beanpost and Wilson eyed each other. Like me they were wondering whether the pressure was causing Yancey to come apart at the seams. I looked at Wilson, and he shrugged.

It was after three o'clock, but we had a long wait until night. If the Germans did pull out, we could slip away in the dark. Even on foot we wouldn't be more than a few hours from our lines.

Metal clattered in the street at the front of the house. We threw ourselves to the floor. A grenade exploded. The house shook and more plaster fell from the ceiling. We listened for sounds of an attack. None came. A curl of black smoke seeped through a broken shutter. We raised ourselves cautiously. Yancey was the last to do so.

"Anything out there?" he asked timorously.

"Nothing," Beanpost answered, peeping from a window.

"I'll check the posts," Yancey said.

We watched him crawl from the room, his pants baggy, his pigeon-toed combat boots scraping the floor. I waited until he was up the steps before speaking to Wilson and Beanpost.

"You think he's all right?" I whispered.

320

"I don't know," Wilson said. "He's acting half nuts about those maps."

"He hasn't done anything really wrong so far," Beanpost argued. "Except he's been slow to react."

I wasn't convinced. Slowness to react could be a sign of something worse. We were all scared, but Yancey's fear seemed to work differently, reducing him to at least momentary helplessness.

From the kitchen came new pounding on the trap door. Because Yancey was upstairs, I crawled in there. The room was dark, and I switched on the light. The Professor was sitting in a straight chair, his legs crossed. I didn't see Smooth. Yancey came into the kitchen.

"What's the matter?" he asked the Professor.

Instead of answering, the Professor shrugged evasively. I was certain I already knew.

"Open the trap door and quiet them down," Yancey ordered.

Though reluctant to do so, the Professor unlatched the trap door. The old man was on the ladder and talking fast. He tried to come up. Yancey kicked at him. The German was pointing into the darkness.

"What's he saying?" Yancey asked the Professor.

"He's pretty excited," the Professor answered, still trying to protect Smooth. "It's difficult to keep up with him."

From the darkness came a giggle. Yancey heard it. He looked around the kitchen and pantry.

"Where's Smooth?" he demanded. "Smooth!" he shouted into the hole.

The old woman was standing right behind her husband on the ladder. Both were talking rapidly and gesturing into the dark. Smooth came out of the dark. He was grinning and straightening his clothes. The servant girl followed him. She was so fat her dress seemed to hold her flesh together rather than cover it. She squinted up at us, her eyes shining in the light.

"You call me?" Smooth asked.

"Come out of there!" Yancey said. "And quick!"

Smooth pulled the elderly couple off the ladder so that he could climb up. He was still grinning. The girl attempted to follow. He had to shove her back to shut the trap door. He pushed the latch into place.

"You deserted your post," Yancey charged him. "You could be shot."

"Aw hell, Captain, we just been sitting here in the dark. The Professor and me can't even see out."

"We might have been attacked. Your presence could've made the difference between success and failure."

"You told us you didn't think we was going to get attacked again."

"Never mind what I told you. I ought to have you shot. Did you rape that girl?"

"Captain, I tell you the truth, she practically raped me."

"You're in trouble, mister. You go down into that basement once more and you're in bad trouble. Understand me?"

"Sure, Captain," Smooth answered, slouching against the wall. He brought out a cigarette.

Yancey glared and ran a shaky hand across his dry lips. When he realized I was watching, he turned the glare on me.

"This is my last warning for you to stay at your post," Yancey said. "I'd just as soon court-martial two men as one. Get back on the double."

I went back to the window. Yancey switched off the light and followed me. He sat by the piano and scowled.

Another grenade exploded in the street. This one was closer to the house. Fragments from the metal canister blasted what remained of the shutters and pocked the ceiling. The house rattled. No great damage was done, but we huddled on the floor.

Upstairs something thudded. Honeycutt yelled in fright. Men scrambled. There was an explosion right over the parlor. Chunks of plaster fell from the ceiling, and a beam poked through like a fractured bone. For a moment I believed the house was coming in on us. We struggled to uncover ourselves. The plaster made us look like ghosts, and we were coughing loudly.

I looked for Yancey. He was protected by an outcropping of the piano, and he had covered his head with his hands. He was shaking. I waited for him to get up. When he did not, I crawled among rubble to the steps.

"What is it?" I yelled.

"Grenade," Timberlake answered from the back bedroom. "It came right in the front window."

"Anybody hurt?"

"Hell yes, I am," Honeycutt said.

I went up the stairs. Black Hatfield and Timberlake were helping Honeycutt who was not wounded as badly as first appeared. The German grenades were more powder than metal. As a result the

322

danger was concussion rather than fragments. Honeycutt was mostly addled. He was also bleeding from the nose and ears. His face was speckled as if he had chicken pox. Timberlake was sprinkling sulpha powder on him. They had dragged him to the back bedroom.

A grenade missed the front window and exploded in the street. The next one, however, dropped into the bedroom and exploded. Furniture was smashed, and walls were collapsing. Holes were driven into the floor. The house sagged.

"What do we do?" Timberlake asked. Like Black Hatfield and me, he was lying flat.

A few more grenades and the house would be knocked to pieces. Another one came, but it too struck the side and fell into the street. The thrower was probably on the second floor across from us. He would be tossing the grenade toward our window in the underhand style of a softball pitcher. Perhaps he exposed himself each time he threw.

I left Timberlake with Honeycutt and ran downstairs. I climbed through the wreckage of the parlor. Yancey had not moved. He continued to lie face down and quake. I got Wilson and Beanpost to their windows. From the kitchen I brought in Smooth and the Professor as well. I called Carter from the hallway. I explained to them that the instant the next grenade was thrown they had to rise up and start shooting. They were all frightened, yet they stayed by the windows.

I ran back upstairs. In the rear bedroom I told Timberlake and Black Hatfield to follow me to the front. They looked at me as if I were crazy, but they came. We crawled over plaster, broken furniture, and holes in the floor. We crouched by the windows. Timberlake and Black Hatfield understood I was counting on the Germans missing the next time. If they did not, a grenade would sail into the room past us. I hoped we could hide among the rubble.

A grenade clattered against the side of the house and fell into the street. My heart pounded.

"Now!" I shouted.

I wanted to cringe, but I made myself rise to the window. Across the street I saw a German soldier. He was directly opposite me, and his hand was still extended in the follow-through of throwing the grenade. I, like Black Hatfield, Timberlake, and the men downstairs started firing wildly.

Our bullets chipped at the house. Guns over there were shooting back. Tiny red flashes of muzzle blast sparked in dark windows.

Pieces of stone, wood, and plaster flew about our heads. The grenade thrower tried to duck, but one of our bullets hit him. He was driven backward out of sight. We dived to the floor.

We crawled to the rear bedroom and panted among plaster. The barrel of my carbine was hot. I'd used up the best part of a clip. After a while the firing across the street died. Apparently the loss of their thrower kept the Germans from trying again. There were no more grenades.

36

Before going downstairs, I took an ammunition count and sent Timberlake and Black Hatfield to their posts in the front bedroom. They made themselves nests in the rubble.

Honeycutt, though in pain, insisted he could watch the back. His bleeding had slowed, but his eyes were cocked. He looked as if he were trying to make a funny face.

At the foot of the steps Yancey crawled toward me. Peering from under his helmet, he resembled a crab. He was powder white, the plaster dust sticking to the sweat of his face. He was on his belly. I tried to get around him, but he held out a hand.

"You did the right thing," he told me hoarsely. "That's why I stayed clear of it. I could see you were taking the proper action, and there was no sense of me interfering."

He was lying. He had been unable to move during the grenade attack. Every muscle and bone of him had been shaking in terror. He was still shaking, and fear brightened his eyes.

"I don't want you to think I resent your taking the initiative," he said, his voice quivering. "I want what's right for all of us here. We can use any ideas we can get. But I expect you to remember I'm in command. I have the helm now. You get back to your post, and I'll make the rounds."

He crawled past me and went up the steps. Ignoring his orders, I moved among the rubble to see whether anybody had been hurt and to continue the ammunition count. No one was wounded, but I figured we had less than six cartridges per man. I sent Smooth, the Professor, and Carter back to their posts. I sat by Wilson. We could hear Yancey upstairs. When he came down, he was still trembling.

"We're intact," he said. "Now I think we ought to reassess the situation. We have to make some decisions."

We watched him. He couldn't stop shaking, and new sweat glistered on him in spite of the white plaster dust. He rubbed his face with a handkerchief. The handkerchief left swipes of shiny skin among the dirt. His eyes rolled.

"Obviously the Heinies have stronger forces than I first believed," he said. "I'd like to get everybody's idea of what we should do."

We knew why he wanted our ideas. He no longer had any of his own. Under our stares, he straightened a little, attempting to act more authoritative, but he couldn't hide his indecision or fear.

"You're not deaf, are you?" he asked. "I told you I wanted your suggestions. Maybe we can put together a plan. What about you, Beanpost?"

"Sir, maybe you just better take it easy," Beanpost answered. A gentle spirit not equipped for hate, he was sorry for Yancey.

"Don't talk like that to me," Yancey said angrily. "I'm not incapacitated if that's what you're implying. I'm in no way incapacitated."

In truth he was again recovering. It was as if each threat drove him into some hole deep within himself from which he emerged as danger subsided. He was emerging now.

"I'm in command here," he told us, continuing to wipe at his face. "I make the decisions and right now I'm calling for a reassessment of the situation."

He scowled at each of us as if he'd been challenged. Outside in the street flames crackled on the trucks, and black smoke occasionally drifted through the windows.

"Personally I think we've beaten Jerry," Yancey continued, his shaking almost under control. "They're realizing they've bitten off more than they can chew. Chances are good they'll break off the action. That being the case, we can sneak out of here tonight."

I wasn't at all sure he was right. The fact the Germans hadn't left made it seem doubtful they would leave now. In addition they might expect us to try to get out after dark. They had nothing to lose by waiting. On the other hand a possibility existed that Yancey was correct.

"If we do try a break-out, we ought to notify the men up the street," I said. "We can talk to them in pig Latin. Somebody up there'll understand, and the Germans won't."

"I've already considered that," Yancey answered, glaring at me. "Naturally I'll notify the others. What's more it just so happens I've been sitting here thinking of using pig Latin too."

He pouted and cleaned his glasses with a handkerchief. He took off his helmet to rub the handkerchief over his head. He must have continued to dye his hair all through the war, for now some of that dye had faded and we saw gray. He looked sixty.

"At the proper time I'll notify the men up the street," he went on. "It's still much too early for that. The best thing we can do is sit here quietly and let Jerry stew. Let him worry about our intentions."

We waited. I lay on my back and looked up through a broken window toward the dirty sky. From time to time our house creaked as if the grenades had caused some fundamental change in its structure. I found myself again growing sleepy. The ebbing fright left me numb. I was still afraid, but the pitch was lower and deadening.

"I should imagine we're missed by now," Yancey said. His shaking had quieted. It was twenty minutes to four. "Corps is certainly aware we haven't completed our mission. They're probably looking for us. They'll be here in jig time, and we won't have to break out."

"Aw, Captain, we're a laundry outfit," Wilson told him. "Who the hell would ever miss us?"

"Don't talk like that. We're as important as anybody to the Army. It's my estimate we're missed and that they're searching for us. That's why I'm considering revising my plan about the break-out after dark."

We all knew what his words meant. Whether the plan was good or not, he was losing his nerve about it. He was thinking it was safer to sit tight. If we didn't expose ourselves, we wouldn't get shot at. In my opinion, however, the Germans could outwait us. We'd eventually have to attempt escape.

Before any of us answered Yancey, we heard a plane. We turned our eyes upward as if we could see through the ceiling. My first thought was it might be a tactical plane sent by the Germans. I lay on the floor staring up at the small strip of sky I could watch between houses. I saw the plane as it flew over, but I was unable to identify it.

Moments later it came back, this time lower. It passed over town very fast. Instinctively we balled up on the floor. Yancey had pushed back under the brow of the piano. To our relief the engine didn't have the throbbing quality associated with German aircraft. Furthermore the plane didn't return.

"One of ours," Yancey said, wiggling out from under the piano. He clapped his hands. "It has to be one of ours. The Luftwaffe's been destroyed. That pilot was American and saw our trucks."

He was very happy, and I found myself believing there was at least a chance he was right. If the pilot was American, he might be radioing in what he'd seen. His report could start the wheels of our release rolling.

"They'll be here quickly," Yancey said, rubbing his dusty, fat hands. "Right at this minute that pilot is speaking to his squadron command. Air intelligence will put two and two together. They'll send a relief column—probably armor—for us. I know I'll catch hell for being lost, but I've got the maps. If they're fair, they'll have to admit the fault lies with the maps."

He was gleeful. He still wore his binoculars around his neck. The cracked lens of his glasses hid one eye. The other appeared particularly large and watery. Elsewhere he might have appeared comical —like a clown in a war skit.

"I'm going to put in good reports on you men too," he said, nodding at Wilson and Beanpost as well as indicating those upstairs and in the kitchen. He didn't look at me. "You all have acted damn fine. I don't want to give away any secrets, but some of you are going to be put in for the bronze star. I'll see to it personally."

I felt my lips twist. Yancey was trying a bribe pure and simple. He was in effect offering decorations to them for covering for him. I glanced at Wilson and Beanpost to see whether they realized it. They did, and their faces were averted from Yancey.

"In fact I'll put in for one silver star and several bronze stars. Under the circumstances I believe that's a reasonable request. Moreover I think we're entitled to the combat infantryman's badge, and I intend to ask for it. I suppose we'll get a certain amount of publicity. It isn't everyday a Quartermaster unit holds off a German attack. They'll probably have something about us in *Stars and Stripes* or *YANK*."

He looked as if he were tasting that. He was smiling, and the one eye I could see was dreamy. He was probably thinking of sending the clippings to Martha to impress her with what a hero he was. He wouldn't impress her long because if I did nothing else I'd write her the truth about him.

"They might take our pictures," Yancey said. "And maybe a general will come down from Corps to award us decorations. Actually they'd do well to make a big thing of this. They could send us to the States to sell war bonds."

"Why don't you shut up a while?" Carter asked from the hallway where he was guarding the door.

Carter hadn't spoken since entering the house. He'd been more afraid than he'd known was possible, and the knowledge had shaken his faith in himself. He was brooding about his fear. Some of his clean boyishness had dropped away, and he appeared older. He was older.

Like the rest of us, Yancey was startled. Carter was the last person from whom we would have expected insubordination. He had been our model soldier—dedicated, military, aggressive. Yancey blinked, and his mouth worked a moment before his lips formed words.

"Now look here you got to remember who you're talking to," Yancey said. "I can understand a man under tension might forget his place, but after all I'm in charge here. I'm responsible. I have to remind you I'm your superior. Now we've all had a difficult time and because of that fact I'm willing to overlook remarks. I'm willing to let bygones be bygones. The truth is we ought to stick together. We've been under fire and have a bond."

He kept talking. His lips seemed to work faster than the words which came from them. Spit sprayed from his mouth, and the voice whined on. As he spoke, none of us looked at him. He was aware of it. His voice became more strident. He was pleading with us.

Shots up the street caused him to roll his eyes and abruptly stop talking. The firing sounded like an attack. We heard grenades and automatic weapons. We could see nothing.

Then, as we crouched fearfully, we heard another kind of sound. It was a loud *whoosh*—a noise like that of a man blowing out a match, yet greatly amplified. We stared at one another.

"Flame thrower," Yancey whispered, terror contorting his face. He pushed back under the brow of the piano.

The shooting slowed. We heard the *whoosh* again, this time followed by a scream—the rising, agonized wail of a tortured man giving up his life. I felt the hair rise on me. Up the street was shouting. We heard men running. Grenades exploded. The shooting became sporadic. Black wisps of smoke drifted across the sky.

In another moment all was quiet. I was sweating. Like the others I lay balled on the floor and thought of being burned alive. I couldn't get the scream out of my ears. I believed I smelled burnt flesh.

"Maybe we ought to try to contact them," Wilson said weakly. He was curled and trembling.

I looked at Yancey. He had covered his head and lay shaking. He wasn't going to do anything. I rolled onto my back and cupped my hands.

"Golden eagle?" I croaked.

There was no reply.

"Boomer?" I called. "Page?"

I got no answer. I turned to my belly and buried my face in my arms. I was shaking as bad as Yancey. A few minutes later we heard more shots. They came from a greater distance and sounded like a volley. The shots had to mean the Germans were finishing off those men they'd taken prisoner.

At eighteen minutes after four a voice using the perfect English of a BBC announcer spoke from the house across the street.

"They can't hear you," the voice said. "They're dead."

Fear was clenching me like a fist. There was a definite sickening stench in the air.

"And you chaps are next," the voice told us—unhurried, cultured, and amused.

37

None of us moved. We lay shaking on the floor. Yancey was pushed back against the piano, every part of him jerking violently. His soft body knocked against the footboard. His helmet banged on the floor. When he got nerve enough to raise his head, his eye darted about in panic.

"They got us," he said shrilly. "There's nothing we can do against a flame thrower. Somebody find a sheet. We'll put out a white flag."

Still nobody moved. Each of us was bound by his own terror. Of all the things I feared, burning to death was the worst. I imagined my own flesh sizzling. I wanted to mash my eyes and become an embryo.

Yet somebody had to take charge. Yancey had gone altogether to pieces. He was a repulsive sight lying under the piano, and to have obeyed him would have been to become like him. Furthermore there had been that last evil volley of shots. If the Germans were taking no prisoners, the only chance we had was to fight.

"We've got to try," I whispered urgently to the others. They turned their heads a little. "Otherwise we're dead. They'll use a house to attack from. They'll set up a covering fire to protect the man with the flame thrower. He has to show himself. We might get him before he can do much damage."

"No!" Yancey protested. He was in a seizure of shaking. He hugged himself as if freezing. "They got us beat I tell you. The only chance we have is to surrender. Now get the sheet. That's an order."

Smooth and the Professor crawled in from the kitchen. Timberlake and Black Hatfield were creeping down the steps.

"We can pile stuff at the windows," I went on, talking fast. "All we need is space to shoot from. The flame thrower can't hit the whole house at once. Somebody's sure to have a shot."

"I give the orders here," Yancey said, his helmet clanging against a pedal of the piano. "I've assessed the situation, and it's my judgment we have to fly the white flag."

"Let's get started," I told them, crawling across the floor. I began to push a table toward a window. "Turn the sofa up on end."

For a moment nobody budged. Most of them rated me and certainly hadn't elected me to command. They might refuse to do what I asked. I went on pushing the table over rubble to the window. Carter wiggled into the room and took hold of the sofa.

The others stirred. Wilson and Beanpost helped Carter with the sofa. Smooth and the Professor dragged in furniture from the dining room. Black Hatfield and Timberlake ran up the steps where they grabbed mattresses from the beds and stuffed them into windows. The activity drew fire from across the street. Bullets plunked into the mattresses.

Most of the work had to be done on the front of the house. At the back both upstairs and down, the shutters were still in good condition. Moreover the flame thrower was likely to take the shortest course.

Honeycutt had recovered enough to use a carbine. I decided to bring Smooth upstairs as well. We could wait on the landing and rush to the side of the house exposed to covering fire. If we were lucky, we'd have a few seconds before the flame thrower was put in use.

I went downstairs for Smooth. Yancey was still pressed against the piano. He glistened with sweat.

"I'll have you court-martialed," he said to me as I passed. "I'll have all of you court-martialed. This is a deliberate disregard of orders. You'll be sent to jail. You'll spend twenty years in jail. You'll be old men when they let you out."

Nobody listened to him. We were all at work blocking up windows. The whole success of what we were trying to do depended on our shooting back quickly and accurately in the face of intense German fire.

I remembered Yancey's submachine gun, went to him, and pulled it from his side. He reached for it, but I knocked his hand away. I also jerked the clip from his belt.

"You'll pay for this," he threatened me, his face contorted. "You think the authorities will take your word over mine? They'll hang you."

I went up the steps and gave the submachine gun to Black Hatfield who checked it over. He counted the bullets in the clip and worked the bolt. He raised the gun to his shoulder to get the feel of it. Lastly he let a cartridge slide into the chamber and snapped on the safety.

Black Hatfield, Timberlake, Honeycutt, Smooth, and I waited on the hall landing. Downstairs Wilson, Beanpost, Carter, and the Professor lay in the dining room—ready to move quickly to the front or back of the house.

I heard a scraping sound. I looked over the railing and saw Yancey. He had come from the piano and was scurrying into a dark, protected corner under the steps.

I made the rounds once more, slipping through the house with my carbine. I talked to the men in the dining room.

"Remember they can't hit every window at once with that thing," I told them, attempting to sound a lot more positive than I felt. "As soon as they start shooting, let go with everything we got."

We grew rigid with waiting. We heard no sounds from the Germans, yet it was easy to imagine them sneaking through shadowy passages in preparation. If they didn't set up covering fire, they had us. We could be cooked even before we reached a window. I found myself caressing the flesh of my throat.

From the street came the noise of boots striking cobblestones, and we flung ourselves about. The footsteps, however, were not those of men in attack but had the regular rhythm of persons promenading. We rushed to the front windows and flattened ourselves against the walls to peek out.

Coming down the street from our right was a German soldier who marched at attention. He was holding a sword which had a white handkerchief tied to the blade. Behind him, walking leisurely and smoking a cigarette, was a slim, wasp-waisted officer. The officer looked as if he might be dressed for a parade. His gray uniform was immaculate, his black boots shined. He wore black gloves, and his pants flared out widely.

"Don't anybody shoot!" I called.

"It might be a trick," Timberlake warned me.

"It might. You all watch for the flame thrower. I'll go down and talk to the officer."

I ran down the steps. Carter and Beanpost came to the hall to help me move the furniture away from the door. Holding my carbine, I straightened my shoulders, opened the door, and stepped out.

The two Germans stood facing me. The private, hulking and stolid, remained at attention, the sword held upright in front of his face. The lieutenant was relaxed and smiling. He was a young man of twenty or so. He was delicately, almost fragilely built. He was pretty with his blond hair and girl's complexion. I smelled the odor of cologne.

I had quickly glanced at his blouse. He was not infantry. Instead twin zigzags of lightning were there—the insignia of the SS. He had seen my eyes move, and he showed his perfect teeth.

"They have very fine sulphur baths here," he said in the voice of the BBC announcer. He waved a gloved hand. "A pity you're not tourists."

His voice was mocking. As he spoke, his blue eyes first searched for my rank and then attempted to see around me into the house. The private with the sword took three paces to the rear so that he was behind the lieutenant. The private remained at attention.

The narrow street itself was clogged with our equipment and trucks—some of which were still burning. Smoke from them had blackened the fronts of buildings. I looked beyond the lieutenant to the house directly across from our own. In the shadows behind windows I believed I saw flickers of movement.

"You're in charge here?" the lieutenant asked.

"Yes."

"Then you must realize we have you," he said, knocking the ash from his cigarette. It was an American cigarette, and I knew where he'd gotten it. "You're contained. I can send my men for you any time I wish."

"Why bother to talk?" I asked.

He laughed. It was almost a giggle—high-pitched, feminine, full of glee. Along his cheek was a short scar.

tical Yankee warrior," he said. "Do you think I enjoy

ow," I answered, again looking at the SS insignia on the
blouse. "You might."
e Waffen SS," he said, standing straighter, his smile
ake no pride in butchery."
ke no pride in butchery, what happened to the men
eet?" I asked, indicating the direction where WO Page
s had been.
sted," he answered, raising the palms of his gloved
y were foolish to do so. The war's almost over. They
een prisoners only a short time. Why die?"
it sound reasonable and attractive except that I feared
s convinced he had shot the others after they were
agreement with this man would be meaningless. We
ce at all if we gave up. If we fought, we might have a

just pull out and allow us to leave?" I asked.
estion. We of the Elite Corps have certain rules. You
e have our pride. We were in this village when you en-
n't pretend we didn't see you. Moreover your presence
ny superiors."
by certain rules too. We don't turn ourselves over to the
got a reputation for killing prisoners."
u we're of the Waffen SS. We're fighters, not execu-
e you my word as an officer you will not be harmed."
emptation. Giving up could mean the terror was over.
e taken someplace safe and be able to wait out the end

I didn't know enough to make any distinction between
branches of the SS, but I did know that WO Page and
re dead.
' I told the lieutenant.
annoyed, but only for an instant. He dropped his ciga-
isted his boot on it.
 honestly that in your place I'd give up. We have a
ilometers to the west. If all else fails, I can radio for it."
d a tank, you'd have already radioed for it," I answered,
to bluff it out. By appearing sure, I might stop an at-

stubborn and stupid man," the lieutenant told me. He

333

stepped back, and the private with the sword
of him. They started away. I turned to the do
ing, Yancey came out and pushed past me.
and his watery brown eye seemed enormou:
cracked lens of his dirty glasses.

"Wait!" he called to the Germans.

The private and lieutenant stopped. Whe
Yancey's rank, he touched his cap in a salut
appraisingly. I was thinking that Yancey's fr
vitation to attack. I grabbed his arm and tried t
jerked loose.

"Take your hands off," he ordered me. "You
martialed."

"Get inside," I whispered.

"I'm in command here," Yancey answered. l

The German lieutenant watched. Then he s:
ward us. I considered getting the others to help
He moved farther into the street.

"I'm in charge here," he told the lieutena
men, and I make the decisions."

"But of course," the lieutenant answered, bow
"I've been explaining to your representative tl
you to die. Obviously you're not even a combat
no disgrace in surrender."

"What are your terms?" Yancey asked, his v
eager.

"You will lay down your weapons and walk i:
your hands clasped behind your heads. As for u
protocol of the Geneva Convention."

Yancey's face went slack. Parts of it were still
sticking to his sweat. He kept licking his lips.

"I'll need some time."

"You may have thirty minutes. During that pe
fired upon. You have my word as an officer."

The German saluted and walked down the stre
toward the house. Any chance of making the lieu
were strong and capable of holding out had been e
cey's behavior. His appearance begged them to cc
lowed him into the house. Inside, I started piling
the door.

"What do you think you're doing?" Yancey asked me. "I haven't ordered that door blocked."

I continued piling up the furniture. Carter helped me. The other men were gathered in the hall. They stood together at the bottom of the steps.

"Get back to your posts," I told them.

"No," Yancey said. "We have thirty minutes."

"You can't trust an SS officer."

"That's only your opinion," Yancey argued, his hands beginning to move excitedly. "I believe we have to assess the situation realistically, not emotionally. I want everybody in on this."

As he talked, I imagined Krauts slipping around the house and sticking the nozzles of flame throwers through windows. The others, however, were listening to Yancey who worked on their fright.

"I want to be realistic," he said. "No good leader will uselessly sacrifice men. Why should he? Useless death secures no military objective. We're Quartermaster troops, not infantry. We can't be expected to stand up against an enemy assault."

He was telling them words they wished to hear. Like a salesman warming to his pitch, his spiel came faster.

"The German lieutenant was telling the truth when he said he has us. We know they got a flame thrower, and there's at least the possibility of a tank. We'd be crazy to try to hold out against such weapons. I admit it's not a very pleasant prospect to be taken prisoner, but it won't help the war for us to die either. We'll have to spend only a short time in a POW camp. That won't be so bad."

His words were oily persuasive. As he talked, he smiled about him. The men stared at him, their expressions hungering for hope.

"Of course it's my decision," Yancey said. "I'm in command here. I must do what I think's proper and correct. I just want everybody to understand my reasoning on the matter."

No one moved. They wished to believe him, yet they doubted. They were balancing the promise of his words against the way he'd acted earlier. It was Black Hatfield who spoke first. His jaw chewed lazily on his cud of tobacco.

"What you think?" he said to me.

The others also turned to me. In spite of my lack of rank, they were asking me to decide. Yancey understood. His tongue flicked out.

"I think we better get back to the windows," I told them. "If we

335

give up, they'll stand us against a wall and shoot us. That's what happened to WO Page and the cooks."

"You don't know that," Yancey protested.

"We can beat the flame thrower," I went on, not really sure but trying to sound so. "As for a tank, I believe that's bluff. If he had a tank, he'd use it."

"I don't mind discussing this," Yancey said, but he was alarmed that the decision was being taken from him. "I must repeat, however, that I'm the officer in charge here and I'll make the final determination."

"A prison camp might not be so bad," Smooth said. "We could catch up on our sleep."

"You don't know that you'll ever see a prison camp," I told him. "They might be digging your grave right now."

"It's my decision," Yancey insisted, looking more desperate. "My best judgment tells me the German officer is right. He promises to honor the Geneva Convention. We have no choice except to put up the white flag. Somebody get the sheet."

Still nobody moved. Some of them wanted to, but doing so would have meant lining up with Yancey who was repulsive to them. His reasoning might be good, but his very being tainted it.

"Get the sheet," he ordered Timberlake who was closest to the steps. "The rest of you clear the stuff away from the door."

Instead of obeying, we merely looked at him. Yancey turned to me. Sweat shone on him.

"Did you hear my order?" he asked.

"Let's vote on it," I told the others.

Yancey scowled. Where he had pleaded, he now tried to threaten.

"I want to be reasonable," he said. "I've never liked pulling my rank. You men, however, are being insubordinate. I'm the one who has to make the final decisions. I've made this one. Now let's move the furniture away from the door. That's a direct order."

"I vote to stay," I said to the others.

"I forbid this," Yancey told them. "I absolutely forbid it."

"I'll stay too," Wilson said.

"You can't do this," Yancey complained.

My eyes went to Beanpost. He smiled apologetically.

"Go," he said.

"Go," Smooth agreed, acting sheepish.

"I'm in charge here," Yancey threatened.

"Stay," Black Hatfield said.

"Stay," Honeycutt said.

"You can't do this," Yancey protested. "I'm your commanding officer."

Carter was next. His face was flushed, and he wouldn't raise his eyes.

"Go," he whispered, full of shame.

"Go," Timberlake said.

That left the decision up to the Professor. The slight, graying, most unmilitary of men stood in the doorway to the parlor. He was white from plaster and seemed to be thinking of something else entirely rather than the trouble he was in. I believed I knew how he would vote. He was not meant to be a warrior. War was the inconvenience which kept him from his cozy study lined with books.

"Stay," he said.

Everybody was surprised by his vote, including the Professor himself. Not counting Yancey, the Professor had given those of us who wished to stay the majority. I wasn't going to allow Yancey to cast a ballot.

"Back to your posts," I said quickly.

"You can't do this," Yancey told them. "It's against every Army rule and regulation."

"Same plan as before," I said.

They began to move. Yancey, panicked, hurried from one to the other of them and clutched at their jackets or arms as he tried to talk them out of it. They pulled loose from him and went on.

"I'm in charge here," he shouted. "I'm a captain in the U. S. Army. You'll do as I tell you. I'm warning you."

They returned to their places. In the dining room were the Professor, Wilson, Carter, and Beanpost. Upstairs on the landing Timberlake, Honeycutt, Black Hatfield, Smooth, and I waited. Honeycutt's eyes were still cocked.

Black Hatfield's canteen was empty and he went down to the kitchen to refill it. A moment later we heard a yell from Yancey. I ran to the first floor. Yancey, holding his nose, was crouched among rubble near the piano. Blood seeped through his fingers. Black Hatfield was jerking the .45 from the oxblood holster.

"He hit me," Yancey said, pointing a shaking hand at Black Hatfield. "He'll be shot for that."

Black Hatfield spat. A thick gob of tobacco juice narrowly missed

Yancey's face and caused him to pull back. Black Hatfield straightened, stuck the pistol in his belt, and went on up the steps.

"Seize him!" Yancey shouted. "Put him under arrest! Do you hear me? That's a direct order. If you don't obey, you're just as guilty as he is."

Blood continued to drip from his fingers. Nobody moved to help him. From the dining room the men watched passively. I left Yancey to go upstairs to the landing.

"I'll have the whole lot of you court-martialed," Yancey yelled in the parlor. "You'll spend the rest of your lives in prison."

He threatened and blustered until the thirty minutes were almost gone. He then scurried for the dark corner under the steps. We heard him begin to cry.

From the front bedroom I peeped around a mattress at the house across the street. There was no sign of movement. I crawled back to the landing and kept looking at my watch. We squatted, listening to the muffled sounds of Yancey weeping.

"We'll have to react fast," I told them, but they knew it as well as I. I'd spoken out of anxiousness. My tongue felt swollen, and my mouth tasted of plaster.

The Germans did not come. Thirty minutes grew into an hour and still we heard nothing from them. I began to hope the lieutenant did not want to make the attack. Or perhaps the flame thrower itself had become damaged in some way. The men were relaxing.

I couldn't allow that. Letting time pass might be some sort of trick to wear us down. I made trips to the first floor to keep Wilson and the others ready. I returned to the landing and waited next to Black Hatfield, who chewed tobacco in a mechanical fashion. My knees were sore from kneeling.

Shooting blasted the silence, and my first impulse was to lie flat. I forced myself to crawl into the front bedroom. At the same time I was shouting for the others. Black Hatfield, Timberlake, Smooth, and Honeycutt followed me. I lunged to a mattress and stuck my carbine out a hole. Bullets were thumping into the mattress and chipping at windows and walls.

"Watch for the thrower!" I kept yelling. "That's all we need!"

"There!" Beanpost hollered from downstairs. "There!"

We all saw it at the same instant. We had expected the flame thrower to appear at a window, but the front door of the house was flung open, and a young German soldier ran out. He was bent over

338

grotesquely, the hump of a dark tank on his back. He couldn't have been much over eighteen, and even from where we were we saw his fright. He was trying to reach the cover of a burnt-out truck. His right hand worked the flint wheel on the nozzle of the hose. I, like the others, started firing rapidly.

Germans in the house were shooting at us. We could see their helmeted heads. I felt the heat of a bullet close to my ear. The young German was having trouble with the flame thrower. He acted as if he wished to get back to the house. The lieutenant was shouting at him.

Flint sprayed sparks, and the sparks brought a yellow flame to the end of the nozzle. Still crouching behind a truck, the young German twisted a valve. A long cone of a roaring yellow torch licked out at us. The fire seared the front of our house. Chairs, tables, mattresses, and rugs we had stuffed into windows were burning. Timberlake screamed, dived to the floor, and pawed at his face.

The terrible heat drove me back. Like Smooth and Honeycutt, I lay on the floor. Only Black Hatfield was still shooting. He was using Yancey's submachine gun. Bullets plunked around him, and the beard smoked on his face.

He stopped shooting and hollered. I pulled myself up to the window. The German had been hit. He was spinning drunkenly and attempting to get to the house he had come from. Somebody downstairs shot, and a bullet hit the tank strapped to the young German's shoulders.

A column of hissing yellow fire burst over him and enclosed him. He howled in agony. He ran two steps, fell, and rolled in the flames which were pouring over him from his own misshapen back. He clawed at the flames, fell onto his side, and kicked. He was turning black. Even after his screams stopped, he continued to jerk. His flesh bubbled and stank. Flames rose as high as the roof.

At the horror of the sight, shooting from both houses stopped. Germans were watching at windows just as we were. The body in the street had become a strip of charred bacon. Fire ran from him into the gutters. Trucks were burning. Downstairs somebody vomited.

The Germans remembered what they were supposed to be doing and again started shooting at us. We, however, lay gasping and sick among rubble. Smoke choked us and made us cough. Timberlake screamed. After a while the shooting stopped.

339

38

Timberlake continued to scream. We crawled to his side and dragged him to the landing where he writhed in pain. His face had been badly burned. It shone slick pink, and all his hair was gone. We gave him water.

Smooth's head had been creased by a bullet. He kept touching the spot. Black Hatfield had been burned. He dabbed at himself with a plug of tobacco.

I left Timberlake with Honeycutt and Smooth and ran down the steps. Flames crackled at windows, and curtains were burning. Men sprawled on the floor. Wilson had been burned on his face, chest, and arms. He, like all of us, was coughing from smoke. Carter had been the one who vomited.

We had to put out the fires. I crawled from man to man and shook shoulders. Like spirits from the dead they stirred. Gagging from smoke, we pulled down burning curtains and stomped on them. We brought water in pans from the kitchen and threw it on flaming furniture. Upstairs Honeycutt and Smooth pushed burning mattresses from windows.

While we fought the fire, I was afraid we would be attacked. I peered with blurred, stinging eyes through smoke at the house across the street. Occasionally shots came from it.

The few pieces of shutters hanging on the front of our house were smoldering. We beat at the flames inside. Our faces were black. We stumbled among rubble and fell. I passed the dark corner under the steps where Yancey was. He was balled up and quivering.

Timberlake screamed from pain. I found a jar of grease in the kitchen and carried it upstairs to spread on his face. Honeycutt and Smooth held his hands.

Timberlake became chilled. We covered him with a blanket and left him in the back bedroom near Batten's body.

I saved a little of the grease for Wilson. We peeled off his shirt and patted the grease on. We helped him into the dining room where he lay with his arms at his sides, biting his lip against the pain.

As soon as the fires were out, men went to their posts and counted their ammunition. Including what was left in Yancey's pistol, we

340

had a couple of rounds per person. The submachine gun was empty. Black Hatfield removed the cartridges from the pistol and put them into the submachine gun's clip.

We slumped by the windows. With our blackened, stark faces we resembled creatures from Hell. Timberlake continued to scream. The sky was turning dark with night. Fires burned in the gutters. A stork sailed over the roof.

Instead of relief, darkness brought a new danger. Men went to sleep. They couldn't help it. I crawled among them in an attempt to keep them awake. I'd get those on one floor up only to have those on the other again fall asleep.

I decided to put them on shifts. In that way half could sleep and half watch. I numbered everybody except Wilson and Timberlake. The odd numbers took the first shift.

Though the house directly across the street from us was dark, farther up the line were lights. I wondered whether people in the town could be going about the ordinary routines of life while I lay in a trench of rubble. Perhaps they were telling children bedtime stories or even saying prayers.

At nine o'clock the even numbers went on guard, and a few minutes later we heard music. It seemed to float down from the sky. I had the crazy sensation I was already dead. The music, *Siegfried's Rhine Journey*, was being played by a symphony orchestra. I turned my face upward. Sleeping men wakened and rose from the floor.

We realized the music must be coming from a radio in the house across the street. Still it had a sweet, unearthly sound as if falling from the heavens. We remained motionless until it stopped. A trumpet fanfare followed, and a German announcer talked excitedly. The Professor interpreted.

"The German Army has just won another victory by consolidating its forces nearer the Elbe," the Professor explained. "It's a way of saying they're still retreating."

Again music started. This time it was not serious, but the deep, vibrating voice of a chanteuse. I understood only the word *"Liebe."*

I needed sleep. I asked Beanpost to take charge while I rested. I crawled to the dining room and lay beside Wilson who was breathing quietly. I closed my eyes. Just as I was sinking into blackness, somebody shook my shoulder. I sat up quickly. It was Yancey.

"Why don't you just shoot me?" he asked.

"Get back to your rathole."

"You've ruined me," he said. He started crying. He was still holding my shoulder. I pushed his hand away roughly.

"Get back or I'll kick hell out of you," I told him.

He crawled off into the dark. I could hear him moving through the rubble. I lay back and went to sleep.

Beanpost woke me. He said Black Hatfield had called. I hurried to the steps, my feet crunching on fallen plaster. Black Hatfield was standing at the top of the steps and looking at the ceiling.

"Listen," he said.

I listened but heard nothing.

"There's something on the roof," he told me.

I heard it—a light scraping sound moving toward the chimney.

"An animal," I whispered.

"Maybe," he answered.

We were both thinking it could be a man. The houses were so close together a person could step easily from one roof to the next. Smooth and Honeycutt gathered with us in the dark.

The scraping reached the chimney, and something rattled down a flue. In the parlor a sputtering grenade rolled from the fireplace and exploded. The house shifted under our feet. More plaster fell. Downstairs men were shouting and trying to escape.

The German on the roof changed flues. His second grenade spun out of the front bedroom fireplace. We all dived into the back before the grenade went off. The house shook, and clouds of plaster dust billowed around us. We pushed Timberlake under the bed. To protect ourselves, we stuffed rugs and bedclothes into the fireplace. A grenade exploded above them, tearing chunks out of the wall and sending stones flying about the room.

Black Hatfield got up and flung himself to the landing. I believed at first he was running out on us. He, however, pulled a chiffonier from the bedroom, climbed on top it, and shoved his hands up through a small door in the ceiling. He wiggled through a hole which led to an attic.

Shaking and unsure, I pulled myself after him. In the dark I had to feel my way. The attic was only a few feet high and sloped with the roof. I slid on my belly. Black Hatfield was in front of me. As we moved toward the chimney, another grenade went off in the house.

Black Hatfield reached the chimney. He pressed the muzzle of Yancey's submachine gun against the roof and pulled the trigger. Stubby bullets chewed up through the tiles.

He had come out right under the German. We heard the man

yell in surprise and pain. He fell, scratched at the roof, and clattered down. He rolled off into the street.

A grenade he'd meant to drop skidded along after him. It caught in a gutter. When it exploded, it knocked off an end of the attic. Black Hatfield and I covered our heads. Tiles and roofing beat on our backs. We raised our faces slowly. We could look out a hole to the house next door and beyond it to the sky.

We climbed down to the second floor. Germans on both sides of our house were shooting. Bullets cracked into the tiles. I thought it must be an attack and yelled to the others. We crawled to the windows. No Germans were coming. The shooting stopped.

I crawled around to find out who was hurt. Everybody had grenade splinters in him. Beanpost's face was badly cut, and he held a handkerchief against it. My own back was bleeding. I took off my shirt, and the Professor sprinkled sulpha powder on me.

We lay at the windows. From across the street the music continued. A chanteuse was singing another ballad. *"Liebe, Liebe, Liebe . . ."*

39

At eleven o'clock the radio started playing Viennese waltzes which, as if in a dream, made me think of beer gardens, students singing, and the Emperor Franz Josef. Occasionally pieces of our house fell among us. Yancey was still balled up in the dark under the steps.

The men on guard were sleeping. Halfheartedly I crawled among them to shake them awake. Carter called to me. He had taken Beanpost's place at the window. I climbed over the fallen plaster. He whispered he'd caught sight of something moving on the other side of the burnt-out trucks. I squinted but was able to see nothing.

For thirty minutes I waited with him. He was more ashamed of himself than ever. He had been terrified, wished to surrender, vomited, and now had given a false alarm.

I sat with my back against the wall and dozed. A sound from the kitchen jerked me awake. I crawled to the dining room where I bumped into the Professor. I heard noise in the pantry.

"What is it?" I asked the Professor.

"I'm not sure," he answered.

The sound continued. Something was definitely happening on the floor. While the professor held his carbine ready, we tiptoed in, and I lighted a match.

The sight was like looking at an enlarged pornographic photograph. Smooth's buttocks were directly below me. The fat thighs of the servant girl were spread under him. Her dress was half over her face. Her big arms clutched his small back. His pants were down around his skinny ankles.

"Goddammit, Smooth!" I said. He had slipped down through the house in the dark while I was asleep.

"Just a second," he told me, breathing like a man who had been running a long distance.

The match burned the tips of my fingers. I threw it to the floor. Smooth kept on. The Professor and I turned our backs. We listened to him finish, change position, and fix his clothes. In the darkness the dim whiteness of the girl was just visible.

"You sonofabitch," I said to Smooth when he stood.

"Now wait a minute," he told me. "She wanted it. She climbed the ladder and scratched on the door. If I'm going to get the hell shot out of me, I might as well have a little. I mean I wouldn't want one of those fuzzies to go to waste."

"Get upstairs."

"Just a second. Come on, honey."

In the dark he helped the girl. He raised the trap door for her and held her arm while she, dazed, climbed down. It was a sort of chivalry. He bolted the trap door over her.

I herded him up the steps. We felt our way through the broken house. I made him go in with Black Hatfield.

"If he tries to leave again, shoot him in the pecker," I told Black Hatfield.

"Aw," Smooth said.

"Right in the pecker. I mean it."

Black Hatfield nodded and spat.

As I was leaving the bedroom, Carter called me. I hurried downstairs and joined him at the front window. We stared into the dark. The radio across the street was playing chamber music. I could see nothing. Carter had given a second false alarm.

I remained next to him, resting my cheek against the wall. Immediately I was asleep. The next thing I knew he was shaking me. I heard the sound of boots running on cobblestones. I grabbed my carbine and yelled a warning to the others.

The attack started with grenades thrown into the street. They exploded among burnt-out trucks and blasted cobblestones against the house. At the same time automatic weapons and rifles began shooting at us. When the grenades stopped, dark shapes ran among the trucks. Something was happening at the front of the house. Carter and I crawled to the hall. A grenade placed in front of the door exploded and knocked us over. Smoke and rubble filled the hallway.

In the smoking darkness a hunched shape was attempting to get past the jagged pieces of the door. Carter and I lay helpless on our backs. The Professor, who had run in from the kitchen, started shooting. Black Hatfield, Smooth, and Honeycutt were firing from the landing. The shape at the door staggered. He was holding another grenade and dropped it just as two more shapes that moved with peculiar hobbling gaits joined him. The grenade went off, slamming them down.

The explosion took the impetus out of their attack. Germans hesitated among trucks in the street. The lieutenant was yelling angrily at them. The men, however, were backing away and fading into the darkness. Some ran to the house across from ours and were let in the door.

Carter and I lay coughing violently in the smoke and swirling dust. We were so addled from concussion we couldn't get our balance. My head ached and throbbed. Black Hatfield and Smooth came down the steps to help the Professor at the door. Just outside was the German who had dropped the grenade. He flopped on the cobblestones. The Professor reached out and dragged him in by the collar. Black Hatfield got the German's rifle.

Black Hatfield barricaded the door. He and the Professor pulled the German over rubble into the dining room. Smooth helped Carter and me. We followed Black Hatfield who had lighted a match and was bending over to inspect the German.

Instead of a young, blond SS soldier, we stared at a man seventy or older who wore the tattered brassard of the *Volksturm*. He looked like somebody's grandfather, and he was dead.

Black Hatfield and Smooth carried him upstairs to put him under the blanket with Batten. I thought of the peculiar hobbled gait I'd seen. The attackers were so old they were bent and crippled with age.

We had used all except four rounds of our own ammunition. We had the dead German's rifle and a clip of cartridges. We couldn't stop any sort of sustained assault, even if the attackers were old men.

Across the street the radio continued to play—this time Strauss' *Tales from the Vienna Woods*.

40

The radio was left on. We heard news broadcasts and more music. Occasionally bullets thunked against the house.

Up the street a party was going on. We could hear snatches of singing and laughter.

As Yancey would have said, I was reassessing the situation. In spite of what the last attack had done to us, the presence of the *Volksturm* was a good sign. It meant no large SS unit was nearby. Probably the lieutenant had rounded up the *Volksturm* on his own initiative. He commanded a ragtag force and perhaps could not again drive the old men across the street.

At just after one o'clock the radio clicked off abruptly. In Oxfordian tones the German lieutenant spoke from across the street.

"May we collect our dead?" he asked.

We thought it might be a trick but couldn't refuse him. We didn't have the ammunition to do so. I tried to make my own voice calm as I answered.

"Permission granted."

We peeked from windows. Germans with flashlights came from the house across the street. They picked up men and carried them inside. In a blanket they collected the charcoal remains of the youngster who'd used the flame thrower. As the Germans returned to the house, their flashlights went out.

The radio was not cut back on. Except for bursts of sound from the party, the night became perfectly quiet. Black Hatfield, Honeycutt, Smooth, Carter, the Professor, and I posted a feeble guard. We slapped our own faces to remain awake.

"The tank's on the way," the German lieutenant called. "It'll be here early in the morning."

"You don't have a tank," I yelled without exposing myself.

"Oh, we have an enormous one. It possesses a magnificent snout which will sniff you out."

He translated that into German. Soldiers in the house with him laughed. They sounded drunk.

"If it has a snout, we'll cut it off," I answered, bluffing to keep him from knowing how badly hurt we were.

"Why don't you let me speak with your captain?" he asked.

"The captain's resting."

"Eternally?"

"At the moment he's not inclined to speak. Why don't you give yourselves up? You could grow fat in an American prison camp."

"Oh no. To allow you to take us prisoner would mean you had won. We're not ready to concede that."

He stopped talking. Slowly, wearily, I made the rounds. As I approached the steps, Yancey crawled from beneath them and grabbed my arm. He was trembling.

"Do we have a chance?" he whispered to me.

"We have a chance," I said, refusing to show my doubt to him.

"What happens if we get out of here?"

"That's not up to me."

"They'll want to know about everybody. They'll ask questions. What'll you tell them?"

"You know what I'll tell them."

"Please, Charley. I'll pay you. I'll make you rich if you cover for me."

I shoved him aside. In so doing, I touched the hardness of the other grenade wired to his field jacket. I'd forgotten it. I wrenched it loose, ripping his jacket. He retreated to his darkness under the steps.

I carried the grenade upstairs. Everybody except Black Hatfield was asleep. I gave him the grenade. He laid it on the floor beside the German rifle.

For ten minutes the radio played American jazz. Then the music cut off. There were announcements followed by a steady hum.

From two-thirty till four nothing happened. I kept falling asleep. At four a plane flew over. Nobody spoke of our earlier hope for rescue. My head beat with pain.

As I lay on my side among rubble, a grenade clattered into the parlor. Rubble saved me. The grenade rolled into a trough of it before exploding. Plaster shot all over the place but absorbed the metal. Believing we were under attack, I flung myself about. There were, however, no sounds of shooting or of men running.

347

The Professor cried out. I crawled to him. He had been closer to the grenade and was bloody. I helped him into the dining room. He was bleeding from so many places I didn't know how to start on his wounds. Carter helped me sprinkle him with sulpha powder.

That was only the first grenade. A quarter of an hour later a second one came through the parlor window. Though nobody was close, the concussion beat on us, and the house was being knocked apart.

The Germans were sending men into the dark to sneak along the street among the burnt-out trucks. The men were able to approach unseen and toss grenades into windows. If they kept it up, they'd eventually blow the house down on us.

Carter, still living with his shame, came to lie beside me. He whispered that if the Germans were able to send men into the street, so could we. He was scared badly but he wanted to creep among trucks farther up the line and find one not burned. There might be a can of gasoline.

Carter removed his helmet, emptied his pockets, and untied his shoes. He was shaking. He breathed deeply before crawling through the rubble of the parlor. He climbed into a window and dropped out quietly onto the street.

I went up the steps to caution men about shooting at movement which might be Carter. While we waited, the Germans could have walked across the street and into the door.

I went downstairs and lay behind the dining-room table. I listened for Carter. When I figured he must be dead, I heard scratching at the window. I pressed myself down, not knowing whether it was Carter or another grenade.

Carter tumbled onto the plaster. The sound caused the Germans to start shooting. He scrambled to the dining room where he collapsed alongside me. He was breathing hard, shaking, and hugging a partly filled jerrycan of gasoline.

"Christ!" he whispered. "I brushed against somebody out there."

We got wine bottles. There were a dozen in the pantry and a whole boxful in the cellar. By the light of a match I could see the old German couple huddled on the ground peering at me. They stood and jabbered. The fat girl smiled.

Carter and I slopped gasoline into the wine bottles, trying to finish before another grenade came in a window. We carried the bottles upstairs. Smooth and Honeycutt tore off strips of sheet to make wicks. We lined up the bottles by Black Hatfield.

348

"Throw one out now," I told him. "Then we'll keep throwing them at intervals until morning. We want to let them know we can light up the street."

I struck a match to a wick. Black Hatfield quickly tossed the bottle into the street at the front of the house. It burst, sending a puddle of yellow flames across the cobblestones. In the blaze of light we saw two Germans crawling under a burnt-out trailer. They ducked back. Black Hatfield pulled the pin on Yancey's grenade and threw it. It exploded among the trucks.

The Germans in the house across the street were shooting. They did so as long as the gasoline burned. When it was out completely, they stopped.

Black Hatfield and I waited eight minutes before throwing another bottle. This time the flames burned in an empty street. Fire licked around the fenders of a jeep which had a blackened red-light-siren on it.

There were more sounds from the radio. We heard a telegraph key on short wave. That was followed by a comedian doing his act in Spanish. The audience laughed.

Downstairs the Professor called. I went to him in the dining room where he lay with Wilson and Beanpost. He'd heard noise at the rear of the house. I ran up the steps, and Black Hatfield threw a bottle of gasoline from a back window. We saw an old man running down the street, a grenade in his hand. He appeared decrepit.

I checked Timberlake. He was dead. We put him with Batten and the body of the *Volksturmer*.

I went downstairs. Wilson was unconscious. Beanpost was moaning. The Professor was lying on his back, his clothes covered with plaster and blood.

In case of attack, only Black Hatfield, Carter, Smooth, Honeycutt, and I could fight—and not much at that with our supply of ammo. I hoped the Germans would not realize what a pitiful condition we were in.

I sent Honeycutt down to be with Carter, and I stayed upstairs with Black Hatfield and Smooth. Periodically we threw bottles of gasoline into the street. With the sixth bottle we caught a cluster of old men crouching behind a truck. The flaring gasoline made them flee. Black Hatfield and I shot. We hit one of the men. Others beat on the door of the house across the street until they were let in.

Black Hatfield and I were out of ammunition. I went downstairs to get a single cartridge from Honeycutt. Smooth turned his over to Black Hatfield. We had to use them well.

The old man who'd been hit was still alive on the street. Even with gasoline we couldn't see him because he was under one of the trucks. We heard him. He groaned and pleaded. He should have been sunning himself or playing checkers in a park instead of dying. He cried out for thirty minutes.

"You can help him!" I shouted at the house across the street. "We'll hold our fire."

"I'm not certain he ought to be helped," the lieutenant answered. His tongue sounded thick. "Did you ever witness such a miserable attack?"

"He's one of yours."

"He makes me slightly ashamed. I will nevertheless send for him."

Two members of the *Volksturm* with flashlights came from the house, found the old man, and carried him inside. As if to show us nothing had changed, the Germans fired at us.

Nobody was hit. We sprawled in the dark, rising occasionally to throw a bottle of gasoline. We waited for the sky to lighten. Under the steps Yancey sniffled.

41

There were moments during the rest of the night when we were all asleep. The Germans could have had us simply by walking quietly across the street and climbing into the first-floor windows.

My head slumped against broken plaster. My body seemed too heavy to move. Honeycutt snored loudly. In and out of my sleep I heard the hum of the radio.

When it grew light, I forced myself up a little. A ground mist lay over the town, and the air smelled wet. Birds were singing.

I looked at Black Hatfield. He was propped in his nest of rubble by a window. Bottles of gasoline were stuck into debris. His head had fallen forward, and the cud of tobacco had dropped from his mouth. I thought he might be dead and shook him. He roused, stuffed the tobacco into his mouth, and began chewing.

I crawled through the house. Men lay with their eyes closed, their legs drawn up. As I drew close to Beanpost, I saw he was dead. He was stiff. I covered him as best I could with a tablecloth.

Wilson's throat rattled each time he breathed. Though the Professor's wounds had stopped bleeding, moving hurt him badly. I found Smooth in the pantry with the girl. They lay sleeping against each other.

Yancey was awake. He blinked out at me from the shadows under the steps. He was like an animal in his lair.

I went back upstairs and sat by Black Hatfield. Our stomachs ached and rumbled. We had long ago eaten our potatoes. We drank water.

By eight o'clock the ground mist had lifted, but there was still no sign of the Germans. Then, like a knife, the radio came on. A chorus of young men sang *Deutschland über alles* as if it were a rousing college song. News and announcements were next. Though I couldn't understand the speaker, he sounded absolutely confident.

In a kind of fever I remembered talk of German secret weapons. Perhaps somewhere they had yet another million blond men they were going to spring on the world. I went downstairs to where the Professor lay and asked him what was being said.

"More of the same," he told me, his face bloody, his voice weak. "They're advancing to the rear."

I crawled back up the stairs. I was no longer scheming. In case of attack, all we could do would be fire our two rounds of ammunition and surrender. I wondered whether we should put our hands over our heads and shout *Kamerad* as the Germans reportedly did.

I decided I might as well get a white flag ready. I pulled a piece of sheet from rubble and tied it onto the leg of a chair. Black Hatfield watched. He chewed but said nothing. I laid the white flag on the floor at my side.

The radio was loud. It played an operetta. I gave Black Hatfield my bullet. At the first sign of attack, he could shoot and I'd throw gasoline. If doing so didn't stop the Germans, I'd stick the white flag out the window and wave it. Perhaps the old men would treat us kindly.

At a few minutes after nine I heard boots striking the cobblestones. I reached for a bottle of gasoline, shouted to alert them on the first floor, and lighted a match. Black Hatfield shifted his German rifle. Down the street the private carrying a sword with a handkerchief attached to the blade was followed by the young, girlish-looking lieutenant. Quickly I crawled across the floor to the submachine gun Black Hatfield had thrown into a corner. It was empty, but the lieutenant didn't know it.

I went to the door. Carter helped me pull apart the flimsy barricade we had built, and I stepped across the broken doorsill to the crumbling stoop. The lieutenant was waiting. He was freshly shaved and smelled strongly of the same cologne.

"Did you enjoy your breakfast?" he asked, his eyes moving to the submachine gun I was holding. He smiled as if we had a joke between us. "I myself had fresh eggs, small, tender sausages, and real coffee borrowed from some of your friends. I can offer you the same."

"I'm stuffed," I answered, making myself stare into his pale blue eyes. "I had caviar and brandy."

"You're a good poker player," the lieutenant told me, the thumb of his gloved left hand playing across the tips of his fingers. "This, however, is no longer a game. Why die?"

"We're not going to die," I said. "We expect a relief column any moment. Besides if you could kill us, you'd have done it before now. You shot your wad."

The lieutenant's lips seemed artificially red, and they didn't entirely lose their smile. The smile, though, didn't count because the eyes were deadly.

"Where is your captain?" he asked me curtly.

"Resting."

"I wish to speak with him."

"He gave orders not to be disturbed."

The lieutenant became angry. Without his uniform, he could have been one of the boys in the chorus. His expression was that of a cross child.

"I'm informed you have German nationals in the house. I request their release. The tank is on its way."

I knew what he was really after. He was not being a humanitarian but hoping by questioning the elderly couple to find out how many of us were wounded and the amount of ammo we had left. I attempted to smile in the same insolent manner.

"They won't be hurt," I told him.

"How can you protect them from a tank?"

"There's no tank coming."

"We will see," he answered haughtily and turned to leave. The sword-carrying private hurried to get in front of him. I returned to the house. Carter, Smooth, Black Hatfield, and Honeycutt were waiting.

"What do we do?" they asked, their faces ancient.

"He's still bluffing," I said. "If he had anything else to throw at us, he'd have done it. We've taken their worst. Let's not hand ourselves over for nothing."

"But what if he ain't bluffing?" Honeycutt wanted to know.

"Make more white flags. If things get too rough, we can wave them."

They made the flags. Each man carried one to his post. I went with Black Hatfield. He settled into his nest of rubble, and I sat with my back against the wall. Music from the radio drifted across the street. We waited.

By noon we'd heard nothing further from the Germans. Every hour I made the rounds. Nobody said anything, but they all thought the Germans had pulled out. I thought it myself, yet I hardly dared believe.

"Let's put something up and see if it draws fire," Carter suggested.

He found an umbrella, set his helmet on it, and moved the helmet across a window. There were no shots. He grinned. In spite of his pain, the Professor, who had been watching, licked his lips and pushed up to an elbow.

"We made it," Smooth said jubilantly. "By God we did."

"Don't get excited," I warned them. "It might be a trick, and anyway we can't do anything before dark."

But the hope had caught us up, and we were certain we were going to get out. Hunger and relief made me dizzy. I drank water thirstily and carried some to the Professor. He sighed.

Yancey crept out from under the steps. He slid among rubble and came into the dining room. He blinked behind his cracked glasses. His face was grooved by tears worn into plaster dust. The goggles on his netted helmet had been knocked crooked. Binoculars still hung from his neck.

We could also smell him. Apparently during the attack which had blown down the door he had dirtied himself.

"We been in this together," Yancey said. He was on his knees in the doorway and held out a trembling hand. "We ought to get out of it together."

"Beat it for God's sake," Smooth told him. Smooth was holding his nose.

"I'm begging you guys," Yancey said. "Don't crucify me."

We backed off from him, our faces twisted by contempt and disgust.

"I'll pay you," he offered. "I got plenty of money. I'll give you ten thousand dollars each. You can buy yourselves a house and a car."

Angrily we moved toward Yancey.

"Get out!" Carter ordered.

"I'm one of you," Yancey pleaded. He was backing away. "We've been through this together. I tried. God knows I tried."

"Get the hell away from us," I told him and swung at him. He scampered off, his mouth open, his brown eye watering. With his head hanging he crawled to his place under the steps. Like a dog fixing its bed, he circled before lying down.

The sun had come out hot, and the house grew warm. We lay dozing in the afternoon heat. I no longer tried to keep anybody at his post. Smooth was in the pantry with the German girl. Honeycutt snored. We heard the radio playing.

In the distance was another sound. At first it was faint. Each of us tensed and sat up slowly. I wanted it to be some sort of defective tractor a farmer was driving into town. As the noise grew louder, however, the faces around me were transformed from hopefulness to terror. We turned east as if drawn by strings.

Black Hatfield was the first to move. He ran for the stairs. I followed him, and on the landing we listened. The clanking was coming from the street at the back of the house. We opened shutters and pressed to the wall to look. We saw nothing.

The clanking stopped, but we heard the engine. It sounded as if it were about to conk out. The thing moved some more. From the noise I guessed it was damaged and limping along. It had probably been patched up to come after us. Again it stopped. The engine stalled. They were trying to start it. We still couldn't see anything. I didn't want to see anything.

"Get the white flags!" I shouted. "Stick them out!"

I got mine from the floor of the front bedroom and waved it out the back. At other windows men were doing the same. The engine sputtered and backfired.

"We surrender!" I yelled out my window. "*Kamerad!*"

The men downstairs shouted also, but we got no reply from the silent houses across the street. The tank, still backfiring, drew closer.

"Everybody to the basement!" I hollered.

Black Hatfield and I ran for the steps. As we reached the landing, a shell screamed into explosion. It hit the back corner of the house, and the house rose off the ground. The corner collapsed, and part of the roof fell with it. Chunks of ceiling crashed down. Beams stuck through at crazy angles.

Black Hatfield and I had been knocked flat. We lay covering our heads and choking as the air around us turned black with whirling dust and debris. Somebody was crying. I smelled the filthy cordite. Red tiles from the roof clattered down. Another shell would cause the house to fall. I felt my way down the shaky steps. Black Hatfield was ahead of me.

At the bottom was Yancey, an indistinct shape in the dust. He crawled past me. He was coughing and wailing. His glasses had been knocked off, and without them he looked naked. He was reeling and stinking. He started up the steps.

"Get back here!" I shouted at him.

He didn't turn. I kept thinking the next shell would be coming, but it didn't. The Germans were having trouble with the gun. The twisting dust was settling. The house was cracked so badly shafts of sunlight stuck through it from all directions.

I abandoned Yancey and crawled over rubble to the kitchen. Black Hatfield and Honeycutt were digging with their hands. The trap door was covered by debris, and they couldn't raise it. I hurried back for Yancey who was at the top of the steps. Cursing and trembling, I went after him.

The steps were just hanging to the wall. They gave under my weight. I believed they would crash under me before I reached the landing. Pieces of the house were still falling. I coughed and spit out dust.

Yancey turned into the front bedroom. I followed and grabbed at his foot. He kicked loose. God he stank. He was black, and tears streaked his face. He continued to wail. We both had difficulty moving over the rubble. The tilting floor was close to giving. Frantic, I crawled to the landing and held to spokes in the railing.

Yancey came out of the bedroom. His mouth hung open. He was shaking so badly his teeth tapped together. He looked like a turtle. In his left hand he had a wine bottle full of gasoline. He moaned.

"You can't throw it from here, you goddamned fool!" I said to him, furious even in my fright.

He didn't answer. He didn't seem to hear. Instead he moved to the chiffonier Black Hatfield had set up earlier under the attic. Yancey righted the chiffonier before climbing on. It tilted with the floor, and he almost lost his balance.

He put the wine bottle of gasoline inside his field jacket and

355

reached for the hole in the ceiling. I lay coughing among the black dust. Yancey was so fat he had difficulty pulling himself up. His feet danced on air. At any instant I expected another shell, and I cringed. Yancey scraped into the attic.

I climbed on the chiffonier to look after him. I pushed my head up into the hole which instead of being dark was now bright from sunshine pouring through the blasted and caved-in roof.

Yancey was crawling on a board laid across beams. The beams were crooked and sagging. I saw them bend under his weight. If they gave, he would fall not only to the second floor but on to the first as well. He was shaking so hard his soft body thumped against the wood. His teeth knocked together.

I lowered myself to the chiffonier. I meant to run down the steps and find something to bury myself under. Just as I was about to release my grip on the frame of the hole, the chiffonier dropped away from me like the trap door of the gallows. I was left dangling. The entire landing and stairs crashed down among the rubble of the hall. I kicked a foot into the attic and pulled myself the rest of the way up. Timbers were giving under me.

I hugged a beam. Around me were the shattered ribs of the roof. Yancey himself had reached the end of the attic where he was pushing stones and tiles out of his way. They banged down through the house. He crawled to the hole made by the German grenade. I understood then what he intended. He could move from the hole to the roof of the next house.

I pressed to my beam. Tiles crashed down through the house. Yancey was crawling slowly, carefully, testing the area in front of him by shoving with the palms of his hands. From where I lay I could see the stains on his pants. Motes of dust swirled about him in the sunlight.

At the edge Yancey rose to his knees and tottered a moment before throwing himself awkwardly to the roof of the next house. His arms and legs straddled the peak of colored tiles as if he were riding a runaway horse. His eyes were closed and his breath coming fast. He whimpered.

He began squirming forward. I waited for shots from houses on both sides of the street. Either the Germans had left or their heads were ducked because they expected another shell from the tank. Still Yancey's plan seemed hopeless. He was at least fifty yards from the tank. He could never reach it across the roofs.

The Germans were working on the tank. I heard a sledge hammer pounding metal. I lowered my head to attempt to find a way down. I looked through the house to the first floor. From the rubble of the dining room stuck the legs of a man. Batten, long dead, lay face upward—mouth agape, his eyes covered by dust.

I again watched Yancey. He was pulling himself slowly along the crown of the roof. When he reached the middle of it, a German at the front of the house yelled. There was a shot, and a bullet chipped into a tile. Yancey swung both legs to the side away from the shot. As he kept going, his paratrooper boots slipped. His feet flew out from under him. He slammed against the tile. I heard him grunt.

From the back of the house he was an easy target, but nobody saw him yet. The hammering on the tank continued. A second shot from the front of the house sent a bullet smashing into the tiles within a foot of Yancey's fat fingers. He'd almost reached the end of the roof, but he was still a long way from the tank.

He scurried to the chimney in a clumsy, crab-like fashion. He was able to hide behind it from the Germans at the front. I heard them calling to each other. Running on the cobblestones meant somebody was being sent to warn the tank.

Pieces of house clattered around me and bounced to the floors below. The beam I held seemed to be sinking. I was shaking as badly as Yancey. I held the beam so tight my arms ached.

The tank started up. Gears ground, and iron treads clanked. The commander must have decided to move closer to reduce the angle he had to shoot from. The runner hadn't reached him yet. If the tank came far enough, Yancey might have a chance with the bottle of gasoline.

He was squatting behind the chimney, keeping himself hidden from the Germans at the front of the house. Once he looked in my direction. In the flash of his sweating black face I saw his wild terror. It was as if he suddenly understood where he was and wanted to flee. He started crying.

With a palsied hand he groped in his field jacket for the bottle. A shot from the front of the house chipped stone out of the chimney. Farther up the street a German was yelling. The tank clanked closer.

Yancey held the wine bottle under his chin while he searched his pockets. My God, I thought, he's forgotten matches. He found them in his hip pocket and struck one. It went out quickly. He tried others. Each time the flame died before he could get it to the wick. On the fifth attempt he let go of the chimney to shield the match. The wick caught, but he was slipping down the roof. He clawed with one hand and pulled himself part of the way back.

Shots continued from the front of the house. Yancey's face was shiny black with crying and sweat. He was whimpering. He sounded like a rabbit feeling the talons. He sobbed openly and shook like a man with ague.

I heard the tank stop, but I couldn't tell how close it was to Yancey. The gears were grinding. Weeping, Yancey held to a flue of the chimney and raised himself to peep over the edge of the roof. There was more shouting among the Germans. Yancey shrank back. He must have seen the tank. Never letting go of the chimney, he tossed the bottle in the awkward, sweeping fashion of a man doing the breast stroke badly. The bottle arched over the edge of the roof and fell away.

I couldn't tell whether he'd hit the tank or not. I thought not because the engine was still running, and the tank was backing off. Then there was a yell, followed by subdued popping noises. A wisp of black smoke rose above the roof. Amid more popping a man screamed. Flaming gasoline seeping into the tank had ignited ammunition.

Yancey was hugging the chimney. From the back of the house an automatic weapon began to fire. Bits of tile splattered along the roof. Yancey jerked and cried out. He slipped a little. He caught at the crown of the roof and held it. His face was pressed against the colored tiles. He was bawling.

The big ammunition in the tank began to go. Men were shouting at each other. A flash of flame whished up above the roof and was followed by a perfectly formed smoke ring. There was another scream. The engine was still idling, and ammunition continued to explode.

Rifle shots came from the back of the house. Bullets thunked into Yancey's soft flesh. The force of them knocked him hard against the roof. He kicked. Dark blood spurted. He clenched his eyes and howled.

Behind the house the automatic weapon fired a second burst. Bullets chipped the tiles and stitched the length of Yancey's body. He gave one last small, frightened cry before letting go and slipping down the roof. The shooting stopped. He rolled ungracefully along the tiles. On the edge of the roof a gutter slowed him. He dropped over and out of sight.

42

In the street flames crackled and more ammunition exploded. For a long time I clutched the beam. I couldn't move. If the Germans rushed the house, they would be able to pick me off like a bird in a tree.

I felt the sun on the back of my neck. After a while I opened my eyes. A column of black smoke twisted into the sky from the burning tank. I looked down to the first floor. Nobody seemed to live. From across the street the radio played a dance number. Like a lover I held my beam.

It was at least an hour before I heard somebody below. I thought it was my executioner. I imagined the pretty German lieutenant's amusement as he raised his pistol to shoot me.

It wasn't the German lieutenant but Black Hatfield. He was creeping among the rubble. His face was black with grime.

"You all right?" he called softly.

"I can't move," I whispered.

"You got to move. Come on now."

I was afraid even my breathing might shake the beam. It had broken loose on one end. My best chance was in shinnying toward the secured side and reducing the leverage. Each time I pulled myself along, however, the beam quivered and sank.

"Keep going!" Black Hatfield ordered me.

I did, but only barely. I was breathing hard and sweating. The beam was giving. Nails pulling from wood screeched. I went faster. I lunged for the side of the attic and was able to grab a heavy joist which allowed me to lift part of my weight off the beam.

I was now over the front bedroom or what was left of it. The floor was torn and sloping. If I dropped, I didn't know whether it would hold me or not. I slipped my legs from the beam and let them hang. Reluctantly I released my hold. I fell through the house until I hit the rubble-laden floor. It gave under me a little, but I caught a pipe sticking from a wall. Plaster and rubble fell. I was sucking for breath.

Now I had to get from the second floor to the first. Moving very slowly, I worked my way along the wall. I made detours around parts of the room which were missing. I crawled across shivering cross-beams. Part of the wall crumbled, covering me with plaster.

I reached what had once been the landing. Sunlight flooded in from above. Black Hatfield sat among piles of rubble, watching me.

"You'll have to jump," he said.

Not quite I wouldn't. Again I hung by my fingers, this time from the door sill of the bedroom. When I let go, I tumbled into the rubble. Pieces of house fell about me, and dust flew up. I looked right through a large gap in the front to the house directly across the street. Instinctively I dived to my belly and covered my head.

Black Hatfield tapped me on the shoulder and motioned me to follow. We picked a path among the debris. The parlor was covered with hills of rubble. In the dining room Wilson was groaning. Carter, looking old and ghostly, was dead—a hunk of shell in his chest. His hands were held over his stomach as if it ached. Black Hatfield and I lined him up with Batten, Timberlake, Beanpost, and the *Volksturmer*. We'd had to pull Beanpost down from where he was lodged between rafters.

We heard scratching from what had been the kitchen. A whole corner of it was gone. We crawled among rubble, staying low to keep from exposing ourselves to the houses across the street. We found the Professor caught under the overturned stove. We dug him out and wiped the dust from him. We helped him to the dining room.

Somebody was pounding on the trap door, but we could do nothing about it. The trap door was covered by several feet of rubble, and we'd be easy targets trying to move it. Instead we lay in the dining room near the dead. I gave Wilson some water.

At dark there was more pounding on the trap door. Black Hatfield and I crawled into what was left of the pantry and began to clear rubble away. The job took several hours because we had to work quietly so as not to draw fire. When we finally had the trap door uncovered, it would raise only a few inches. Black Hatfield pried it with a broken rifle.

Smooth climbed part way up the ladder. The German girl was close behind him. She kept hugging his legs, and he pushed at her.

"Should I come out?" he asked.

"It don't make no difference," Black Hatfield answered.

"I think I'll stay," Smooth told us as he looked at the condition of the house.

From below, the old German woman could see too. When she

understood how bad the damage was, she shrilled her grief. Her voice sounded like a dog's mourning death.

We heard nothing from the Germans across the street. If they were plotting against us, they were wasting their time. They could walk to the house and have us for coming inside. There wasn't much to have.

I considered going down into the cellar, but it seemed too much effort to move. I lay on the rubble and saw stars through ribs of the house. The moon brightened the dark.

Honeycutt was still missing. Black Hatfield picked among the rubble and found him under a pile of debris. Rather he found a shoe, and the shoe was attached to a foot. He and I dug around it. Honeycutt wasn't breathing. His head had been crushed, and most of the bones in his body were broken. He was limp as a jellyfish.

During the night, the radio across the street played American dance music from London. The skeletonized house was a cage around us. We waited for the Germans to come.

"They might be gone," the Professor whispered.

"They might," I answered, not believing it this time because I had believed it too often before.

Wilson groaned periodically. From the cellar came the muffled cries of the old woman. Smooth wanted out. He couldn't stand the noise. He made the German girl stay below.

The night air was cool. It lowered on us damp and fresh. Our cramping stomachs rumbled and gurgled from lack of food. Several times my imagination tricked me into believing I saw dark shapes sneaking toward us, but the Germans never came. The radio signed off. We heard static.

We slept. It made no difference. There was nothing to guard. My head lay against roofing tiles. I heard a dog barking. Occasionally a piece of house tumbled down. Moonlight shone on the ghostly dead.

I awoke with light on my face. The sky was pearl gray, and clouds swept across the broken roof. Black Hatfield sat back against a pile of rubble with his eyes open. The Professor was stretched out as if on a cross. Smooth slept curled up. Wilson was still living, but just barely.

We couldn't wait any longer. We didn't even have to talk it over. I found one of the white flags we'd made the day before and crawled to the front of the house. Smooth and Black Hatfield came with me. We could have left the house by any of a dozen holes, but we chose the front door. We pushed aside what was left of it, stood, and walked slowly into the street.

"We surrender!" I croaked.

The radio started playing *Deutschland über alles*. We crouched as if to run, expecting shouts of discovery and shooting. I held the flag high. No Germans appeared.

Black Hatfield walked toward the house where the radio was. He knocked on the door as if paying a social call. Nobody answered. Warily he pushed it open.

Like sleepwalkers Smooth and I followed him inside. The first floor was a shambles. Empty cartridge cases, smashed furniture, and broken glass lay about. In the center of the room was the radio, sitting on a table. Beside it lay an overturned wine bottle. We smelled the stink of German uniforms and Turkish tobacco. Black Hatfield snapped off the radio.

We crept upstairs. Those rooms, also filthy, were empty. We returned to the street and walked past burnt-out trucks. We crossed the awful spot on the cobblestones where the flame thrower had exploded. I was still holding the white flag.

We reached an alley which led behind the house we had fought from. We peeped around a corner at the tank. It was blackened from fire and swollen because of shells which had exploded inside. Timidly we approached. I put out a shaky hand to touch the side of the tank. The iron was still warm.

The German dead had been carried away, but Yancey lay on the cobblestones where he had fallen from the roof. He was face down, his arms over his head. One of his fat pale legs was twisted under him. I knelt and turned him over gently. His body was stiff, and his glasses were gone.

In death he looked absolutely terrified.

43

We lifted him and took him into the house to lay beside the others. Black Hatfield moved among our trucks. Though he found one not burned, he was unable to get it out of the blocked street.

He searched houses. All were empty, but he came across a German shotgun and some shells. He brought back a stale loaf of dark bread. We chewed without taste.

Smooth let the servant girl and elderly couple up from the cellar. The old woman walked from room to room of her shattered home, raising and dropping broken objects—a picture, the head of a figurine, a part of the piano. All the while she sniffled and whined. The old man sat on a straight chair and stared at a torn wall. Smooth offered him bread, but the old man wouldn't eat.

The servant girl, smudged and blowsy, followed Smooth around. Whenever he was still, she approached and stood close. She looked adoringly at him. Her actions were making Smooth nervous.

He, Black Hatfield, and I talked. We decided we'd have to get out of the town even if it meant leaving Wilson and the Professor. The Germans could come back any minute.

We covered the dead. Smooth talked to the German girl in the short-course polyglot he'd learned with her in the basement. She promised she would look after Wilson and the Professor until we returned. She explained to the old man. He sat perfectly still in the chair and didn't seem to hear.

The Professor refused to be left. He made us help him walk. We moved down the street among the silent houses. Black Hatfield was still scouting. He searched for the rest of the men from our unit. He found WO Page and four cooks in a building. They were burned black, and they had been long dead.

We jogged out of the town. Smooth and I were half-carrying the Professor. We were ready to turn into the woods at the sound of either vehicles or troops. We saw German civilians, who ran on sighting us.

We kept going all morning. Black Hatfield led us. He carried the German shotgun like a hunter. The bouncing we gave the Professor hurt him, but he didn't cry out. The sun was so hot we sweated. We filled our canteens at a stream beside the road.

At noon we reached a junction. By then we were exhausted and lay in the shade of the woods to rest. As we were doing so, we heard the engine of a truck. We crawled deeper into the woods and peeked around trees. The truck came closer. We saw it was American.

Smooth, Black Hatfield, and I ran out of the woods and waved. We hadn't considered what we might look like to others. We were unshaved, bloody, and blackened. Instead of slowing, the Negro driver speeded up. He ducked over the wheel, and his eyes were wide. He was escaping from what he must have believed were wild men who lived in the forest. We stood in the road, looking after him. He drove off at full speed.

We lifted the Professor and plodded in the same direction the truck had taken. We followed less than twenty minutes before we heard jeeps. There were two of those as well as the truck with the Negro driver. One of the jeeps had a machine gun mounted on it, and the truck was full of both MPs and infantrymen. They jumped to the ground and deployed along the road. Smooth and I held our hands over our heads. A sergeant of MPs came toward us. He was bent over a submachine gun and watching the woods.

"Who the hell are you?" he called.

I did the talking. While I explained, MPs and infantrymen closed in around us. Others ran through the woods. They scowled as if they didn't believe what I was saying. An infantryman snatched Black Hatfield's German shotgun. The MPs whispered about it. They thought us agents—like the paratrooper priests who had been dropped during the Bulge and who had carried Schmiessers under their cassocks. The sergeant held the submachine gun on us and ordered us searched.

We were herded to the truck. The Professor, splotched with blood, was so weak he almost fainted, but the infantrymen glared at him threateningly. I asked for a cigarette. Nobody would give me one.

They drove us to the regimental headquarters of an infantry division preparing for an attack. The MPs took the Professor to an aid station. Black Hatfield, Smooth, and I were turned over to a captain from G-2. We were separated and questioned. I had to tell my story over again and point out on a map where I believed I'd been.

"Where'd you learn your English, Kraut?" the captain asked me.

I was too tired to bother to answer. I let my head fall forward and slumped in the chair. The captain shook me. A medic came in to give me a tetanus shot. I'd forgotten I was wounded.

The captain formed up a convoy which consisted of an armored car and five trucks of infantry. I had to ride in a jeep with the captain. The MP sergeant sat in back pointing his submachine gun at my head. The captain asked for directions on how to return to the town. I gave them as best I could.

When we drew close, the captain stopped the convoy on the road above the town. He searched the terrain with his binoculars. He left me under guard while he talked with other officers and noncoms. The armored car moved a hundred yards ahead. We followed slowly until it halted near the outskirts.

"I got an idea," the captain said to me. "You lead us in."

I climbed from the jeep and went down the road to the armored car. I walked in front of it. It rumbled and clanked behind me. The infantrymen were dismounting and fanning out. German soldiers could have returned, but I was too beat to care much. I stumbled over cobblestones to the barricade where our laundry trailers had been stopped.

Infantrymen spread through the streets and ran from house to house. I continued on to the demolished home Wilson was in. The German servant girl sat with him. He was unconscious but still alive. A medic ran up, knelt, and began to work over him.

The captain looked at our dead. He talked with the MP sergeant. The medic got a litter to put Wilson on. They strapped it to a jeep, and the jeep left immediately.

A truck backed up for the dead. They, Yancey among them, were loaded into the rear and the tailgate closed. The infantrymen, many of whom had never been in action before, gawked at the corpses and the battleground around them. They examined the tank and looked up at the roof where Yancey had been. The German servant girl moved among them, peering into their faces and asking, "Smooth? Smooth?"

The rest of the men from the laundry unit were found. They were not all dead as I'd supposed but locked in a stone barn outside of town. They came out afraid and blinking in the sunlight. After capture, the Germans had not hurt them. They had even been fed some cheese. They were awed by the battle scene.

The captain's attitude toward me had changed. He had become very polite. In the jeep riding back nobody guarded me. My head lolled from side to side. He left the convoy to take me to a field hospital set up in a meadow full of buttercups. I was given another shot of tetanus before I could explain I'd already had one.

A medic walked me to a ward. Black Hatfield, Smooth, and the Professor were there. Cleaned up and in pajamas, they lay with the stillness of death. The Professor and Black Hatfield were bandaged. A nurse washed me, and a doctor dressed my wounds. The nurse gave me a blue 88 sleeping pill I didn't need.

They kept us asleep for thirty-six hours. When we woke, we felt drugged, but some of the gauntness was gone from our faces and some of the hollowness from our eyes.

None of us was badly hurt. The Professor was covered with wounds, but each was superficial. My back and shoulders were spot-

365

ted with shrapnel which the doctors were able to pick out without taking me to the operating room. Black Hatfield had a piece of metal in his neck. He squinted at the nurses who fooled with his bandage. Smooth was untouched.

We sat on the edges of our cots, talking very little but sticking together against others in the ward as if our experience had somehow set us apart from them. We smoked and ran our hands through our hair. The nurses brought us colored bathrobes. We were allowed to sun ourselves outside the tent.

Officers questioned us. A team from division intelligence arrived and went over the whole business. We answered the questions automatically, not really concerned with whether we were believed or not. A full colonel interrogated me. He had a male secretary taking notes.

"And you say your commanding officer blamed his maps?" the colonel asked.

We stayed at the field hospital ten days. During that time we were treated like royalty. The medics deferred to us, and we were pointed at as we moved about the area. Smooth found himself a nurse who met him each evening after dark in the blanket tent.

At the end of the ten days we were driven by ambulance to a train station in France and sent to a general hospital in Paris. The hospital was a complex of modern brick buildings and grassy lawns. The four of us were put into one sunny room. We had a radio, a pretty nurse, and a Red Cross woman who came daily to bring us magazines.

"They're going to ship us to the States," Smooth said. In less than twenty-four hours he had developed an arrangement with a petite French girl who worked in the kitchen. She would slip into the linen closet with him. "I got it from authority."

As in the field hospital, we led privileged lives. We were allowed to sleep late in the mornings, and nothing was required of us other than we stay clean. Smooth's little French girl made our beds as well as brought our meals. We could go to movies, read, or play cards. Black Hatfield strummed feuding chords on his guitar and smuggled in cognac with which we laced our coffee. When doctors did appear, they acted more concerned with pleasing than treating us.

The Red Cross woman brought an article about us which appeared in YANK. Our blundering into a German town and holding off attack were made to seem glamorous and daring. The story was carried by a lot of newspapers in the States. An official Army photographer came to the hospital to take our pictures. A detailed account appeared in a national magazine. My mother wrote a long letter, telling me how proud she was.

"They might use us to sell war bonds," Smooth said. He had now made connection with several of the little French girls who flitted about the wards. He was turning the linen closet into a harem. "We might have to go to places like Hollywood and kiss pretty movie stars to win the war."

Perhaps somebody did mean to use us for publicity purposes, but if so, the plan fell through because of the end in Germany. Everybody had been expecting it, and there was a big celebration in Paris. Most of us at the hospital had a few quiet drinks. On some of the wards the pale, shrunken forms of men near death lay motionless and rebuked celebration. Late that night Smooth made his first hit with our pretty nurse, introducing her to the delights of the linen closet after she was a little tight. The French girls were angry.

I wanted to know what had happened to our dead. A chaplain who made the rounds of the wards found out for me. They had been buried in a military cemetery near Nancy. I requested to see it, as did the Professor who was covered with scabs. We had to argue with a doctor before he would lend us a jeep and a driver.

The cemetery was just being laid out. Kentucky blue grass had been planted, but large portions of the area were muddy. Only a few crosses had been knocked together. None of the colored troops could tell us in what section of the field Yancey and the others were. The Professor and I went back to Paris without finding them.

I guess it was the visit to the cemetery that started me thinking about Yancey. I'd deliberately been avoiding that, allowing my mind to function around him, closing him off whenever he intruded. Riding back to Paris, however, I looked at the new green arching over the road and the spring sunshine on my hands. I could no longer avoid him. He was down under that muddy earth, and I owed him my life.

It was more than just owing him life. In a way he had been right because we should have surrendered to the Germans earlier. We wouldn't have been shot as I'd believed, and Carter, Honeycutt, Batten, Timberlake, and Beanpost would not have died for nothing. I was responsible for their being dead.

In addition I felt I'd denied Yancey a living salvation, that I'd acted out of hate for him and a wish to destroy him. I'd cut off his

367

balls. On that roof he had been a quaking, slobbering animal, but he had been brave as well. His courage was all the higher because of the size of his terror.

So I felt guilty not only about the others, but also him. He'd been bad, but he could never have been as awful as I considered him and done what he had.

I brooded about Yancey. I couldn't stop, and the only relief I had from it was drinking. I drank enough cognac to get me through the day and night without sweating, yet even a bottle wouldn't let me forget entirely. One evening while quietly drunk I questioned the Professor.

"How did the sonofabitch do it?" I asked of Yancey.

"I'm going to give you a pompous lecture," the Professor said, adjusting his glasses. He and the others had been watching me for days. "Human beings are now and then capable of rising above themselves. Only now and then, but it's the best part of us. No matter how corrupt, degraded, and filthy we become, we can commit acts which are far more than the total of ourselves. If I've learned anything, it's that a man brave for one second—and everybody has a second of bravery in him—can change the course of history."

The Professor was pompous and certainly too fancily academic. He was already lecturing his classes. I remained confused and tortured. Only one thing I was sure of. Toward the end I'd been more of a coward than Yancey was. I'd waved white flags and clutched my beam in writhing fright while he crawled along that roof. Thus I was now sick with the sight of myself. I'd been scorched, and I felt I'd not heal if I lived to be a hundred. I could never again trust myself.

Wilson was to fly home. Doctors had sliced off his left arm, and he was wrapped like a mummy. We all went to see him, but he couldn't speak through the Vaseline gauze. We stood by while they loaded him into the ambulance which took him to the airport.

Smooth, Black Hatfield, the Professor, and I stayed on at the hospital, though there was no longer any reason for it. Black Hatfield's bandages had been removed, and the Professor's scabs peeled off. Smooth wasted from his activities in the linen closet.

I continued to drink too much, and it was beginning to scare me. I slept as long as I could, yet there were still too many hours to be got through. Without a load I was unable to escape the corpses or the guilt about Yancey.

On a Friday morning we were roused by our pretty nurse who

368

sent us to supply for new uniforms. We believed we were going to be shipped out, but that afternoon an infantry lieutenant led us from the hospital to a formation on the parade ground. We were marched at attention in front of ranks, and a general approached.

The Professor, Black Hatfield, Smooth, Wilson in absentia, and I were given purple hearts and bronze stars. An adjutant read the commendation.

"For courage greatly above and beyond the call of duty in organizing resistance in a service unit against attacks by the enemy, for driving off that enemy and adding glory to the United States Army and the United States of America, these decorations are hereby presented."

As the medals were fastened to my blouse, I stood stiffly in the sunlight and hoped the general couldn't smell my breath. Once Yancey had received medals he didn't deserve, and now I was doing the same. The commendation mocked me. The general shook my limp hand.

At the same ceremony our dead—Carter, Honeycutt, Batten, Timberlake, and Beanpost—were awarded bronze stars and Marvin Yankovitch Yancey the Legion of Merit. Again the adjutant read flowery phrases. Reporters took our pictures. As soon as the formation was dismissed, I hurried to the ward where I tore off the medals. I went into Paris and got drunk.

At the first of the week the adjutant sent for me. He was a major with a bushy mustache who had his office on the first floor of the brick headquarters building. He was uncertain what to do with Yancey's medals.

"Send them to his wife," I said, thinking of the elegant Martha and the way the memory of her could still hurt.

"Well, that's the problem. She's married again. Maybe she wouldn't want the medals."

"I'm sure she will. Send the commendation too. She'll appreciate that."

"You really think so?" the major asked.

"I'd bet a million on it. They'll provide her with beautiful memories."

Perhaps I shouldn't have told the major what I did. Martha had plenty of justification from Marvin for the way she treated him. We all had justification. That was the confusing part. Anyway I wished I'd kept my mouth shut.

The same morning I received a letter from my mother. She enclosed a write-up about me which had been in the Richmond newspaper. She said that all the family were bragging on me and that Mr. Edwards had called from the bank to congratulate her. She, however, was worried that I was still in the hospital. I wrote a long, gentle letter I hoped would please and reassure her.

Through the intelligence system he'd developed in his linen closet, Smooth told us we'd soon be leaving. His information was correct. We learned we were going to the States.

I wanted to visit the cemetery once more. The doctor got me a jeep from the motor pool, and I drove out by myself. The place was a lot neater than when I'd first seen it—the blue grass was growing and sprinklers threw whirls of water over the grass and the freshly painted white crosses. A Negro private helped me locate Yancey's grave.

I didn't have any real reason to be there because I could do nothing about the buried. I was a little drunk, and I stood alone among the plain of crosses. A Frenchman was selling roses, so I bought a bunch and put them on the damp hump of earth. I smoked a cigarette before walking back to the jeep.

I drove to Paris. It was dark by the time I reached the city, and I stopped at a bistro to have a last drink. As I entered, I had a bad scare. Sitting at a table with his back to me was Yancey. He waved his arms and talked excitedly and loudly. When I stepped closer, I saw, of course, it was not Yancey, but my heart was pounding.

Tipsily I walked to the rolypoly soldier and put my arms around him. He was surprised and outraged.

"What the hell you doing?" he said, standing and knocking me backward.

"Stay dead," I told him. "Please stay dead."

He and others stared as I left the bistro and turned up the dark street toward the jeep and the hospital.

Hamilton Basso
  The View from Pompey's
    Head
Richard Bausch
  Real Presence
  Take Me Back
Robert Bausch
  On the Way Home
Doris Betts
  The Astronomer and Other
    Stories
  The Gentle Insurrection and
    Other Stories
Sydney Blair
  Buffalo
Sheila Bosworth
  Almost Innocent
  Slow Poison
David Bottoms
  Easter Weekend
Erskine Caldwell
  Poor Fool
Fred Chappell
  Dagon
  The Gaudy Place
  The Inkling
  It Is Time, Lord
Kelly Cherry
  Augusta Played
  In the Wink of an Eye
Vicki Covington
  Bird of Paradise
Elizabeth Cox
  The Ragged Way People
    Fall Out of Love
R. H. W. Dillard
  The Book of Changes
Ellen Douglas
  A Family's Affairs
  A Lifetime Burning
  The Rock Cried Out
  Where the Dreams Cross
Percival Everett
  Cutting Lisa
  Suder
Peter Feibleman
  The Daughters of Necessity
  A Place Without Twilight
Candace Flynt
  Mother Love

William Price Fox
  Dixiana Moon
George Garrett
  An Evening Performance
  Do, Lord, Remember Me
  The Magic Striptease
  The Finished Man
Reginald Gibbons
  Sweetbitter
Ellen Gilchrist
  The Annunciation
  In the Land of Dreamy
    Dreams
Marianne Gingher
  Bobby Rex's Greatest Hit
Shirley Ann Grau
  The Hard Blue Sky
  The House on Coliseum
    Street
  The Keepers of the House
  Roadwalkers
Ben Greer
  Slammer
Barry Hannah
  The Tennis Handsome
Donald Hays
  The Dixie Association
William Hoffman
  Yancey's War
William Humphrey
  Home from the Hill
  The Ordways
Mac Hyman
  No Time For Sergeants
Madison Jones
  A Cry of Absence
Nancy Lemann
  Lives of the Saints
  Malaise
  Sportsman's Paradise
Beverly Lowry
  Come Back, Lolly Ray
Clarence Major
  Such Was the Season
Valerie Martin
  A Recent Martyr
  Set in Motion
Willie Morris
  The Last of the Southern
    Girls

Padgett Powell
  Mrs. Hollingsworth's Men
Louis D. Rubin, Jr.
  The Golden Weather
  Surfaces of a Diamond
Evelyn Scott
  The Wave
Lee Smith
  The Last Day the Dogbushes
    Bloomed
Elizabeth Spencer
  Landscapes of the Heart
  The Night Travellers
  The Salt Line
  This Crooked Way
  The Voice at the Back Door
Max Steele
  Debby
Virgil Suárez
  Latin Jazz
Walter Sullivan
  The Long, Long Love
  Sojourn of a Stranger
Allen Tate
  The Fathers
Peter Taylor
  In the Miro District and
    Other Stories
  The Widows of Thornton
Robert Penn Warren
  Band of Angels
  Brother to Dragons
  Flood
  World Enough and Time
Walter White
  Flight
James Wilcox
  Guest of a Sinner
  Miss Undine's Living Room
  North Gladiola
Joan Williams
  The Morning and the
    Evening
  The Wintering
Christine Wiltz
  Glass House
Thomas Wolfe
  The Hills Beyond
  The Web and the Rock